The Call to Shakabaz

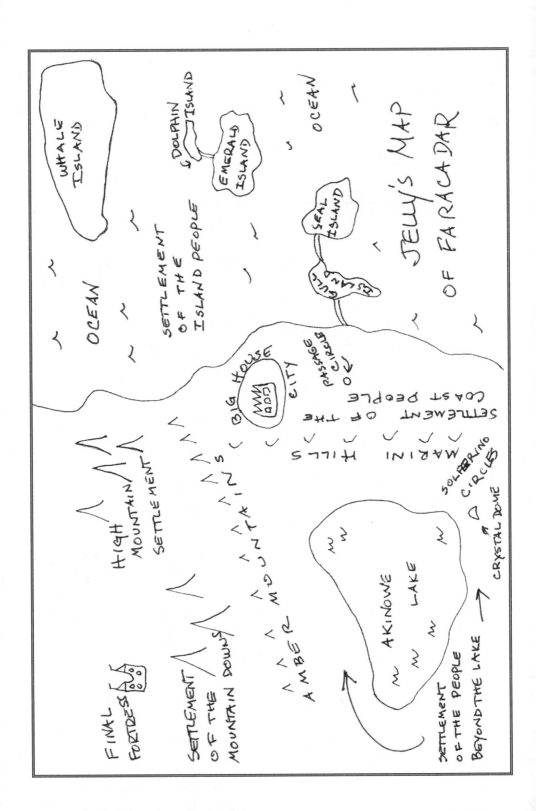

The Call to Shakabaz

Amy Wachspress

Woza Books
Books that Raise the Spirits

The Call to Shakabaz

Copyright © 2007 by Amy Wachspress

Cover design: Amy Wachspress and Cypress House
Cover collage: Amy Wachspress
Cover silhouette: Sandra Lindström
Book design: Cypress House
"Lift Every Voice and Sing", from *Saint Peter Relates an Incident* by James Weldon Johnson, copyright 1917, 1921, 1935 by James Weldon Johnson, copyright renewed (c) 1963 by Grace Nail Johnson. Used by permission of Viking Penguin, a division of Penguin Group (USA) Inc.

Publisher's Cataloging-in-Publication Data

Wachspress, Amy.
  The call to Shakabaz / by Amy Wachspress. -- 1st ed. -- Ukiah, Calif. : Woza Books, 2007.
    p. ; cm.
    ISBN-13: 978-0-9788350-2-6
    ISBN-10: 0-9788350-2-6
    Audience: ages 9-14.

Summary: Four children and their parrot travel to the fantasy land of Faracadar on a mission to retrieve the Staff of Shakabaz and free the land from the clutches of the evil enchanter Sissrath.

1. Courage--Fiction. 2. Fantasy fiction. 3. Young adult fiction.
4. Adventure stories. I. Title.
  PS3623.A247 C35 2006   2006932279
  813.6--dc22 0610

Printed in Canada
2 4 6 8 9 7 5 3 1

For my mother, Natalie Wachspress, who believed in my talent long before I did; and my father, Eugene Wachspress, who read aloud to me when I was a child (with the best silly voices).

For my remarkable children, Yael, Akili, and Sudi, who tramped through the pages of many an adventure with me in the twilight hours before bedtime. And for the grandchildren I hope to read to on some future evening.

For all the children who marched to prevent and protest the War on Iraq. Keep marching and speaking, dear ones. Keep faith that there is a peaceful path to justice.

For Ron, who makes my dreams come true every day.

Contents

Chapter One ✦ The Amulets • 1

Chapter Two ✦ The People Beyond the Lake • 14

Chapter Three ✦ The Hunt • 24

Chapter Four ✦ Sun Power • 36

Chapter Five ✦ Akinowe Lake • 50

Chapter Six ✦ Jelly and the Crystal Dome • 62

Chapter Seven ✦ Meddling Sprites • 73

Chapter Eight ✦ The Coast People • 87

Chapter Nine ✦ The Island People • 104

Chapter Ten ✦ The History Lesson • 117

Chapter Eleven ✦ Vengeance • 130

Chapter Twelve ✦ Big House City • 141

Chapter Thirteen ✦ Captured • 152

Chapter Fourteen ✦ Into the Amber Mountains • 166

Chapter Fifteen ✦ Geebachings • 179

Chapter Sixteen ✦ The High Mountain People • 194

Chapter Seventeen ✦ The Final Fortress • 207

Chapter Eighteen ✦ Satyagraha • 222

Chapter Nineteen ✦ The Battle of Truth • 235

Chapter Twenty ✦ The Return of the Four • 251

Chapter One

The Amulets

In the blue-gray pre-dawn light, Doshmisi awoke in terror, her heart beating wildly in her ears and a muffled shout in her throat. The tall, sinister man in the long robe had pursued her in her dreams ever since Mama died. She never saw his face. Sometimes his claw-like hands reached for her. The most frightening thing about him, that penetrating voice, lingered in Doshmisi's thoughts. He always said the same thing: your mother can't protect you here. She can't protect me anywhere, Doshmisi thought sadly. Her mother, Deborah Goodacre, had died of a heart attack one stormy night two months earlier.

Doshmisi looked out the window at the familiar pattern sketched by the branches of the giant chinquapin tree in the moments before a glorious June morning burst forth to reveal its secrets. She was safe and sound in the heavy carved wooden bed in her very own room in Aunt Alice's large welcoming farmhouse on Manzanita Ranch. Until they moved to Manzanita Ranch, Doshmisi and her brothers Denzel and Sonjay and her sister Maia had shared one room in a small apartment in the city. Doshmisi sometimes felt like a princess when she woke up in that tall bed, snuggled up all cozy under a fluffy comforter and a handmade quilt.

Suddenly she remembered it was Midsummer, the longest day of the year, which was a special event in her family. That cheered her and made her want to go back to sleep for awhile so she wouldn't be tired later on. Then she heard a murmuring voice on the other side of the wall in Aunt Alice's study. Her aunt usually got up early to tend to her animals up at the barn, but not this early.

Doshmisi stealthily stepped out of bed and padded across the floor to her door, which she opened as quietly as possible. She could hear Aunt Alice's voice in the next room quite distinctly, although her aunt spoke softly into the phone.

"Bobby, we have no choice. With Debbie gone, the whole land is in danger. And you know perfectly well that we can't go back ourselves. I don't see any other way. We have to send the children," Aunt Alice said.

Uncle Bobby and Uncle Martin, Aunt Alice's younger brothers, would be driving up from the city to Manzanita Ranch to celebrate Midsummer's Eve later that day. Uncle Bobby played the saxophone in a band and Uncle Martin designed airplanes. Aunt Alice said nothing for a moment, apparently listening to Bobby.

"May I remind you that Debbie was even younger than Sonjay the first time we went? Oh, if only we could explain some of it to them then it wouldn't be so hard!" Aunt Alice exclaimed with a frustrated tone to her voice.

Doshmisi waited while Bobby said something again and then Aunt Alice answered, "I know, I know, the amulets won't work properly if they come to them at the first with prior knowledge. I wish it weren't so complicated."

She listened to Bobby on the other end of the line and then she said, "You're right of course, they will be in danger. But at least they will have the amulets. OK. See you later. Love to Lena and the kids." Aunt Alice hung up. Doshmisi quickly closed her door and crawled back into bed. Aunt Alice's conversation disturbed her even more than the tall man who pursued her in her dreams because Aunt Alice was for real.

At fourteen, Doshmisi was the oldest of the Goodacre children and she felt responsible for looking after the others. Mama's death had left them orphaned. Their father had disappeared when Sonjay was a baby and even though Mama always said that Daddy would return to them as soon as he could, they figured they'd never see him again. Since their father was nowhere in sight when Mama died, Doshmisi and Denzel (who was thirteen), Maia (who was eleven), and Sonjay (who was ten), moved to Manzanita Ranch to live with their Aunt Alice on six hundred acres of forest. Aunt Alice had never married and she had no children.

The Goodacres could not get used to living in the country. They viewed trees and deer as boring neighbors compared to the friends they had left behind in the city. But if they couldn't have Mama, there was no question that they wanted to live with Aunt Alice, who loved them like a second mother. Doshmisi couldn't imagine that Aunt Alice would send them into danger. Not their Aunt Alice, who made them laugh with her silly sense of humor and cooked delicious food (like fruit pies and chicken enchiladas), and who loved to read them stories out loud before bed. Aunt Alice always read fantasy adventures about magical make-believe places. She liked to ponder over what the people in the stories chose to do and often asked the children what they would have done in the same situation. "Now if you had been turned into a dragon, and you couldn't talk, how would you let the others know it was you and that you wouldn't burn them up with your terrible fire-breath?" Doshmisi could hear Aunt Alice's voice in her head, asking those questions. She smiled.

Even though the Goodacre children loved Aunt Alice, they had a hard time getting used to living at Manzanita Ranch. Aunt Alice worked from dawn to sunset in her gardens and orchards and taking care of her animals. She always had lots of chores for the children to help with, willing or not. She liked to milk goats and grow tomatoes and the children liked to go to the movies and the mall. She was a country person and they were city people. They were just different from each other, as simple as that.

It drove Doshmisi crazy that Aunt Alice didn't have a TV. Back in the city, she used to go to her friends' houses after school to watch the soap operas. They would make popcorn in the microwave and put on nail polish and discuss what folks in the "stories" (as they called them) ought to do. Aunt Alice had no TV and no microwave and Doshmisi had no friends to go visit. She could make new friends, but everyone lived in town, and Doshmisi lived out a dirt road in the middle of nowhere. As she curled back into her bed, she wished for something interesting to happen, something unusual and good, something *not* dangerous. With that wish, she drifted back to sleep.

The sun was high in the sky and Doshmisi knew the others had probably eaten breakfast by the time she woke up later. She hurried to get dressed. She took pride in her stylish appearance and always dressed with care. Short and slender, she had dark chocolate-brown skin and almost shoulder-length hair that she straightened so she could fix it all different ways. She never wore plain T-shirts, only nice tops. She wanted to look especially good on Midsummer's Eve because her uncles were coming. She was so preoccupied with her appearance that she forgot Aunt Alice's pre-dawn phone conversation.

On Midsummer, Denzel hopped out of bed early. Uncle Martin and Uncle Bobby would be here today, he thought happily. In the kitchen, he found Aunt Alice drinking a cup of coffee. "You're up early," she commented.

"Couldn't sleep no more," Denzel said, as he stuffed a banana muffin into his mouth.

"Couldn't sleep *any* more," Aunt Alice corrected. "Boy, slow down before you choke on that muffin. Why don't you go pick me some cherries so I can make a pie?"

He didn't mind picking the cherries because he loved Aunt Alice's pie. She gave him a basket and he headed out into the fresh morning.

Denzel had already shot up taller than Doshmisi. He was the lightest brown of the four children, with big eyes and big hands. Girls had just started noticing his good looks when he left the city. He missed his friends back in the 'hood almost as much as he missed Mama. Manzanita Ranch was a frustrating place to live. He couldn't skateboard on pine needles and even though Aunt Alice tried to set up Mama's computer, it didn't do everything it used to do and for some reason it wouldn't load his games anymore. You could only count on it if you had to write a paper for school and Denzel didn't like to write. Aunt Alice kept suggesting that he "go take apart the car." She had an old Toyota that didn't run anymore and she kept telling Denzel he could take the engine apart to see how it worked (or didn't).

"I'm only thirteen years old," he told her. "I don't know nothin' about car engines!"

"Anything," Aunt Alice corrected him, "you don't know anything. If you took the car apart then you *would* know something."

He had found a thick book in Aunt Alice's library entitled *A Beginner's Guide to the Way Things Work*. The book intrigued him and he had glanced through it with some interest. But that book wasn't anywhere near as much fun as kickin' it with his friends, shooting some hoops, listening to music, or checking out the newest video games at the mall.

As he headed across the front yard, he wished for some excitement at Manzanita Ranch. That's when he decided not to go straight to the orchard. Instead he walked down the driveway and turned onto a worn path surrounded by raspberry brambles. The path led to a crooked cabin with a padlock on the door. Aunt Alice had warned the children to stay away from that cabin and so of course they had snuck right over there to check it out, but when they peeked in the windows they saw nothing inside except a broken bench. On this morning, Denzel felt like flirting with danger and the cabin had been forbidden. As he picked some raspberries, he glanced in the direction of the cabin. He suddenly stopped in his tracks. A thin ribbon of smoke threaded up from the chimney.

Denzel cautiously crept along the path toward the cabin. As he drew near, he caught a glimpse of a figure through the window. He couldn't make out details of the figure very well, but to him the figure didn't exactly seem like a person. He had the distinct and unsettling feeling that an alien creature inhabited the cabin. Then the creature lifted an object over its head and Denzel thought the object looked like an axe. Denzel tried to duck behind a tree, but his foot caught on a root. He sprawled into a raspberry bramble, which clung to his clothes and scratched his skin. The raspberries he had picked flew out of the basket and scattered among the tree's roots. Denzel ripped himself out of the grasp of the brambles and fled down the path without looking back.

For Maia the most exciting thing in Aunt Alice's house was a large exotic parrot named Bayard Rustin. Aunt Alice had named him after a civil rights leader whom she admired. Bayard Rustin did not have a cage but instead perched on a branch affixed to a corner of the front parlor.

His red, blue, green, and yellow coloring stood out so brilliantly that it made your eyes hurt to look at him. He could talk, but nothing that he said made any sense. His favorite phrase was "hyacinth is a fool." When Maia asked Aunt Alice about hyacinth, her aunt told her a hyacinth was a blue flower. Maia liked to prompt Bayard Rustin to speak and then she would puzzle over his pronouncements.

When Maia woke up on Midsummer, she went to see Bayard Rustin first thing and wished him a good morning.

The parrot promptly told her "amethyst makes spice cake." She stroked his head and gave him a few strawberries she had saved for him. Then she followed her nose into the kitchen because she smelled fresh muffins.

"Aunt Alice, this morning Bayard Rustin said 'amethyst makes spice cake.' What do you suppose that means?" Maia asked. "Isn't amethyst a precious gem?"

"That bird certainly has a mind of his own," Aunt Alice answered. "Baby, would you please pick some flowers for the table? I put a couple of vases out in the dining room and my clippers are on the counter. You know how to make such a nice bouquet." Maia blushed at the praise.

Maia had coffee-and-cream-colored skin, exquisite almond-shaped eyes, and she wore her hair in one long French braid straight down her back. She was a quiet, shy person and she felt self-conscious because she was overweight as a result of her terrible sweet tooth. She had a passion for music and she loved to play Aunt Alice's old upright piano with the carved curlicues that stood stoutly on lion's claw legs in the front parlor. Her music helped her adjust to her new home in the country. But sometimes Maia longed to go back to the apartment in the city and sit in the overstuffed easy chair and look at the portrait of Dr. Martin Luther King, Jr. that used to hang over the couch. Maia imagined that Dr. King looked out of the picture at her with understanding eyes. His eyes put her at peace. Sonjay had the portrait of Dr. King hanging in his bedroom now and Maia still looked at it sometimes. She felt a little lost with so many of the familiar things from the city in unfamiliar places at Manzanita Ranch.

Just as Maia picked up the clippers from the counter, Denzel burst into the kitchen with startling news. "Aunt Alice, someone, or some*thing*

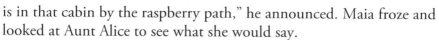

is in that cabin by the raspberry path," he announced. Maia froze and looked at Aunt Alice to see what she would say.

"I told you to stay away from there," Aunt Alice snapped, clearly annoyed.

"But I thought you would want to know. Hey, I was just picking some raspberries and then I saw smoke coming out of the chimney so I went for a closer look. There's something in that cabin."

Aunt Alice responded sternly, "Listen, I don't want to hear anything more about this. I know exactly what is going on at that cabin and I want you to stay away from there. And not a word about this to anyone. You too, Maia, not a word. To anyone. You understand me?"

Aunt Alice sounded angry and not at all alarmed. Maia and Denzel exchanged a confused look behind her back.

Midsummer found Sonjay at the basketball hoop as usual. He threw the ball at the hoop and missed. He was getting rusty and that made him mad. He was already mad this morning. He had been looking forward to Midsummer's Eve and now it was spoiled. No one else he knew made the kind of fuss over Midsummer's Eve that his family did. The Goodacres had gone to Manzanita Ranch on the first day of summer in June every year. Mama never missed spending Midsummer's Eve with her older sister and brothers. And Sonjay loved his cousins; Uncle Martin's girls and Uncle Bobby's boys. But this year the cousins weren't coming. Uncle Bobby and Uncle Martin weren't bringing their families. It would be hard enough to do Midsummer without Mama, but it seemed really unfair to have to do it without their cousins. And the grown-ups wouldn't give them a good reason why, which bothered Sonjay most of all.

Sonjay was compact and wiry, with powerful muscles for a little boy. He had a broad fleshy mouth and long eyelashes and he seemed larger than life because he had so much energy. He had darker skin than the other children and his hair curled tighter. Living at Manzanita Ranch was hardest on Sonjay because he couldn't just step out the front door into the street for a good game of basketball. Aunt Alice put up a basketball hoop on a tree for him. He appreciated her effort, but that lonely hoop on the tree just didn't cut it. Sonjay hated the peace and quiet at Manzanita Ranch. He needed something going on. He wished he could just step out the front door and have it happening.

He took aim at the hoop and tried again. This time the ball went in. Then he heard Doshmisi's voice. "They're here," she shouted. Sonjay ran to the house and from there he could see Uncle Bobby's deep blue Oldsmobile at the yard gate. The car came up the driveway and stopped by the front porch.

Before Uncle Martin had walked three steps from the car, Sonjay took a flying leap and slammed into his uncle's wide chest like a misbehaved dog. Uncle Martin staggered backwards against the car, laughing, and took the blow in stride as he embraced his enthusiastic nephew. Uncle Bobby exchanged a look with Aunt Alice that seemed to ask how she was managing with the children. Doshmisi saw Aunt Alice smile. In an instant Uncle Bobby and Uncle Martin challenged the children to a game of basketball. Sonjay's gleeful whoops and hollers could probably be heard in Brazil.

They played basketball and then badminton. Uncle Bobby stole the hose from Aunt Alice while she was watering her flowers and he sprayed the children. But Denzel got his payback in a surprise attack on Uncle Bobby with a giant water balloon.

By dinner time, when the enticing smells of country cooking crept through the house, the children had worked up a huge appetite. Uncle Martin barbecued hamburgers and hot dogs on the grill and Aunt Alice made melt-in-your-mouth buttery biscuits. The best part was Aunt Alice's cherry pie with vanilla ice cream. Her old-fashioned cherry pie with the criss-cross crust could whisper your name like nothing else on the table.

After dinner, they sat on the screened-in porch, safe from the biting bugs, and made each other laugh with their stories. Darkness had not yet settled in when Uncle Martin sent the children upstairs to get ready for bed. They grumbled and complained that it was still light out, but it did no good. Aunt Alice fussed and fussed, making them each take a shower and brush their teeth, and tucking them in and kissing them each goodnight.

Just before she fell asleep, Doshmisi remembered the strange phone conversation she had overheard as the day had started and she decided she would have to look up the word "amulet" in the dictionary in the morning. But the morning turned out to be much further off than Doshmisi could ever have imagined.

Doshmisi awoke in pitch darkness to Aunt Alice's insistent gentle voice. "Dosh, it's time to get up," Aunt Alice said. "We don't want to be late." She turned on the light next to Doshmisi's bed.

Outside the night insects chirped loudly at the moon.

"It's not time to get up. Check it out, it's the middle of the night," Doshmisi mumbled as she turned the light back out and curled tighter into her bed.

But Aunt Alice turned the light on again and shook her shoulder and handed her some clothes. "Put these on quickly. Choose a sweater to take. Do as I say. I have to go wake Maia. Are you awake?"

Doshmisi blinked her eyes against the brightness of the light and sat up. Why did Aunt Alice want her to put on long pants and a sweater on a warm summer night? Why did she need to get out of bed at all? Her sleep-filled mind suddenly snapped alert as she remembered the phone conversation she had overheard the day before. She emerged from her room to find Uncle Bobby and Uncle Martin gently prodding Denzel and Sonjay down the stairs. Aunt Alice, with Bayard Rustin perched on her shoulder, led a sleepy Maia by the hand. They trooped through the house and stepped lightly across the lawn.

"Where are we going?" Sonjay asked, rubbing his eyes. It angered Doshmisi that the grown-ups had dragged him out of bed too. He's so little, Doshmisi thought. But she also knew that he wouldn't want to be left out if something unusual or exciting was happening.

They walked down the driveway and through the gate, then turned down the raspberry path to the deserted cabin. As they approached, they saw a light shining in the window and the cabin didn't look as crooked as usual. In fact, it looked downright cheerful and inviting. Denzel and Maia exchanged a curious look.

The whole posse stopped at the door and Uncle Martin knocked twice, then paused, then knocked again four times. His knock sounded like a code. "Amethyst," he called through the door in a loud voice, "we're here, open the door."

A very old, very wrinkled, tiny woman opened the door. Tufts of bristly, loud red hair poked out from a bright pink kerchief on her head. Her hair was so red, it was alarming. In fact, her skin was alarmingly red too. Her skin, actually dark brown, glowed with a fire engine redness. She wiped her hands on her white ruffled apron and peered at them through thick spectacles. Immediately, Bayard flew to her shoulder and called out "Amethyst makes spice cake."

"The children?" Amethyst questioned as she stroked Bayard affectionately.

"It's OK. They're Debbie's," Aunt Alice explained. She put a hand on Amethyst's arm and told her softly, "Debbie passed over into spirit this year. We have brought her children. Since Debbie has passed, we are worried that the people are in danger and we think the children must retrieve the Staff of Shakabaz from Sissrath. The time has come."

Amethyst nodded solemnly in agreement. "Of course," she said. "Some of the elders suspected that Debbie had passed. Sissrath is making motions. He wouldn't dare if she still lived. You are right, as long as he has Shakabaz in his possession, the people remain in great danger." Aunt Alice looked anxiously at Uncle Martin.

"Debbie's children," Amethyst cackled, and she patted their cheeks and shoulders with her calloused and gnarled hands, chuckling, as the children trooped past her through the doorway. "So big," she muttered. Then she turned to Aunt Alice and shook her head sadly and tsk-tsked. "Debbie has truly passed? Sissrath exacted his price then."

"It seems he did," Aunt Alice replied quietly. Amethyst brushed away tears with the corner of her apron. "But we will make a new start, I see, with these four. That is an exciting prospect, don't you think?" She quickly brightened.

"Sure enough," Bobby answered.

Doshmisi squinted in the glaring light of the cabin. She glanced at her brothers and sister and they stared back at her with questioning eyes. The cabin looked nothing like it had when they had investigated it a few weeks before. No longer bare, it had a bright fire in the hearth and a big iron cook stove, from which emerged lovely smells of something sweet baking. A round table with chairs stood in the center on a forest-green braided rug. Amethyst had set the table with care for five people. She had placed little tea cups, small plates, forks, and linen napkins.

"Amethyst makes spice cake," Bayard announced. Maia understood what he meant this time.

"And you shall have some," Amethyst told the bird. "Oh my, I hope I have enough cake for all these children."

"Don't worry about that, you always make way too much," Uncle Bobby reassured her. "So sorry we're late. We had to get the children up and dressed. This is Doshmisi, Denzel, Maia, and Sonjay. And this," he said to the children, grandly, with a sweep of his hand in the direction of the little woman, "is Amethyst the Gatekeeper."

"So pleased to meet you, sons and daughters of Debbie," Amethyst curtsied, which looked more like a sort of a little bob of her stout body.

Sonjay stepped forward gallantly and took Amethyst's hand and shook it. He surprised Doshmisi with his formality, but the gesture seemed so correct that she followed his lead, as did the others in turn. Amethyst looked quite pleased by the hand-shaking. "Oh my," she said suddenly, her face clouding over, "then, a new four must actually pass into Faracadar this year! Very exciting indeed. I have not administered such a passage in a long time. And we haven't much time." She instantly scurried around the cabin in a flurry of activity, pulling jars of colorful powder down from the cupboards and searching the closet for heaven knew what. Aunt Alice motioned the children to the table where they each took a seat. Uncle Bobby sat down too and Uncle Martin drew up an extra chair. "Can we help with anything?" asked Aunt Alice.

"Why yes," Amethyst replied breathlessly from the depths of a trunk that had swallowed the upper half of her body. "Please help yourselves to tea and cake. Cake's in the oven. Make sure Bayard gets his piece. Now where did I put the...? Oh my!" Amethyst whirled around to face Aunt Alice, "Did you bring the amulets?" she asked in a tizzy.

"Yes, of course," Uncle Martin replied, "Don't worry. We have them." So saying, Uncle Martin and Uncle Bobby each produced a necklace from their pockets and Aunt Alice drew out two necklaces from hers. Amethyst stopped scurrying around and approached the table to examine the handiwork of the amulets. The children leaned forward eagerly to see the mysterious objects. The metal of the amulet chains looked like copper but with a glimmering green and blue sheen to it that made it shimmer in a way that copper never shimmered. Each of the chains held a medallion as big around as a walnut, and each medallion looked as if made out of a different unidentifiable material. When she examined them more closely, Doshmisi saw that the medallions each had their own unique markings in strange characters that she could not read.

Denzel asked, "What do these markings mean? Do they spell something?"

"The markings aren't letters, but they do have meaning. The meaning changes depending upon the wearer," Uncle Martin told them, with a longing look at the medallion that rested in his palm.

"We can't tell you much because you must come to the amulets innocent of knowledge the first time," Aunt Alice said. "We entered that way. But our time has passed and now it is up to you. Go to Faracadar. Recover the Staff of Shakabaz from Sissrath. This task is your calling and these amulets will help you. They belonged to each of us and to your mother and we wore them a long time ago to help us protect a great many wonderful creatures from harm."

"When you wear the amulets, no one can take them from you unless they first take your life," Uncle Martin told the children.

"Enough, Martin," Aunt Alice raised a hand to silence him.

"The time has come for us to pass these on," Uncle Bobby said, stroking the object in his hand. It seemed like he and Uncle Martin could hardly part with their amulets.

Then Uncle Martin solemnly placed his amulet around Denzel's neck. "This belonged to me, the Amulet of Metal. Now it is yours." He turned it face up on Denzel's chest. "Wear it well and with ingenuity."

Uncle Bobby placed his amulet around Maia's neck. "This one

belonged to me, the Amulet of Watersong, and it is now yours. Wear it well and with creativity."

Doshmisi wanted to run away when Aunt Alice approached her because it all seemed strange and frightening, but she forced herself to stand and accept the amulet that Aunt Alice placed around her neck. "This was mine, it is the Amulet of the Trees. Now it is yours. Wear it well and with compassion."

Then Aunt Alice turned to Sonjay and knelt on the floor to bring herself to eye-level with him. She placed a fourth amulet around his neck. "This amulet belongs to you, the youngest, and it is the Amulet of Heartfire. It belonged to your mother, also the youngest. Wear it well, with courage and a hunger for the truth."

"Nearly midnight," Amethyst said with urgency, "almost time."

Chapter Two

The People Beyond the Lake

"**D**o you think we could have one piece of spice cake before you zap us?" Sonjay begged. "I'll pass on the tea," he added, eyeing with suspicion the teapot, from which there wafted a seaweedy smell.

Bayard called enthusiastically, "Amethyst makes spice cake." Aunt Alice took the spice cake out of the oven and gave the first piece to Bayard, who set upon it with furious fervor, flinging crumbs across his back as he tore chunks off with his powerful beak. Unlike the tea, the spice cake smelled heavenly to the children.

"Yes, yes, of course, cake," Amethyst muttered distractedly. "Martin come help me with these things."

As the children ate the warm, tangy cake, Uncle Martin helped Amethyst set out four large silky cushions in a row on the floor and then she placed four roughly carved sticks in a square around each cushion.

"The passage sticks," Aunt Alice pronounced. "My own first trip seems like such a short time ago."

Those sticks made Doshmisi anxious. Perhaps all of this would have thrilled her if she had a clue about what was going on, but it seemed like any minute Amethyst planned to zap them (as Sonjay had put it) into the unknown on a pillow and she didn't feel prepared for an adventure of this magnitude. She had hoped for something to liven up her summer, but purchasing a large screen TV would have done the trick nicely.

Uncle Martin produced a knapsack that he put on Denzel's back. "I packed you a few things that might come in handy. I wish your Great

Uncle Charles had done the same for me, but he was Old School and he just threw me in sink-or-swim."

Aunt Alice pressed a dog-eared book into Doshmisi's hands. "Here's my herbal. Never mind the stains on the pages, just read what it says and follow the directions. Here's the carry-case so you can buckle it around your waist."

Amethyst took a metallic bowl off the mantelpiece and handed it to Maia. Upon examination, Maia discovered eight bowls in progressively smaller sizes nested into each other. "You must take Raffia's water organ. It saved her life and mine once and it may save yours," Amethyst told Maia, as she produced a small canvas sack for Maia to put the bowls into. Maia wondered how a musical instrument could save someone's life. Doshmisi wondered what they needed to have their lives saved *from*.

"Have you finished your cake? Good. Then sit on the cushions, and keep your fingers and toes within the sticks," Amethyst commanded, steering Maia toward the cushions.

"But what about me?" Sonjay demanded in alarm. "Don't I get anything to take with me that might save *my* life?"

"You already have everything you need, baby," Aunt Alice reassured him, "you don't need any powerful objects or tools."

Sonjay stood firmly, unmoving, and looked worried.

"Get on up outta here," Aunt Alice made a shooing motion with her hands.

But Sonjay stubbornly refused to budge. "No, I think I want something," he insisted. So Aunt Alice turned and eyed Bayard Rustin, "Go ahead, go with them this time. I know you've wanted to for ages. But do come back to me." Aunt Alice kissed Bayard fondly on the top of his bright green head and shrugged him off her arm.

"Hyacinth is a fool," Bayard Rustin called as he flew to Sonjay's shoulder. Amethyst laughed heartily at that utterance. "I suggest you keep your thoughts to yourself in Faracadar if you value your feathers," Amethyst told him.

The children seated themselves on the cushions. Bayard Rustin perched on Sonjay's shoulder. Doshmisi strapped her book around her waist with shaky hands. She almost blurted out that she would rather not go. Then she glanced over at Sonjay, who had seemed so little to her since Mama's death, and she saw his eyes shining brightly with excitement. How did he become so brave all of a sudden?

Opening an array of jars of brightly colored powder, Amethyst muttered to herself, "Two pinches of the aquamarine and four of the yellow, or maybe three of the yellow, now what was the magenta? Hmm, definitely four of the yellow. Four corners. Four yellow. Yes."

"Tell them about the return," Uncle Bobby prompted Amethyst.

Amethyst looked up abruptly from her powders. "Oh my," she said in a flustered voice, "Thank you, Martin. I almost forgot." Then she told the children, "You must go to Angel's Gate on the thirty-fifth day of Loma for your return. If you miss the appointed time, well, then I don't know exactly when I can bring you back."

"That's important," Aunt Alice emphasized. "Angel's Gate. The thirty-fifth day of Loma. We always got there early to be on the safe side. Denzel, repeat it."

Denzel obediently recited "Angel's Gate, thirty-fifth day of Loma."

Just as Doshmisi wondered what Amethyst may have forgotten to tell them entirely and how on earth Aunt Alice could tell them to do anything to be on the safe side under the circumstances, a burst of brightly colored powder surrounded her and she felt herself swept backwards as if sucked through a wind tunnel. Her ears buzzed and she closed her eyes tightly as she held onto the edges of her cushion with clenched fingers.

When she reached the end of the wind tunnel, the air current forced Doshmisi out and deposited her with a loud popping noise in a freestanding doorway made of heavy dark wood. The sun dazzled her and made her blink and wince. Wisps of green smoke rose from her shoulders. Seconds later Denzel and Maia appeared in their own doorways with popping sounds of their own. She had to laugh at Sonjay when he popped through with Bayard; in fact they all laughed, because he brought a huge cloud of bright yellow with him. Bird and boy choked and snorted yellow smoke.

"I think Amethyst used too much yellow on you, man," Denzel said to Sonjay, waving the smoke away from his brother's face.

The sight of Sonjay steaming with yellow mist set them off and the children fell into a fit of giggles. Meanwhile, the doorways through which they had come crumbled into splinters on the ground and dissolved into the earth in puffs of colorful smoke.

"Where the heck are we?" Denzel burst out. This sent them into more gales of laughter because they hadn't a clue where they had landed. They lay on the ground, helplessly holding their sides and trying to catch their breath between guffaws.

Finally, one by one, they sat up, gasping for air as their laughter subsided, and peered around at the brilliant landscape. They seemed to have arrived at midday in the first rush of early summer in a small meadow loaded with vibrant wildflowers in every shade of red imaginable. The color of everything around them burst forth so brightly that they squinted, their eyes throbbing as they took in their dazzling surroundings. Although the land looked like summer, the air that touched their skin had a soft coolness to it, nothing like the harsh dry heat of Manzanita Ranch. Unlike the sun they had always known, the sun that beat down on them here was four or five times as large as the sun at home and had a green tinge to it. They discovered immediately that they could look straight at it without burning their eyes. Surrounding the sun, in every corner of the sky, they saw glittering jewel-like points of light. The lights seemed like stars visible in daylight, in rich shades of midnight blue, turquoise, forest green, wine red, sunflower yellow, and other more subtle tints. The children gazed above them in wonder at the strange and beautiful sky until Sonjay suggested to Denzel, "Hey, let's check out what Uncle Martin put in your knapsack."

Denzel kneeled down, put the knapsack in front of him, and undid the buckle in front. Inside he found an insulated lunch sack with a couple of Ziploc bags of ice and a stack of meatloaf sandwiches.

"Better save those for when we get hungry," Doshmisi advised sensibly.

Then Denzel found four pairs of sunglasses, which he handed out to the others. The children put them on with relief, dizzy from the overwhelming brightness of everything around them. Uncle Martin had packed a good Swiss army knife, which Denzel put in his pocket for safekeeping. He also discovered a small tool kit of mostly screw drivers and wrenches, a coil of rope, a roll of duct tape, a flashlight that used AA batteries, and a solar battery charger with AA batteries in it. They found four good metal canteens of water with carrying straps, which they slung over their shoulders so that they hung at their hips.

They were so intent on the contents of the knapsack, that they did not notice the boy approaching them across the meadow. The boy stopped in his tracks and stared. His mouth dropped open. The brown and tan shepherd at his side looked up at him questioningly and then began to bark. At the sound of the barking, the Goodacres looked up from the knapsack. Bayard, who had perched in a nearby bush to munch berries, flew immediately to Sonjay's shoulder. The boy, who had skin dark brown as cloves and seemed even more red around the edges and in the hair than Amethyst, bolted toward the children at a run. He arrived panting and grinning broadly.

"I can't believe you came!" he exclaimed. "Every year Crystal sends me and no one comes. But this year you came." He looked puzzled for a moment. "You're a different four. You're young. Who are you?"

"Debbie's four," Bayard cried out. "Debbie's four."

"I'm Doshmisi, these are my brothers Denzel and Sonjay and my sister Maia. Who are you?" Doshmisi asked.

"I'm Jasper. Amethyst the Gatekeeper is my grandmother. And I was supposed to be here when you arrived. You won't tell that I was late, will you?" he asked anxiously. "I just didn't think you would come. No one ever does. Every year they send me out and no one shows up. But this year you came. What a great surprise for my mother. Just in time too, she's not doing well." At that moment his dog barked and he knelt down to pet her. "This is Cocoa."

"Cocoa," Bayard called. "Cocoa." Bayard flew to Cocoa's back and perched there. Cocoa didn't seem to mind. On the contrary, she looked pleased to have a parrot riding on her.

"That's Bayard Rustin," Sonjay pointed at the parrot.

"I know who he is," Jasper said. "I have heard about him from people in my circle."

"Your circle?" Maia asked, puzzled.

"Yes, you've arrived in one of the circles of the Settlement of the People Beyond the Lake. How are you related to the old four?" Jasper asked with growing excitement.

"Our mother is," Denzel faltered, "well, our mother was Debbie. She died. We were sent here by our Aunt Alice and our uncles."

Jasper's face fell. "Your mother passed into spirit?"

Denzel and Doshmisi nodded. The others remained silent.

Jasper shook his head from side to side. "Crystal was right. She said she has the Star Blood Fever because Debbie passed over. Sons and daughters of Debbie, please come with me to meet Crystal, my mother. She will know what to do." With that, Jasper turned and set out across the meadow at a fast pace. He appeared to be a little older than Doshmisi. He had long legs and the Goodacres had a hard time keeping up with him. Cocoa trotted along with Bayard still sitting on her back. They crossed the meadow and then followed a wide path that cut through a sparsely wooded grove. The path swiftly trailed into a manicured yard surrounding a tidy farmhouse with a red picket fence and a roof made of large, shiny leaves. The Goodacres followed Jasper through the crimson wooden door and into the house in silence.

Just inside, in an alcove with benches on either side, Jasper sat down and removed his shoes. He told the Goodacres to do the same. Denzel felt reluctant to leave his good Nikes behind, but it didn't strike him as a smart idea to argue over it. They entered a cozy living room with a scarlet bouquet of gladiolas on the coffee table, a thick burgundy rug on the floor, and a long maroon couch. At one end of the couch lay a thin, light-skinned brown woman with pale pink hair. She was propped up on pillows and covered with a light patchwork quilt. She looked like she had dozed off while reading. Her book lay on her chest.

Jasper gently touched her arm and called her name, "Crystal. Crystal, wake up, they have finally arrived."

Crystal murmured. Her eyelids fluttered open. Although at first glance Crystal looked old, the Goodacres could see that she had the eyes of a younger woman. Those eyes burned right through the children with their intense gaze. This did not scare them, but rather it welcomed them. A girl a little bit older than Jasper entered the room, wiping her hands on her apron and looking quizzically at Jasper and at the Goodacres.

Jasper turned to her and spoke excitedly. "They came. This time they came. You'll never guess. Their mother was Debbie. She passed into spirit. And so they came!"

"Did you bring the Amulet of the Trees?" The girl asked with hope and wonder.

"Yes, I have it," Doshmisi answered.

"And you have Alice's herbal?" The girl asked with unconcealed growing excitement.

Doshmisi nodded assent. "Oh my," the girl exclaimed. "Crystal! They arrived in time." Without warning, the girl burst into tears.

Crystal tried to prop herself up a little higher on her pillows with her elbows. She motioned to the girl. "Quickly, go find your father." The girl raced out of the room.

Jasper turned to the Goodacres. "That was my sister, Ruby, and this is my mom, Crystal," he told them. He introduced each of them to his mother.

"Is Ruby OK?" Sonjay asked.

Crystal called the Goodacres to come closer so she could see them better. "My daughter is just happy to see you. I have been gravely ill and she thinks that now that you have arrived with the herbal and the Amulet of the Trees that you will make me well. But we shall see."

Doshmisi replied in dismay, "But I don't know what to do with the herbal. I don't know anything."

"I know dear," Crystal told her. "It's your first time, so you'll have to figure it out from scratch. Alice would have known, but it is not for her to do. You will simply have to do the best that you can. Let's see Alice's herbal."

Doshmisi produced the worn little book from it's case which she wore around her waist. She handed it to Crystal.

"Do you see this dent on the cover?" Crystal asked.

The Goodacres and Jasper leaned in to peer at the book. They saw the dent. "If you place the Amulet of the Trees in that indentation, and place the book on the chest of the one you wish to heal, the book will turn to the page with the recipe for the correct medicine and instructions on how to administer it. Then you must follow the directions and perhaps it will work and perhaps it won't. One never knows. Especially with a healer, such as yourself, who has only just begun to use the herbal. But you would not have received the amulet if you did not have the talent of healing. The eldest always has the talent of healing."

"I'll try," Doshmisi told her. But inside she felt terrified, for she knew in her heart that Crystal was dying and that her family expected Doshmisi to save her life. Maia placed her hand gently on Doshmisi's arm in encouragement. Just then Ruby returned with Jasper's father, who shook hands with the Goodacres. The whole family had deep brown skin edged in bright red color with hair as red as the red crayon in the Crayola box; except for Crystal, whose illness must have drained most of the color out of her.

Crystal said, "I thought that your mother had probably passed over when I became ill. We were star blood sisters, your mother and I, and it often happens when one blood sister dies before her time that the other takes ill with the Star Blood Fever. Perhaps you can do nothing to help me, but we have only one way to find out."

It astonished the Goodacres that this foreign woman claimed a blood sisterhood with their mother. Doshmisi went to Crystal and nervously began to remove the amulet from around her neck. Crystal stopped her. "Hold on. You must never take the amulet from your neck," she told her. "I see they have told you nothing. If I regain some of my strength then I can explain a little. But you must travel to the islands to see Clover the Griot as soon as possible. She keeps the history. Listen up, sons and daughters of Debbie: never remove your amulet from your neck."

Doshmisi leaned forward so that the amulet could reach the herbal where it lay on Crystal's chest, and she pressed it into the indentation in the book. The moment the amulet touched the cover, the book began to glow with fluorescent green light. The light reminded Maia of the way radioactive objects looked in cartoons. Doshmisi held the amulet against the green shimmering book and requested, "Tell me what to do." She had to concentrate on holding the amulet in place as the green shimmer traveled up her arms and across her own chest.

"Now *that* is hecka cool!" Sonjay blurted, grinning.

Suddenly the book burst open of its own accord in a shower of green sparks and stood at the ready with a page for Doshmisi.

Doshmisi lifted the book from Crystal's chest and read out loud, "Star Blood Fever to be cured with star brush tea. Next it lists the ingredients. Then how much water to boil and how long to steep it. You drink three cups in an hour and then one cup every three hours for two days and two nights. That's all it says." Doshmisi looked up in panic, "I don't have these ingredients, you know."

"Mark the page," Crystal instructed weakly. She whispered to her husband, "Granite, you must hunt for the ingredients."

"My mother has lain near to death for two months," Ruby told Doshmisi, "but she has clung to life in the hope that you would come this summer with the Amulet of the Trees. And now you have arrived. We must find these ingredients. She has suffered so much while she waited for you. You have to save her."

"We'll find them," Sonjay told Ruby with determination. "Somehow."

"Now I see why Compost is headed this way," Granite said grimly.

"Compost?" Ruby exclaimed, her forehead puckered with worry.

"He has been sighted on the road traveling to our circle," Granite informed.

"Compost?" Sonjay asked. "Isn't compost kitchen garbage?"

"Well, yes," Granite replied, "but it's also the name of Sissrath's chief agent. His real name is Comice."

"He's named after a kind of a pear called Comice," Jasper contributed. "But no one calls him that. Everyone calls him Compost."

"To his face?" Denzel asked.

"Yeah, he likes it. Go figure," Jasper answered.

"He smells really bad," Ruby told them. "And he's proud of it so he likes to have people call him Compost. He considers it a compliment."

"That's messed up," Sonjay shook his head in disbelief.

"I would imagine Sissrath has awaited your return as eagerly as we have," Crystal speculated. "Because he can't wait to get rid of you. Beware of Compost. If he finds you, he'll take you directly to Sissrath. They must suspect your arrival."

"Compost has a sensitive nose," Granite added. "He can smell an ant on a blade of grass from ten yards away. He loves smelly things. Just like a dog. That's why he enjoys smelling like compost."

"The recipe," Ruby reminded them.

"Yes. The recipe." Granite turned his attention back to the recipe page, "We have some of these ingredients at the Garden, like sarafan and sage. Raspberries grow wild down by the pond."

"I know exactly where to find them," Jasper said.

Granite continued to study the page. "I think I know these ingredients and Jade the Gardener will help us with some of them. But I've never heard of star brush."

"We can ask Jade about it," Ruby assured her father.

Doshmisi suggested, "Let's copy out the list and divide it up. We'll follow Granite's instructions about where to look." Ruby gave Doshmisi a pencil and paper and Doshmisi began to copy the ingredients.

"We need flush grass and it's tough to cut. I'll take the boys with me to get that first while you girls go see Jade at the Garden. Jasper," Granite ordered, "go get Sheba and Tom for the girls to ride to the Garden. Take Denzel with you. I'll go get the tools we need."

Someone had to stay with Crystal, and they could see how much Ruby wanted to contribute to the hunt for the ingredients, so Maia offered to remain at the house.

As soon as Granite left, Ruby explained, "Each circle in our settlement has its own community garden. Everyone works in the Garden and we take whatever food we need from it. We have goats that produce milk and cheese. Some of us grow things at our houses also just because we like to; but mainly our food comes from the circle's Garden. Many of the ingredients in this recipe grow in the Garden."

Just then Sonjay, who had gone outside to the front of the house, burst into the room waving his arms frantically. "Check it out, you've got tigers in your front yard!" he shouted. "We gotta warn Granite and Denzel and Jasper!"

Ruby slowly turned a surprised face to Sonjay. Through the window Doshmisi and Maia saw two enormous white tigers lunge toward the house. The hair on the back of Doshmisi's neck stood up and Maia shrieked.

Chapter Three

The Hunt

Ruby burst into laughter. "That's Sheba and Tom," she cried. "Our tigers."

From the couch, Crystal spoke up faintly, "Ruby, they're not accustomed to tame tigers. Tigers are dangerous where they come from. Now explain to them, don't laugh at them."

But Ruby could not stop laughing at the horrified expressions on the faces of her guests.

"These are domesticated tigers," Crystal told them. "We keep them as pets and farm animals and, in our land, we ride them the way you ride horses in your land. You will find them swifter than horses and more intelligent. Your mother described horses to me. We don't have them here."

"And the tigers don't eat you?" Sonjay asked, incredulously.

"Not at all," Ruby replied, still giggling to herself. "They only eat fruit, leaves, and grasses. Look at their tiny teeth." Sure enough, when the children looked at their mouths, the tigers had the small teeth of a sheep or a goat, despite their body size and their large, clawed paws. "Oh you should have seen your faces," Ruby started laughing all over again.

"Sweet," Sonjay commented, and he went outside to check out Sheba and Tom.

"They travel very fast if they wish," Crystal said.

"You don't expect me to ride one of those, do you?" Doshmisi exclaimed, horrified.

"They won't hurt you," Ruby said. "We raised them from kittens.

You will love riding them, trust me."

"You are one of the Four," Crystal told Doshmisi, "you must show courage."

Doshmisi didn't want to show courage.

But then Granite returned with his tools and Jasper and Denzel appeared in the yard next to the tigers and it was time to go hunt for the ingredients for star brush tea. Bayard sat perched on Sheba's head and Denzel scratched Tom between the ears as Doshmisi ventured timidly out of the house. She could hear the big cats purring loudly. "You get to ride the tiger," Denzel told Doshmisi, jealously, as soon as she emerged. "You lucky dog. Man, I wish I had offered to go to the Garden. Look at these cats. Aren't they about the coolest animals you've ever seen?"

Bayard pecked Sheba lightly on the top of the head and Sheba growled playfully. Granite laughed at the bird and turned to Denzel, "You'll get a chance to ride one soon enough. I promise. But right now we men have important work of our own to do. Ruby, keep a sharp eye out for any sign of Compost and his officers on the road."

"I will," Ruby jumped astride Tom and gestured toward Sheba. Doshmisi unconsciously wrapped her hand tightly around her amulet through her shirt as she held her breath and walked over to the enormous cat with the big green eyes. Sheba nudged Doshmisi's hip with her nose, as if to say "It's alright, I'm gentle." With her heart beating wildly in her ears, Doshmisi mounted the tiger.

"Wrap your legs underneath and use them to hang on," Ruby advised. "You can grab the scruff of her neck to keep your balance, she won't mind."

Doshmisi glimpsed Sonjay hopping from one foot to the other in front of the house with excitement and calling to her "you go girl" as she headed down the path on Sheba, but he soon disappeared out of sight. The tigers increased their pace and Doshmisi had to concentrate on keeping the rhythm of the big cat's movements so she wouldn't fall off.

The path swiftly flowed into a dirt road, marked with tiger footprints. Once on the road, the tigers picked up their pace. They passed many farmhouses set back from the road, each one with a neat little yard that contained flowers and fruit trees. At some of the houses, people waved to Ruby as she rode past. She waved back. The people they passed glowed with different shades of red, from deep burgundy to practically pink. At the Garden, the tigers came to a halt in front of a corral in which several yellow-brown, striped tigers lazed. Ruby dismounted and opened the gate to the corral for Tom to go inside. Tom made straight for a large trough of lettuce. Doshmisi stepped down from Sheba with weak and wobbly legs.

Ruby led Doshmisi into a cluttered office adjoining a gardening shed, where she breathlessly informed a woman in faded overalls, "Jade, this is Doshmisi, daughter of Debbie, and she has come from the Farland just today. She has the Amulet of the Trees and she promised to try to make Crystal get well, and we…"

"Whoa, whoa, wait," Jade held up a callused, muddy hand, "slow down." She turned to Doshmisi. "The daughter of Debbie?" Her eyes widened in amazement as she scrutinized Doshmisi.

"And you have come wearing the Amulet of the Trees? Four of you have come?" Jade inquired.

"Yes," Doshmisi replied. "My sister stayed with Crystal and my brothers went with Granite to hunt for the ingredients for the medicine listed in Aunt Alice's herbal. That's why we rode over here, to ask for your help. We need some things to make the medicine for Crystal."

"Of course," Jade responded. "Well you must be the oldest, then. And I suppose you are starting from scratch and have no experience in the healing arts." Jade sighed and Doshmisi felt inadequate. "You will soon learn. Let's have a look," Jade reached for the book.

Doshmisi set the herbal on the desk. She had marked the page with a rubber band and memorized the page number. She feared that if she closed the book completely it wouldn't open again or the page number might move because the herbal acted like an enchanted thing. So she had put the thick rubber band around it to keep her place.

"My father has gone to gather the flush grass and raspberry leaves and some of the other wild ingredients. He will track down this one here and this one and this one down here," Ruby pointed to the page. "But we need a few things that grow in the Garden and none of us have a clue about the star brush. Have you ever heard of star brush?"

Jade studied the recipe. "I can help you with these," she said. Ruby looked relieved. "I bet your father won't know about the high thistle, but I know. It grows at the top of the oak trees around High Road Pond. Ruby come help me gather some of these things and then go tell your father where to find the high thistle. As for the star brush, only Doshmisi can obtain that." She turned to Doshmisi, "Follow that trail down there to the Grove of Shakabaz and the trees will help you once you enter the woods."

Doshmisi started at Jade's words, for she remembered that Aunt Alice had told them before they left that they must find the Staff of Shakabaz and take it away from someone. "Is that the same Shakabaz as the staff?" she asked Jade.

"Yes. The staff comes from the Grove of Shakabaz," Jade told her. "Sissrath possesses the Staff of Shakabaz and how he got his greasy hands on it is a long story for another time because you must make haste. It may take you some time to hunt down the star brush." Jade rose and, grabbing a couple of baskets, headed out into the magnificent garden that spread like a jeweled carpet in all directions. Ruby followed her. Doshmisi turned her steps toward the trail that Jade had pointed out.

Following the trail, Doshmisi soon found herself surrounded by trees. Some she recognized as evergreens like the ones at Manzanita Ranch but most of them looked like oaks and maples and the kinds of trees that put down deep roots. They boasted the light green new leaves of spring and early summer. The trees increased in size as she walked and before long the darkness of deep woods beneath a high tree canopy engulfed her. Thick vines crisscrossed above her head. The sound of her footsteps became muffled in the mossy forest bottom. The trail remained plain and clear so she did not fear losing her way, but she did fear unknown creatures hiding in the forest.

When she reached the heart of the woods, she came upon a clearing scarred with half a dozen enormous craters and on the far side of the clearing stood the largest trees she had ever seen in her life. She did not recognize them and could not identify them. They looked like some sort of red oak trees, as wide as the old growth California redwoods she had seen a few times in her life, but not nearly as tall. The bases of some of the trunks looked as big around as small cabins in which whole families could live. For just a moment she felt as though someone was calling to her, not in words, but in a deep way. A call straight to her heart. Like lightning or an evening breeze.

She skirted the craters in the clearing and entered the safe harbor of the grove of giant red oaks. As she stepped in among the giants, she heard a rush of whispers inside her head and a great heaviness overtook her limbs so that she had to sit down on the springy ground strewn with pine needles, moss, twigs, fallen lichens, and leaves. The Amulet of the Trees began to shimmer with green iridescence as it had when she had inserted it into the herbal. She closed her eyes and a communication entered her head, not in speech, but in images and understanding. In thought and energy. She would later describe it as the language of the trees, for she knew that in her heart she heard the trees "speaking" to her.

They welcomed her with their rough, green grace and embraced her in their fashion. She could feel a deep sorrow among them, but sensed their joy at her presence, their hope at her arrival. She did not know how long she sat soaking in the wordless messages sent to her by the trees before she remembered her mission.

She focused her mind on the image of Crystal, lying on the maroon couch, sick almost to death, and with the herbal on her chest, open to the recipe for star brush tea. She could feel a rippling sigh go through the trees. Then an image came into her mind of a scrubby plant with sharp-pointed, tiny pale purply flowers. She saw the image of this plant growing between the enormous, raised, outstretched roots of a large tree in the grove. Doshmisi opened her eyes and looked around. She stood up and continued on into the grove for a short distance until she recognized the purple flowers that she had seen in her mind's eye. Not even knowing why, she closed her eyes again and sent a wordless message to the trees of the Grove of Shakabaz, asking permission to pick the scrubby plant with it's milky-pale violet-tinged flowers from between the arms of the tree roots. She received permission and then bent to gather the plant, which she knew could only be star brush. She did not know how much to pick, but after she had gathered a little bundle in the crook of her arm, the trees let her know she had taken enough for the task at hand. She thanked them in the new silent language that she had learned from them and returned the way she came.

This time, as she crossed the clearing of craters, she felt such sorrow that she thought her heart would break. Each crater called out to her in excruciating pain. But when she entered the forest that lay between her and the Garden, she felt the joy of young and hopeful trees. She felt as though the trees recognized her and their spirits rejoiced at her presence. She put the star brush down on the ground at her feet and held the Amulet of the Trees with both hands and closed her eyes. Her spirit danced up into the treetops with the wordless voices that surrounded her. She thought she would never feel so happy and so much at home again as she did in that moment.

Then she opened her eyes and picked up the star brush and continued back out of the woods and into the Garden where Jade eagerly awaited her. It surprised her to realize that the bright afternoon had faded and the enormous greenish sun of Faracadar poised ready to duck its cheerful head behind the horizon. Jade certainly looked pleased to see the star brush.

"I sent Ruby on ahead to tell Granite where to find the high thistle. Sheba will take you back. I can see that you have spoken with the ancient ones; they've left their imprint in your eyes," Jade gently rubbed her thumb across Doshmisi's forehead just above the bridge of her nose. She hugged Doshmisi quickly then helped her mount Sheba. After her experience in the Grove of Shakabaz, Doshmisi didn't feel as frightened of Sheba. In fact, she felt completely calm, as if nothing evil could touch her while the trees watched over her. She clung to the star brush with one hand and the tiger with the other and wondered at how far she had traveled from her familiar life in the little apartment in the city.

While Doshmisi was communicating with the ancient trees, the boys and Granite were cutting the flush grass and gathering other ingredients. At first, Granite was so intent on finding and cutting the flush grass, that he didn't review the list that Maia had made for him of the wild ingredients needed for the medicine. Denzel, Jasper, and Granite worked hard sawing at the tough fronds that looked like thick wheat but resisted the knife. Cocoa wandered around, poking her nose into every hollow stump and gopher mound, sniffing and snorting eagerly. Sonjay walked a short distance from the grassland to High Road Pond to pick raspberry leaves. Bayard flitted off to eat raspberries and explore.

Sonjay ate some of the juicy berries while he picked the leaves. Suddenly, Bayard circled overhead calling "skeeter, skeeter." He quickly flew to Granite, alighting on his shoulder with the same frantic cry. "Skeeter, skeeter."

Granite combed the sky with his eyes and shouted urgently, "Sonjay, come back here, now!" Sonjay did not question the command. He ran back to the others.

"Quick, lay down on the ground." Granite threw Denzel and Sonjay onto the ground in the tall grass and covered them completely with a red and white checkered tablecloth. "You can talk, but don't move," he instructed. "Don't move a hair." Then Granite sat down on Denzel's back and motioned Jasper to sit on Sonjay.

"Am I hurting you?" Granite asked anxiously.

"You're kind of heavy," Denzel's muffled voice emerged from under the tablecloth. "What's up? Why are you sitting on me?"

"Sorry, I'll explain in a minute. Jasper grab that bag of fruit and spread it out between us. Pretend we're having a picnic," Granite urgently directed his son.

Meanwhile, Bayard perched in a nearby tree and continued to repeat that one word "skeeter."

"What's Bayard saying?" Sonjay asked. "What's going on out there?"

"It's a skeeter," Granite said. "Don't try to look at it because if you can see the skeeter then it can see you."

"It's a white bird," Jasper told them, "with horrible big yellow eyes. It can see for miles."

"It can see a spider on a blade of grass from half a mile away," Granite elaborated. "Compost uses skeeters as spies. It's probably out here hunting for you. Lucky for us that Bayard saw it before it got close."

"Can you see it right now?" Denzel asked.

"Yes, it's flying overhead," Jasper whispered.

"It can't hear you," Granite told Jasper. "You don't have to whisper."

Bayard took off out of the tree to follow the skeeter. Granite and Jasper pretended to eat some fruit.

"It flew out of sight," Jasper finally told them with relief.

"Then can you please get off my back?" Sonjay asked.

"Wait a minute," Granite cautioned. "We have to make sure it's not coming back."

But Bayard flew to them an instant later and squawked "party's over."

"It's probably heading on up the High Road," Granite speculated. "I bet it just flew over here by chance." Granite and Jasper stood up and helped Denzel and Sonjay out from under the tablecloth.

"That's the first time someone had a picnic on me," Sonjay muttered, brushing off his clothes.

With a glance overhead, Granite unfolded his list. He nodded his head several times and then a worried expression came over his face. He led them into a wooded area where they collected several roots and leaves at his direction. But he kept unfolding his list and rereading it nervously and then refolding it, his forehead knotted. Sonjay finally asked, "Is something wrong?"

"Sort of. I thought I knew these ingredients but actually I don't know one of them," Granite answered.

When they came out of the woods, they saw Ruby riding astride Tom through the grassland on the other side of the pond. She shouted something that they couldn't make out.

It sounds like she said, "I throw hair to fry the high whistle," Denzel pronounced.

Jasper and Sonjay broke into laughter. "That doesn't mean anything. Man, you know you can't hear her from way out here," Sonjay said.

"I can hear her," Granite said, straining for the sound, as Ruby drew near.

"Don't worry," Ruby shouted. They could hear that. And when she came within earshot they heard her clearly as she called, "I know where to find the high thistle."

Granite's face relaxed with relief. "She knows the last ingredient, the one that I didn't recognize."

Ruby arrived, breathless and flushed, dismounted Tom and sent him down to the pond to drink. "Did you see the skeeter in time?" she asked right away.

"Yes," her father replied. "Bayard warned us."

Ruby nodded, "It went down the High Road. It's long gone. Hey, Jade said to tell you that the high thistle grows at the top of the tall oaks that ring the High Road Pond. She said you wouldn't know it. I dropped the Garden ingredients off at the house. Crystal is sleeping. Jade sent Doshmisi into the Grove of Shakabaz for the star brush."

"Shakabaz?" Sonjay exclaimed. "Denzel, isn't that the name of that thingamajig we're supposed to find?"

"Yeah, man," Denzel replied. He turned to Granite, "Aunt Alice told us we have to take the Staff of Shakabaz from this dude named Sissrath."

Granite laughed, "Oh she did, did she? That 'dude' only happens to be the most powerful enchanter in Faracadar and the chief advisor, or should I say chief taskmaster, of High Chief Hyacinth."

At the mention of the name "Hyacinth," Bayard dove down from a great height to call out to them "Hyacinth is a fool." And then he perched on Sonjay's shoulder.

"Hush," said Granite. "Even if it's true, you mustn't say it out loud. Sissrath will pluck you and eat you as an appetizer and you'll get the rest of us killed." He looked around as if half-expecting to find one of Sissrath's spies listening.

"It's getting late," Ruby reminded them, "and we still need the high thistle." As the sun sank in the sky and the evening air became cooler, Granite walked over to one of the oak trees that ringed the pond and looked up into its branches.

"How do we pick that high thistle way up there before it gets dark out?" Jasper asked his father.

"I don't know," Granite scratched his head and continued to look up into the tree. They stared up at the towering oak. "Jade says it grows at the very top of the tree?" he asked Ruby.

"The very top," Ruby confirmed. "That's what Jade said. The high thistle grows at the top of the oak trees that ring the pond."

From his perch on Sonjay's shoulder, Bayard repeated the words "high thistle" several times. He cocked his head one way and then the other, eyeing the top of the tree with his one-sided bird vision.

Sonjay echoed the bird, saying "high thistle."

Suddenly Bayard leapt off Sonjay's shoulder with a clatter of wings and flew to the top of the oak tree, where he pecked at the uppermost branches. Sonjay watched him for a moment and then he shouted, "Look, Bayard is picking the high thistle!" Sure enough, the bird flew back down with several bristly sprigs of something resembling spiky, red mistletoe in his mouth, dropped them at Granite's feet, and then returned to the top of the tree. In no time at all, Bayard had collected a big bunch of high thistle and the search party turned their steps back toward the house.

Doshmisi arrived at Crystal and Granite's house at sunset to find the others eagerly waiting for her with all the ingredients from the recipe spread out on the dining room table. At Crystal's instruction, Maia had made a vegetable soup for dinner and set it out in the kitchen with homemade bread that Ruby had baked earlier in the day.

Sonjay ate the bread, but the soup looked to him like it had an awful lot of green things floating in it. Suddenly he remembered the meatloaf sandwiches that Uncle Martin had packed for them and he retrieved them from Denzel's knapsack.

Doshmisi prepared to cut up the meatloaf sandwiches and share them with their hosts, when Ruby asked, "Are those animal sandwiches?"

"Meatloaf," Denzel told her.

"We don't eat animals," Ruby informed them, with a shocked expression.

"Only the Mountain People eat animals," Jasper explained. "None of the other peoples eat things that walk or swim or fly."

Doshmisi reluctantly started to put away the meatloaf sandwiches, but Sonjay would not allow that. He took a big, fat sandwich outside and sat on the top step and wolfed it down. Denzel soon joined him with a sandwich of his own. Now the Goodacres realized why Uncle Martin had packed the sandwiches. It looked like they might have to go a long time before they would eat meat again.

"We gotta find those Mountain People before we starve to death," Sonjay declared. "You understand what I'm saying?"

"Yeah, man, I hear you. I'm not sure how long I'm gonna last without a burger and fries," Denzel replied, and he even ate the crusts on his sandwich.

The boys looked out at the yard, which had grown dark since the sun went down. The land around them looked more ordinary at night, when the brightness of the colors didn't blare at them so loudly. But the sky reminded them that they were not at Manzanita Ranch. The colorful stars shone above them with a much greater intensity than during the daytime. And they did not see a moon anywhere.

"I can't believe we're really here," Denzel said. "This isn't a dream is it?"

"Pretty realistic dream," Sonjay replied.

"Very realistic," Denzel agreed.

The boys went back into the house, where they could smell the first brew of the star brush tea steeping in the kitchen. Doshmisi had not eaten her soup until she had set the tea to steep and now she sat with her soup bowl balanced on her knees in a chair next to Crystal.

"Hey what happened to the moon?" Sonjay asked.

"We don't have one," Crystal answered simply.

Sonjay made a low whistle as he mulled over the idea of no moon.

"Maia can share Ruby's bed," Crystal told Granite, "and you should set up the cots in Jasper's room for the boys."

"What about Doshmisi?" Granite asked.

"I'm going to sleep here, next to Crystal, so I can make the tea every three hours during the night," Doshmisi said.

Denzel looked at his sister in surprise. He knew how much she hated having her sleep interrupted, and he valued his life too much to ever try to wake her up in the morning. But here she offered to wake up all night long to make tea for Crystal. He looked at her as if to say

"Have you lost it?" but Doshmisi shrugged off his look and finished her soup.

Granite set up the cots in Jasper's room. Doshmisi looked in the bottom of Denzel's knapsack and found toothbrushes, much to Sonjay's dismay.

"Who ever heard of taking your toothbrush with you on an adventure?" Sonjay rolled his eyes and grumbled.

"When the adventure is over, you don't want rotten teeth, do you?" Doshmisi asked.

"How do you know they even have tooth rot here?" Sonjay demanded. But Doshmisi pointed to the bathroom and gave him what Sonjay called "the look" so he went to clean his teeth without further argument.

Granite made up a bed for Doshmisi on a pad on the floor next to Crystal, who had already dozed off. Before he went to his own room, Granite self-consciously took Doshmisi's hands in his large, work-worn ones. "I don't know how to thank you," he told her awkwardly.

Doshmisi looked up into his kind face and said, "I know what it feels like to have your mother die. If I can protect Ruby and Jasper from that then it's worth it."

"Raspberries," squawked Bayard sleepily from his perch on the back of a chair.

"Did you keep an eye on how much that bird ate today?" Doshmisi asked Granite.

"I'm afraid I didn't," Granite answered.

"He's going to get so fat that he won't be able to fly by the time we leave this place if I don't watch him," Doshmisi said with a smile.

"Goodnight, daughter of Debbie," Granite said and went up the narrow stairs to his room.

Doshmisi laid down on her mat on the floor, which she found perfectly comfortable, set her alarm to wake herself up for the next brew of tea, and soon wandered into a wonderful dream in which she talked to large, wise trees.

Chapter Four

Sun Power

Denzel slept later than usual. When he awoke, he found the other beds empty and the sun peeked gaily through the bedroom window. He hurriedly pulled on his jeans. He had left his baseball cap behind at Manzanita Ranch and his head felt bare without it. He bolted down the stairs to find everyone else perching giant cups of cocoa on their knees where they sat around the living room. Crystal, no longer propped on pillows, but sitting up straight on her own on the couch, held court. Crystal's hair had turned a deeper shade of pink during the night and her skin, which had looked rather gray when she went to bed, had a rosier tone to it. She looked rested and stronger. Crystal glanced up as Denzel descended the stairs.

"Lookin' good this morning, Crystal," Denzel gave her the thumbs-up.

"I feel much better," Crystal responded. "Your sister jumped in with both feet and I guarantee you that she will soon be an expert in the healing arts, just like Alice before her."

Ruby poured Denzel a steaming cup of cocoa and handed it to him. Denzel noted that Doshmisi looked tired.

"Crystal just told us a story about one of her adventures with Mama back in the day," Maia told Denzel. Denzel wanted to hear the story, but Crystal shooed them into the kitchen where Granite flipped giant blueberry pancakes on a griddle, then stacked them up on plates and smothered them with syrup. Bayard perched on the edge of a bucket full of blueberries and picked them out one at a time with his sharp beak.

Doshmisi had brewed another cup of tea for Crystal and she started to take it to her when Crystal surprised them by turning up in the doorway of the kitchen, swaying slightly. Ruby burst into tears.

"*Now* what's the matter?" Sonjay asked.

"Crystal hasn't stood up and walked on her own for a few weeks," Granite said as he put his arms around his daughter.

"I don't get it," Sonjay pondered aloud, "Ruby always cries when good things happen. What does she do when bad things happen?"

"Boy, you have a lot to learn about women," Granite told Sonjay.

Crystal ran her hand affectionately across Sonjay's head and then sat in a chair at the table to sip the miraculous healing tea that Doshmisi had brewed.

Sonjay attacked a giant pancake. "So what kind of sports do you play here? Can we meet some more of the people in your circle?" Sonjay asked between mouthfuls of pancake.

"I'll take you to the center this morning if you like," Jasper offered. "I can't wait to share the news of my mother's cure."

"You will do no such thing," Crystal told her son abruptly. "As soon as word gets out that I'm cured then Sissrath will know for certain that the Four have returned. He will have Compost turn over every rock in the circle looking for them."

"That is why you must leave," Granite informed his guests. "This is the first place Sissrath will look for you."

"My sister needs to get some sleep before we travel anywhere," Denzel insisted, looking at Doshmisi worriedly.

"I guess I didn't have a restful night," Doshmisi confessed. "And I'm not good at sleeping when it's so light out."

"Then first thing tomorrow, you must go," Crystal instructed.

"Go where?" Maia asked.

"To see Clover the Griot on Whale Island. She keeps the history there at the library and she has the wisdom to answer your questions so you can figure out what you must do," Crystal told them.

Jasper set his cocoa cup down in the saucer and looked up at his father. "You know I must go as their guide. I have trained for this my whole life."

Granite sighed, "Yes, I know it. I have regained my wife only to lose my son."

"No loss, just separated for a time," Crystal told him, covering his hand with hers. "And he has prepared for this long and hard and for this purpose the circle has protected him from the tax collectors."

"Hold on, I'm lost," Denzel said shaking his head. "Let's rewind to the part about Jasper preparing for this his whole life and explain what the heck you're talking about."

"We've waited for many years for the return of the Four," Jasper said. "And as more and more time passed, we figured out that the old four would probably not return but we've hoped for a new four to replace them. And we knew that if a new four came, they would need a guide. The circle chose me and I trained as a guide. The Four always come through the gate in our circle. So we thought that if you came, you would arrive here, and so you would need someone from our circle to take you to Clover the Griot and to Big House City, the ruling center for our land, and to wherever you need to go."

"But you see," Granite told them, "everyone knows that the Four come through the gate in our circle. Everyone including Hyacinth and Sissrath and his spies and warriors. As soon as word of Crystal's recovery spreads, others will guess that you have arrived in the land."

"What makes Sissrath so nasty, anyway?" Sonjay asked hotly. "I'm tired of hearing Sissrath this and Sissrath that. What makes everyone so afraid of him?"

"He's a mighty enchanter who rose up from the Mountain People," Crystal told them. "The Mountain People live in the Amber Mountains. They have the ability to harness their knowledge of the mysteries of nature and enchantment to exercise tremendous power. The wisest and most skilled enchanters come from the Mountain People. While many of them, through years and years of study, become the eyes and arms of wisdom; others, like Sissrath, have ruined themselves with their lust for wealth and power. He uses his skills to serve only his own purposes. He has no soul. He has terrorized High Chief Hyacinth into doing his bidding. And he invented the coins to enslave the people throughout the land."

"With his ridiculous coins and his efforts to gain more and more power, he has broken the peace of the people," Granite continued. "The people say that Sissrath invented the coins just so that he could collect them himself and have the most in the land. We think he invented them so that he would have a way to measure the fact that he is the most wealthy person in Faracadar."

"You mean before he invented money, or the coins as you call them, you didn't have any? How did you buy things? Like shoes or blankets or chairs or things?" Denzel asked.

"We don't need to buy things. We trade. We have never needed these raggedy in-between coins and we still don't need them," Granite said bitterly. "Everyone in the circle has skills and talents and we can share them, we always have. The Garden belongs to everyone and we work there together and we eat what we grow. But now Sissrath demands coins from the citizens every year."

"A tax," Maia said.

"Exactly," Granite continued. "He makes us pay a tax and the only way for the people to get coins to pay the tax is for us to send the young people of our circles to serve in Sissrath's army. The young people go to Big House City where they serve Sissrath and the royal family."

"And in exchange, they receive coins for their service, which they send home to the circles for their parents to use to pay the taxes," Ruby interjected.

"That's right," Granite said. "Every year, the tax collectors come to the circles where the people either pay taxes or send their sons and daughters. So families have started scrambling to gather coins so they can pay up and not have to send their children away to Sissrath's army. Some people have started to ask for coins for the services and goods they used to provide to their neighbors only in trade, or as their contribution to the circle. With each passing day, people become more dependent on the coins and use the old trade system less."

"So the coins have started making some people rich and some people poor?" Doshmisi asked, as she began to understand the meaning of Granite's explanation.

"Yes. Our son Mica is serving in the army to help pay the circle's tax because we have no other source of coins," Granite told them. "Sissrath's taxes have also resulted in people working as spies for coins. People spy for Sissrath in order to protect their own children."

"What happens if the circle can't pay the tax collectors and you refuse to send your children?" Maia asked.

Granite and Crystal exchanged a look of fear.

"He has burned down some rebel circles," Jasper said quietly.

"He killed and scattered the people," Ruby added sadly.

"Before we left our world, Aunt Alice told us that we have to take back the Staff of Shakabaz from Sissrath. If we do that, will he lose his power?" Sonjay asked.

"No, he will still have the powers of a skilled enchanter," Crystal answered. "But he will lose the special powers he receives from possession of Shakabaz. Also, the people will fear him much less and I think that High Chief Hyacinth could then be persuaded to break away from him. The high chief is not a bad man. He just lacks spine."

"So how do we take this Shakabaz away from him?" Sonjay asked.

"We kind of thought you would figure that out," Jasper said hopefully.

"How wonderful if you could take Shakabaz from him," Granite sighed.

"You absolutely must go speak with Clover, and the sooner the better," Crystal told them urgently. "She will answer your questions. She can tell you the true history of your mother, your uncles, and your aunt, and the properties of Shakabaz. I don't even know for sure if what I have heard has full truth in it. Only Clover can tell you the truth. And you will need the power of truth to accomplish the task of retrieving Shakabaz."

"Some say that Shakabaz can create and destroy life, just like the Great Spirit," Ruby said, almost in a whisper.

"One story among many, and Clover will know for sure," Crystal amended firmly.

"What do you call this circle?" Maia asked shyly.

Crystal and Granite fell silent and did not readily answer.

"We used to call it the Circle of the Gate," Jasper told them. "But

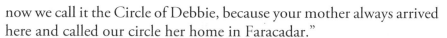

now we call it the Circle of Debbie, because your mother always arrived here and called our circle her home in Faracadar."

"Now you see why you can't stay here," Crystal said. "Because Sissrath will look here for you first; in fact, it seems that Compost is already on his way."

The Goodacres had a great many things to think about after breakfast. Doshmisi stayed at the house and continued to brew the tea for Crystal. She showed Ruby how to do it for the coming night. Jasper took Denzel, Maia, and Sonjay for a ride on the tigers so they could get used to them. Granite had to leave to do his designated chores at the circle.

After lunch, when Granite returned, he had a letter from his elder son Mica with him. The family sat down eagerly to hear him read the news. Granite told the Goodacres that before Mica went into the army, he and some of his friends in the circle had tried to figure out how to build a kind of solar panel to collect energy from the sun. Mica wrote about continuing his work on this project at Big House City with some of his companions in the army. Most of his letter had to do with this work, which excited him tremendously.

After Granite finished reading the letter out loud, Denzel asked, "What type of energy do you use here to operate your lights and water pumps and stuff?"

"We have one among us who works as our battery maker," Granite explained. "He builds batteries from chemicals that he brews from plants grown in the Garden. When the batteries run out of energy, we return them to him and he takes them apart and replaces them with fresh chemicals. But Mica had this idea that we could collect energy from the sun to recharge the batteries instead of constantly rebuilding them. He was trying to build something he called a solar collector when he left for the army."

"Now that's a trip because I know exactly what he has in mind, wait right here," Denzel interrupted Granite. He ran up to his room and pulled open the knapsack that Uncle Martin had given him. He rummaged through it for the solar battery charger and ran back downstairs to show it to Granite.

As Granite turned the little charger around in his large hands, Denzel told him, "where I come from, we already use solar panels to gather energy. This is one of them. It's a small one to charge small batteries. I started checking out how these things work before we came to your land and I know something about them."

Granite studied Denzel's face, then handed the solar charger back to him. "Your great uncle, Charles, taught us how to make batteries in the first place. He too wore the Amulet of Metal. I think you should meet our battery maker. I'll take you to him." As Denzel followed Granite from the house, he realized that the amulet resting on his chest had become warm and it glowed faintly with a red light.

Granite led Denzel to the paddock where the tigers lazed in the sun. He called two of the tigers to him, he and Denzel mounted, and they proceeded through the woods. "I don't want to take the main road," Granite called to Denzel over his shoulder, "because we don't want to run into Compost's spies."

They soon arrived at a cottage surrounded by heaps of parts of mechanical things in various stages of disintegration. Granite rode right past the cottage and out to a large barn from which emerged the sound of hammering. He hopped off his tiger and beckoned Denzel inside, where workbenches loaded with strange objects and tools spilled over onto the floor. Gadgets and gizmos in varying states of assembly and disassembly covered every horizontal surface. A large man, deep burgundy in color and quite bald, tinkered at one of the workbenches. He had enormous, muscular hands.

"Meet our circle's battery maker, Diamond," Granite said. He turned to Diamond, "You must swear to me that you will keep silent about this young man. Our lives may depend on it."

Denzel drew the amulet out of his shirt and held it up in front of his face. It had begun to throb with a strong red glow as soon as he had entered Diamond's workshop.

Diamond gasped, "He is one of the Four."

"Denzel, Son of Debbie," Granite confirmed with a note of satisfaction in his voice. "Arrived yesterday with three others. The new four. Debbie passed into spirit." A shadow passed over Diamond's face at this news. Granite continued, "Denzel has something you must see, which is why I brought him here. Do you remember Mica's idea that we can capture energy from the sun?"

"Of course. We've been writing to each other about it. I have a drawing here that he sent me just today."

"Yes, I received it too." Granite turned to Denzel, "Show him the solar charger."

Denzel removed the charger from his pocket and handed it to Diamond. "I brought this solar panel. Actually, Uncle Martin put it in my bag. It's a small one," he explained. "We have large ones, too, where I come from. I know how these things work. I could probably help you build one so that you can use power from the sun to recharge your batteries instead of rebuilding them all the time."

"Here," Diamond took a paper from his pocket and handed it to Denzel, "Mica sent me this."

Denzel studied Mica's drawing while Diamond turned the solar charger around in his hands. "Do you have wire? And a sheet of glass and a glass cutter?" Denzel asked.

Diamond laughed. "I have everything," he said waving his arm in an arc to encompass his kingdom of chaos. In no time at all the two of them lost themselves in Diamond's kingdom. They decided to sacrifice Denzel's charger to their task and pulled it apart to see exactly how it went together. Denzel figured out how to bend and fit the wire on a larger scale. While they worked, Granite paced outside the door of the barn. After awhile, it occurred to Denzel that Granite had stuck around to stand guard. Denzel went to the doorway.

Granite stopped pacing and they looked at each other. "Go home, Granite. Go check on Crystal. I'm going to stay here for awhile to work with Diamond. The skeeter can't see inside the barn." Denzel didn't generally tell grown-ups what to do, but it seemed like the right thing to say.

Diamond emerged from the workshop, wiping his hand on a rag, "Denzel's right. You should go home to Crystal. How is she?"

"Doshmisi, the eldest of the Four, has cured her with a tea," Granite told Diamond.

"Wonderful news, and all the more reason why you belong at home. We may need to work on into the evening and he can spend the night here if necessary. I'll bring him back safely to you before breakfast. I promise."

"You know that Compost is on his way?" Granite asked, worriedly.

"I have heard. Just leave Denzel with me for one night. If we can solve this problem and build this thing, then it will change the energy game, not just in this circle but throughout the settlements," Diamond's eyes glistened with anticipation. "Think what it will mean to Mica."

Granite reluctantly turned to go. "I'll leave Quincy with you for Denzel to ride back in the morning. Perhaps you should show Denzel how to bed him down for the night, since he will travel with him soon."

"I'm on it," Diamond told him. "Quincy will do just fine with my tiger in the paddock."

Denzel and Diamond worked through the evening, stopping only for some hastily made peanut butter sandwiches. Denzel fitted the large panel together while Diamond reassembled Denzel's little panel for him to take with him to show to other battery makers in other circles in the days to come. By the time they finished building the large panel, the sun had gone down and night had crept into the corners of the barn.

Then Denzel noticed some metal wheel-holders in Diamond's shop that he figured could work as skateboard trucks and it gave him an idea. He scrounged up a nice flat piece of wood and had Diamond find him the kind of wheels he needed. To Diamond's amazement, Denzel made himself a skateboard. He glued some sandpaper to the top of it and trimmed the edges. It looked pretty good in the end, all things considered. When he tried it out on the floor of the shop, it worked. So he made a second one for Sonjay while showing Diamond how to make one that Denzel could give to Jasper. Diamond produced some rope from which he made carrying slings for the skateboards. The skateboards really pleased Denzel, and this made Diamond feel like he had given Denzel something in return for the solar panel.

After they completed the skateboards, the two of them left the shop and walked up to the house under an inky black, moonless sky dotted with a zillion colorful stars arranged in constellations completely unfamiliar to Denzel. He and Diamond happily fell asleep on deep, squishy couches amid the piles of parts and pieces sprawled across the living room. Denzel felt at home in the battery maker's untidy house of inventions. Just before he nodded off, he noted that the Amulet of Metal, which had glowed with red light all day long, had finally gone dark, although it retained a warmth to it where it lay on his chest.

Diamond and Denzel awoke at first light. Diamond fixed Denzel a cup of sweet coffee with cream. Denzel had never had coffee before and he discovered that he liked it. They proceeded to Diamond's workshop and hooked the solar panel up to one of Diamond's batteries. Diamond took the panel and battery outside and aimed the panel at the sun.

After they set up the panel to collect energy from the sun, Denzel went into Diamond's barn, cleared a few objects out of the way, and showed Diamond an ollie and a kickflip on the skateboard. He messed up the kickflip the first time but landed it the second. "I'm a little out of practice," he told Diamond. While they waited for the sun to do its work with the solar panel, Denzel checked out what he could do on the rough-hewn skateboard until Diamond said, "Let's take a look at our invention. The sun is high enough in the sky and I promised I'd take you back to Granite for breakfast. So let's give it a shot."

Diamond connected the battery to a little water fountain in his yard. "This was a completely dead battery," Diamond told Denzel. But as soon as he touched the wire to the fountain it spurted water out of the mouth of a little ebony dolphin. Diamond sat down right there on the ground and laughed with a deep rumbling laugh. "Terrific. Absolutely terrific. Magnificent. Wait until Mica hears this. He was right all along. This completely changes the energy game. You have no idea. Absolutely no idea."

"I wish I could meet Mica," Denzel said wistfully.

"One day, perhaps you will. You might even have a chance to work with him on another one of his projects sometime. He thinks he can figure out a way to talk to people from a great distance through a wire," Diamond told Denzel.

Denzel realized that Mica had figured out the concept of a telephone. He smiled to himself. He didn't think he could help out much with building a telephone right now. He would have to do a lot more reading, studying, and tinkering back at Manzanita Ranch first. If he ever got back to Manzanita Ranch. He wondered if he would have the chance to learn more about how things worked in his own world one day so that he could bring what he learned to Faracadar to help his new friends. If he could do that, he'd have a lot to share with this clever Mica. He imagined bringing a computer to Mica. That would blow him away!

"Let's get you back to Granite," Diamond said, interrupting Denzel's thoughts. "You have to hit the road soon."

When Denzel and Diamond arrived at the house, they found Crystal in the kitchen taking trays of muffins out of the oven. Diamond gave her a warm hug. "Look who's up and busy," he said. She looked marvelous. Her hair had gone a rich maroon color and her face had a returned youthfulness.

"Where did everyone go?" Denzel asked.

"Down to the pond to pick raspberries. It was the only way to keep that loud-mouthed bird of yours quiet! They'll be back any minute," Crystal told Denzel. "Do you want a glass of cider?"

Denzel and Diamond sat down at the table with tall glasses of cool apple cider. The morning sun cast an amber tint to the kitchen, promising a clear and beautiful day. Denzel had only taken one sip of his cider when the others burst into the kitchen with baskets full of raspberries, bright and juicy. Cocoa barked gleefully, Bayard squawked "raspberries," and the young people talked and laughed together at once.

"Hey," Granite greeted Denzel and Diamond, "Any luck?"

"Extremely successful," Diamond told him. "Beyond my wildest dreams. Wait until you see what I can do with what Denzel has shown me. Wait until Mica sees. He knew all along. If they hadn't taken him away for that ridiculous army, I think he would have figured this out last year. I miss him."

"We all do," Granite agreed.

They sat around the kitchen table like one big family, celebrating the return of Crystal's health and the success of the solar panel, until Sonjay leaned across the table abruptly and demanded of Crystal, with an authority in his voice that startled his sisters and brother, "Before we ride off looking for Clover, I want to know more about this place and what we're doing here. What can you tell me that I should know?"

Silence fell like a curtain over the breakfast party.

Crystal pushed herself back in her chair and surveyed Sonjay seriously. "What can I tell you that will be helpful? Well. The People Beyond the Lake, like us here in this circle, have a reputation as inventors and mechanics and engineers. The Island People produce our greatest healers and most gifted farmers. The Coast People are mostly artists and musicians, dancers and writers. And the Mountain People are generally the wisest ones because they have the greatest ability to use the energy of enchantments in Faracadar. The Mountain People are shy, private people who keep to themselves, but they are also the most capable of leadership and from among them have come our greatest enchanters. Although these descriptions of our peoples generally hold true, they're not entirely true since people can be quite different. And each settlement has its own healers and mechanics and leaders and musicians of course. For the most part, we live in our own settlements made up of small communities called circles. The high chief governs the land from the seat of power at Big House City."

"Who chooses the high chief?" Denzel asked.

"The position of high chief is inherited and has come down through the royal line. Right now we have High Chief Hyacinth," Crystal told him.

"Hyacinth is a fool," Bayard interjected energetically.

"He says that all the time. I used to wonder what it meant until we came here," Maia said.

"I wouldn't exactly call Hyacinth a fool. He's weak-willed, frightens easily, and bows to the influence of others. He doesn't keep it a secret that he would rather care for his animals than rule the people. He didn't want the job of high chief in the first place. He was next in line for it. And he's terrified of Sissrath. I think he would actually rule very well, with justice and kindness, if he could get out from under Sissrath's thumb." Crystal sighed, "Our Mountain People are a mystery and a trial. They have the power to do such good, but also such evil. Sissrath's use of Shakabaz is a case in point."

"Shakabaz came from one of the trees in the grove of ancient trees beside the Garden, didn't it?" Doshmisi wanted to learn more about the trees.

"Yes, it did. A mighty and wise red oak named Shakabaz, the oldest tree in the land, once lived in the grove right here in this circle. The people of Faracadar recognized Shakabaz as one of our greatest teachers. Perhaps Doshmisi saw the scars in the ground from where they ripped out the oldest red oaks during the Battle of Blood Winter. Shakabaz fell during that battle and as the mighty tree lay dying it commanded your mother, who was not much older than Sonjay at the time, to have a staff made from the wood at the core of the massive trunk. It broke our hearts to do so, but the elders of the circle cut into the dead tree and removed the core and gave it to the finest woodcarver of the Coast People who fashioned a strong and beautiful staff from the precious piece of wood. Then the greatest enchanter who ever lived, Hazamon, took the staff and wove a deep power into it. In your mother's hands, the staff performed mighty enchantments and protected the people from harm. Your mother carried Shakabaz with her always until Sissrath stole it from her. The staff has potent powers and Sissrath uses it to do harm to people who will not bend to his will. I expect Shakabaz rightfully belongs to Sonjay. From the youngest to the youngest. That is how it usually goes with the Four." Crystal opened her mouth to say something further but the words never came out because at that moment there was a knock at the door.

Jade from the Garden poked her head into the kitchen tentatively. "Sorry to bother you. Compost has been seen traveling on the High Road. Sniffing his way here. You would have to smell that man to believe him. I came to warn the Four, I think they had better hurry on their way."

Diamond told Denzel quickly, "Wherever you travel from here, please take your small solar charger and show it to the battery maker in as many circles as you can reach." He handed Denzel a piece of paper, "I've written here precise instructions so that other battery makers can make their own solar panels like ours. Tell them to send word to me if they have any questions." He gave Denzel the paper and winked at him.

"It has been a pleasure to work with you. I leave you to your journey." He shook Denzel's hand and then disappeared.

After Diamond took his leave, Crystal told the others, "Jasper will take you to the Coast People, who will care for you and replenish your supplies on your way to Clover in the islands. You have brought me back to health, and for that I am truly grateful, but I am one person only. To bring our land back to health, you must find a way to take back Shakabaz."

Chapter Five

Akinowe Lake

The household became a flurry of activity, with Granite fitting saddlebags on the tigers and Ruby packing food and Crystal helping Jasper decide what to take with him and the Goodacres gathering their things. Then, in the midst of everything, Denzel remembered the skateboards and insisted on giving Jasper a board and showing him how it worked. The boys went to the barn for a quick trial run. While the boys tried out the skateboards, Crystal wrapped a few herbs for Doshmisi to take with her, attempting to explain the properties of each of them as she tied them up in bits of cloth. Doshmisi took a large bundle of fresh lavender since it smelled wonderful and reminded her of Aunt Alice.

Ruby gave Maia a little flute that she called a timber flute. "Because you carry the Amulet of Watersong," she explained, but Maia didn't know what she meant. They had soon done the things that needed doing. Crystal and Granite took Jasper into the house alone to bid him farewell. Ruby started crying yet again when they emerged and she gave her brother a hug. "Good luck. Be careful," she told him, wiping her eyes.

Crystal embraced Doshmisi. "I owe you my life, daughter of Debbie. May you have the courage and wisdom of your mother."

The travelers mounted their tigers, who turned their large padded feet to the path and set out on the journey. Bayard sat perched on Sonjay's shoulder and Cocoa followed close at the heels of Tom, Jasper's tiger. They rode out from the house in haste and constantly on the lookout for Compost and his officers. Once they hit the open road at a fast pace, the travelers felt a rush of excitement as they struck out on their own. They were optimistic and in good spirits, despite the knowledge that Compost lurked nearby.

Maia and Doshmisi began to sing an old Motown song that Mama liked. The song was called "Ain't No Mountain High Enough." It was actually a love song, but it sure made a good traveling song. They soon came to a large clearing with many paths leading from it. Jasper led them out through a heavily wooded glade with thick moss along the ground and tiny pinpricks of intense sunlight penetrating the forest canopy. As soon as they entered among the trees, Doshmisi received communication from them welcoming her and her fellow travelers. She could sense that word of her arrival in the woods spread out before them in waves as the leaves rippled slightly in a sudden breeze. If she closed her eyes, she could feel the breeze on her face, but it felt like the gentle brush of leaves on her skin. The hair on the back of Sheba's neck stood up, as if electrified, but this didn't cause the tiger to slow her pace.

"Are you OK?" Maia asked Doshmisi with concern, as she came alongside her on the narrow path. "What's up?"

Doshmisi opened her eyes, "I'm fine. It's the trees, they speak to me in their own language." Maia eyed her sister curiously and then dropped back to make it easier for her own tiger, Cora, to move freely on the path.

They rode in single file throughout the afternoon as the tigers kept up a brisk pace. At dusk, Doshmisi had a call from the trees to turn off the path. She shouted ahead to Jasper to stop and she dismounted Sheba. "I have to go in here. The trees have something to show me." This seemed to make perfect sense to Jasper, but Sonjay exclaimed, "What in the heck?"

"She can talk with the trees," Maia explained to her brother, riding up next to him.

"No fair," Sonjay pouted, "I want to talk with the trees. How come the oldest gets to talk to trees, why can't the youngest talk to trees?"

"Oh stop whining," Denzel snapped. He looked worried, as his sister disappeared into the thick forest that grew darker by the moment. He was tired and hungry.

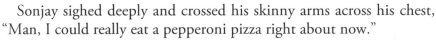

Sonjay sighed deeply and crossed his skinny arms across his chest, "Man, I could really eat a pepperoni pizza right about now."

"You've got that right," Denzel agreed.

Jasper dismounted and walked over to Denzel, with Cocoa at his heels, her tongue hanging out as she panted and dribbled. "I think we should stop here for the night. It's well-sheltered. I can see a little stream just there. We should make Akinowe Lake by tomorrow afternoon."

"You're the guide, whatever you say," Denzel responded.

While they waited for Doshmisi to return, they set up a makeshift camp. Maia took the tigers and Cocoa to the stream to drink. Bayard flew to the top of a tree for a look around. The boys unpacked their saddlebags and made up beds.

Doshmisi emerged from the forest, picked up one of her saddlebags, and emptied it out on the ground, "I found some kind of fruit in there that the trees want to give to us. I'll be right back." She disappeared again and soon returned with the saddlebag full of a pale lavender fruit that looked like a fuzzy golf ball.

Jasper hopped excitedly from one foot to the other. "Mannafruit!" he exclaimed. "Amazing. How did you find them?"

"The trees led me to them," Doshmisi answered. "How do we eat them?"

"Just like an apple only much slower and with smaller bites because they fill you up in an instant," Jasper explained. "What fabulous luck. I've never eaten one, but I know exactly what they are. I've seen pictures. They taste like whatever you imagine them to taste like. If you close your eyes, and imagine your favorite food, they taste just like it, only more so."

Sonjay immediately picked one up, closed his eyes, said "pepperoni pizza," and took a huge bite. Then he spit it out. "Ugh, this isn't like a pizza. It tastes like chalk. Are you playing with us?" he asked Jasper.

"I didn't get a chance to finish. For mannafruit to work, you have to be grateful," Jasper said.

"Grateful?" Denzel asked.

"Grateful?" Sonjay raised his eyebrows.

"Yeah, you have to be grateful to the tree for giving you the mannafruit, or it won't taste good."

"How do we be grateful?" Sonjay demanded.

"You know," Doshmisi told him condescendingly, "You have to *thank* the tree for letting you eat its fruit. Just think thankfulness when you eat it."

Sonjay closed his eyes and murmured "Thank you, thank you, thank you, oh wonderful trees." He took another tentative bite. A small one. But a look of pleasure spread across his face this time. He chewed and swallowed and then he said fervently, "Oh thank you, thank you, *thank you!*"

"Pepperoni pizza?" Denzel asked.

"Pepperoni pizza," Sonjay replied.

Denzel took a bite of his mannafruit and chewed appreciatively. "Thin crust with extra cheese. Yes."

Jasper and Maia ate theirs and as smiles spread across their faces, Doshmisi finally took a bite of her own mannafruit, with a thought of thankfulness to the tree that provided it, and imagined Aunt Alice's spaghetti. It tasted heavenly.

"What's yours?" she asked Jasper and Maia.

"Crystal's squash soup," Jasper answered.

"Mama's fresh baked bread," Maia said. Immediately Doshmisi, Denzel, and Sonjay echoed her, "Mama's fresh baked bread? Oh yeah!" They each took another bite.

None of them could finish even one little globe of the fruit because it filled them up so quickly. As night flowed over them, they fell exhausted into their makeshift beds. Jasper kept watch for a few hours and then woke Denzel, who took the next watch. Maia watched after him and then Jasper again. They didn't wake Doshmisi or Sonjay. The tigers slept curled up together. Cocoa slept at Jasper's feet. Bayard remained perched in a tree where he could keep a lookout. The travelers passed the night undisturbed.

In the morning Maia insisted that they eat the food that Crystal had packed and save the mannafruit for when their other food ran out. Jasper told them that if they didn't break the mannafruit open then the small lavender balls would keep for weeks and weeks, but once they bit into them, the fruit would turn bad within a few hours. Jasper counted it as a good sign that Doshmisi had found them because the trees evaded most travelers and only made themselves known to those they trusted. He said that they could expect Doshmisi to find more mannafruit in the days to come. Before they set out, Doshmisi went back into the forest for more mannafruit and sure enough she found the trees again without difficulty.

While Doshmisi went for mannafruit, the others packed up their camp. As Maia picked up her bedroll, a brilliant red, orange, and turquoise butterfly alighted on her arm. "Oh look," she exclaimed. "Isn't it the most beautiful butterfly you have ever seen?"

Jasper came to see. "It looks like one of Percival's tribe. It has the Percival turquoise eyes."

"How can you see its eyes?" Maia asked, incredulously.

"Those large circular markings on the wings are called eyes. They don't see with them. Percival's tribe of butterflies has those turquoise circles and we call them butterfly eyes," Jasper explained.

"Well whatever you call them, they're exquisite," Maia admired the delicate creature that perched on her finger.

After Doshmisi returned with a saddlebag full of mannafruit, they mounted their tigers and continued along the path behind Jasper's lead. The butterfly flitted around Maia's head for over an hour as she rode along, until Doshmisi teased, "Who's your new friend?"

"I don't know," Maia giggled, "but she's beautiful isn't she?" The butterfly seemed to flutter even more. After awhile it disappeared, only to return soon afterward with more butterflies that circled Maia's head as she rode along. Sometimes they alighted briefly on her arms and then fluttered up into the air again. Maia loved her butterfly escort.

The travelers wound uphill on a path surrounded sometimes by small meadows dotted generously with bright purple wild iris, buttercup, miniature magenta columbine, and other flowers less familiar to the Goodacres, and sometimes by expanses of tall wild grasses, that looked like sedge and rye, and sometimes by trees. The trees along the path did not grow as thick as in the forest they had passed through the previous afternoon. When they looked up into the sky, they could see the colorful stars winking at them even in broad daylight as usual.

The path became wider and seemed more like a road. They passed no other travelers, which Jasper took as a bad sign. "I think Compost travels somewhere on this road, otherwise we would see people on it," he called to the others with concern. "Look sharp."

Only moments after Jasper's warning, a tiny puff of dust appeared ahead of them on the road and a terrible smell like rotting vegetables wafted to them on the breeze. "Into the field, quickly," Jasper called to them. "That's Compost up ahead! I can smell him."

The travelers tumbled off their tigers and rolled down into the tall grass by the side of the road. The tigers took off at a fast clip to crouch behind some nearby boulders. Jasper led the Goodacres, who crept behind him on their bellies, further into the grass and away from the road. They found a ditch and eased down into it. The smell of rot had become quite strong and a group of armed soldiers appeared, led by the filthiest person the Goodacres had ever seen. They peered up at the road through the blades of tall grass as Compost and his soldiers came to a halt. Compost sniffed the air suspiciously. He had the nappiest uncombed hair and a film of dirt and dust covered his yellowish brown skin. He jumped down off his tiger and his fat stomach wiggled like Jell-O over his belt. He held his nose high as he sniffed noisily.

"I smell something foul," he told his followers.

"Probably smells his own breath," Sonjay whispered, and Denzel clapped a hand over Sonjay's mouth.

Compost started to walk out into the field right toward the hidden travelers, sniffing as he went. Doshmisi realized any moment he might smell them out there hiding. She slowly reached down to the bag at her side and pulled out the wrapped herbs given to her by Crystal. She unwrapped the lavender and laid it out in the open. The pungent, clean scent of the purple flowers filled the air. Compost reared back and covered his nose with his hand. "No, no, not here," he muttered, "that's not them." He walked in a different direction, looking confused. Doshmisi had thrown him off with the strong scent of the lavender. He banged around in the tall grass for a little longer. Then he returned to the soldiers on the road. He ordered them off their tigers and had them fan out to search the grass. Meanwhile Compost returned to his tiger and lifted a birdcage off the tiger's back.

"Skeeter," Jasper breathed almost noiselessly. "It will see us for sure."

Denzel looked around in panic, thinking fast, searching for a better hiding place.

Just then, Maia pointed to her arm. The others soon saw that her butterfly friends had come back and they sat perched all over Maia. Then, as they watched, more and more butterflies filled the air and came to rest on the travelers. Up on the road, Compost released the skeeter from its cage, but by the time the skeeter took to the air, the butterflies had completely covered the travelers, so thick that not a hair of them remained visible. The butterflies covered the field in all directions from the spot where the travelers lay. Thousands of millions of butterflies had instantly appeared and made the entire landscape disappear under the bright festivity of their red-orange-turquoise wings.

The travelers could hear the skeeter squawking overhead in frustration and the soldiers returning to the road. "Never mind," Compost told them. "This field is altogether too cheerful for me." His soldiers laughed at that comment. Compost called the skeeter back to him. Then the search party mounted their tigers and proceeded down the road, while those they sought remained hidden behind them in the field, covered by butterflies and shielded from Compost's sensitive nose by the scent of lavender.

The travelers lay in the field for a long time to make sure that Compost had truly gone. After awhile, the butterflies began to fly away. Maia thanked them in a soft, quiet voice. In the end, when the butterflies had taken to the air, one particularly large butterfly, three times as large as the others, settled on Maia's hand.

"Look at this one," she told the others. "Look how big it is, and I think it's nodding its head at me."

"Butterflies can't nod," Denzel said.

"This one can," Maia told him, and when he looked it certainly seemed like the butterfly nodded its head.

"I think you have Percival himself," Jasper said with a note of awe in his voice.

"Who would think that a creature so small would save our lives?"

Maia wondered. Then Percival took to flight with the rest of his tribe, which drifted away. The tigers bounded joyfully across the field from their hiding place behind the boulders, where the butterflies had concealed them too.

"Let's go," Jasper said. "I think we can make Akinowe Lake by sunset, which would be great because I want you to see the view from the top before we go down to the shore."

Everyone felt relieved and much safer knowing that Compost had passed them on the road. In the late afternoon, they reached the rise of a hill and when they came over the top, a sweeping view of the valley spread before them in all its splendor. The trees were fluffed out full with the new leaves of early summer in every shade of green, the light glancing off them in silver-gold glimmers. The crowning jewel of the landscape, Akinowe Lake, shimmered iridescent blue below them.

"I've never seen anything that blue outside of a Disney movie," Maia murmured, as they pulled the tigers to a halt to gaze in awe. Denzel whistled through his teeth. Dim and hazy purple hills rose on the far side of the lake. On their side of the lake the ground sloped down away from them gradually to the shore. Birds swooped on graceful wings from treetop to treetop and called to each other, their various songs echoing in the valley below. Bayard gave a cry of pure glee and swooped in a wide arc away toward the lake.

Doshmisi saw smoke coming from the trees in tiny threads at one end of the lake and at the other she could make out tended fields and pastures of farms, dotted with houses. "Who lives around the lake?" she asked Jasper.

"On that end, where you see the smoke from the chimneys, are the last of the circles of the People Beyond the Lake and on the other end, where you see farmland fanning out, the circles of the Coast People begin. The Coast People love the water and so they live next to it. Just on the other side of those hills we'll come to the ocean. Most of the Coast People live near the beach, but some of them live here around the lake. It is said that the lake has healing properties and many people have come to it for a cure, but no one knows how the healing properties work exactly." Jasper explained this while they continued to enjoy the panoramic view. Sonjay thought it looked almost prehistoric and he half expected to see dinosaurs and pterodactyls emerge from the landscape.

"If they can't figure it out, why do they say it heals people?" Doshmisi asked.

"Because every once in awhile, someone who has gone to the lake as a last resort, has come away healed. But no one knows why it works for those people. Just after Hyacinth's mother died, his father grieved so heavily that he wouldn't eat and he fell ill. But then his cousin took him to the lake and he came away healed. It's a famous story," Jasper explained. "Come, let's head down."

They ambled their way along the dirt road that wound around and back on itself until it settled in the valley floor and took them to the edge of the lake. Jasper told them "The Solferinos live here. They have ancestors who are a mixture of Coast People and People Beyond the Lake. These people have lived here where the two settlements meet for hundreds of years. Sometimes, because of their closeness to each other, People Beyond the Lake and Coast People marry each other and we call their children Solferinos. A lot of Solferinos marry back into the People Beyond the Lake or the Coast People and go to live in those circles. But right beside the lake you can always meet Solferinos. Here, and also on the other side of the lake, straight across over there," he pointed but they could see little among the gathering shadows of nightfall.

Jasper led them to the edge of the circle and asked a deep purplish man in indigo overalls where they could make camp for the night. He directed them to an inviting portion of lakefront with a sand beach and lean-tos for passing travelers. The boys took one lean-to and the girls took another. They ate mannafruit for dinner as they watched the tigers play on the dark beach.

When a dull orange oval loomed above the trees and rose into the sky, Doshmisi asked in wonder "What is it?"

"The lesser sun," Jasper told her. "It usually hides behind the greater sun. But in every season it appears in the night sky for just two nights. The wild mango musk cactus around the lake bloom giant melon-scented flowers at midnight on the nights when the lesser sun comes out."

"Wild mango musk cactus? The lesser sun?" Doshmisi echoed softly.

It gave her a chill to look at the lesser sun and reminded her that she couldn't count on things in Faracadar to act like things at home.

"It's not very bright," Doshmisi observed.

"It's an old, old star," Jasper explained. "Nearly dead now. We are lucky to have the greater sun, a much younger star, with many years of warmth left in it."

The travelers sat on the edge of the boys' lean-to and admired the lesser sun for awhile. Just before going to sleep, they shared two mannafruit between them for dessert and Sonjay imagined a hot fudge sundae with extra hot fudge. He smacked his lips so hard that he startled Bayard, who flew up to the top of a lean-to and eyed him skeptically. "I could get very used to this mannafruit," Sonjay proclaimed.

The travelers fell asleep under the eerie orange light of the lesser sun as they listened to the hypnotic lapping of the water.

The water still lapped rhythmically when Doshmisi awoke a few hours later in deep night. The strange, oblong lesser sun had moved to the other side of the sky and the air around her carried a strong sweet scent coming from pale blossoms as big as basketballs that burst from spiky plants around the lake. Wild mango musk cactus blossoms, Doshmisi thought to herself. The air burst with the scent of ripe cantaloupe melons, honey-sweet, like the kind Aunt Alice grew in her garden.

The trees spoke to Doshmisi in their fashion and beckoned her to the water's edge. She left the lean-to quietly, without waking Maia, and padded down the sand to the sparkling water. The lesser sun reflected in the water and shed a dim golden light on the sand and trees. She leaned over the edge of the water and there, instead of her own reflection in the water, she saw Mama, as alive as ever. Doshmisi gasped and jumped backward from the water's edge. But then the thought of seeing her mother again overcame her fear of the supernatural and she returned to her position, leaning out over the lake, so that she could see the image in the water.

"I'm so glad you came tonight, baby," Mama said. "I hoped you would come to see me at Akinowe one day."

"I don't understand," Doshmisi said. She felt tears, hot on her cheeks.

"Don't cry, baby girl. Things are as they must be. I am at peace in spirit. You're doing well. You look so grown up. I know you miss me, but I'm always with you."

"Oh, Mama, I never got to tell you good-bye. And, and" she stammered, "and I wanted you to know that I'd look after the others for you. Because I'm the oldest. I wished that I could have told you that. I wanted to make that promise."

"I know. That's why I have come to you at Akinowe," Mama said, "to tell you that you don't have to look after the others. That's not your job. The others will look after themselves and you have Aunt Alice and your uncles and many friends and perhaps, one day, your father. You're not responsible for the others. You're only responsible for you. So put it down, Dosh, put the burden down. Just take care of yourself. You have your own destiny and that will be enough work for you to do."

"If you had spoken with me one last time, would you have told me this?" Doshmisi asked.

"I *am* speaking with you one last time. And yes, that is what I have come to tell you. You're a beautiful, smart young woman with the gift of healing. Do what you need to do to develop your own self, and don't take on your sister and brothers. And Dosh, don't take on the universe. Just do what you can do. I guarantee you it will be more than enough to ask of yourself and more than enough to make a difference," Mama told her. "Do you hear me?"

"I hear you," Doshmisi said, and a tremendous warmth filled her.

"Promise?" Mama asked.

"I promise," Doshmisi replied.

"So, tell me, can you figure out the secret of the lake?" Mama asked. "Since you are a healer, do you know how it works now?"

Doshmisi thought for a long moment. She recalled Jasper's story about Hyacinth's father and she thought about seeing her own mother beyond death, and suddenly she knew the secret of the lake. She looked into Mama's eyes that wavered in the ripples of the lake's surface.

"Of course," she said. "It heals a person who has lost someone unexpectedly to death by allowing one last conversation, doesn't it?"

Mama nodded. "Yes. But only on a night of the lesser sun. Only then, and only for those who have suffered loss of sudden death without closure."

"Should I wake the others and bring them to see you?" Doshmisi asked.

"No, I'm near them always. And they left nothing unsaid with me. They're at peace. Only you were not at peace."

"But now I am," Doshmisi said.

"Now you are," Mama agreed. "You'll do well here because you have Faracadar in your blood. I must go now, but give my love to Clover when you see her. I'm sorry I couldn't tell you about this before I left you, or even now. But all of you will do just fine. Do what you believe is right, in your heart, and you will be just fine."

"I love you," Doshmisi said.

"I love you, Dosh, my baby girl. Always," Mama told her, as her image faded out of the water and Doshmisi could no longer see her face.

Doshmisi touched the water with her fingertips. She stood a long time gazing out over the healing lake before she returned to the lean-to and fell again into sleep. Peaceful sleep.

Chapter Six

Jelly and the Crystal Dome

In the morning the travelers went for a swim in the lake before breakfast. Denzel and Jasper swam out toward the middle and raced back. Jasper won, but Denzel didn't mind. Bayard thought it made great sport to buzz the boys' heads while they swam so he swooped down on them, cawing with glee. Doshmisi remained pensive and quiet, but no one noticed. She didn't want to tell the others about her conversation with Mama. It was private and hers alone.

Cocoa seemed to think that the lake was the best thing that had happened on their journey so far and she ran in and out of the water barking madly. Maia threw a fat stick into the ripples and Cocoa swam out for it, returning it to Maia's feet with yips of excitement in anticipation of Maia tossing the stick again. Sonjay floated on his back and looked at the sky and then stood at the water's edge where he skipped stones off the surface.

After their swim, they changed out of their wet clothes and laid them on the edge of the lean-tos to dry. Then, leading the tigers behind them, they walked into the circle to find breakfast. A boy directed them to what he called the Tollhouse where he said they provided food for wayfarers. At the Tollhouse, a jolly balding man with inky purple-black skin and a pale orchid-colored beard welcomed them. "Sit down, sit down," he said, gesturing to a long table, one of several in a large hall with a high wood-beamed ceiling.

The man's wife came out of a kitchen in the back, took one look at the travelers and commented, "What have we here, Jelly? These look like royalty by their color. Haven't eaten breakfast yet? Well, we can fix that!" She bustled back into the kitchen.

"You're a little late for breakfast," Jelly boomed. "But hold on, the missus can make a fast pancake. Coffee? We have a pot on."

"I'll have coffee," Sonjay answered immediately, sitting up straight, his eyes flashing.

"No you will not," Doshmisi frowned.

"That's just what we need is Sonjay on caffeine," Maia giggled.

"Milk," Doshmisi replied to Jelly. "We'll have milk all around."

"Actually, I'll take the coffee, thanks," Jasper said a little timidly.

"Me too," Denzel raised his hand as if in school. He remembered the wonderful strong coffee Diamond had made for him. Sonjay started to open his mouth but Doshmisi shot him the look so he popped it shut again. He knew how to pick his battles, and this would not be one of them.

They saw no one else in the room, presumably because any other wayfarers had already eaten and left. Jelly and his wife sat down at the end of the bench to satisfy their curiosity while the travelers ate their pancakes. "You must have come from Big House City, by the looks of you," Mrs. Jelly prodded.

Doshmisi looked at Denzel, and Denzel looked at Jasper, and Maia and Sonjay bowed their heads over their pancakes in embarrassment because it didn't seem wise to give out too much information about themselves, yet Jelly and Mrs. Jelly were so friendly and hospitable that it made them feel rude for not answering.

"They fear for their safety," Jasper explained finally.

Then Jelly's eyes opened wide and Mrs. Jelly clapped a hand over her mouth. "It's true then," Jelly said in a stage whisper. "We heard but we did not believe."

"We heard a rumor," Mrs. Jelly told them, "that you had come into the land to force Sissrath to abandon the taxes. But we didn't believe it really. I thought it the idle gossip of wishful thinkers."

"You can't force Sissrath to do anything while he holds Shakabaz, you know," Jelly told them ruefully.

"So we've heard," Denzel replied.

"Then you intend to take the staff from him?" Jelly's eyes nearly popped out of his big jolly face and Mrs. Jelly leaned forward on the table in obvious disbelief to take a better look at the children who thought they could undertake such a feat.

"We don't know what we intend to do. For now, we intend to stay out of the way until we have more information and it has been difficult to stay out of the way in this land where news flies faster than the parrots." Doshmisi could not keep the irritation out of her voice. Jelly and his wife both sat back a notch on the bench, straightened their backs, and pretended to zip up an imaginary zipper on their lips. They did this at exactly the same moment, their motions completely synchronized, and they looked so funny doing it that the travelers burst into laughter.

"Well," Jelly said, "the secret of your presence is safe with us. We are trustworthy people. My wife and I come from families who have lived in this place since the mountains and the waters separated. The Solferinos are the communicators of Faracadar," he stated with a note of pride in his voice.

"I'm satisfied just laying eyes on you," Mrs. Jelly pronounced.

Jelly took a pancake and offered it to Cocoa who eagerly gulped it down.

"Look at her," Mrs. Jelly complained disapprovingly. "I work so hard at cooking good food and she doesn't take the time to taste it."

"It's the smell that counts for her," Jelly said. "And look how much she appreciates your cooking." Cocoa wagged her tail in agreement, looking pleased with herself.

"She says thanks," Jasper told Mrs. Jelly. "Look, she's smiling." Cocoa wagged her tail even harder and barked because she knew she had their attention.

After the travelers finished their breakfast, Jelly took off his apron and asked, "Would you like to see the Crystal Communication Dome, which gave our circle its name? If you come with me, I'll give you the grand tour."

Jasper's eyes grew wide with excitement. "You mean we can go inside the Dome?"

"Of course. Here at the Dome Circle, the forces of nature converge in exactly the correct and necessary manner. That's why we have such a fine Tollhouse here for travelers," Jelly boasted. "A lot of visitors come to our circle to see the Dome and to send messages from it. Follow me."

"Yes, please," Jasper responded eagerly. The Goodacres wondered what Jelly and Jasper meant by the Dome, but judging from Jasper's excitement, they surmised it must be something truly amazing.

Fed and rested, the tigers awaited their riders in the corral outside the Tollhouse. Jelly mounted his own plump, dark brown tiger and the travelers mounted their tigers and they proceeded on a path that led through a grove of eucalyptus trees with their characteristic scent and the bark that peeled away in shreds. They continued up a hill until they reached the top where they arrived at a building that resembled an observatory. It had a rounded roof made entirely of glass, like a giant greenhouse. Inside, they climbed stone stairs that wound up to a top floor. The entire structure looked ancient.

At the top of the stairs, they passed through a heavy wooden door into a room so bright with the sparkle of daylight that the travelers winced. Prisms of color flashed on the floor in changing geometric patterns. Crystals embedded in the lower band of glass at the base of the rounded ceiling encircled the enormous room. In the center of the room was a large raised pedestal on which stood a gigantic crystal that seemed to throb as it glowed with a vaguely violet light. Tables surrounded the central pedestal, fanning out to the edges of the room. On the tables were screens resembling computer monitors, but they had no keyboard or computer attached. People of varying shades of purple, wearing long white frock coats, either sat at the monitors adjusting knobs or scurried between the tables.

"The crystal diode, which you see in the center of this room, is older than some of the stars in the sky. With its energy we power the most sophisticated communication system in Faracadar," Jelly explained with pride and enthusiasm.

"How does it work?" Jasper asked.

"What does it do?" Sonjay asked.

"What a beautiful room," Maia turned slowly around and around, holding her hands out to catch the rainbows cast by the crystal prisms embedded in the glass walls.

Jelly reached over to a stand next to the door and picked up several paper sunglasses, which he passed to the visitors. "I suggest you put these on. It might give you a headache to stay in here without them."

Jelly waved his arm in the direction of the crystal and explained what they saw. "The crystal diode works as a transmitter. The energy field created by the crystal when it receives direct sunlight allows it to transmit and receive images across great distances. Because of the Dome's central location, we have the ability to transmit communication images just about everywhere, except for a few locations in the Amber Mountains. I'll show you."

They walked to the nearest table and looked over the shoulder of a young man who worked the controls at the base of a screen. An image of a greenish woman appeared on the screen. She was sending a birthday greeting.

"Where is she?" Jelly asked the man at the controls.

"On Dolphin Island," the man told him.

"And where is she transmitting to?" Jelly asked.

"We'll forward her message to her son at Big House City in just a moment," the man said.

Jelly picked up a piece of paper and a pencil and said, "Let me draw you a map of Faracadar." On the far left he wrote "Settlement of the People Beyond the Lake." Then, to the right of that, he drew an oval and labeled it "Akinowe Lake." On his map, the Settlement of the People Beyond the Lake extended below Akinowe Lake. Along the bottom and toward the right side of Akinowe Lake he wrote in "Solferinos" and he noted the Crystal Dome right there. Then much farther to the right of that he drew a line going up and down. To the right of the line he wrote "ocean." In the ocean he drew a series of five islands and wrote alongside them "Settlement of the Island People." Down the edge of the ocean, across the beaches, he wrote "Settlement of the Coast People." He filled in a few other things on the map, like the Marini Hills at the end of Akinowe Lake and the Passage Circle between the hills and the ocean. Toward the top of the Coast People's Settlement and inland from the ocean, he marked Big House City. Then extending to the left of Big House City and above Akinowe Lake, he wrote "Amber Mountains" and indicated the High Mountain Settlement, the Settlement of the Mountain Downs, and finally, way up in the top left-hand corner, the Final Fortress. The Goodacres peered over his shoulder at the map as it took shape.

When Jelly completed the map, he pointed to an island in the ocean. "This is a map of Faracadar and the lady you saw on that screen is way over here on this island. The image message she sent will go to her son who lives up here in Big House City. The crystal in this room acts as the receiver and the transmitter." The travelers looked up from the map with new respect for the crystal that glittered in the center of the sparkling bright room.

"May I keep that map?" Sonjay asked.

Jelly folded it in half and handed it to him with a grin. "Of course. I made it for you."

"Can someone send a message to all the circles at once?" Denzel asked.

"Oh yes. There would be a delay, of course; a different delay for each place. And some of the remote places in the Amber Mountains can't receive."

"So it doesn't transmit in real time?" Denzel asked.

Jelly looked puzzled. "Real time?" he asked. "Wait, let me get someone who knows the technical aspects of the crystal." Jelly loped across the room to a glass booth in which several people sat at desks. He spoke to a woman who rose and followed him.

"This is Violet," Jelly gestured toward the tiny woman, "the director of the central communication team here at the Crystal Dome. She can answer your questions."

Violet had delicate bones and short-cropped hair, like a man's, and she wore large dangling metal earrings and an ear cuff and a lot of bracelets on both wrists. She had light skin of a dusty brown color tinged by a vibrant violet shade that almost made her quiver with energy. She had large gray-violet eyes that peered at the travelers now through violet-tinted glasses. "What did you want to know?" she asked in a soft but business-like voice.

They felt somehow honored by her presence, and none more than Denzel, who replied humbly, "I wondered if you can send a message to all the circles at once."

"Yes, we can," Violet told him, "but it would arrive at different times at different places, depending on the distance."

"So you can't send in real time?" Denzel forgot to feel shy as he became more engrossed in understanding how the crystal worked.

"Correct. The delay is not much, but it's significant enough that we rarely attempt to carry on a conversation. People just send singular messages. The delay to the nearest circles is only a few minutes, however to places farther out, like Whale Island or the Amber Mountains, it can take as much as a day for a message to carry, a little longer in overcast weather. The crystals work best in bright sunlight."

"You say crystals," Denzel noted. "Does that mean that each village, I mean circle," he corrected himself, "has a crystal?"

"Why yes. And a communicator who sends and receives the messages," Violet explained.

"Kind of like a wireless radio, only not in real time," Denzel muttered to himself.

"Why hasn't Sissrath tried to destroy the crystal here at the Dome?" Sonjay piped up.

Violet and Jelly exchanged a shocked glance, but immediately recovered. "Because he uses it as a strategic tool to maintain control," Violet answered.

"Why don't the people use it to organize against him?" Sonjay asked.

Several nearby workers glanced up sharply. Fear flickered across Jelly's face and in Violet's eyes. "Hush," Violet hissed, and she turned smartly on her little heel and snapped, "Follow me." They followed her back to her private office in the glass booth where she closed the door and spun around. "Do you want to get us killed?" Violet asked shakily.

"Did I say that out loud? My bad." Sonjay looked apologetic.

"Sissrath has spies and agents everywhere," Violet reminded them. "We walk a thin line here at the Dome. If he suspects that anyone might use the crystals to organize against him then he will place his agents here and remove the rest of us. In order to maintain access to the crystals and to have people here who truly understand how to use them and maintain them, we must bend to his will enough for him to feel secure in leaving us here. Do you understand?" Sonjay appeared to take things more seriously as he nodded assent.

"I have a message I need to send to all the circles," Denzel told Violet. "Don't worry, it's not political. It's scientific. But I can't transmit it myself. It would put me in danger, it would put all of us in danger. The person who needs to actually transmit it lives at Debbie's Circle. Does he need to travel here or can you take a transmission from him and send it out?"

"Oh we can receive from him and then send it out, that's not a problem," Violet replied.

"What do you have in mind?" Jasper asked Denzel.

"I want to have Diamond do a demonstration on how to build a solar panel and send it out to all the battery makers at once," Denzel explained, animatedly.

"You have a blueprint for a solar panel? Does it work?" Violet asked, her love of science apparent in the excitement in her voice.

"I made one with Diamond a couple of days ago and it works. The crystal can help us share the information about how to make one with people in other settlements," Denzel replied. He could feel his amulet getting warm inside his shirt.

Sonjay pointed at Denzel's chest. "Your amulet wants a word with you, man," he said. Doshmisi and Maia laughed.

Denzel blushed and pulled the red glowing amulet from his shirt. He held it in his hand and stared at it, "Kind of like having a light bulb go off over your head every time you have a bright idea. It's getting embarrassing." But Jasper, Jelly, and Violet looked weak in the knees at the sight of the amulet.

Violet leaned against her desk for support and covered her mouth with her hand. She let out a small gasp, "You are the Four." She turned to Jelly and choked out, "They're the Four."

"It would seem so," Jelly replied to Violet. "I figured they must have royal blood of course by their color, but I didn't dare hope. My wife knew, right enough. That woman is always right. Could make a man crazy, it could. She said they were the Four."

"So, how do I send a message to Diamond?" Denzel asked in a matter-of-fact voice, stuffing the glowing amulet back inside his shirt.

"I'll hook you up. Come with me," Violet replied, efficiently. "And we'll have to send a couple of extra communicators out to Debbie's Circle to help send messages back and forth to Diamond. I'm sure that he'll receive a lot of messages once the word goes out."

"And questions," Denzel added. "A lot of people will have questions."

Violet took the travelers to a station where Jasper sent a message to Diamond. Before the travelers left the Dome, Violet took Denzel back to her office alone. She produced a small purple velvet box from her top drawer. "I think you may find this handy." Violet opened the box to reveal a small, flat crystal, the size of a quarter. "This is a traveling communicator," she told Denzel. "I designed it myself and it's the only one I have. You can use it from anywhere to send me a message and I can forward the message for you. The message will come in on my private screen here. You simply need to catch a ray of sunlight with the crystal. Then speak. Unfortunately, I can't reply through the crystal. I think it will work only once before the energy leaves it. But do not hesitate to use it when there is need. And I wish you strength and speed with your mission, whatever it may be."

Denzel asked Violet if she had any news of Compost's whereabouts and she replied that as far as they could tell he had arrived at Debbie's Circle and set up camp.

The travelers left the Dome reluctantly, not only because of the beauty of the place but also because something about the energy of the crystals made them feel joyous and hopeful. Outside, they found Cocoa sleeping with the tigers and Bayard perched in a nearby tree preening himself. As soon as Bayard caught sight of them, he cawed loudly, "Hit the road." They returned to the edge of Akinowe Lake to retrieve their dry clothes and then stopped in at the Tollhouse to pick up sandwiches that Mrs. Jelly insisted on making for them.

The sunny morning had vanished and storm clouds rolled in. The air smelled damp and felt heavy with moisture. "Looks like rain," Jasper said.

"If I might be so bold," Jelly told them at the Tollhouse, "you must realize by now that many will figure out your identity because of your appearance."

"I think I get it," Maia said. "Because we're just plain brown, and don't have a bright color in our skin, we must look to people here as if we have no color. So we stand out."

"Correct," Jelly confirmed. "In Faracadar, people with no color come from the royal line. High Chief Hyacinth is bland, as we call it. It means he has plain brown skin like you."

"Oh no," Doshmisi said quickly, "We aren't royalty. This is just the way African American people look in our land."

Jelly's eyebrows shot up and he started to say something, but just then a small boy of about five years old, with skin like black grapes and thick large curls absolutely the same color as Aunt Alice's prize delphiniums, appeared out of nowhere and tugged urgently at Jelly's pants leg. The Goodacres stared at him in amazement because his feet did not touch the ground. He hovered six inches off the grass beneath him. Jelly gave the miraculous floating boy his full attention, not like you normally would to a small child interrupting a conversation. "What do you want, Jack?" he asked.

"Sissrath r-rides out Big House," the boy stammered. "Go go go. Four go. Jack go. Go Passage. Off t-to Passage." He seemed exhausted by the effort of speaking and he touched the ground with one of his feet, which made him bob up and down like a helium balloon.

"You must leave here immediately," Jelly told the travelers. "Jackal says that he can see Sissrath riding out from Big House City. Perhaps Sissrath knows your whereabouts. Jackal is my nephew. He says he should go with you and I agree. You could definitely use the services of an intuit."

"An intuit?" Sonjay and Doshmisi asked at the same time.

"I'll explain later," Jasper told them hastily. "You can ride with me," he said to Jackal and hoisted the child up in front of him onto his tiger. "An intuit will help us a lot," he assured the others.

"Wait, wait," Doshmisi hesitated. "How can we take such a small child with us? We can't take care of him."

"He's small but not as childish as you would think," Jelly told her. "He can take care of himself better than you can."

"Fast." Jackal exclaimed. "Fast. Fast. Ride."

"He says that we must leave," Jasper told the others.

"You kill me, how come you didn't tell me you speak intuit?" Denzel teased Jasper as they turned the tigers toward the road. "You're multi-talented, man."

"You don't have to speak intuit to figure out he wants us to get out-ta here," Sonjay said.

Jasper smiled, "C'mon, let's go, and I'll explain to you about intu-its later."

Large rain drops began to fall. Jelly ducked into the Tollhouse as he shouted after them, "Be careful. Jack, try to slow down and speak slow-ly so they can understand you. Come back to us. Keep safe and come back to us. Strength and wisdom go with you!"

Chapter Seven

Meddling Sprites

Putting on hooded cloaks to repel the summer rain that attempted to drench them, the travelers rode swiftly through the Solferino Settlement, passing several circles along the road. Jasper pressed forward, trying to make it into the Marini Hills by nightfall. He had told the others that no people lived in the hills and that they would find many good places to hide themselves away quietly for the night. The rain fell heavy at times and just drizzled at others, leaving the air freshly cleansed.

They began climbing into the densely forested hills just before sunset, following a well-maintained road that wound up into the trees ahead. As soon as they entered the woods, a sweet scent permeated the air. It smelled kind of like the spices on a pizza, but more flowery and vaguely perfumed. Either the thick tree canopy held the rain from seeping through or else the rain had thinned. The air remained damp but no raindrops pelted them.

Soon they came to a clearing by a brook and there Jasper halted to allow the tigers to water. Jack had fallen asleep nestled in front of Jasper on the tiger's back. Jasper lifted him gently down and placed him on a soft, mossy mound. The travelers drank deeply from their canteens of water and Maia removed Mrs. Jelly's sandwiches from the bag slung over her shoulder. Mrs. Jelly had given her the bag and Maia loved it because of the beautiful lavender, pink, and violet flowers embroidered on it. Her timber flute and water organ fit snugly inside it.

Between bites, Denzel asked Jasper, "So what's the deal with intuits? They float off the ground? How come you wanted to bring him with us?"

"An intuit can see things from far away and know things unknown to other people. An intuit has an extra sense, a sense of intuition that most people can't develop," Jasper answered.

"We call that a sixth sense," Doshmisi said.

"That's exactly it. We call it that too," Jasper continued. "An intuit has a sixth sense and can use telepathy. Like today, when he could see Sissrath leaving Big House City. He had a vision of Sissrath and his Special Forces riding out. The minds of intuits move very quickly and their thoughts whiz by so fast that they can hardly speak. They think in abstractions, like images and sounds, and they have trouble with words. So it's a little difficult to figure out what they're trying to tell you. Sometimes, when they get upset or excited, they become speechless, they can't put any of their thoughts into words. Most of the time they emit a strong electrical charge. The charge lifts them right off the ground with its energy. Unfortunately, they don't live very long. They burn up at a young age. The best intuits are usually young children. I can understand the words of intuits because I used to have an intuit friend at home while I was growing up. But like I said, they don't live very long; not much past sixteen or so." Jasper glanced at Jack sadly, then he looked down at his sandwich. "Intuits sleep soundly," Jasper added. "We should save him something to eat because he will probably sleep until the morning and he'll wake up hungry."

"So where should we make camp for the night?" Sonjay asked.

"How much farther to the top of these hills?" Doshmisi wanted to know.

"What is the plan for tomorrow?" Denzel added.

"Hold on," Jasper replied, unable to answer all the questions fast enough. "It's my job to take you to Clover the Griot on Whale Island before Sissrath or Compost can find you. On the other side of these hills we'll come to the circles of the Coast People, who live up and down the beaches of the ocean. The Coast Settlement is bigger than the others because there are almost twice as many Coast People as any of the other people. When we get to the Passage Circle, on the Coast, we can cross to the islands by a combination of ferries and bridges. Right now we're in the Marini Hills, which are particularly safe for secret travelers because of the scent of the trees, which makes it difficult for dogs to track through here. Even Compost can't sniff us out in here. If we can make camp a little deeper into the woods, I guarantee you that no one will find us. When Jack wakes up, I expect he'll know something about Sissrath and Compost. As your guide, I have the job of getting you to Clover safely. After that," Jasper shrugged, "well, after you meet with Clover then you just tell me what you want me to do next. I'll do whatever you want me to do. Take you wherever you want me to take you. You're the Four. I don't make plans for you, you make plans for me."

"This Clover the Griot person better have a lot of answers," said Sonjay skeptically, "because I don't know nothin' about where I want to go or what I want to do."

"Maybe we'll just wake up in bed at home in the morning," Maia suggested.

"No way," Doshmisi said with resignation. "This is real and eventually we'll have to make some decisions." The Goodacres looked at each other with fear in their eyes because they knew that the people in this land were depending on them to do something miraculous and they didn't have a clue how. "We're the Four," Doshmisi echoed Jasper's words grimly.

"Well, if Sissrath is as evil and dangerous as they say, then you all are going to be the three as soon as I see him coz I'll be outta there," Sonjay joked.

"Come on," said Jasper, "let's use the last of the light to gain some distance." They mounted their tireless tigers and continued on into the deep hill forest until the lesser sun shyly peeked it's pale orange nose between the leaves. Then they tumbled off the tigers in a stand of tall, tall fir trees whose crowns disappeared in the shadows above. They bedded down on springy pine needles for the night. The air remained damp, but the rain had stopped falling.

The travelers slept soundly, as if drugged, as if they had a spell cast on them, as perhaps they did. For while they slept, brightly glowing little creatures emerged from the forest and formed a ring around them. The little creatures nodded to each other and pointed and spoke in a silent mindspeak. They screwed up their luminous white little faces in puzzlement and the males stroked their long misty beards and the females scratched their fair heads. One of them boldly tiptoed to Sonjay and touched his shirt where it covered the amulet. The oldest among them, who had a silver-white beard that flowed to his knees, sat down on a rock and stared at the travelers in puzzlement, wringing his hands and furrowing his brow and muttering to himself almost inaudibly "what to do, what to do?" The other little creatures watched him expectantly. Finally, looking anxious, the oldest gave a command and the creatures hopped on silent feet among the travelers, dipping and dodging and plucking and carrying and then they disappeared into the woods bearing aloft three skateboards and a number of other items.

The travelers awoke groggy and stiff on an overcast and cool morning. Clouds blocked the sun like fat wooly sheep grazing across the sky. No rain fell. They crawled one by one to a little spring that emerged like a biblical miracle from a large gray rock. They gratefully washed up in the crystal water and drank deeply. The water tasted cool and sweet. The beautiful herbal scent of the trees permeated everything and made them lazy and not at all in the mood for hard riding. Jasper petted Cocoa, "Even you smell good this morning, girl."

None of them could quite wake up completely, until Doshmisi screamed and tore wildly through her bed roll and belongings that lay on the ground. "I've been robbed," she shouted. She looked out frantically among the trees, as if a clue would reveal itself there. The others ran to her in alarm.

"My herbal. It's gone. It's completely gone. Someone must have robbed it during the night." Fighting back tears, Doshmisi held up the empty case. She had worn it around her waist ever since Aunt Alice had given her the valuable book. Everyone immediately jerked wide awake as they checked their belongings. Sonjay's hand went to his throat where he felt for the chain of his amulet and when the others saw his hand fly up, they checked theirs too. Then Maia said softly, "Remember, they can't be taken from us while we live."

They soon discovered that Denzel's knapsack was gone, with everything in it. Maia's water organ was missing and so was Jasper's compass and the three skateboards. The morning suddenly seemed less pleasant and the forest felt sinister and hostile and falsely seductive in its beauty.

Denzel turned on Jasper accusingly, "You said no one could find us here. You said it was safe. It's not safe. We should have taken turns standing guard."

"Because we felt safe, we weren't watchful," Doshmisi added reproachfully.

"I don't understand it. I thought we *were* safe," Jasper defended himself angrily. "The Marini Hills are safe. Are you blaming me? Listen, I don't know what happened. I'm not one of the Four. You guys are the Four. I'm just the guide, OK? You figure out the hard stuff. I just have to get you to Whale Island." Jasper whirled on his heel and headed off to round up the tigers.

"Yeah? Well you're some guide, man! You led us right into some kind of a trap!" Denzel shouted at Jasper's retreating back, kicking up a heap of pine needles with his toe in fury.

Sonjay called Bayard to him to make sure the bird was alright. Bayard perched on Sonjay's shoulder and cocked his head back and forth in an agitated manner. "Sprites, sprites, sprites," he said, but the robbery had distracted everyone so much that they paid him no mind so he flew off ahead on the trail, as if to check for safety.

Jasper returned with the tigers, sullen and silent.

"Ahead. On ahead," Jack told them, pointing down the trail after Bayard. Then he rubbed his stomach, looking at Jasper, apparently undisturbed by the anxiety over the robbery.

"He's hungry," Jasper said shortly.

Maia gave Jackal the last sandwich in her bag, which they had saved for him the night before, and she passed around some slightly battered bananas to the others. "This is all the food that we have left," Maia told them.

"What about that mannafruit?" Sonjay asked.

"I had it in my knapsack," Denzel said. "It got stolen in the safe, safe hills," he added sarcastically.

"Well maybe Dosh can find some more," Sonjay said hopefully.

"These trees don't seem friendly," Doshmisi told him. "I don't think I can find mannafruit here."

"Since we have nothing to eat, we might as well just ride. I'll stop for the tigers to water sometime this afternoon. Otherwise, you'll have to signal to me if you want to stop," Jasper told them curtly. Then he picked Jack up, mounted his tiger, and took off without another word.

"Whatever," Denzel muttered sullenly as they scrambled onto their tigers to catch up with Jasper.

Jasper rode far out in front all day long, and didn't look back, as if he hoped he would lose the Goodacres. Silent tears rolled down Maia's cheeks as they tried to keep up with the bobbing red dot way ahead of them along the trail. She felt sorry for herself. At least Doshmisi had used her herbal to heal Crystal. Maia had never used the water organ. She hadn't even learned how the nested cups worked to make music and now she would never hear how they sounded.

Denzel remained in a foul mood. He felt like a chump, getting ripped off like that. If Jasper hadn't made him feel so comfortable he never would have dropped his guard. He did blame Jasper and he was angry with him and thought Jasper should apologize and at least admit he had messed up, not get angry back. And what was up with that comment about them figuring it out because they were the Four? This wasn't their land and they had to depend on people, like Jasper, to give them accurate information. Jasper was stupid.

Doshmisi felt terrible. She blamed herself. If she was smarter and had her wits about her, this kind of thing wouldn't have happened. She should have tried to communicate with the trees as soon as she entered the forest. Now the trees had closed up and wouldn't speak because they could tell that she didn't trust them. She knew Denzel blamed Jasper, but Jasper sort of had a point: they were the Four. How come they couldn't figure things out better? And what would Aunt Alice say when she found out that Doshmisi had lost the precious herbal? She felt so irresponsible as she imagined the people she could have healed with it. Why didn't she *feel* like one of "the Four"? Why didn't she know what to do?

Sonjay decided he didn't want to think about the robbery. If he had nothing to eat and he had to ride all day without stopping, he refused to feel bad on top of it. So he said out loud to himself the names of his favorite basketball players and he watched Bayard fly above in the trees and he looked closely at the flowers they passed along the way and before long he started to whistle and, despite everything, he had a pleasant ride through the Marini Hills on little more than sheer determination.

Jasper rode fast and did not look back. They stopped briefly in the afternoon by a stream for water and no one spoke. Denzel and Jasper ignored each other. And so they passed through the beautiful scented Marini Hills in miserable silence, with the Goodacres, except for Sonjay, feeling threatened and angry and scared.

In the evening, they came to a place where the trees thinned out making it possible to see below to where the hills sloped downward to the ocean. They could vaguely make out the ocean in the distance, but it looked like part of the sky from so far away. A cool, damp, salty breeze wafted in among the trees. The travelers shivered and pulled on their sweaters. They were hungry but they had nothing to eat. Jasper just kept riding silently out in front. As the warmth of the sun disappeared and the shadows of the far end of the day began to gather, Doshmisi rode swiftly on ahead to catch up with Jasper so she could ask him if they could stop and make a fire to warm up.

Jasper shrugged, "Whatever you say."

They stood despondently, watching, as Denzel started a campfire. Jasper made no move to help him. When the fire had taken and Denzel could feed it with larger logs, Jasper said, "I'm going to take Jack and go look for something to eat before it gets dark. But I want you to know that I've made a decision. I'll guide you to Clover, because that's my job. Then I'm going home. I don't think you'll need me after that since I'm such a bad guide." He turned sharply before anyone could respond and disappeared into the blue shadows of dusk with Jack floating along beside him and Cocoa trailing absently behind.

Doshmisi and Maia stared miserably into the fire and Denzel frowned, tight and closed in his anger. Sonjay stood at the edge of the little clearing where they had made camp and looked off into the distance in the direction of the ocean. His stomach rumbled. Then he looked more carefully, alert and watchful. He thought he saw something moving below where the hillside sloped away from the forest. At first it just looked like a glowing movement, low to the ground. Then, right before his eyes, a long string of lights burst into radiance out of thin air. The lights bobbed up and down. "Whoa, check it out," Sonjay said softly. No one heard him so he called back to the others, louder, "Yo, you guys, check it out, what *is* that?" He pointed.

The others left the warmth of the fire and came to stand next to Sonjay. They peered down the hill. "What *is* that?" Sonjay repeated.

"Torches, or lanterns maybe." Denzel squinted.

"And people carrying them," Doshmisi added.

"People hiking up the hill toward us," Denzel said.

"It looks like a necklace of light," Maia whispered.

"For real. Hey, what do you figure makes that glow down on the ground?" Sonjay asked. No one answered. No one knew.

They stood and watched the progress of the lights below them, not knowing what to do. Who, or what, was making its way up the hill toward them?

When Jasper returned to the campfire, he found the Four staring down the slope at the necklace of lights and his curiosity overcame his anger. He walked over beside them and when he saw the lights, his jaw dropped in amazement. Jack, who floated at Jasper's elbow, gurgled happily, "Welcome welcome welcome. Lost and found."

"Someone is coming this way," Doshmisi said.

"Lots of someones," Sonjay added.

"I can see that," Jasper snapped.

"After what happened last night," Denzel remarked, "I think we should put the fire out and hide until we can check out if they want to help us or harm us."

Jack tapped Jasper's arm and said, "Welcome welcome welcome."

"It's OK," Jasper spoke absently, almost to himself, "Jack says they're friendly. He gets that they're coming to welcome you. They look like a party of Coast People coming out to meet you. But how did they know you were here? Do you think they know you're the Four? How could they know that?"

Jasper turned to the intuit and asked, "Jack, how could they know that?"

"Lost and found," Jack said cryptically.

Denzel exploded, "How do you know they're friendly? You thought no one could find us in the Marini Hills and we got ripped off up there. You know what? A lot of very bad messed up stuff happens in the world and you could walk us right into another trap with your everything-is-just-great attitude. You understand what I'm saying?"

"Oh give it a rest, Denzel," Doshmisi snapped.

Sonjay hated how mean everyone kept acting toward each other. It made him more frightened than anything else. He, for one, would rather face Sissrath than his own family at the moment. "I'm going down to meet them," he said deliberately.

"No you're not," Denzel told him.

"You're not the boss of me," Sonjay said stubbornly. "And if you don't believe Jack and Jasper then tough. I do believe them."

Doshmisi looked worried, "I don't know if going to meet them is a good idea, Sonjay."

"Jack is the intuit and he says they're coming to welcome us. I believe him," Sonjay repeated, and before anyone could stop him he mounted his tiger and took off down the hill, with Bayard perched on his shoulder. Jasper picked up Jack and followed close behind. Doshmisi shrugged at Denzel and fell in behind Jasper, with Maia at her side. Denzel kicked dirt on the fire to extinguish it and reluctantly brought up the rear. He didn't like this one bit.

Darkness had completely blanketed the hillside by the time the two groups of travelers met each other on the trail that led down out of the Marini Hills. But the light from the lanterns carried by the welcomers lit the landscape and illuminated the welcomers' faces. They were indeed Coast People. No question about it. The cobalt blueness in their skin radiated under the lantern light. They had such delighted, open, excited faces, that Sonjay knew at once that Jack had been right. These were friends, not enemies. The Coast People formed a circle around the travelers while their leader, a portly man with a high, black and blue, striped, cat-in-the-hat-type hat and positively turquoise eyes, stepped into the middle of the circle with his large hand outstretched.

"Welcome, welcome sons and daughters of Debbie. We are most honored and delighted by your presence and wish to be of service to you in any way possible," the leader proclaimed in a booming voice. He then proceeded to shake hands with each of the Goodacres and then with Jasper and Jack. Cocoa sat right up and held out her paw as if performing for a treat so the man shook hands with her too, laughing jovially.

"Hold on, how do you know we are the sons and daughters of Debbie?" Denzel asked suspiciously, still trapped in the bad taste left by the robbery the night before.

From between the legs of the Coast People, tiny creatures no more than two feet high emerged shyly. They were as white as bleached sheets and glowed with an unearthly light. Their glow was what had made that strange shimmer across the ground that the travelers had wondered about up on the hill. The creatures peered at the travelers with clear eyes, that had no color, like water, and their pale clothing had a cobwebby quality. From their shoulder blades protruded papery thin wings. They looked quite fragile. The females had long, long straight white hair, that fell to the backs of their knees. The males had white beards and the oldest one had a beard that flowed to the ground. When the oldest one held out his hands toward her, Doshmisi gasped, for in his hands he held the herbal. In fact, she realized, he held it out to return it to her.

She took it from him gently, asking incredulously, "Where did you find this?"

The creature cleared his throat nervously, and explained, "Didn't mean to cause worry but had to show Governor Jay something for proof you understand and couldn't quite figure it out, you understand. What to do, what to do?" He wrung his little hands.

Then the other tiny creatures produced Maia's water organ and Denzel's knapsack and Jasper's compass and finally, carried aloft over the heads of a dozen or more creatures, the three skateboards emerged.

"I hope you can forgive Bumblebee. Sprites solve problems in unusual ways," Governor Jay (the man in the cat-in-the-hat hat with the turquoise eyes) told them. "Bumblebee is the leader of the sprites. Sprites have their own ways of doing business. Doesn't make much sense to us people. But it works for them. Bumblebee figured the only way to convince us down at the circle that the Four were headed our way was to show us some of your objects of enchantment. And I must say, he produced an impressive array. Those boards on wheels are something else. Couldn't figure those out. Hope you didn't suffer much over the temporary loss. Bumblebee meant no harm. Sprites have a reputation for unpredictability and peculiarity so I doubt we would have believed Bumblebee if he hadn't shown us the objects. But now he has returned them to your safekeeping and set it right again. And because of him, we have come to welcome you to the Coast Settlement. We are most honored and delighted by your presence and wish to be of service to you in any way possible."

Bumblebee tugged at Governor Jay's pants leg and informed, "You already said that. Honored and delighted. Already. You said that."

"Yes, yes, I'm repeating myself. This is just too exciting. We have come to escort you to the Passage Circle," Governor Jay exclaimed.

"Wait," Sonjay held up a hand. He pointed to the sprite leader and then he pointed to the ground between his feet. "Mr. Bumblebee," he called, "come over here."

Bumblebee cleared his throat self-consciously and cleared it again and then proceeded to the spot in front of Sonjay. His head bowed low so that he almost tripped over his beard and his delicate wings drooped slightly.

"Mr. Bumblebee," Sonjay said to him quietly, "fortunately nothing terrible came of this but if you couldn't get our things back to us and we needed them then something very bad could have happened. You mustn't steal, even if it seems like borrowing. Bad things are still bad even if they make good things happen. Stealing our things made bad energy. Do you understand what I'm saying?"

"Yes sir," Bumblebee said miserably, looking like a disciplined puppy. "Bad things are still bad even if they make good things happen. Yes sir."

"OK, then," Sonjay said and he held out his hand. Bumblebee's face lit up as he took it and they shook solemnly. "I am Sonjay, youngest of the Four, and I am pleased to meet you Mr. Bumblebee, leader of the sprites."

"And you Chief Sonjay, pleased sir." Bumblebee pumped Sonjay's hand energetically.

Meanwhile, Doshmisi wondered to herself at how grown-up Sonjay acted. How did he know what to say to Bumblebee? Sonjay seemed like the only one of them who knew how to act like one of the Four. It made her proud of him and jealous at the same time.

"Hungry," Jack blurted out. "Hungry, hungry, hungry." He bounced up and down in the air rubbing his little stomach.

Bayard wheeled overhead and came to perch on Sonjay's shoulder and announced loudly "supper-time."

"Oh my word. When was your last meal?" Governor Jay asked.

"Our friendly sprites 'borrowed' our food," Denzel remarked.

Governor Jay quickly called forward some of his people and they set up a wooden folding table and placed on it fruits and cheeses and bread and sweet muffins with butter, which the travelers dove into greedily. Bayard received his own personal bowl of berries and enthusiastically gobbled them up between shouts of "divine." Only Denzel held back and did not pounce immediately on the food with the others. He stood aside, brooding, digging his foot into the ground.

The sprites stared out of large, curious eyes at the travelers as they ate and the Coast People came forward to shyly ask questions about the journey.

Denzel tapped Jasper on the shoulder and motioned with his head, "Can I have a word with you, man? In private?"

"Sure. Step into my office," Jasper said with a wan smile. The two of them slipped through the ring of people and sprites that had gathered around the table and stepped quietly away where no one could overhear them.

Denzel looked back behind them at the shadows of the trees in the hills they had traveled through that day. Then his eyes met Jasper's. "I don't know how to say this." He took a deep breath. "I'm sorry. The forest was safe and there was an explanation for the robbery. You were straight up and I acted like a punk."

"It's OK," Jasper said. "I lost my temper too."

"I don't blame you for losing yours, I really lost mine, big time," Denzel continued. "But I promise you that I'll never doubt you again. Never." Denzel put out his hand and Jasper took it. They shook. "From now on, I'm your man one hundred percent. I've got your back. No matter what."

"It's all history," Jasper said, a little awed at the commitment he had just received from one of the Four. "We'll just go forward from here."

"Then you'll stick with us after we talk to Clover? We need you. Not just as a guide. We need you as a friend," Denzel told him.

"Yeah, I'll stay. I just got mad. I didn't really mean what I said about going home. This is the greatest adventure of my life and I wouldn't want to go home in the middle of it. But you know what? You don't need me as bad as you think. You guys are the Four. Don't you get what that means?" Jasper asked earnestly.

"We don't. I wish we did," Denzel shook his head sadly, discouraged. "I don't know what I'm doing here. I'm making this up as I go along, believe me. And without you to explain some of this stuff to me, I'd be totally lost. I just hope that after we talk to Clover things will make more sense. C'mon," Denzel put his hand on Jasper's shoulder, "let's go eat."

The other travelers noticed when Jasper and Denzel returned and they sighed with relief to see that the two had made up. Doshmisi put her hand on Jasper's arm and said softly, "Are we OK?" She touched his chest with her fingertips then touched her own chest, "I mean you and me. Are we OK?" She looked at him anxiously out of her large brown eyes.

Jasper flushed and felt warm all over. His job of leading them safely to Clover had absorbed him so completely that he had not given much thought to other things and now he noticed that Doshmisi was very pretty. "Um hum," he sputtered, "yeah, we're fine, just fine." Doshmisi broke into a grin. She felt much better now that she had eaten something and Jasper and Denzel had made their peace with each other.

Governor Jay asked, "So should we return to the circle?"

"Now?" Doshmisi asked incredulously.

"You bet. We're not that far away, maybe an hour's hike, and we don't plan to sleep out here, do we?" he asked kindly.

"I guess not," Doshmisi answered wearily. She did not feel like traveling further, but she found the thought of a bed for the night attractive.

"After I get something to eat, I know I can do an hour's hike," Denzel told the governor. He had his old energy back. That good energy. Not the bad energy of anger. The good energy made him feel more confident.

"Well you eat," Governor Jay, told him hospitably, "and then we'll move out. Many others back at the settlement eagerly wait to welcome you in a manner such as befits the Four."

Chapter Eight

The Coast People

"Which among you holds the Amulet of Watersong?" Governor Jay asked.

Maia raised her hand self-consciously.

"If you wear the Amulet of Watersong, then you are a musician," Governor Jay announced. He turned to his people and commanded, "Bring her a drum!"

The sprites hopped up and down excitedly as the people brought forward at least a dozen drums made out of wood and gourds and other materials the Goodacres could not recognize. Governor Jay chose six small drums, each very different, each with a carrying strap. He lined them up in a row. "I present to you a selection of our best travel drums. Choose one for yourself as a gift from my people," he told Maia.

Maia looked in amazement at the beautiful drums. The gourd-drums had beaded strings woven around them so that the beads would rattle in beat with the drum when played. The wooden drums had extraordinary carved pictures on their sides.

"They're so beautiful. I don't know," Maia said, wondering which one to choose.

"Close your eyes and choose by sound," Bumblebee advised. "By sound," echoed the sprites.

Maia tapped the drums one at a time, at first timidly with her fingertips and then harder with the palm of her hand, until she had no doubt in her mind and she chose the reddish wooden one with the carvings of flying birds.

Sonjay grumbled to no one in particular, "Great, just my luck. Dosh

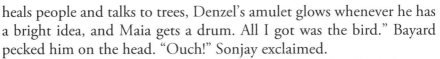

heals people and talks to trees, Denzel's amulet glows whenever he has a bright idea, and Maia gets a drum. All I got was the bird." Bayard pecked him on the head. "Ouch!" Sonjay exclaimed.

The travelers didn't mount their tigers, but instead walked along in among the welcomers through the grasses and heather and succulents that grew along the path toward the ocean. The Coast People and the sprites produced flutes, pipes, thumb-harps, drums, small guitars, and an assortment of hand-held instruments that the Goodacres had never seen before. Some of the Coast People simply banged two polished sticks together in rhythm. Before long, the whole posse danced along the path. Maia carried her new drum slung over her shoulder by the strap and contributed to the rhythm, oblivious to the fact that her amulet cast a radiant blue glow in front of her.

At first, the sprites whirled and danced along on the ground, but soon they flitted into the air on their papery wings and sang with heavenly voices. In no time at all the moving music jam reached the edge of the Passage Circle and more Coast People hurried out to meet them and greet them and join in the merriment. When they arrived at the circle, the music and dancing swelled.

The Coast People had lit the central plaza of the circle with lanterns. Denzel noticed that the lanterns consisted of a clear, enclosed box inside which hundreds of small glowing bugs gathered around some type of bar of food. The lanterns efficiently illuminated everything and made everyone clearly visible.

The men and boys from the circle wore their hair in dreadlocks and the women and girls had theirs braided in long braids, with intricate braiding patterns cornrowed across their scalps where the braids started. The Coast People went barefoot and wore lightweight shorts in plain solid colors, and sweaters because of the nippy night breeze that came off the ocean. They had strikingly blue eyes in every shade of intense blue; eyes that contrasted with their richly dark bluish skin. Most of the Coast People had Asian eyes, exquisitely angled in shape.

Once the travelers reached the plaza, the people and sprites increased the level of the music, bringing out more and larger instruments that they could not have carried in the welcome party. One instrument required three people to play it and looked like a canoe strung across with fat strings. Even though night had fallen long before, the circle obviously had no intention of going to sleep. But Doshmisi, exhausted from the long and emotionally difficult day, asked Governor Jay where she could find a bed. He beckoned to a woman. "This is Ginger. While you stay among us, Ginger and her sister Cinnamon will look after you at their house."

Doshmisi went into the crowd to retrieve Sonjay, who yawned and did not complain when she dragged him from the celebration, responding obediently for a change. Taking Jack by the hand, Jasper joined Doshmisi as he and Denzel sleepily followed Ginger into the dark. They could not reach Maia, who had become entirely swallowed up in the crowd of musicians.

Ginger led the weary travelers away from the plaza and music, lighting their path with a hand-held lantern. When they reached the house she told them to "go on upstairs where you can see the ocean." She followed them up a huge central staircase to their rooms, large and airy with open windows facing the water. The boys had one room and Doshmisi had another. The bed looked so inviting that Doshmisi nearly fainted with relief and fell asleep practically before she finished lying down.

At first light, the morning fog tiptoed into the room on padded toes and tickled Doshmisi awake with damp fingers. At first she didn't remember where she was. Then the events of the night before came back to her. She snuggled down between the cozy blankets and gazed out the open windows where the fog obscured her view. She listened to the gentle rhythm of Maia's even breathing in the bed next to her. The softness of the bed and the soothing sound of the waves lulled Doshmisi back to sleep. When she awoke again later, the sun had climbed the sky, the fog had burned off, she heard the hum of voices coming from the boys' room next door, and she felt deeply rested and ready to face whatever the day might bring. In the distance she could see the gray-blue ocean through the open window.

The room contained hardly any furniture. She saw a tall wardrobe and, opening it, discovered clothes inside that fit her perfectly. She changed into a pair of green pants and an aqua sleeveless shirt, then threw on a fat warm sweater and left the room.

The enormous house seemed to have endless rooms. The bedrooms on the second floor opened off of a square terrace that framed the central staircase and formed the middle of the house. Doshmisi descended the staircase and then walked around behind the stairs through a back hallway. She passed a double door that led to a greenhouse and through the windows of the greenhouse she could see a field of silver plants stretching away into the distance.

In the kitchen, Ginger bustled around making breakfast. Two little girls stood in front of music stands in a corner of the kitchen and practiced a violin and flute duet. They stopped when Doshmisi entered the room. Ginger motioned to them to continue, but they ignored her and stared at Doshmisi.

"How did you sleep?" Ginger asked.

"Great," Doshmisi answered. "I hope it's OK that I borrowed some clean clothes."

"I put the clothes there for you. I'm glad you found them. Are the others awake?"

"I think the boys are. But not Maia."

"That doesn't surprise me. She stayed up nearly all night with the musicians. What a talent for drumming she has; and her timber flute didn't sound half bad either." It astonished Doshmisi to hear this report about her shy little sister.

"What are those people doing out there in the silver fields?" Doshmisi inquired curiously.

"Nipping back the silver spark. Have you heard about the silver spark?" Ginger asked.

Doshmisi shook her head "no."

"You would have great interest in it, I should think," Ginger told her, "since it has powerful healing properties. It only grows here in this one place where the bacteria in the soil protect the silver spark roots. People have tried to transplant silver sparks to other places, but they won't move, the stubborn things. So far, they only grow in the Passage Circle. Silver spark can heal a person who clings to life by a thread. It has the power to reconnect the spirit to the body, even when the spirit has almost entirely left. Look for it in your herbal. It will tell you all about it."

Doshmisi took the herbal out of its case instantly and opened it, wondering where it described the properties of healing plants. She flipped through the pages and then discovered an index at the back of the book. She did not remember ever seeing the index in the herbal. Seeing it now, she could not believe she hadn't noticed it before. Ginger watched her intently. "Objects of enchantment work in their own mysterious ways, don't they?" She winked at Doshmisi. "Why don't you fetch your brothers for breakfast. Let Maia sleep."

Doshmisi went through the dining room and back to the front of the big staircase. This time, she stepped into the front entranceway of the house, and she glanced out the window. She stopped short when she saw a long line of people stretching right down the street. Some sat on folding chairs. The hum of their quiet conversations drifted into the house. Some instinct caused Doshmisi to duck back into the interior of the house without being seen. Just then, the boys descended the stairs.

"Good morning," Jasper greeted.

"Come here," Doshmisi grabbed Denzel's arm, and the others followed. She opened the door to the front entranceway a crack and pointed. They looked at the line of people and then ducked their heads back in.

"What's up with that?" Doshmisi asked.

At that moment Ginger emerged and shooed them into the kitchen.

Jack sang out to Jasper "safe, safe, safe."

"I guess we don't have to worry about Sissrath today?" Sonjay asked Jasper.

Jasper replied, "Yeah, I'd say Jack believes it's safe for us to stay here today."

Jack bobbed up and down like a bouncing ball, grinning, and repeating "safe, safe, safe."

"You've made your point," Jasper told him. "It's safe to stay here today." With that, Jack stopped speaking altogether and floated happily around the kitchen, touching everything.

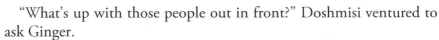

"What's up with those people out in front?" Doshmisi ventured to ask Ginger.

"They came to see you," Ginger replied.

"You mean the Four?"

"No, you."

"Just me?" Doshmisi's eyes grew large and fear gripped her chest. She looked to the others for help but they said nothing.

"Just you. You carry the Amulet of the Trees and the herbal."

"So what do they want from me?" A note of panic entered Doshmisi's voice.

"Healing," Ginger explained.

"But I don't have a clue how to ..." Doshmisi's throat went dry and she could not continue.

"You just think you don't know how. But the oldest always has the gift of healing. Not to worry. When you start seeing them, you'll figure it out, one by one," Ginger assured her.

"When I *start seeing them*?" Doshmisi repeated in horror.

"Why yes. You can't turn them away. They have faith in you. First have breakfast and then we'll show you the clinic you can use to receive them."

"We have to reach Clover, as soon as possible. I can't possibly stay here to see all those people," Doshmisi protested.

"Don't worry about getting to Clover today," Jasper told her. "Jack will let us know the minute Compost makes a move or if Sissrath heads this way. For now we're safe."

"But I *want* to see Clover, to get enough information to figure things out," Doshmisi insisted.

"We all do," Denzel said. "But if Jasper says it's safe to stay here then I'm behind him. He's the man." Denzel softly punched Jasper's arm affectionately.

Doshmisi remembered the day before, when they had doubted Jasper and been wrong. Now he said it was safe to stay here. Well maybe so, but she couldn't possibly heal all those people out front. She needed an excuse to leave.

"Dosh," Jasper said quietly. It was the first time he had called her by her nickname, the one only the family used. "You can do it. You healed

Crystal. You know how. It will just come to you, with help from the herbal. I'll meet them with you if you want me to."

"You'll stay with me when they come in?" Doshmisi asked him.

"If you want me to," Jasper answered.

"Two of my daughters are prepared to assist you," Ginger said.

At that moment Maia appeared in the doorway, rubbing her eyes and smoothing her hair.

"Hey, little maestro," Ginger greeted her. "You rocked last night."

Maia shrugged and, saying nothing, sat in a chair at the table. The others stared at her and wondered what she had actually done the night before at the music jam.

Ginger served them breakfast and when they finished, she told them to help themselves to the clothing in their rooms and suggested they go out into the circle to meet the people.

"But what about Sissrath's spies?" Sonjay asked.

"No need to worry about them here," Ginger assured them. "Our circle resists Sissrath."

"Besides, Jack says it's safe today," Denzel reminded him.

"You come with me," Ginger motioned to Doshmisi and led her and Jasper out of the kitchen, through the greenhouse, to another building a short distance from the house. It was a little clinic, with a waiting room, two examination rooms, a bathroom, a kitchen, and an office.

"My husband used to work here," Ginger told Doshmisi with a note of sadness in her voice. "My daughters, Grace and Harmony, used to help their father here in the clinic and they can help you. Just tell them what to do. That door goes to the brew kitchen, where you will find herbs and other healing substances. Grace can help you find anything in there and she does a good job brewing. Harmony does especially well out front with the people while they wait. I'll be in the silver spark fields if you need me."

Harmony went out to the waiting room and Grace showed Doshmisi around the brew kitchen. Doshmisi surprised herself by recognizing quite a few of the herbal names on the labels. She even saw a jar of the high thistle and another one of the star brush. She looked up at Jasper nervously and he assured her, "You can do this."

"Tell me again," she pleaded.

"You can do this," he took her hand and squeezed.

"I can do this," she repeated.

Grace took a pale green coat from its hook off the back of the door and handed it to Doshmisi, who took off her sweater and put on the coat. When they returned to the office, she could hear people entering the waiting room. She unsnapped the herbal's carrying case. She could feel the amulet on her chest begin to grow warm against her skin. Jasper pointed at it. Sure enough, a green glow emanated from her shirtfront. She simply had to put the herbal on the patient's chest and read what it told her when it chose the right page. How hard could that be? No more difficult than what she had done for Crystal. Grace would even brew the recipes for her.

"OK," she took a deep breath and said "send the first one in."

After breakfast, Maia left the house with Raffia's water organ, determined to find someone to teach her how it worked. As she walked along the path to the central plaza, she recognized faces from the night before. People waved and smiled at her and many bowed their heads in her direction. As she greeted these people in passing, she felt like one of the Four for the first time. She had earned their respect and she knew it. She had the ability to make music and here, among the Coast People, that counted for something.

She didn't see any sprites and she wondered if they had returned to the Marini Hills. When she arrived at the plaza, she noticed a group of young people drumming together. As she stood and listened to their rhythm, a passerby stopped to wish her good day. She recognized him from the night before.

"Would you please help me figure something out?" she asked him politely.

"Certainly," he replied, eager to assist her.

Maia pulled open her bag and showed the man her water organ. "Amethyst the Gatekeeper gave this to me and I don't know how it works."

"That's a water organ, by the looks of it," the man said.

"Yes, a water organ. Amethyst said it once belonged to Raffia. But I don't know how to play it and I'm wondering if you can tell me who might teach me," Maia explained.

The man grinned broadly, "Well, you can ask Raffia herself. She usually spends her mornings over at Braiders Cottage. Do you know how to get there from here?"

"I don't know how to get anywhere," Maia told him.

"I would say you know how to get into the rhythm," the man chuckled. "Here, I'll show you the way to Braiders Cottage." He led her down a street that ended in a small grassy field loaded with tiny brilliant blue flowers with yellow dot centers. Square gray stones set into the grass formed a path to the door of a cottage at the far end of the field. Maia followed the gray stone path and arrived at the cottage, from which she could hear women's voices raised in song. She pushed open the door and found a room full of women braiding each other's hair. The braiders sat up on chairs while those whose heads were being braided sat on the floor on piles of cushions. The room smelled delicious with the heavy scent of coconut oil and other perfumes.

When Maia entered, the singing stopped and the women cooed over her. "Did you want your hair braided in a pattern of the Passage Circle?" they exclaimed with excitement, thinking she had come for the braiding.

"Oh no, no thank you. I'm actually looking for Raffia," Maia told them.

They parted and turned toward an old woman with powder blue hair that tumbled in tiny braids to her waist. She worked on the hair of a child who sat between her legs, her crooked fingers moving as fast as a hummingbird's wings across the child's head. Her eyes gazed straight ahead blankly and Maia realized that Raffia was blind.

"What do you seek from me?" Raffia asked, without so much as pausing from her task.

"I am Maia. Amethyst the Gatekeeper gave me your water organ and told me that perhaps it might save my life one day, but I don't know how to play it. Please, would you teach me?" Maia inquired.

"I know who you are," Raffia answered. She stopped braiding and held her hands out, "Give me the water organ." The child between her legs scooted out of the way. Maia removed the water organ from its bag and placed it in Raffia's hands. Raffia's face lit up as she felt the eight nesting cups, one in the next, in order by size. "I never thought I would touch this instrument again. I gave it as a gift to Amethyst. It did indeed save my life once, and hers as well. Bring me a jug of water and I'll show you how to play it."

Raffia slid off her chair and onto a cushion on the floor. She lined up the eight cups in a row in front of her and then instructed Maia to pour water into each cup from the jug. "How much water?" Maia wanted to know.

"It doesn't matter," Raffia replied. "This is not an ordinary water organ. The great enchanter Hazamon made it a long, long time ago. The cups need only have the water element within them and they will create their sound." Once the cups had water in them, Raffia licked the tips of her fingers and ran them around the rims of the cups. A lovely pure sound floated from each cup as she played it. The sound reminded Maia of the crisp, tropical music of the Trinidad steel drums that so oddly resembled organ music. Raffia played a tune that Maia recognized from the previous night.

Raffia stopped playing the water organ abruptly. "Your turn," she said as she felt behind her and sat back up on her chair.

Maia sat down on the cushion in front of the water organ. She licked one finger and ran it around the largest cup. A pure and sweet sound came from the cup, making the women in the room gasp with delight. Maia looked up in astonishment.

"I told you. This is no ordinary water organ," Raffia said softly with a coy smile.

Maia licked several fingers and repeated the tune that Raffia had just played, but under her fingers it became an exquisite and intensely moving piece of music that reverberated through the room. Her amulet grew warm as it glowed with eerie blue light on Maia's chest. Maia had never known an instrument easier to play than that water organ. She barely needed to touch it to draw the music out of it. She felt as though it responded to her fingers intuitively and anticipated the notes she would play next. She forced herself to stop before she became too caught up in the music. When she leaned back and removed her hands from the water organ, the last note hung in the air with a life of its own and then drifted away into silence. The Amulet of Watersong fell dark. The women in the cottage clapped their hands with delight and the children pointed to the windows, where a flock of blue birds perched on the sills, attracted by the music.

"Now you know how it works," Raffia said quietly. "Use it when you have need."

Maia carefully poured the water back into the jug. Someone gave her a towel, with which she wiped out the cups and nestled them back together, then she returned them to the sack. The women watched her, unmoving, until she put the water organ away out of sight. Then one of the women clapped her hands and the braiders jumped back to work.

"You must let us braid your hair," they tried to persuade Maia, who at first resisted. She had always taken pride in her single long braid. But she truly loved the beautiful braiding on the heads of the women of the Coast People. So she decided to let them do hers. As soon as she agreed to it, everyone wanted to work on Maia's hair. Raffia started each braid off, creating an elaborate cornrowed pattern on Maia's head. After Raffia started the braids, the other women extended them and took them to Maia's waist. The braiders had such a pleasant and mesmerizing touch that Maia fell asleep as the women worked and sang over her hair.

While Doshmisi and Jasper treated patients in the clinic and Maia visited Braiders Cottage, Denzel and Sonjay made the discovery that if intuits couldn't talk very well, they sure could skateboard.

Denzel found the perfect spot, that looked strikingly like a basketball court. The court was smooth and worked well for the unrefined skateboards Denzel had made at Diamond's shop. Denzel and Sonjay flew back and forth, practicing ollies, kickflips, and other tricks.

Pretty soon Jack appeared with a half a dozen intuits, all bobbing up and down just inches above the ground. They watched Denzel and Sonjay for a few minutes and then crossed their legs and sat, floating several inches above the grass next to the court, with their chins in their hands. They concentrated on the skateboarding with rapt attention. They pointed and poked each other and laughed in unison and generally acted like any small children. They didn't speak, or at least they didn't use words, although they shouted and laughed and made lots of noise. Sonjay guessed they communicated with some kind of mental telepathy. However they communicated, they seemed to have a roaring great time together. Of course, it didn't take a sixth sense to figure out that those intuits wanted to try out the skateboards. So Sonjay sat down on the ground and handed his board to Jack, who hopped on enthusiastically. The instant Jack's feet touched the skateboard, they stuck to it as if glued on and both the boy and the board hovered over the ground.

"Denzel," Sonjay called to his brother, "check it out. When Jack uses the skateboard he turns it into a hoverboard. Sweet."

Sure enough, the board floated over the ground and little Jack, who had never even seen a skateboard before in his life, proceeded to maneuver moves in mid-air that had taken Sonjay months to master on the ground. Jack's skateboarding totally blew Denzel away. He sat down next to Sonjay and handed his board over to one of Jack's little intuit buddies. Denzel and Sonjay watched in amazement for nearly an hour as the intuits took turns on the skateboards. They whizzed through the air, kicking around, flipping the skateboards as if they weighed nothing, in fluid and graceful motions. They landed every trick every time.

When Sonjay and Denzel got hungry at midday, they left the skateboards in Jack's safekeeping and promised the intuits that they would bring Jasper's skateboard for them. Then they walked to Cinnamon and Ginger's for lunch. While they ate, a young man came to the back door of the kitchen. He knocked politely and flashed a smile full of dazzling white teeth at Ginger, who laughed when she saw him.

"Now what coaxed you out of the shop and into the daylight?" she teased.

"I come looking for the one of the metal," he answered.

"I should have known. He's right here," Ginger told the man, putting her hands on her hips. She turned to Denzel. "This is one of our battery makers, and he's absolutely a mad scientist. Not much entices him to crawl out from the battery barn. But I guess you're a main attraction." She gestured with her head in the direction of the visitor, who took the gesture as an encouragement and entered the kitchen where he pumped Denzel's hand awkwardly in an enthusiastic handshake.

"Everyone calls me Mole. You must be Denzel. Pleased to meet you, mahn. Honored. I've come to fetch you for the battery barn. We be needin' some help out there." Mole smiled and shifted restlessly from foot to foot. Denzel found it amusing that the man spoke with a Rasta-sounding accent. He looked like a Rastafarian too, with his long dreadlocks. He had a handsome face, but when he moved he jerked self-consciously, like the sort of person who doesn't know exactly how to act around people very well. He had dirty fingernails and muscular, calloused hands.

Denzel remembered the transmission he had asked Diamond to make and he wondered how the battery makers here in the Passage Circle had progressed so far with their solar panel. "Did you get your message from Diamond?" he asked Mole.

"Yah mahn," Mole answered. "And we be havin' some questions. Will you come?"

Denzel gulped down the rest of his sandwich and grabbed a piece of fruit that strongly resembled a blue apple from the bowl in the middle of the table. "You want to come?" he asked his brother.

"Nah, I'm going back out to skateboard," Sonjay replied.

Located just off the central plaza, the battery barn was an enormous warehouse-type structure with a high ceiling and a lot of floor space. Benches and tables covered in all manner of objects in various stages of disassembly and reassembly filled the inside. Tools, machinery, parts, and chemicals covered the racks and shelves on the walls and littered the floor. Denzel wondered how anyone could find anything in there. It looked like Diamond's shop times twelve. A big set of double doors opened out into a large yard and a cool breeze fanned in across the room. Mole introduced Denzel to the other six battery makers, who obviously did much more than make and repair batteries in this shop.

Mole and his fix-it buddies had partially built a big solar panel. In half a second they had Denzel scratching his head and working with them on the project. After Denzel helped the battery makers figure out how to wire the solar panel to a battery, they showed Denzel a small car they had built that ran on used cooking oil. Denzel suggested they run an electric car with a solar panel and they discussed this possibility. They proudly revealed the biggest project in the shop, an elegant windmill made from a lightweight metallic material. Denzel felt at home with the battery makers. His amulet glowed warmly against his chest and he could practically feel the little wheels turning in his brain as he discussed with them their various inventions. He wished more than anything that he understood electronics, and that he could teach these Coast People how to build a computer chip. That would have been sweet. When he returned to Manzanita Ranch, he would have a lot of studying to do. If he returned. He didn't want to think about that.

After lunch, Sonjay discovered to his great delight that the skateboarding court had filled up with young people from the circle. The boys and girls from the Passage Circle couldn't skateboard through the air with the greatest of ease like the intuits, but they did catch on to how the boards worked on the ground and everyone wanted to try it. Now *this* was more like his idea of a good adventure. He wished that Denzel had made more skateboards.

While he sat on the edge of the court and watched, Sonjay talked with the other boys and girls who had turned up. He wanted to learn as much as he could about Faracadar.

"Do you go to school?" he asked them.

"Yeah. But not right now. We're on vacation. We go to school here at the circle until we finish and then if we want to we go to Big House City to keep studying something complicated, like healing or communications or gardening, stuff like that."

"Is that how you get a job?" Sonjay asked.

"What do you mean?" they asked.

"How do you make money?"

"Money? You mean Sissrath's coins?"

"I mean money to buy things. You do buy things, don't you?"

"Like what? What would we buy?"

"How about food, do you buy food?"

"We get it from the Garden."

"Clothes, then, how do you get clothes?"

"From the weaver families."

"Do you ever need to have new furniture?"

"Yes, the carpenters make it for us."

"How do you get a house here?"

"If someone needs one, then we build it."

"Well, don't you need money for anything?" Sonjay asked. He was beginning to understand what Crystal had tried to explain to them about the coins and how much better things worked before Sissrath invented money.

The Coast children looked at each other nervously. "People have to pay coins to Sissrath. Or they're supposed to, anyway; otherwise he gets mad. But we usually don't have any coins. So we're supposed to send people to serve in Sissrath's army and to work at the Big House. He pays them coins to give to us so we can give the coins back to him. Go figure." The boy speaking lowered his voice to a whisper, "Dumb, huh?"

"No one needs coins except Sissrath," they nodded their heads solemnly, like a bunch of old folks, in agreement.

Ginger's sister Cinnamon served the travelers dinner late that evening. They ate a simple meal of thick vegetable stew with an abundance of big chunks of freshly baked bread and butter. The Goodacres did not have the best relationship with vegetables, but they were getting used to them since that's what they had to eat in Faracadar and they were usually hungry enough to feel grateful for whatever they received.

Maia looked resplendent that evening with her hair in braids, and everyone admired the design. Weary from a long day working at the clinic, Doshmisi had a pang of jealousy that Maia had gotten her hair done, but it made her glad to see her sister so happy.

Denzel described some of the inventions underway at the battery barn and Sonjay asked Denzel if he thought he could get the battery makers to put together a few more boards and maybe a couple of ramps. Denzel promised to look into it. Sonjay turned to Jack and

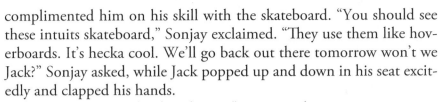

complimented him on his skill with the skateboard. "You should see these intuits skateboard," Sonjay exclaimed. "They use them like hoverboards. It's hecka cool. We'll go back out there tomorrow won't we Jack?" Sonjay asked, while Jack popped up and down in his seat excitedly and clapped his hands.

"Well that sure makes him happy," Jasper said.

Cinnamon added, "Intuits have few pleasures. They suffer from the visions and messages they receive. They rarely get to have fun like other children. I think I'll have to go to the court tomorrow just to see them skateboard."

Doshmisi asked Jasper, "Is it safe for us to stay here tomorrow?" She hoped to help more people at the clinic.

Jasper pulled Jack down out of the air by the ankle and demanded the full attention of the intuit. "Jack, we're depending on you," he told him. "You must let us know the minute Compost leaves Debbie's Circle or if Sissrath heads this way. If anything changes, tell me right away. Understand?"

Jack nodded solemnly and shaped his lips around the word "safe."

"According to our communicator, Compost has camped out at Debbie's Circle," Cinnamon informed them. "Sissrath has gone to meet him there. It looks like they think you have not come into the land yet. But as soon as they figure out their mistake, they will come looking for you."

"Jack will let us know when they make a move, won't you Jack?" Jasper asked the intuit confidently.

Jack pointed at each of the Four in turn and stated "safe, safe, safe, and safe." The next morning he greeted them again with his declaration of safety. He rose early and waited in the kitchen until each of the Four had emerged from their bedrooms, then he touched their amulets through their shirts with the tips of his small purply fingers, staring into their eyes with his large violet ones, and told them "safe." He didn't leave the house with the skateboards until he had assured each of the Four of another safe day in the Passage Circle.

Denzel and the battery makers built the intuits two ramps and a grinding bar. Denzel showed them how to do a few tricks. He found them helmets and insisted that they wear them if they were doing tricks on the ramps, because of the way they flew through the air. He didn't want them to bash their valuable little psychic brains out. Denzel also taught a few of the young people from the circle how to make skateboards and pretty soon a variety of colorful skateboards appeared in the possession of their proud owners. After Denzel hooked up the skateboarders, he turned his full attention to Mole's windmill, which fascinated him. He spent the whole night at the battery barn, tinkering, and the next day he slept until noon.

Meanwhile, Sonjay spent his time at the makeshift skate park, asking questions and learning about Faracadar. He went to Braiders Cottage and had the braiders lock his hair into dreads. Afterward he looked very different, with tiny twists all over his head. When Denzel saw it he asked him, "What'd you do that for, man? You'll never get a comb through that mess." But Doshmisi thought the little dreadlocks made Sonjay look more commanding. He looked capable, like a leader you could trust. Or was that some other change in him that had nothing to do with his hair?

On the morning of their fourth day in the Passage Circle, the moment they had dreaded arrived. At dawn, Jack woke the entire household with his blood-curdling screams. "Not safe," he shrieked. Rocking back and forth on the edge of his bed, with his small hands over his ears, and his face screwed up in terror, he shouted over and over again "not safe, not safe, not safe." Jasper soothed Jack with quiet words and succeeded in getting him to stop screaming.

Sonjay immediately took charge. "Denzel, go to the battery barn and borrow any useful tools you think we should take with us. Maia, help Ginger pack us some food. Remember to fill the canteens with water. Doshmisi, give Jack something to calm him down because we need to take him with us, then go close up your clinic. Take whatever medicines you can carry that might protect us or save us if we get hurt. Jasper, call Cinnamon in here to watch Jack and then go help Dosh at the clinic. I'll find Bayard and get the tigers. Go quickly. We're outta here." After bossing everyone around, Sonjay flew out the door. The others stared after him for a moment and then, without questioning, they ran to do what he had ordered.

Chapter Nine

The Island People

The travelers fled the Passage Circle on a path that led straight to the ocean and the Island Settlement beyond. Doshmisi thought back to her hasty departure from the little clinic. After carefully wrapping as many medicinal herbs as she could easily carry in swatches of cloth, she had stood in the doorway and fought back tears. Even though she had spent only a short time in the clinic, it felt like home. Taking one last look around, she caught a glimpse of herself in the oval mirror mounted on the wall and her appearance astonished her. Before she came to Faracadar, Doshmisi had always had a strong sense of fashion and had worked hard at her appearance. But in the Passage Circle she worked hard at the clinic and did not have time to think about her hair or her nails or her clothes. In the mirror she saw her hair pulled back in a scrappy ponytail. She couldn't remember any time in her life that she had forgotten to do her hair.

When she returned to the house from the clinic, Doshmisi asked Cinnamon for a hat. Cinnamon offered her a circular woven hat in several shades of green. It reminded Doshmisi of the kufi hats she had seen some of the Black Muslims wear, but the colors of it made her think of the panoramic view of the trees in the valley spread out before them as the travelers had approached Akinowe Lake.

"This will work perfectly for a journey to the islands," Cinnamon told her. "My old friend Fern on Emerald Island gave it to me." Doshmisi tucked her hair up into the hat and pulled on a comfortable, baggy sweater. So much for fashion. To cheer herself up, she put on a pair of dangling metal earrings shaped like dolphins, a gift from one of her patients. Now, as Sheba the tiger leaned from side to side in her descent toward the crashing waves on the beach, Doshmisi felt the tiny metal dolphins tickle her neck.

Denzel had gone on ahead, telling them he would meet up with them on the beach, and she could see him at the water's edge with some of his battery maker friends. They leaned together, deep in a discussion that focused on a giant windmill perched on the edge of the surf. The patients at the clinic had absorbed so much of her attention, that only now, as she watched Denzel scurry around the windmill, pointing and calling out to his friends, did Doshmisi realize how involved he had become in his projects at the battery barn.

Maia, who had ridden behind Doshmisi, spurred her tiger Cora to a run, passing Doshmisi and bounding down the sandy slope. Then Doshmisi saw a group of dreadlocked young drummers near Denzel and his friends. Maia made a beeline for her night-drumming companions. Together they had pounded out rhythms in the central plaza under the moonless sky of jewel-like stars. Maia jumped from Cora's back to embrace each of them in turn.

Doshmisi arrived on the beach flanked by Sonjay and Jasper. Bayard perched on Sonjay's shoulder, his favorite spot. Cocoa trotted alongside Jasper who held Jack in front of him on his tiger. The tea Doshmisi gave Jack to calm him down had made him sleepy. He leaned against Jasper with his eyes closed.

Jasper called to Doshmisi and Sonjay, "We have a choice. We can either travel the bridges to the closer islands and then catch the Emerald Island Ferry further out where the bridges stop or we can wait here for the next ferry to Seal Island.

Before Doshmisi could even open her mouth with a suggestion, Sonjay called back to Jasper, "Let's do the bridges. I want to get out of the Passage Circle as soon as possible. We can wait for the other ferry further out." Jasper glanced at Doshmisi to see what she thought, but she just nodded her head toward Sonjay to indicate that she would follow his decision.

Doshmisi, Jasper, and Sonjay rode out onto the beach and joined

Denzel, who mounted his tiger while he called last minute instructions to Mole and the others. The battery makers filed past him solemnly and shook his hand. Doshmisi noticed how rough Denzel's hands had become. He had several nicks and cuts on them and his fingernails had grown dirty and ragged. He had a smear of grease on his cheek. She called over to him and motioned for him to rub his face. He brushed the grease with the back of his hand and made it worse. Meanwhile, Maia sobbed as she mounted her tiger and pulled up beside the others.

"You'll see them again in a few days," Doshmisi comforted her.

"That's just it," Maia said, wiping her tears, "I have a bad feeling. I feel like the drummers are in danger. I'm scared that I *won't* see them again."

Doshmisi's eyes met Jasper's. After working beside him so closely in the clinic, she could recognize what his expressions and gestures meant. She could see in his eyes that Maia's words troubled him. And that worried Doshmisi. A terrible sense that something dreadful waited just around the corner hung over them as they proceeded swiftly down the beach and rode out onto the ocean bridge leading to Gull Island.

Maia's drummer friends remained on the beach, where they drummed wildly for her benefit as she departed. When the travelers had ridden a few yards out on the bridge, Maia dropped to the back of the group and turned. She drummed a response to her friends on her travel drum and then waved her arm in the air. As she caught up with the others, she continued to drum softly in rhythm with the drummers on the beach. Even when she could no longer hear them or see them, Maia beat out a rhythm that echoed the one the drummers had sent to her as the travelers crossed the bridge and rode swiftly across Gull Island, and then continued on to the next bridge.

As they rode, the heavy fog that had engulfed them during their departure thinned and soon the sun dazzled them from an electric blue sky. A herd of fat puffy clouds lazed playfully in the distance over the water. On the second island out, Seal Island, graceful cypress trees surrounded them. Doshmisi closed her eyes to listen to what the trees would tell her. Their comforting energy gave her strength.

The travelers reached the far side of Seal Island by late afternoon. Jasper halted at the edge of a pungent eucalyptus grove. He got down off his tiger and took Jack down after him. The others dismounted stiffly and sent the tigers back into the eucalyptus trees to find some greens to eat. The medicinal tea Doshmisi had given Jack had worn off. He sat quietly on Jasper's jacket. It made Sonjay sad to see Jack so subdued as he remembered vividly the little boy's shouts of glee as he popped ollies and kickflips on the skateboard only the day before. The travelers ate sandwiches and drank water from their canteens. Doshmisi wanted to walk among the trees to see if they had anything important to tell her so she followed the tigers into the eucalyptus grove while the others sat in a circle and stared down the beach at the ferry dock.

"We'll pick up the ferry at that dock," Jasper told them. "We still have enough daylight left to make the next island today. We'll stop there for the night."

"That must be Emerald Island," Sonjay observed.

Jasper looked surprised, "Yes, it is. How did you know that?"

"Third island out," Sonjay replied. Then he counted off on his fingers, "Gull Island, Seal Island, Emerald Island, Dolphin Island, Whale Island."

"You've had a geography lesson," Jasper sounded impressed.

"What do you think I did all day while you guys were fooling around at that clinic?" Sonjay grinned. "Besides, Jelly put it on his map," he admitted sheepishly.

Denzel touched Jack gently on the arm and asked him, "Is it safe on the Emerald Island?"

Jack rolled his eyes. "Keep moving," he said grimly.

When Doshmisi returned from her walk in the woods, she had some mannafruit for them. They split one to cheer themselves up and Doshmisi put the rest of them away in her bag. "What was yours?" she asked Denzel after they had each bitten into their piece.

"Ginger's carrot cake," Denzel mumbled.

Sonjay fell over laughing, "Man, you could have had pizza or barbecue and you want carrot cake? Now that's messed up!"

"It was a good carrot cake. Don't mess with me," Denzel knocked Sonjay down playfully and sat on his chest. He tickled him under the armpits and Sonjay screamed for mercy. Denzel noticed out of the corner of his eye that Jack had cracked a weak smile at their antics. Bayard buzzed Denzel's head and squawked at him until he got off Sonjay.

"Ferry's on its way in," Jasper announced. Sure enough, they could see the ferry in the distance heading toward the dock. They gathered their things, rounded up the tigers, and headed down the beach. Jasper made them put their hoods up to hide their faces a little from view. They stood aside to allow the incoming travelers to disembark and then they filed onto the deck of the large wooden boat.

Deep forest green in color, the ferry had a yellow railing that wrapped around the deck like a ribbon on a package. The deck itself was made of planks of polished wood. Sea gulls and other sea birds circled in the air above it. Maia thought it looked beautiful when it came across the water to the dock and she loved it even more when she stood on the deck. She took out her timber flute, sat down on a bench in the prow, and began to play. A few wide-eyed children congregated around her to listen. They clapped their hands and hummed along. Jasper left Jack to listen to Maia with the other children.

Sonjay and Denzel went up to the captain's room that housed the controls for the ship, where they could talk to the navigator and the captain.

Jasper stood at the yellow railing next to Doshmisi. He thought that she looked good in her new green hat, but he couldn't seem to form the words to tell her so.

"You miss the clinic, don't you?" he asked her instead.

She nodded. "Sure enough. But I'll probably find plenty of healing to do someplace else."

"I miss the clinic too," Jasper said wistfully. "I felt useful there, like I could make a difference for people." He looked at his feet, embarrassed and not really able to express himself.

"Maybe you'll decide to study healing when you get older," Doshmisi suggested.

"I doubt it. I was trained as a guide."

"You're a very good one," Doshmisi told him. She thought she could see him blushing but couldn't tell for sure since he had that reddish color of the People Beyond the Lake to begin with. "How long until we reach Clover?" she asked to change the subject.

"We'll spend the night on Emerald Island and we should arrive at Whale Island before dark tomorrow. A bridge goes from Emerald Island to Dolphin Island and then we have a long ferry ride out to Whale Island. You'll like Whale Island. Many plants and animals can survive only on Whale Island and nowhere else because of the unique ecology of the island. We call it a rainforest. Do you have those in the Farland?"

"I'm not sure. I know we used to," Doshmisi answered, "but I think they might have disappeared."

"What do you mean disappeared? Where did they go?" Jasper asked in confusion.

"Well, some big companies" she paused "do you know what a big company is?"

Jasper shook his head "no" because he didn't know what she meant by a company.

She had to think how to explain this to him. "Well some people where I come from make a lot of money by cutting down the rare trees in the rainforest and selling them and other people get rich off products they make out of dead plants and animals from the rainforests. I think the people getting rich have destroyed most of the rainforests," Doshmisi told him. "We studied it in school. I don't remember if we have any rainforests left."

"They ruined the rainforest just to get coins? I don't get it. Who would want money instead of trees?" Jasper tried to process this idea.

"Crazy, huh?" Doshmisi agreed and then she looked off into the sunset as they approached Emerald Island. The huge green-tinged ball of the sun dropping down over the island as they glided in at the dock made a beautiful sight. The captain came down and stood at the gate and saluted the Four as they disembarked. Denzel and Sonjay shook hands with him.

They made their way into the circle surrounding the little harbor where the ferry docked. Jasper stopped a passerby to ask for directions to the Willow-wisp Inn, owned by Cinnamon's friend Fern. Leaving the animals outside (except for Bayard who rode on Sonjay's shoulder as usual), the travelers entered the inn. A man greeted them at the entrance and Sonjay asked if they could speak to Fern. The man went into the kitchen while the travelers waited in a dining hall furnished with shiny dark wooden tables and chairs elaborately carved with leaves and flowers and birds. Ferns of many shapes and sizes decorated the room.

Fern emerged from the kitchen, wiping her hands on an olive-green bib apron. Slender and beautiful, with high cheekbones and long eyelashes, she had a deep forest green cast to her dark brown skin. She wore an ear cuff on her left ear and a delicate sparkly nose ring stud on the side of her nose. She had three or four holes in each earlobe with silvery green earrings dangling from each hole, and a stack of thin silvery green bracelets on each wrist. She wore her hair short under a hat similar to the one Doshmisi had on. In fact, Fern pointed at Doshmisi's hat and said, "Looks like Cinnamon sent you, judging by that hat, which I recognize. I'm glad she passed it along, it suits you." She stepped forward and held out her hand, "Fern. Pleased to meet you." Then, as her gaze passed over the entire group, she gasped, and pulled her hand back, covering her mouth. "Hold on," she said. "You're the Four, aren't you? Cinnamon sent me the Four. Oh my."

"We're on our way to see Clover," Sonjay told Fern, trusting her completely since she was a friend of Cinnamon's. "Can we sleep here tonight?"

"Yes, yes of course. Do you need anything? Do you want something to eat?" Fern became flustered. Sonjay accepted Fern's offer of food on behalf of all the weary travelers and he introduced them each to Fern, who called her inn staff to her and issued instructions, sending the travelers to rooms and preparing to serve them a late meal. When they sat down to eat, they invited Fern to sit with them and Sonjay gave her the latest news from the Passage Circle. The others remained quiet, grateful to Sonjay for doing all the talking. Everyone felt raw after tearing themselves away from their friends in the Passage Circle in such haste. Right after they ate, they went up the stairs to their rooms for the night. Jasper made certain that the tigers received food and water and that a stable hand bedded them down comfortably.

Doshmisi felt as though she had just put her head on the pillow when Jasper shook her shoulder urgently a few hours later, awakening her from a sound sleep. She swam up to consciousness. Jack floated eerily next to her bed in the dim light and told her, "Compost coming. Hide. Hide."

"Get your things together. Meet me in the dining room," Jasper told her.

Doshmisi jumped out of bed and grabbed her bag and canteen. She made sure she had all her belongings. As she ran out of the room, the man who had greeted them upon their arrival entered with fresh bedding to remake the bed and remove every trace of Doshmisi's recent presence.

In the dining room, Jack, Maia, and Denzel waited for her with Fern, who commanded tersely "follow me." She led them out behind the Willow-wisp to the barn where Sonjay and Jasper had started herding the tigers through a trapdoor in the barn floor and down a flight of stairs beyond. "You can hide in here. Someone will come for you when you can come out. I must go back to the inn and remove any evidence. Compost can sniff a flea in a sandstorm. Quick, get inside and we'll cover the door with hay."

The travelers hurried down the stairs into a chamber of stone underneath the barn. Sitting on the cold floor, surrounded by inky darkness, they could hear the scrape of a pitchfork moving hay above them. Doshmisi felt for Maia and the sisters leaned against a stone wall together, clasping each other's hands.

"What is this place?" Denzel asked from a few feet to their left.

"Part of the Underground Pathway," Jasper said. "Those who oppose Sissrath can sometimes escape his grasp by hiding in the Marini Hills or the Amber Mountains. The Willow-wisp is a secret safe house on the Underground Pathway from Whale Island. Sissrath's enemies sometimes hide here while passing through. Many of the circles have safe houses."

"Like the Underground Railroad," Maia pointed out and Doshmisi nodded her head in agreement, but then realized that Maia couldn't see her in the darkness.

"What's that smell?" Denzel asked.

"Sweet grasses," Jasper answered. "They must be spreading them in the barn to cover our scent from Compost's nose."

"Quiet," Jack urged. "Quiet."

"You mustn't speak," Jasper told them. "Not a word, not a sneeze. Not until Fern returns." Jasper pulled Cocoa into his lap and stroked her ears. She understood that she had to keep still. Bayard Rustin did not make so much as a peep. They waited in silence. Alert, tense, listening.

It seemed like they had sat in the underground chamber for hours before they heard a rattling sound approaching from the barnyard. Maia squeezed Doshmisi's hand. The barn door opened and the floor creaked above their heads. The smell of decomposing broccoli filled their nostrils and nearly made them gag. Compost had arrived.

"What do you keep in here?" Compost's voice snarled.

Fern replied, "Our hay, for bedding down the tigers of our guests."

"A lot of sweet grass in here," Compost sniffed loudly.

"Tigers like to eat it," Fern said curtly.

"I see." He walked slowly from one end of the barn to the other. Underneath Compost's measured footsteps, Sonjay held his breath.

Another person entered the barn. "What do you think, Compost?" asked a voice as chilling as a cemetery in February. The voice made the travelers shiver and their skin crawled. At the sound of that voice, the hair on the back of Doshmisi's neck stood up. She stuffed her hand in her mouth to avoid screaming. It was the voice in her dream. The voice of the sinister man who had chased her through her nightmares in the months since Mama's death. She could hear that voice in her head saying "your mother can't protect you here." She trembled and Maia put her arms around her sister in terror.

"I think perhaps a search enchantment might be in order," Compost suggested. "I just have this feeling."

At that moment, Jack silently reached over and took Doshmisi's hand in the dark and then he took Sonjay's hand. They could vaguely see him floating above the stone floor and his face had a slight violet glow to it, not bright at all, but enough that they could see him close his eyes in concentration.

"How's that?" asked the chilling voice.

"A feeling, Master, Sir, that they might..." but Compost's voice trailed off and faltered. He suddenly sounded uncertain.

"Go on."

"Never mind. I think we should have searched the coast more

carefully," Compost suggested. "I had their scent the strongest down at the water. I'm losing it out here." A note of frustration entered Compost's voice.

"Then let us return and look more carefully," the steely voice agreed. "I will send a friend to watch the waters out here in case we have missed something."

"Do you wish to return now or in the morning, Master?" Compost asked.

"It is nearly morning. Let's rest for a couple of hours and breakfast before continuing."

Compost clapped his hands and ordered Fern, "Show Master Sissrath to a bed and feed our tigers some of this sweet grass." With a final sniff in the doorway, Compost left the barn and Fern closed the door behind him.

Jack released Doshmisi's hand and floated back to Jasper's side where he dropped feebly to the floor and fell into an exhausted sleep. The voice of Sissrath hovered in the barn even after his departure and filled the travelers with such dread that none of them dared speak for fear he might discover them even from the distance of the inn. One by one, they drifted off to sleep in the dark chamber, hopeful that Sissrath and Compost would leave the islands in the morning.

To their great relief, they awoke to Fern's voice calling down to them from above. "They left. We're moving the hay and sweet grass and we'll get you out shortly."

The travelers soon emerged, blinking in the bright light of the mid-morning sun.

Fern hugged each of them in turn, glad to see them safe and sound. "I thought they would find you for sure when Compost suggested the search enchantment, but then he changed his mind. You must have good luck," she told them.

"Not luck. An intuit." Jasper smiled smugly. "Jack scrambled Compost's intuition. He sent him confusing messages."

"Of course," Fern exclaimed. "Great work Jack. You protected the Four."

Jack looked pleased with himself.

"Now we have to get you out of here. Sissrath and Compost are heading back the way they came. They think you eluded them at the Passage Circle. You should make a run to see Clover now, before they come back this way," Fern advised. She gave them each a sack of food she had packed for them and they headed toward the bridge that led off of Dolphin Island. Jack had a gloomy look, but at least he had no premonition of disaster. Before nightfall the others would wonder why he hadn't seen the danger that lurked in the ocean depths, preparing to strike out at them later that day. But their day's journey started out most uneventfully, with a trek over the ocean bridge from Emerald Island to Dolphin Island.

The landscape on Dolphin Island resembled a Caribbean paradise, with palm and coconut trees on the beaches and tropical fruit trees like papayas and mangoes in the gardens and yards. The women on Dolphin Island wore their hair short and most of them had little hats like the one Doshmisi wore. The men had their hair cut short too. The Island People wore woven tunics of red, green, yellow, and black. Jasper told the others that people came to Dolphin and Whale Islands to study healing and to seek out the best healers. Doshmisi wished she could stay and study on these islands.

Jasper led them down to the dock on the other side of Dolphin Island in time to catch the afternoon ferry. When the boat docked, and the tigers realized that Jasper expected them to board, they balked. Jasper couldn't understand it. The tigers simply refused to board that ferry. They sat down on the beach and howled like a pack of dogs, pawing the ground and shaking their large heads. They turned their huge sorrowful eyes on Jasper and acted as if heartbroken.

"I don't know why they won't board," Jasper said. "It's not a good sign."

"Are they afraid of water?" Maia asked.

"No, they love water. They're great swimmers," Jasper told her. He turned to Jack, "Do you see anything?" Jack crinkled his little brow anxiously. He shook his head. "Not right, not right," he said, looking worried. Jasper found the captain of the ferry and asked him if he had seen anything unusual on the previous day's journey.

"Well, I didn't see any dolphins out there, if that's what you mean. And I consider that unusual, because they like to play alongside the boat and escort us. But otherwise, we had a normal passage," the captain told him. Jasper explained to him the difficulty with the tigers and he kindly agreed to hold the ferry so that Jasper could find someone to take the tigers and look after them until the travelers returned. Sonjay went with Jasper and they came back before long without the tigers. Fern had told Jasper that if they had any trouble they should look for her sister on Dolphin Island and Jasper had tracked her down. She would keep the tigers for the time being.

Doshmisi felt uneasy about leaving the tigers behind, especially after Maia said she had the feeling that they shouldn't board the ferry. "But it's the only way to Clover," Doshmisi reminded her.

Whale Island lay quite a distance from Dolphin Island. They couldn't see it from the harbor as the ferry pulled out. Maia stood at the railing, scouring the water for any sign of danger. Jack drifted distractedly next to her, biting his lip, and looking as if he were trying to remember something. Maia took his little hand and held it in her own. By all accounts, they should have had an enjoyable voyage. The sun shone out of a clear, tropical sky and the fresh ocean air welcomed them to the furthest islands. But the tigers' refusal to board the ferry made everyone too anxious and put them too much on their guard to relax and enjoy the beautiful day and the beautiful ocean.

Doshmisi couldn't stand to hear Jack muttering "not right" and to watch Maia's worried face so she went below the deck with Jasper. Denzel and Sonjay had again chosen to travel on the bridge with the captain, where they could have their questions answered.

The ferry traveled for more than three hours and Doshmisi eventually fell asleep leaning on Jasper's shoulder. The day lazily approached sunset. But then, as the ferry neared Whale Island, Sonjay on the bridge and Maia, still clinging to the railing, saw at the same time the phosphorescent white scales of something with the appearance of a giant worm glide up out of the water and back down again silently and ominously in the distance. Maia grabbed Jack by the arm and repeated the words he had muttered all afternoon, "Not right."

Sonjay pointed out the snaky object to the captain as it appeared and disappeared again, a little closer than before. "What is that?"

The captain squinted into the sun. He gave a low moaning whistle. "It looks to be a sea serpent," he said in astonishment. "We haven't had one of those in over thirty years. I didn't think they still existed!"

"I don't suppose they're friendly," Denzel muttered grimly.

"Never," the captain said, and then, lowering his voice, he added, "They are agents of evil enchantment. Only Sissrath could have unleashed this beast."

Then Denzel remembered Sissrath's words in the barn at the Willow-wisp. This must be the "friend" he said he would send to watch the waters.

They stared out at the sea serpent in shock, as it rapidly approached the ferry. Suddenly, it reared its spiky head out of the depths of the ocean and spouted water from its nostrils in fury all over the deck of the ferry, completely soaking Maia and Jack with water and sea serpent slime. Maia grabbed Jack and dragged him toward the stairs on the wet and slippery deck. As they stumbled below, the sea serpent whipped around and caught the ferry hard with its tail, cracking the prow of the boat, just below the spot where Maia had stood all afternoon, waiting for this disaster, sensing it coming.

On the bridge, the captain said to Denzel and Sonjay, "If we take in too much water way out here then we won't make it to the harbor."

Sonjay pointed, "Look, it's coming back."

"It could sink us with a couple more blows like that," the captain said, wide-eyed and unbelieving.

For a moment, Sonjay, Denzel, the captain, and the other crew members on the bridge stood mesmerized, watching the sea serpent return. As the hideous spiky head drew nearer and the white-green scales glittered dangerously out on the water, Denzel asked the captain tensely, "What can we do to fight it?"

Before the captain could answer, the sea serpent struck the ferry again with its tail. The ferry shuddered. All at once everyone ran in a million directions in complete pandemonium as panic seized the ferry passengers.

Chapter Ten

The History Lesson

The passengers on the deck stampeded, dragging Maia and Jack along with them in the crush of bodies as they stumbled down the stairs and into the room below the deck where Jasper and Doshmisi, struggling to keep their footing, clung to a metal railing that ran around the wall. The boat lurched and rolled like a crazy bucking bronco beneath their feet. The captain, Denzel, and Sonjay flew past the passengers and down a flight of stairs that led deeper into the depths of the ferry. As they ran past, the captain called, "Grab the railing and hang on."

"What in the heck?" Doshmisi turned a questioning face to her sister.

"Sea serpent," Jack answered for Maia. Then he stuttered, "C-c-couldn't s-see, couldn't s-see."

"We got slimed," Maia looked down at the greenish yellow goo that soaked her clothing. She and Jack and some of the other passengers from the top deck looked dreadful, and they smelled like old tuna fish sandwiches.

"C-couldn't see. Why?" Jack demanded of Jasper in a frenzy, as if Jasper would have an answer.

Meanwhile, Denzel and Sonjay raced to keep up with the captain, who proceeded to the bottom of the boat, ran the length of a long passageway, and stopped at a metal door. He fumbled for a key on his large key ring, found the one he wanted, and opened the door. Inside Denzel and Sonjay saw what looked like a small museum of seafaring objects. The captain strode to a dusty glass case mounted on the wall. In black letters across the top of the case it read "IN CASE OF SEA SERPENT BREAK GLASS AND BLOW HORN." The captain looked around him frantically, shouting "In here, we have to get into this case."

Denzel grabbed an axe-like tool from a nearby bench and thrust it into the case, shattering the glass. The captain carefully removed a large object that looked like a combination bassoon and baritone saxophone, he also took a sheet of music from behind it. The strange wooden horn had a black metal mouthpiece protruding from it. "We need to find someone who can play this thing," he said as he tapped the mouthpiece anxiously.

Sonjay exclaimed, "My sister can play anything." The three of them immediately pounded back up the stairs. When they reached the room below the deck, they found the passengers clinging to the railing on the wall in terror. The ferry navigator stood at the top of the stairs and bellowed, "It's coming back, it's coming back."

Sonjay ran up the stairs past the navigator and onto the deck while Denzel and the captain rushed to Maia. "You need to play this thing," Denzel shouted at Maia. Then he turned to the captain, "Tell her what to do."

"Play this horn," the captain said, struggling to catch his breath, and he thrust the enormous, unwieldy instrument at Maia.

Maia stared at them, dumbfounded. "What do you mean?" she demanded.

"I think that if you play this horn, it will do something to the sea serpent," Denzel explained quickly. Wrapping one arm around the peculiar horn and grabbing Maia's hand with the other, he rushed toward the stairs.

"Wait," the captain cried, tearing after them, "you have to play this music." He clutched the crumpled sheet of music he had grabbed out of the glass case in his clenched fist and he held it out to Maia with a trembling hand. Then Denzel, Maia, and the captain stumbled headlong back up the steps with the horn jostling between them. When they reached the top deck, they gasped at the sight that met their eyes.

The sea serpent's spiked head towered over the boat, its yellow-green eyes flashing with malevolence. It opened its mouth and lunged forward to take a bite out of the stern. At that moment Sonjay spun around on the deck with a long-handled wooden shovel in his hand and he reached up and crammed it into the sea serpent's mouth. The sea serpent howled ferociously and shook its giant scaly head, trying to dislodge the shovel, which forced its mouth wide open. "You think you the boss?" Sonjay shouted at the beast. "Well chew on that."

"Tight," Denzel whistled through his teeth. He raised a closed fist over his head and shouted to his brother, "Hey, Sonjay, you the man."

Meanwhile the captain breathlessly explained to Maia, "If you play this piece of music on this horn supposedly it will drive away sea serpents. Don't ask me how. It's the only thing I can think of. Please, try it. Please."

Maia didn't know much about playing horns, but she could feel her amulet glowing warmly against her chest, which gave her courage. So she took the horn from Denzel resolutely.

"Alright, alright. Here, hold this." Maia pushed the sheet music at the captain, who smoothed it out and held it open and flat across his chest. He looked like a human music stand. Maia tried to arrange her fingers around the instrument, which she thought resembled a sort of giant timber flute, but she found it awkward to play because of its size. She hummed the tune written on the music sheet to herself, then she blew on the mouthpiece and a cloud of dust fizzled out of the end of the horn and billowed around the captain's knees. "How old is this thing?" she asked. The captain sneezed.

Suddenly, rays of blue light burst forth from the front of Maia's shirt as her amulet began to blaze.

"Never mind how old it is, just play it," Denzel shouted to her. "That shovel is going to splinter any second." And sure enough, the shovel bowed and then cracked and then flew apart as the sea serpent continued to roar and shake its chartreuse head. Now the creature appeared angry specifically at Sonjay, who looked around desperately for some other useful object of defense.

Maia blew hard into the ancient horn and a note came out; clear and deep and resonant. At the sound of the note, the sea serpent hesitated, closed its mouth, and looked at the little people on the deck of the ferry with uncertainty. Maia blew a number of other notes, trying to figure out how to play the thing. Then she looked at the music sheet on the captain's chest and she tried to play the tune. By some mysterious good fortune, her fingers found the correct positions and the notes soon followed the music. The horn sounded like the call of sea lions penetrating a deep fog. Below the deck, the panic subsided as the passengers grew silent to listen to the horn. Doshmisi thought that if she could ever hear the singing of mermen, it would sound like that horn. Deep and mournful. Smooth. Rumbling. A sound of great pain and great beauty.

The effect of the sound on the sea serpent was swift and brutal. The monster cried out in agony and shook its head while green goo poured out of its ears.

"Now that's nasty," Sonjay muttered to Denzel as he retreated to his brother's side. "Must be serpent blood."

"Or serpent ear wax," Denzel suggested.

"That's *really* nasty," Sonjay exclaimed.

Maia played the horn long after the monster had fled back across the water and disappeared from sight. Slowly the ferry passengers crept onto the deck to see the retreating sea serpent and to listen to Maia playing the haunting tune on the horn as blue light emanated from her amulet.

The captain returned to the bridge and guided his damaged ship into the harbor at Whale Island, which swiftly came into view after the sea serpent's departure. Maia continued to play a made-up tune on the horn. The voice of the horn resonated far out across the water, so that by the time the ferry finally arrived, curious Island People who had heard the unusual sound mobbed the ferry dock on Whale Island.

A large, forest green woman, wrapped in a colorful shawl and wearing a hat much like Doshmisi's over her gray-green hair, parted the crowd and stood at the end of the dock, her head cocked to one side, listening. "It's the horn that repels the sea serpent," she told those who stood around her. "And," she muttered under her breath inaudibly, "I would bet by the sound of it that one who wears the Amulet of Watersong blows the horn." She stood at the end of the dock until the ferry pulled up and tied down. Then she leapt onto the deck and approached Maia (who still held the horn but no longer played it) extending both of her work-worn hands in a warm greeting.

"You must wear the Amulet of Watersong. Let me take a look at you," the woman's voice cracked with emotion as she continued "oh daughter of Debbie." Tears ran down the woman's cheeks as she embraced Maia. "I am Clover the Griot, and I have long awaited the day of your arrival." Maia fell into Clover's arms and burst into tears, overcome with relief at arriving safely at last in Clover's circle.

Clover dried her own eyes and patted Maia's hair reassuringly, "It was just a sea serpent, and you managed to get the better of it; everything turned out alright." Maia wiped her eyes as Clover released her to greet the others. Clover folded Doshmisi, Denzel, and Sonjay, each in turn, in a big and protective embrace. It felt like coming home and Doshmisi wondered why this woman's greeting had such a powerful affect on them. Clover did not embrace Jack or Jasper, but shook their hands instead, saying to Jasper, "You must be their guide; way to go, young man, way to go."

"Come. We have much to discuss and this place is too open and visible," Clover turned and began to push her way through the press of people.

Island People milled around on the dock, gawking at the Four with curiosity. "Move along. Nothing to see here," Clover instructed the onlookers as she led her visitors off the dock. Once free of the crowd, Clover strode swiftly up the street, past the neat little wooden houses, painted bright colors, with flags and banners flapping gaily from porches and doorframes.

The travelers scurried to keep up with Clover. She led them through a stone gate into an ancient cobblestone courtyard surrounded by cottages and beckoned for them to follow her into one of the cottages.

"Welcome to my home," Clover made a wide arc with her arm. A young woman promptly appeared, rubbing her slender hands on a green and blue plaid apron and Clover introduced her. "Iris lives with me and helps me in my work." She introduced the travelers to Iris, who nodded her head shyly in greeting and retreated to the kitchen while

Clover took her guests into the living room. She pointed at Maia and Jack, "It looks to me like you two need a shower."

"We got slimed," Maia explained.

The travelers took turns using the shower in the tiny bathroom tiled with pictures of sea creatures. Iris brought them delicious tropical fruit smoothies to drink while they waited their turn for the shower. In a short time they found themselves seated expectantly at the round oak table in Clover's kitchen, ready for some explanations. Iris had cooked them scrambled eggs with cheese and she set out a platter of fruit.

"I know why you have come," Clover told them, getting straight to the point. "You have questions for me and I don't know how much you have already figured out."

"Next to nothin'," Denzel snorted.

"We want to know who we are," Doshmisi demanded.

"Of course. Doesn't everyone?" Clover smiled a faint, all-knowing smile and tilted her head in thought for a moment. She closed her eyes and took a deep breath. "Before I tell you who you are, I'm going to tell you who I am. It's my biggest secret and only three people in this land know of it: Jasper's mother Crystal, the enchanter Cardamom, and Iris here. But I want *you* to know who I am. I trust that it will not leave this room." She looked pointedly down her nose at Jasper and Jack and then at each of the Four. "My dear children, Sonjay, Maia, Denzel, Doshmisi: I am your grandmother."

As soon as the words left Clover's lips, the Goodacres knew in their hearts that she spoke the truth.

"They told us that you disappeared somewhere in Africa after Grandaddy passed," Doshmisi said.

"And that nobody knows where you went," Denzel added.

"Does Aunt Alice know you live here?" Sonjay asked.

"She knows I came to Faracadar but no, she doesn't know that I live here on Whale Island. I have kept my true identity a secret. I have the job of preserving the history, an extremely important function as you will one day realize. And something one cannot do while one is busy banging around making history; one must remain rather removed from history to keep the facts straight. When someone needs a reality check, they come to me. Just as you have done."

"But I thought your name was Rosemary," Maia told Clover in confusion.

"When I returned to Faracadar, I changed my name to Clover to protect my privacy and to ensure my safety," their grandmother explained.

"Do you know that Mama passed into spirit?" Maia asked softly.

"Yes, I do," Clover told them, her shoulders drooping slightly. "I no longer have the powers of one of the Four, but I have the gift of sight. I can often see into the distance and sometimes into the mists of the future."

"How do you stay so green?" Sonjay blurted.

"Sonjay, mind your manners," Doshmisi scolded, although she had wondered the same thing herself. Clover threw her head back and laughed heartily. Then she winked at them. "A little secret potion. Color change powder."

"I gotta get me some of that," Sonjay announced.

"Hold on, all in good time," Clover told him.

"So tell us what's up. Why did we get sent here? Why us?" Denzel asked.

"Where to begin?" Clover said, more to herself than anyone else.

"Begin at the beginning," Sonjay suggested.

Clover laughed. "That's too far back. Tell me, have you already guessed who the old four were?" Clover asked.

"Our mother, Aunt Alice, Uncle Bobby, and Uncle Martin," Sonjay answered promptly.

"Do you know your destiny? Do you know the heritage that flows in your veins? Have you heard it whispered in your dreams?" Clover smiled an enigmatic smile. "Your history joins that of Faracadar with your great-grandfather, High Chief Elder."

Doshmisi covered her mouth with her hand in surprise, Denzel's and Maia's eyebrows flew up, and Sonjay's jaw dropped open like in a cartoon.

"Our great-grandfather came from Faracadar?" Denzel tried to understand what that meant about himself.

"You mean our family is from Faracadar?" Sonjay asked.

"Yes, you are part Faracadaran. In fact, you are part *royal* Faracadaran," Clover confirmed. "And so am I, of course. Your great-grandfather, my father, was High Chief Elder. He belonged to the royal family. He had an adventuring spirit. He commissioned a great enchanter named Hazamon, who came from the Mountain People, to help him create Angel's Gate, which allows passage from Faracadar to the Farland and back. The gate has complex properties, which no one, not even Sissrath, fully understands. It only allows passage to a select few and only at select times. And, as you have discovered, passage does not always occur at the site of Angel's Gate. High Chief Elder traveled through the gate to the Farland, where he met your great-grandmother Leona, and fell in love with her the moment he set eyes on her. Now there's a romantic story for another time. He brought her back to Faracadar as his high chieftess. But the people were foolish and they didn't want a foreign high chieftess. High Chief Elder had such great love for Leona that he gave up the throne to his brother, Peep, and came to live out here, on Whale Island, far from Big House City. He founded the library that I now look after. For seven years, Chief Elder and Chieftess Leona lived in simple happiness in a house on the beach. The chief needed no further adventure than that of fatherhood, for they had four children together. You know these four children. Their names are Charles, Henry, Laurel, and Rosemary, that's me. Now Clover."

"Our grandmama," Maia murmured.

"We never met Charles," Denzel said.

"Yes, indeed. Because he lived here. After Peep became the high chief, he summoned the great enchanters from the Amber Mountains and enlisted them to increase his power and his grip on the people of Faracadar. Then a sad thing happened to Chief Elder. Peep, fearing he would lose control of the land one day to his brother's children, decreed that Chieftess Leona and her children must return to the Farland. Chief Elder chose to go with her and he disappeared from Faracadar forever. Peep had the original Angel's Gate disassembled, but the magic of it persisted in pieces of the wood from which it was made that the sprites took into the Marini Hills and kept hidden. Amethyst regained the wood and with the help of Hazamon she refashioned the gate so that eight years after their banishment, Chief Elder's children returned. I am one of those children. To make a long story short, High Chief Charles took the kingdom from Peep and chased Peep's enchanters back to the Downs. The High Mountain People are a private and spiritual sort, who have mastered many mysteries of the universe. They keep to themselves, and most of them would not harm even the tiniest bug. They possess more knowledge of nature and the universe than any creatures living. But the Mountain People of the Downs, well, Sissrath comes from these. Beware of these of the Downs for their hunger for power has corrupted their use of their gift of enchantment."

"So Uncle Charles stayed in Faracadar as the high chief?" Denzel asked.

"Correct," Clover confirmed.

"But you returned to the Farland and married Grandaddy," Doshmisi confirmed.

"That I did," Clover agreed.

"Why?" Sonjay asked. "Why didn't you stay in Faracadar?"

Clover looked down at her hands, folded calmly in front of her. "Because I was the youngest and I felt at the time that the safest place for me to raise my children was in the Farland. Same as your mother. I returned to the Farland and married for the same reason that your mother returned to the Farland and married, to ensure the continuation of the royal line from High Chief Elder. From the youngest to the youngest."

"What do you mean?" Sonjay asked, worriedly, since he was the youngest.

"The royal line comes through the youngest. High Chief Elder was the youngest, and it was his duty to provide four children, to bear the amulets. He did this with Chieftess Leona. Then I came along, the youngest. I grew up and assured the strength of the royal line with Alice, Martin, Bobby, and Debbie, who became the Four for a time."

"And our mother, the youngest, had the four of us," Doshmisi contributed.

"Exactly."

Suddenly everyone looked at Sonjay.

"What?" Sonjay stuck his lip out. "Hey, don't even go there. I'm not getting married anytime soon. Maybe never. So forget it."

Denzel cracked a grin and whistled a few bars of *Here Comes the Bride.*

"Don't make me come over there, man," Sonjay warned him, pointing a finger. Clover smiled indulgently and continued. "Sissrath and his followers believe that the Mountain People are the rightful royal rulers, because they have the gift of enchantment. It angers them that the rest of the land refuses to recognize them as the rulers and their anger consumes them. It makes them prisoners of their own pride and enslaves them. Because he cannot rule outright, Sissrath has made the high chief into a puppet, a high chief in name only."

"How can he get away with that?" Doshmisi could not understand why Hyacinth didn't stand up to Sissrath.

"Many years ago, during the Battle of Blood Winter, Sissrath and others of the Downs felled the greatest of the red oak trees, a mighty red oak named Shakabaz. At the command of Shakabaz itself, an object of extraordinary power was crafted from the dying tree and given to your mother, the youngest, to help her care for the people. But your mother did not keep the Staff of Shakabaz for long. Sissrath stole it from her with enchantment and deception. Shakabaz has certain powers in matters of life and death. Your mother could not gain it back from Sissrath, but she could protect the people from him to some extent. She made a bargain with Sissrath. She traded years of her life in exchange for his bond that he would not, could not use Shakabaz directly in matters of life and death. A deep binding enchantment sealed their bargain and neither one of them could ever break it. Debbie was still young at the time and she imagined she had plenty of years ahead to have four children. Sissrath figured he could use Shakabaz for such powerful enchantment that he could get around the matters of life and death. He thought he got the better end of the bargain since he expected that he had rid himself of the Four. Debbie underestimated how many years she had and how much she would want those years, to see all of you grow up. And Sissrath underestimated the difficulty he would encounter learning how to use Shakabaz and bending it to his will. He also didn't count on the fact that Debbie would retreat to the Farland and successfully have four children."

Silence filled the room as the meaning of Clover's words sunk in: Sissrath had taken their mother's life.

By the time Clover had told them all of this, it had grown pitch dark outside. No cheerful moon peeked over the trees in this land and the lesser sun would not appear again in this season. The travelers could hardly believe this day had started at the Willow-wisp Inn on Emerald Island, since so much had happened. They had a lot to think about.

"Time for bed. I'll tell you more in the morning when I take you over to the library, where I work." Clover pushed herself back from the table and she and Iris hastened to the living room where they made up makeshift beds on the floor for Clover's grandchildren and their friends. Clover tucked them in and kissed each of them goodnight. As she drifted off to sleep, Doshmisi remembered that Mama had told her to give her love to Clover. She would find a private moment to do it in the morning, and it made sense now.

The next day, after breakfast, Clover wanted to take them straight to the library. This suited Denzel, Maia, and Sonjay just fine; but Jasper and Doshmisi had other plans.

"Jack has me worried," Jasper told Clover. Jack had refused to wake up and continued sleeping, curled up on his mat in the living room. Jasper couldn't even wake him up for breakfast. "I think something is wrong, but he can't see it. When the sea serpent came after us, he kept asking me why he didn't see it beforehand," Jasper explained to Clover.

"Perhaps something clouds his vision," Clover suggested.

"Do you think Sissrath knows that Jack is traveling with the Four?" Jasper asked anxiously.

"I seriously doubt that possibility, but maybe Sissrath has figured out a way to block the intuits," Clover thought out loud.

"Exactly. I want to find another intuit to see if others have clouded vision," Jasper said. Clover gave him directions to another intuit's house and Jasper walked off toward the harbor.

As for Doshmisi, she agreed to join them at the library soon. She had made a secret agreement with Iris and they wanted to remain at the house together. Although curious about her mysterious plans, the others didn't question her.

After the others left, Iris asked Doshmisi, "How short do you want it, daughter of Debbie?"

"I want it as short as yours." Doshmisi had decided to cut her hair short. She would wear her woven hat over it like her grandmother. Iris draped a tablecloth around Doshmisi's shoulders and went to work. When Iris finished, Doshmisi looked just like one of the Island People.

"If anyone sees you standing next to Clover, you will give away her secret identity I think," Iris giggled. Doshmisi certainly resembled her grandmother more than ever with the new haircut.

"Now one more thing," Doshmisi instructed Iris. "I want you to pierce my nose, just like yours and Clover's. Can you loan me a small stud to put in it?"

"I have a stud that is exactly right for you. It would please me if you would let me give it to you and it would make me proud to have you wear it," Iris told her. She produced a small emerald gem stone, deep green like the middle of a forest in late afternoon light.

"It's perfect. I love it. Thank you." Doshmisi admired the jewel.

"I am delighted to have one of the Four adopt our style, especially you, the one with the Amulet of the Trees," Iris told her softly. She insisted on giving Doshmisi an ear cuff and some silver-green bracelets for her wrists. When Iris had finished her handiwork, Doshmisi liked her new appearance.

"Now, off to the library with you," Iris said as she pointed Doshmisi in the right direction.

As Doshmisi walked the short distance to join the others, she thought to herself that she did not look forward to making a decision about what to do next. It seemed to her that everything pointed toward a confrontation with Sissrath and she didn't feel brave enough for that. It was entirely possible that she could lose her life here in Faracadar and that thought filled her with fear. When Doshmisi entered the library, Sonjay did a double take that secretly pleased her. Denzel stared in disbelief at his new sister.

Maia burst into tears. "You cut off your hair," she sobbed.

Sonjay said, "Ooh-ooh, girl, Aunt Alice is going to have a hissy fit when she sees that nose ring."

"How do you know we'll ever see Aunt Alice again?" Doshmisi demanded. "Besides, Aunt Alice has been here and she knows what a healer looks like."

The truth in what her sister said stopped Maia's tears.

"You look good with short hair," Jasper complimented her from the doorway, as he returned just at that moment. "You look like one of the great healers. It's just the right style for you." Doshmisi shot him a grateful look.

"So what's up with the intuits?" Denzel asked Jasper.

"Not good," Jasper shook his head ruefully. "I saw three others and none of them will wake up this morning. They act just like Jack, as if in a coma. This has to be Sissrath's handiwork. He doesn't want us to know what he's doing or where he went and so he has blinded the intuits."

"Then we haven't much time," Clover told them with a note of urgency in her voice. "I have more to tell you, now that I have all of you here together, and before you must leave. I want to tell you about your father."

The Goodacres exchanged looks of disbelief.

"Our father?" Maia whispered.

Chapter Eleven

Vengeance

The Goodacres had generally held a low opinion of their father because he abandoned their family. When their mother spoke of him, she said he would return one day, but they never believed her. Now their grandmother told them what had happened.

"Your father knew about Faracadar from the start, but he did not know about your mother's bargain with Sissrath for many years," Clover began. "Your mother thought she could only secure a new four and keep you out of harm's way if she never returned to Faracadar. After Sonjay was born, and your mother had fulfilled her destiny by producing four to inherit the royal line, she confessed to your father that she had traded years of her life to Sissrath to protect our people here. He couldn't bear the thought of losing her while she was still so young, and so he found a way into Faracadar. To this day, no one knows how he did this. Only the one living gatekeeper and those of royal blood have passed through Angel's Gate. But your father passed through and attempted to take back the years of your mother's life from Sissrath. He was unsuccessful and was taken away to the dungeons of the Final Fortress, deep in the Amber Mountains. Few return from the dungeons. None after this many years have passed."

At last the Goodacres understood why Mama always said Daddy would return when he could. Mama thought he was still alive and she believed that he would escape one day.

Clover continued, "The Staff of Shakabaz rightfully belongs to the youngest of the Four. It is an object of power that should have been passed down to you, Sonjay, from your mother. It does not want to belong to Sissrath. It is Sissrath's prisoner and it resists him. It calls to you to release it. It does not wish to do Sissrath's evil work. Even though he cannot use it directly to kill, he has learned a way to use it to turn a certain tree sap into a deadly poison. He puts this poison on the tips of darts. His Special Forces, the soldiers he has hand picked from among the Mountain People of the Downs, are the only ones to possess these darts and with them they terrorize the people. You see, in Faracadar, they have never invented guns. These poison-tipped darts are the most lethal weapons in the land. To protect himself and his own people, Sissrath uses the inner bark of the red oaks to make an armor that prevents the dart poison from penetrating the skin."

"When I visited the Grove of Shakabaz, I saw the craters in the ground where murdered red oaks must have stood," Doshmisi told Clover. Doshmisi remembered the terrible sadness of the trees in the center of the grove.

"Most of the ancient red oaks died during the Battle of Blood Winter. Sissrath has felled two great ones since then to gain the sap for his poison and to make more armor. But your presence in the land completely changes the game," Clover lifted her chin with a touch of pride. "You will break Sissrath's grip on Faracadar if you can take Shakabaz from him. He thinks you are just children with no power to resist him. But I think he underestimates you."

"There's something I don't get," Sonjay said.

"What's that, baby?" Clover encouraged him.

"What's up with Hyacinth? How can Sissrath play him like he does if the people support Hyacinth?"

"Hyacinth is a fool," Bayard uttered vehemently from his usual perch on Sonjay's shoulder.

"You never miss an opportunity to dis the man, do you?" Sonjay sounded annoyed.

Clover wagged a finger at Bayard, "He is not a fool, you mean-spirited bird. He's just not cut out to be a high chief. He would prefer to live quietly with his animals than to rule the land." Then she told her grandchildren, "You and Hyacinth are distant cousins. He is of the

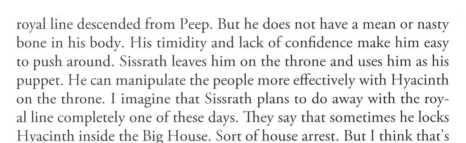

royal line descended from Peep. But he does not have a mean or nasty bone in his body. His timidity and lack of confidence make him easy to push around. Sissrath leaves him on the throne and uses him as his puppet. He can manipulate the people more effectively with Hyacinth on the throne. I imagine that Sissrath plans to do away with the royal line completely one of these days. They say that sometimes he locks Hyacinth inside the Big House. Sort of house arrest. But I think that's just idle gossip. Poor Hyacinth." Clover sighed.

"So what's up with that army?" Denzel asked. "You know, the people who serve in Sissrath's army to earn money for their circles to pay the taxes. Who does Sissrath plan to fight with the army?"

"Ah, yes, the army," Clover replied. "The Special Forces are his real army because they come from his own people and they're loyal to him and loyal to the belief that the Mountain People should rule. As for the rest of the army, the sons and daughters of the land, well, some maintain the Big House, working as servants, and others work on Sissrath's special projects. He also trains many of these young people as a fighting army to fulfill his greatest fantasy, which is to invade the Farland one day. But he can't figure out how to get through Angel's Gate. So he seeks another entrance into the Farland."

"They told me in the Passage Circle about the whales he killed with that sonar stuff," Sonjay interjected. "That's messed up."

"You've got that right," Clover agreed. The others didn't know what had happened to the whales so she explained. "Sissrath uses Shakabaz to send powerful sonar sound waves out through the ocean to detect any land that might lie across the water. He believes that he can reach the Farland across the ocean. But first he must locate the Farland. The sonar waves are so loud that they kill the whales and the dolphins in the waters near them. Many of our whales are hundreds of years old, and they are part of a delicate ocean ecosystem that maintains the green algae. The green algae cleans our air, creating fresh air for us to breathe."

"You mean the whales do something that helps the green algae to live and you need the green algae to make your air?" Maia asked.

"Exactly," Clover replied. "Sissrath keeps making bigger and louder sonar waves. One day he will kill every last one of the whales, who are perhaps the wisest creatures in Faracadar."

"So what will happen if Sissrath kills all the whales?" Sonjay wondered.

"Some scientists say that if the whales die out, then the air will thin and turn to poison and all of the creatures of Faracadar will perish."

"What part of this does Sissrath not understand?" Doshmisi asked in frustration.

"Oh, he understands the scientific explanation. But Sissrath thinks he can keep the green algae alive with the power of enchantment. So he thinks he doesn't need the whales. Arrogant fool. Enchantment is not as powerful as nature or the force of creation. The people have hoped for the return of the Four because they believe that only you can regain Shakabaz for the good of the land. Without Shakabaz, Sissrath is just an ordinary enchanter," Clover concluded.

"How does he force the army to stay at Big House City and serve him?" Denzel asked.

"By means of his greatest weapon. Fear," Clover told them grimly. "The people in the army fear that he will harm them, their families, or their circles if they don't obey."

"He has caused great harm to some already," Jasper spoke up.

"Like Ginger and Cinnamon," Sonjay told the others. "Sissrath threw their husbands in prison because they refused to pay taxes and refused to send their daughters to serve in the army."

"How do you know that?" Maia asked her brother.

"Did you think all I did at the Passage Circle was skateboard? I learned a thing or two." Sonjay looked smug.

At that moment Iris appeared in the doorway, her face twisted with anxiety, "Come quickly, it's Jack."

The travelers ran back to the house to find Jack moaning and shivering under a pile of blankets. Even though he appeared feverish, Clover felt his head and assured them he didn't have a fever.

Bayard perched grimly on the back of a chair and announced "bad news."

"Let me try the herbal," Doshmisi suggested as she unstrapped the book. When she laid the book on Jack's chest, it refused to open. She sat down next to him and took his hand, looking up anxiously at her grandmother. "What do we do now?" she asked.

"I think what you should do is leave Jack with me and get out of here before Sissrath finds you," Clover said with a sigh. "I wish you could stay with me longer. You only just arrived. It's not fair. But these are difficult times. I'll give you some of my color change powder to take with you." Clover went into the kitchen and returned with a wide-mouthed canning jar filled with a bluish-green powder that resembled bath salts. She gave the jar to Doshmisi. "Cardamom invented this powder. It's actually a simple formula and I can easily make more. He made it originally as a birthday gift for your Aunt Alice so that she could pass unnoticed among the people. It will disguise you by tinting you a color, like I did to myself. It brings out your inner color. Just sprinkle it in your hair. If at first it doesn't work, use more. There's plenty in the jar for all of you. I wish we had Cardamom here right now. He would be such a tremendous help."

"Where is he?" Sonjay asked.

"Sissrath holds him prisoner at the Final Fortress. He's heavily guarded both by enchantments and Special Forces. Sissrath uses Shakabaz to diminish Cardamom's powers so he can't escape. Sissrath can inhibit Cardamom's powers, but he can't seem to overpower him. Cardamom's skills are simply too great. And Cardamom's life is protected in the bargain Sissrath made with your mother."

"Maybe we should try to rescue Cardamom," Sonjay suggested. "Wouldn't it help to have an enchanter on our side?"

"I don't know the Amber Mountains very well," Jasper looked worried. "And it would take us quite awhile to travel there and back. Besides, the Final Fortress is Sissrath's stronghold and it would be dangerous and probably foolish to walk right into enemy hands."

"Jasper's right," Clover agreed.

"We need a plan," Denzel reminded them. "There's no point in going anywhere without a plan."

"I want a map of Big House City and more information about the Big House," Sonjay decided.

The discussion ended when Jack let out a bloodcurdling scream of anguish and the herbal on his chest flew open. The little intuit's eyes rolled back in his head and his body went rigid. Doshmisi looked at the page of the herbal, which had only two words on it: silver spark.

Doshmisi's heart sank. She knew that silver spark helped cure people who clung to life only by a thread and sometimes it could save their lives, but often it couldn't.

"Oh no. I don't have any," Clover said softly in dismay.

"I brought some," Doshmisi assured her.

"How old is it? It has to be fresh to work."

"I know. I know. It's fresh enough."

Suddenly, Jack stiffened and fell into a trance-like state. His voice became husky and, for the first time since he had joined the travelers, he spoke more than a few words in a row. "Flames consuming the Passage Circle. Intuits dead. Silver spark fields burning. Children hiding in the caves. Drummers fleeing to the hills. Swordsmen murdering. Fire engulfs. Poison darts. Help. Help the people." Jack fell limp against the bed.

Tears streamed down Maia's cheeks and Denzel looked like thunder as he clenched his fists. His eyes fierce with rage, Sonjay voiced the decision they had all made in that moment. "We must return to the Passage Circle as soon as the ferry can take us. Jasper, go speak to the ferry captain. Dosh, make sure Jack gets some silver spark into him. Clover, I need a good map of Big House City. Denzel, see if you can find us some kind of weapons."

"Beware, for those who carry weapons are likely to have weapons used against them," Clover warned Sonjay.

"And how would you suggest we defend ourselves without weapons?" Sonjay asked of her in frustration.

"I would expect the Four to think of a better way," Clover fired back.

"While I'm thinking, I'm going to carry a weapon," Sonjay asserted firmly. "Will you help me with a map or not?"

"While you carry the weapon, don't forget to think," Clover snapped. "Come with me. I have a map of Big House City in the library."

Less than an hour from the moment Jack had gone into his trance and

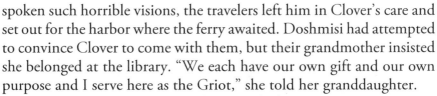

spoken such horrible visions, the travelers left him in Clover's care and set out for the harbor where the ferry awaited. Doshmisi had attempted to convince Clover to come with them, but their grandmother insisted she belonged at the library. "We each have our own gift and our own purpose and I serve here as the Griot," she told her granddaughter.

"When will we see you again?" Maia asked.

"Hopefully during better times," and with these words Clover embraced each of her grandchildren in turn and kissed them goodbye.

The captain assured the travelers that all the ferries were carrying the ancient horn to defend against sea serpents. Then he pointed out to them that the dolphins were running again, which he took as a good sign. The dolphins would not run alongside the ferry if the sea serpent lurked in the water.

As the ferry pulled away from the shore, Doshmisi heard beautiful singing in a language that she strangely understood. It was sort of like the language of the trees, but unlike the messages of trees, the singing came from outside her, from the water all around her. The song told of friends swimming together. She could not see the singers. It puzzled her and she wished she could ask Clover about it, but they had seen Clover and knew as much as they would learn from her for now. When Jasper came and stood by her side, Doshmisi asked, "Do you hear singing?"

He looked at her intently. "No, but I think I know what you hear. Can you tell me the words of the song?"

"It's a playful song. Something like, 'we are swimming together in the bubbles of the leaves of the sea, we are dancing, I'll chase you if you chase me' and such. It's a silly song, like something little children would make up."

"You're probably hearing the dolphins. You must have the rare ability to understand the Seaspeak, the language of dolphins and whales. Dolphins act pretty silly and sing playful songs. The whales, on the other hand, are quite serious and sing about great events of the past and about the days to come. Can you hear the whales?" Jasper asked eagerly. "They might tell us something important."

Try as she might, Doshmisi couldn't hear the whales.

The ferry took the whole afternoon to make its passage to Dolphin Island, where the travelers reclaimed their tigers who joyously licked them in the face with big rough tongues and purred and bounded beside them. On tigerback once again, the travelers set off across the ocean bridge for Emerald Island, where they arrived in cloak of darkness at the Willow-wisp Inn. Fern met them at the door. "I knew you would return as soon as you heard," she said, her face taut with grief and anxiety. "It is said that Sissrath's Special Forces, under the command of Compost, attacked the Passage Circle during the night. Many Coast People lost their lives and Governor Jay lies imprisoned in Big House City. The sprites came out of the hills this evening to bring food to the people. Rumor has it that the Special Forces burned the circle to the ground. But no one from the Passage Circle has come to the inn so I don't know for certain exactly what happened."

"What about Ginger and Cinnamon?" Doshmisi asked.

"Have you heard anything about the drummers?" Maia begged. "What happened to the drummers?"

"I don't know. I have no details," Fern's lip trembled and she bit it to regain her composure.

The travelers spent a restless, gloomy night at the inn, dreading what they would find at the Passage Circle. But they had to wait until the morning to make the ferry crossing to Seal Island. After that they pushed the tigers hard across the ocean bridge to Gull Island, rode without stopping across the island, and proceeded straight on across the bridge leading to the beaches of the Passage Circle. Although they had brought food with them, they never stopped to eat.

In the late afternoon, as they rushed over the last bridge, they could see a thick yellowish mass of smoky air in the distance. By the time they reached the shoreline, they breathed sooty air so thick that it clogged their lungs and made them cough. The beach was deserted. The windmill, that Denzel and his friends had so lovingly erected at the edge of the ocean, lay broken into pieces and scattered on the sand. When Denzel saw it, he dug his heels into his tiger's sides and shot swiftly up the path.

As they came over the last rise of sand dunes and gazed out across the circle, they pulled up short and stopped to stare at the devastation. It looked like a bomb had exploded in the circle. No building had gone untouched. Only the shells of many of the circle's structures remained. Others were burned to the ground. The stone clock tower in the plaza had not burned, but black soot coated it from top to bottom. It stood as a lone landmark amidst the unrecognizable landscape surrounding it. Beyond the plaza and the burned-out homes, the travelers could see the charred remains of the community garden and the fields of silver spark. Smoke drifted off the fields and gardens that gaped out of the ground like open wounds. Makeshift tent-like shelters were visible here and there. Many people camped out on the site where their home had once stood. In the distance, thin threads of smoke rose from campfires on the hillside in the direction of the Marini Hills. The bright glow of sprites wove in and out of the desolate scene.

A light drizzle began to fall and Maia imagined that the sky wept for the destruction of the Passage Circle.

The travelers took their bearings by the location of the clock tower and the burned out silver spark fields. Denzel frantically called to the others, "I'm going to the battery barn. If I don't find you later, send someone to meet me at the clock tower before dark."

"Same for me," Maia shouted, "I have to find out what happened to the drummers."

Doshmisi felt overwhelmed and weary. As a healer, she wanted to do something to help, but she didn't know where to start in the midst of such an enormous disaster. "Let's see if we can find Cinnamon and Ginger," she told Jasper. So she, Sonjay, and Jasper, with Cocoa trotting at their heels, rode to where the big, beautiful house they had stayed in only days before once stood.

When they arrived at the site of the house, they could see that the chimney wall of the kitchen remained standing. Doshmisi and Sonjay leapt off their tigers and raced around to the other side of the wall, where they found Cinnamon stirring a pot that hung over a fire in the fireplace. She looked up at them, her face dull with grief. When she realized who had arrived, her face opened like a treasure chest and she stepped forward to embrace them. Doshmisi cried with relief at the sight of Cinnamon.

"How is Ginger? And your daughters?" Doshmisi demanded.

"Ginger burned her hands while trying to save the silver spark, but she's alive. We fear we lost all the silver spark. If the fire ruined the soil, then we may never grow any again. Our daughters are accounted for, but the Special Forces killed Grace's boyfriend with one of their darts. She's with his family."

"Why did he do this to you?" Sonjay asked.

Cinnamon sighed, "Our circle refuses to pay taxes and refuses to send our sons and daughters to the army. We resist Sissrath. This is the price we pay for our resistance."

"He did this because you harbored us," Doshmisi suggested grimly. "We brought this disaster. He figured out we stayed here and he's trying to hurt us by hurting you."

"I don't know about that. He could have done this to any circle. To Debbie's Circle or to the Dome Circle. He has hated the Passage Circle for a long time. We stick in his side like a thorn," Cinnamon raised her chin defiantly. "And glad of it," she added.

"What can we do to help?" Doshmisi asked.

"Ride out among the people and encourage them. Let them see that you remain unharmed and that Sissrath cannot scare you away from the land," Cinnamon suggested. So Sonjay and Doshmisi rode out among the people and past the blackened silver spark fields and up into the hills where many survivors camped. Just before nightfall, they met Denzel and Maia at the clock tower where they shared news. The battery barn had blown up when the fire started; not surprising since it contained chemicals and explosives. Some of Denzel's battery maker friends died in the explosion. Mole survived because he had fallen asleep on the beach by the windmill. Maia's drummer friends had fled to the safety of the Marini Hills where they still hid, too scared to come out. Some of the Coast People had suffered damage to their hair since Sissrath's men found it amusing to cut off the dreadlocks of the musicians. Raffia died at Braiders Cottage. The intensified vision of the tragedy had killed all the circle's intuits at the beginning of the attack.

Denzel remembered the joyful intuits bouncing through the air on the skateboards like ordinary little children at play and not like those carrying the gift and the burden of intuition. The thought of their death infuriated Denzel.

He had failed to find any weapons among the Island People before leaving Whale Island. As healers, the Island People had no weapons since the purpose of weaponry was the complete opposite of healing. But the more he thought about the death of the intuits and the destruction of the Passage Circle, the more Denzel burned with the need to find a weapon, even if he had to make one himself. He wanted revenge. "It's payback time," Denzel told the others through clenched teeth. "We can't let him get away with this. If Hyacinth, that lame excuse for a high chief, won't do anything to stop this, then the Four will. I say we ride for Big House City in the morning and we take weapons with us and we kill Sissrath."

Jasper looked scared. "He has us way outnumbered. Even if the regular army dares to turn against him, he still has his Special Forces. We can't hope to overpower him."

"We'll have to figure out a pretty good plan then, won't we?" Denzel snapped.

"This isn't like the movies, Denzel," Maia said softly. "The good guys don't necessarily win just because they're good. The good guys might lose."

"I'm with Denzel," Sonjay said boldly. "We should ride against Sissrath. So what if we're outnumbered? We'll lay low, and watch, and wait, and work out a plan. And eventually we'll get him, and when we do we'll tell him, *this* is for the intuits and the musicians and the battery makers. *This* is for burning the Passage Circle. *This* is for Jack. And *this*," Sonjay's face twisted with rage as he made a stabbing motion in the air with his empty hand, "*this* is for murdering my mother!"

"I'm with you," Jasper said.

Maia set her mouth in a grim, straight line, "I am too."

Doshmisi put her closed fist out in front of her and into the space between the travelers where they stood. "For vengeance," she said. Denzel put his hand on top of his sister's and the others in turn each added their hands to the pile as they echoed "vengeance."

Chapter Twelve

Big House City

The travelers spent the night in the burned out remains of Ginger and Cinnamon's once large and beautiful house. In the morning, two sprites with iridescent white hair flowing to their knees flew to the house on translucent wings to bring bread, cheese, and blueberries. The travelers sat with Ginger and Cinnamon and their nine daughters on the ground and ate.

While they ate, Doshmisi looked through her herbal to find healing herbs for burns but she couldn't find anything that the Coast People didn't already know about. She didn't feel very wise or helpful. It disappointed her that she could not offer any remedy to undo some of the damage. Then she remembered something she knew that would help.

"Ginger, Cinnamon, I want you to promise that you will do something for me," Doshmisi demanded. "On the next night when the lesser sun appears in the sky, take everyone from the circle to Akinowe Lake and spend the night there. At midnight, everyone must look into the water of the lake."

"We'll do what you say, of course, but why?" Ginger asked, exchanging a puzzled glance with her sister.

"When I traveled around the lake, I learned the secret of its healing powers. The lake helps heal people who have experienced the sudden death of a loved one. But it only works when the lesser sun appears in the sky. Trust me. If the people of the circle gaze into the waters on the night of the lesser sun, it will help them."

"What will they see?" Denzel asked.

"Each of them will see what they alone need to see," Doshmisi replied mysteriously.

"Now you're starting to sound like one of the Four for real," Sonjay looked at Doshmisi curiously. "How come you didn't tell us that you figured out the secret of Akinowe Lake?"

"I forgot to mention it." Doshmisi didn't want to share her private conversation with Mama. It belonged to her and her alone.

"OK, that's lame," Sonjay shook his head and laughed at her. "That's really lame and you know it."

Doshmisi just shrugged.

"Where will you go from here?" Ginger asked.

"Maybe you better not know," Sonjay told her.

She nodded her head in agreement, "Yes, of course."

After breakfast, Denzel went to meet with Mole to see if he could lay his hands on some weapons. Doshmisi and Sonjay circulated among the people. Doshmisi told them to go to Akinowe Lake on the night of the lesser sun. "You must rebuild this beautiful circle," she said over and over again, for just as Debbie's Circle had become special to her mother, the Passage Circle had a special place in Doshmisi's heart. She had wandered as far as the path to the beach when she heard the music. A single timber flute beckoned with a beautiful melody that lifted and swelled and filled the listener with hope. Doshmisi joined some people who followed the sound of the music to the remains of the central plaza. Other people hurried from other directions, called by the sound of the timber flute.

The source of the music was Maia. She did not play a mournful tune but rather a joyous one, full of spirit. Maia knew that music, the soul of the Coast People, would give them the energy and the hope that they needed to rebuild their circle. As the plaza began to fill with people, Maia set aside the timber flute and began to sing "Let the Circle Be Unbroken." Doshmisi joined her from where she stood. The tune was so simple and the words so easy to follow, that before long Maia had taught the song to everyone in the plaza. Doshmisi had the feeling that the Coast People thought Maia had made the song up there on the spot just for them. She smiled to herself with the knowledge that it

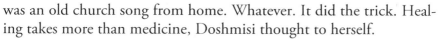

was an old church song from home. Whatever. It did the trick. Healing takes more than medicine, Doshmisi thought to herself.

Pretty soon, the musical instruments that had survived the attack turned up in the plaza. Those who had no instruments found sticks or other objects to use for percussion. Maia, with her amulet aglow, picked up her timber flute again and the others joined her, at first following her music and then taking it from her and making it into something of its own, that belonged to no one and to everyone all at once. It became a community tune of survival from those who had lived to make music together again. And once it started, it swept the people of the Passage Circle away with it. The music swelled and so did the crowd. Maia hoped her drummer friends would hear the music and come out of hiding. She didn't know if the music would carry to wherever they had gone. But if it carried, then the drummers would receive Maia's message begging them to return. The Passage Circle needed the drummers, the heart of the people, to face the task of rebuilding.

As the Coast People lost themselves in the embrace of their beloved music once more, Denzel, Sonjay, and Jasper rejoined Doshmisi and Maia, and together the travelers slipped quietly away. They returned to the site of Ginger and Cinnamon's house to collect their belongings and retrieve the tigers. They found themselves entirely alone since the rest of the circle had gathered in the plaza.

"Did you find weapons?" Doshmisi asked Denzel.

"Mole hooked me up," Denzel replied as he placed a canvas bundle on the ground and carefully unwrapped it to reveal a complicated slingshot. It looked like a toy or an antique, made of crude metal. "It's not what you think," Denzel said.

"I don't know what to think, but I do know I wouldn't trust my life to that thing," Doshmisi told him. "What is it?"

"It shoots this." Denzel took out a small wooden box and removed the lid. Maia, Sonjay, and Doshmisi leaned over and peered inside. The box contained a small wooden dart, with a sharp metallic tip and red and yellow feathers on the back end. "Don't touch it," Denzel cautioned.

"A dart?" Doshmisi asked. "That was the best you could do? We're going to shoot Sissrath with a dart? Oh puleez."

"Poison dart," Jasper hissed without humor. "Do you have any idea what Denzel has here? Or how hard it is to get ahold of one of these?"

"Poison dart," Denzel confirmed. "Mole stole this from one of the men who destroyed the Passage Circle. Remember what Clover told us about these things? In the Special Forces they wear protection, a tough armor made from the inner bark of the ancient red oak trees. But ordinary people have no protection, which makes them easy targets. In fact, the regular army has no armor against these either. Only Sissrath's Special Forces have the armor. If we can catch Sissrath unprotected, without that armor, we can kill him with this thing."

Doshmisi looked at the dart again with increased respect. "If that's what we've got then that's what we'll use."

As they prepared to mount their tigers, Doshmisi called to them, "Hey, wait, let's use some of the color change powder to disguise ourselves before we get any closer to Big House City."

Doshmisi took the jar that Clover had given her out of her bag. "Who wants to go first?" she asked.

Denzel stepped forward. Doshmisi took a tiny pinch of powder and sifted it over his head. It scattered in his hair and, for a second, red dust drifted off Denzel's head. Then Denzel looked the same.

"Try using more," Jasper suggested. Doshmisi took a bigger pinch of powder and flung it over her brother's head. As it landed on him, he suddenly developed a distinct red tinge from head to toe.

"Sweet," Denzel grinned.

"Oooh eee!" Jasper jumped up and down with excitement. "It's going to make you look like the People Beyond the Lake, like me. Wait until Crystal hears about this. She'll love it."

Next Doshmisi threw a pinch of color change powder over Maia's head, and Maia turned a deep, midnight bluish black.

"I guess we're not all going to look like the People Beyond the Lake," Denzel pointed out to Jasper.

"Hey, at least you do," Jasper told him, still pleased, and Denzel gave Jasper a high five.

Much to everyone's shock, the powder gave Sonjay a bold yellowish golden tinge.

"I don't want to be like one of the Mountain People," Sonjay whined. He really looked ferocious. The whites of his eyes had turned yellow, and his fingernails too. The little baby dreadlock twists all over his head had spiky yellow points to them that looked rather shiny.

"Don't reject the yellow so quickly," Jasper told Sonjay. "Mountain People are enchanters and some of the most powerful. Maybe you have the power within you to weave enchantments. Clover said the powder brings out your inner color."

"Then I can guess what color it will turn me," Doshmisi said, as she handed the powder to Maia. "Make me green," she told her sister as she closed her eyes.

Maia threw a pinch of powder over Doshmisi, who immediately took on a forest green glow. "I knew it," Doshmisi exclaimed triumphantly, admiring her arms. "I love it!"

Jasper looked slightly awestruck as he tried to get used to the new appearance of the Four. "It really worked. You look, well, like ordinary people."

"That's the point," Denzel announced, pleased at his red glow. "C'mon, let's get on up outta here!"

They mounted their tigers and followed Jasper onto the road in the direction of Big House City. Their new colors made them feel safer. They could blend in now. On the road to Big House City, they passed many other travelers, all of them Coast People. After they had passed quite a few travelers heading in the direction of the Passage Circle, Jasper called out to a man, "Why do so many travel to the Passage Circle today?"

"We're bringing food and medicine. We heard what happened and we're going to help," the man called back.

"You're not afraid of what Sissrath might do if he finds out that you brought help to the people of the Passage Circle?" Jasper shouted to the man.

"If he burns the Passage Circle today, he will burn our circle tomorrow. We have to stick together," the man answered philosophically and continued on his way.

His reply made the Four even more determined to succeed in their grim mission of assassination.

They rode all afternoon and into the night. Jasper suggested they stop when it grew dark, but the Four agreed that they wanted to push forward to Big House City quickly. They had a lot of work to do there and they hoped to stop Sissrath as soon as possible, before he did more harm. So they rode on into the night, until Sonjay nodded off to sleep and fell from his tiger. Fortunately he didn't hurt himself, but Jasper insisted that they stretch out on the ground right there, in a meadow by the side of the road, and catch some sleep until the sun came up.

When they awoke, they ate some of Doshmisi's mannafruit and continued on their way. The walls of the city appeared in the distance by mid-morning. They halted and Jasper argued with them to find a spot in a nearby grove of fir trees to make a camp to return to for the night. "We can leave the tigers and our bedrolls here and just take our valuables with us into the city," Jasper urged them.

They reluctantly agreed to this. They didn't want to leave their tigers behind, but they could see the good sense in Jasper's suggestion. They chose a secluded camping site and separated out the things they wanted to carry with them. Then Sonjay rolled out a map of the city on the ground and put rocks in the four corners. He rolled out another map of the Big House itself. The travelers stared at the two maps.

Sonjay sat back on his heels and bit his lip. "A web of secret passageways runs through the Big House. No one knows how many. You can see some of them marked on this map. I'm not sure yet how that might help us."

Jasper reminded Sonjay, "Sissrath is an enchanter, remember. He may have blocked these passages with enchantments."

"If he knows about them," Denzel muttered.

"We still don't have a plan," Maia reminded them. "That's always been the problem."

"Exactly," Denzel agreed. "We need more information so we can make a plan. These maps won't help us until we know more about Sissrath. We have to find a way to learn more about his routine, to discover his weaknesses."

"And Hyacinth's routine," Jasper added.

"Hyacinth is a fool," Bayard blurted from Sonjay's shoulder.

As hilarious as it looked, Sonjay was as serious as cancer when he grabbed Bayard's beak and held it shut. "Bayard Rustin, you have *got* to stop saying that. You'll get us killed. Do you understand?"

"How can you tell if a bird understands something you say to it?" Denzel asked, annoyed. "We can't take him with us into the city, you know."

"So what do you suggest I do to keep him from coming?" Sonjay demanded with exasperation.

"Don't let him perch on your shoulder and if he follows us, pretend you don't know him," Denzel suggested. Sonjay shooed Bayard off his shoulder. He had mixed feelings about treating Bayard so badly, but Denzel had a point. Bayard could ruin everything with his loud mouth.

"Let's just go into the city and see what we can scout out," Doshmisi suggested.

"We should split up," Jasper advised. "Sissrath's spies or Special Forces might recognize you despite your new colors just by noticing your ages and sizes."

"Jasper's right," Sonjay agreed. "Just look at us. And if we appear in the city together, with one of the People Beyond the Lake as our guide, right after the destruction of the Passage Circle. It won't take an Einstein to figure it out."

"What's an Einstein?" Jasper asked.

"He was a brilliant scientist in the Farland," Denzel answered.

"Jasper and Denzel should go together, since they both look like People from Beyond the Lake," Sonjay said.

Jasper's face clouded over. "I'm not leaving Dosh," he stated flatly. "Why don't you and Dosh come with me and Denzel can go in with Maia." Denzel and Sonjay exchanged a brotherly look that said *looks like Jasper has something going on with Doshmisi*, but they didn't bug him about it.

"OK," Jasper continued, "today is a market day, so the city will be crowded and chaotic and it'll be less likely for us to be noticed. Just keep your hoods up and don't talk much." The Four nodded their heads in agreement with Jasper's plan. Jasper, Dosh, and Sonjay gave Denzel and Maia a good head start before they turned their own steps toward the city.

Denzel and Maia entered the city through a large stone gate four stories high and as wide as a house. The gate was one of six such gates, each set in the surrounding wall of the city, allowing entrance from every direction. It reminded them of city gates they had seen in movies that took place in ancient civilizations. People with many different colors superimposed on skin in every shade of brown and people of many different sizes, shapes, and ages, streamed into the city through the gates. Outside the city walls they could see stable yards and people who cared for tigers and dogs and other animals left outside while their owners went into the city square.

When they came through into the city, Maia caught her breath and stopped in her tracks. She had never in her life seen a city as beautiful as this one. The enormous marketplace was filled with vendors' booths and people and animals and everyone and everything bustling and laughing and singing. She heard music all around her. The booths consisted of tents or stalls put together with colorful cloths and pieces of wood or beaten metal. Beautiful objects met the eye in every direction: carvings, musical instruments, clothing, fabric, housewares, tools, medicines, food, gadgets, books, plants. Maia felt overwhelmed. And the aroma of spices and herbs and delicious things cooking made her mouth water. She felt jolted coming from the burned out remains of the Passage Circle into this shocking splendor. They had never seen anything like it and they just stood for a few minutes and gazed at the scene, as other market-goers jostled past them.

Maia and Denzel stood on high ground at the wall of the city. The marketplace sloped away below them into a sort of a valley. Beyond the market, in the distance, they could see houses rising up a hillside. At the top of the hill stood a huge mansion, four stories high, with towers at either end and flags flying from the peaks in the roof. Anyone could recognize it right away as the Big House. The Big House rested on the highest point in the city, and Maia and Denzel had an excellent view of it from where they stood at the entrance gate.

"C'mon," Denzel said at last, "let's take a look around." They joined the crowd.

A half an hour later, Sonjay, Doshmisi, and Jasper entered the city by a different gate and also stood transfixed by the awesome spectacle of market day. Doshmisi and Sonjay had grown up in a large city, but Jasper had never seen one, so the bustling marketplace dazzled him even more than it did his companions. Cocoa, poor thing, cowered at Jasper's heels, terrified of all the people.

"Don't worry if we get separated," Sonjay said to the others, "I'll meet you back at camp."

At Sonjay's words, Jasper instinctively reached out and took Doshmisi's hand, "I don't want to lose track of you in the crowd," he explained.

The three travelers wandered from one booth to the next for quite some time, looking at the wonderful things on display. After awhile, Doshmisi realized that the most unusual thing about the market was that hardly anyone there used money. Every booth had more than one person attached to it and runners went out from the booths with items in their hands. They traded what they had brought for other things at the market that they wanted. Practically the whole market operated on a barter basis. In fact, when a few soldiers turned up at one of the food booths and gave the seller coins to buy their food, Doshmisi could tell that the seller didn't really want the money, but he couldn't do anything other than take it. It amazed her that this huge marketplace worked on trade, with almost no money changing hands. When she saw the soldiers at the food booth, she squeezed Jasper's hand. He saw them too. They were Mountain People; probably Special Forces. Jasper and Doshmisi moved a little nearer to them to listen to what they might say.

Doshmisi kept an eye on Sonjay, who had ducked into a dim, grimy booth at the edge of the market, just where the houses and buildings started. She strained to hear the soldiers and at the same time not lose track of her brother. Then, out of the corner of her eye, she caught a swatch of colorful feathers as Bayard appeared out of nowhere and flew into the booth with Sonjay. Doshmisi took off like a shot, with Jasper close on her heels. They arrived at the entrance to the booth just in time to see Bayard perch on Sonjay's shoulder, where the bird fluffed his feathers and tilted his head from one side to the other, eyeing the merchant of the booth.

The merchant was one of the Mountain People. He had straight, golden brown hair, long yellow fingernails, yellow eyes, and he wore an ochre robe. His face was pockmarked and his teeth were brownish. His booth displayed towels with embroidered pictures of a middle-aged man and a girl. Doshmisi had a bad feeling about the merchant. She closed in on Sonjay, to yank him out of there, but he seemed almost mesmerized in that spot as the merchant showed him the towel, saying, "My wife makes these, good likeness to the high chief and his daughter, don't you think?"

"I don't know this bird," Sonjay told the merchant, as he tried to brush Bayard from his shoulder, but the bird just returned the moment Sonjay put his hand down. "Is that the high chief?" Sonjay asked the man.

"I take it you have never seen him in person?" the merchant asked in a syrupy voice as he examined Sonjay with an intense gaze.

"No, never," Sonjay replied. He felt strangely drugged and his voice sounded far away to him.

"Aaaah, well this is the lovely Princess Honeydew and her father High Chief Hyacinth," the merchant stroked the towel like a prize-stroker on a game show.

Doshmisi whispered "oh no" at the mention of the name Hyacinth because she knew all too well what Bayard would do. And sure enough, the parrot leaned in close to the merchant of the booth and, with his beak in the merchant's face, Bayard recited clearly "Hyacinth is a fool."

The merchant, Sonjay, Bayard, Doshmisi, and Jasper froze. The merchant stared at Bayard's face. Then he reached up and removed Sonjay's hood, touched his hair with grimy fingertips, and snatched at Sonjay's arm. Bayard clamped his skinny claws firmly on Sonjay's shoulder, Jasper grabbed the tail of the merchant's robe, Doshmisi clung to Jasper's hand, and like this all of them were propelled out the back of the booth and down an alleyway that led into the buildings of the city. The merchant did nothing to try to free himself from Jasper's grip, but it was all that Jasper could do to keep up with him as he flew through the alley, ducked into a dark doorway, and knocked twice, then four times on a peeling wooden door.

The door opened as if by itself, for there didn't seem to be anyone behind it. The merchant strode across the room and down a flight of moldy stairs into a basement lit by a single lamp. The lamp stood in the middle of a table. Around the table sat six or seven Mountain People, with their yellowy eyes and long straight yellowish hair and long fingernails. Doshmisi realized that other figures lurked on the edges of the room, where she couldn't see them clearly. Several of them moved around behind the merchant to block the exit from the basement. The merchant swept Sonjay into the center of the room and pushing Sonjay's face into the light of the lamp, where the others could see it clearly, the merchant announced with glee, "We're in luck; looky, looky, looky! I believe I found one of the Four right under our noses, in the marketplace!"

Chapter Thirteen

Captured

"I'd say you snagged more than one of the Four," a large, fat woman told the merchant. "Looks to me like you've got three of 'em, y'ole buzzard." The fat woman sat at the table chewing the end of a pipe. She pointed her pipe stem at Doshmisi and Jasper. The merchant reached behind him, batted at his robe, and stared at Doshmisi and Jasper with a befuddled look as he apparently realized for the first time that they had latched onto him.

He quickly recovered and grasped Doshmisi by the wrist, forcing her around and into the light of the lamp next to Sonjay where he could get a better look at her.

Jasper said "I'm not one of the Four, you're mistaken." It was the truth, too. He hoped maybe the merchant would assume Jasper spoke for all of them.

The merchant looked from Doshmisi to Jasper and then back again. "Turn up the lamps," he demanded, without releasing Doshmisi's arm. "The bird said the password. These gotta be the Four."

"Hey, Crumpet, what'd you do to that little one?" a voice asked out of the dark edges of the room.

"I put a numbing enchantment on him. It'll wear off any minute. I didn't want any trouble from him in the marketplace. Draw attention and all that," the merchant answered gruffly.

"You put an enchantment on him?" Jasper exclaimed angrily. "Well, Crumpet, whoever you are, take it off. Take it off now!"

"Don't have kittens," Crumpet chuckled. "It's wearing off already."

"Crumpet? Do I know you?" Jasper asked, peering at their captor more closely. "That name sounds familiar."

Crumpet looked pleased. "It is familiar. I'm the crafty older brother of Cardamom, the great enchanter, held prisoner in the Final Fortress these four long years." Crumpet bowed his head slightly and produced a grin that went halfway to a snarl. He pointed to the woman with the pipe and introduced her, "And this is my fair wife Buttercup."

"And we're in the middle of a secret meeting, in case you forgot, baby-cakes," Buttercup grumbled.

Meanwhile, the Mountain People had lit lamps and brought them over to the table. The lamps flooded the basement with light and the travelers saw that the room held thirty or more tall Mountain People dressed in yellow robes. Some were old, some were young, and not all of them looked as scrappy as Crumpet. Many of the people were strikingly beautiful, with flowing golden brown hair and golden eyes.

As the numbing enchantment wore off, Sonjay became his usual feisty self. "Who are you and why have you kidnapped me?" He stamped his foot indignantly.

"Kidnapped?" Crumpet exclaimed. "Oh no no no. I didn't kidnap you. No, the bird said the password."

"You mean Bayard? What password?" Sonjay demanded.

"Hyacinth is a fool," Crumpet said. And Bayard repeated, "Hyacinth is a fool, Hyacinth is a fool."

"You see," Crumpet turned in a semi-circle to his companions with his arm outstretched and the palm of his hand facing up, as if Bayard's words proved something. Then he pointed to Bayard, "He said the password."

The others in the room all started talking at once, and some of them clapped their hands in excitement. Buttercup warned Crumpet sternly, "You know you better be right about their identity or we're dead. Look at them, they aren't bland. The Four would have the royal color."

Crumpet spluttered in exasperation, "The bird knew the password, woman."

Jasper clicked his fingers together three times and then burst into a grin, "I know who you are. Of course. Cardamom's brother. And

Buttercup. The High Mountain People. You ambushed Compost and took a coffer of Sissrath's coins last spring, right? How did you get into Big House City? I thought Sissrath banned enchanters from entry."

No one answered Jasper, instead an uncomfortable silence fell in the room.

Buttercup leaned across the table and looked Sonjay in the eye. He didn't blink or flinch. "You don't have the color of the Four. Prove to us that you're one of the Four," she commanded.

"Why should we?" Sonjay asked.

"Because if you're not of the Four, we'll have to kill you," she answered smugly. She sat back in her chair, which creaked under the shift in her substantial weight, and crossed her arms on her ample bosom.

"Buttercup," Crumpet whined, "the bird knew the password."

"I'm not going to stake my life on something a bird said," Buttercup snapped.

"It's OK," Jasper told Sonjay. "They come from the High Mountains. They're on our side." Then Jasper said to Buttercup, "I'm not one of the Four but Sonjay and Doshmisi are. They used a color change powder to alter their appearance." Buttercup nodded ever so slightly in acknowledgment but did not take her eyes off Sonjay.

Sonjay's gaze circled the room; he looked every single person in the eye. The Mountain People shifted restlessly. Doshmisi couldn't believe that Jasper had revealed her identity and she wanted to shout out to Sonjay not to give these people any information, but she held her tongue. She had a bad feeling about this and she didn't trust these people, even if Jasper did. She could see that Sonjay trusted them. In fact, Doshmisi could tell by the way he smiled slyly at them as he cast his eyes over the room that he liked them. To Doshmisi's horror, Sonjay reached slowly inside his shirt and lifted out the Amulet of Heartfire and held it up to the light so that everyone could see it.

"Dosh," he said, his voice even and commanding. She didn't move. "Dosh," he snapped his fingers. With her heart beating loudly in her ears, Doshmisi reluctantly drew out her amulet and showed it to the High Mountain People.

Jasper shrugged, "I told you, I'm not one of the Four. I don't have one."

Buttercup kissed the tips of her fingers and touched them reverently to Sonjay's amulet. Sonjay let her do this, without hesitation, as if he had taken the amulet out of his shirt specifically for her to touch it, while Doshmisi quickly returned her amulet to the inside of her shirt.

"Now explain yourselves," Sonjay demanded.

Buttercup leaned back in her chair and took a long, contented draw from her pipe. She smiled a satisfied smile. "OK, Crumpet. Ya done good, baby," she said.

Crumpet pulled up a chair close to Sonjay and leaned forward eagerly into Sonjay's face, "When Sissrath took my brother prisoner, Cardamom sent me a message that one day the Four would return to the land. He said we would know you because you would have a bird with you who knew the password 'Hyacinth is a fool' and your bird knew the password. That's no coincidence. How many parrots go around saying *that*? This must be the same parrot my brother Cardamom gave to Alice on her twenty-first birthday." Crumpet turned to Bayard and said, "Happy birthday dear Alice."

Bayard sang out delightedly "Happy birthday dear Alice, happy birthday to yooooouuuu."

Crumpet's gnarly face burst into a childlike grin. "We," Crumpet waved his arm to encompass all the people in the room, "I mean I and my comrades, have been working on a plan to overthrow Sissrath. Many of us in this room have the gift of enchantment. We must remain in hiding because Sissrath banished the enchanters from Big House City in order to protect his power. He picks his Special Forces carefully from among those who do not have the gift."

"You are working on a plan to overthrow Sissrath? How interesting," Sonjay said, "because we came with the same thought in mind. What a coincidence."

"Coincidence!" Buttercup snorted. "Not highly likely. We were brought together for this purpose."

"So what is your plan?" Crumpet asked Sonjay eagerly.

"What is yours?" Sonjay countered.

"I asked you first," Crumpet said, guardedly.

Sonjay sighed. "Truth? We have no plan. We just arrived and we hoped to learn about the city and Sissrath and to find out some piece of information that would help us come up with a plan. My brother and sister, Denzel and Maia, are also in the city somewhere. We went separately to prevent people from recognizing us. A lot of good that did, with that loud-mouthed bird. This is Jasper, our guide." Doshmisi resigned herself to accepting Sonjay's intuition. He was nearly always right about people, and he seemed to trust these Mountain People completely.

Crumpet looked at Buttercup, who shifted in her chair and put her pipe down. She looked at the others in the room. "What do you think?" she asked her comrades. They seemed to know what she meant with no further explanation. They looked around at each other, then nodded their heads curtly in the affirmative. They had apparently agreed on a decision amongst themselves without even having a discussion. So Buttercup leaned across the table to Sonjay, taking him into her confidence. "We have a plan of sorts. Maybe we can hook up with you and work out something foolproof. We have watched Sissrath for many weeks and we know his ways. Once a month he always takes a bath."

"Whether he needs it or not," a pretty young woman with high cheekbones giggled.

Buttercup scowled at the girl, who ignored her and kept giggling.

"He takes a bath. Do you know the significance of an enchanter taking a bath?" Buttercup asked.

Doshmisi and Sonjay looked mystified.

"Yeah, well, didn't think so," Buttercup said. "OK, here's the deal. When an enchanter takes a bath, any enchantments the enchanter has put on himself, or herself, wash off. They have to redo the enchantments afterwards."

"But what does that have to do with Sissrath?" Doshmisi asked, noting that these Mountain People probably looked so grimy because they didn't bathe much.

Buttercup waved a hand toward the giggly girl, "This is my daughter Daisy. Daisy, you explain." Buttercup picked up her pipe, took a long draw on it, and closed her mouth in a firm line. She sat back in her chair, as if exhausted by telling the little bit she had already told.

Daisy came forward. She appeared to be about Sonjay's age and she had corn-kernel yellow hair braided into two braids. She had freckles on her broad, flat nose. She looked fresh and honest. She spoke in a lilting, sing-song voice that made it hard to take her seriously. "Sissrath weaves enchantments around himself. His enchantments make him look younger and larger than for real and more fierce and frightening. He uses his enchantments to make others fear him and to protect him from attackers. He has all sorts of enchantments and he keeps changing them. That's why he hates to take a bath, because a bath weakens personal enchantments and they fall apart. After his bath, he stays up all night reweaving his enchantments. But on the night of his bath, his enchantments go down the drain with the dirt. He's vulnerable. You know what vulnerable means, right? He can be attacked easily. He has few defenses. On the night of his bath, he sends the Special Forces away because he doesn't want anyone to overhear the words of his enchantments. His strength goes into his enchanting, which weakens him." Daisy paused and rubbed her hands together with glee, giggling wildly. "On the night of his bath, we can kill him."

"We will use a secret passageway that Crumpet knows to get into Sissrath's private chamber on the night of his bath, which happens to be tomorrow night. Crumpet will stun him with a new enchantment that he recently developed. It's difficult to get close to Sissrath when he wears his enchantments. But on the night of his bath, we will have our one chance for this month. If Crumpet can stun him, then we think we can assassinate him."

"That sounds like a reasonable plan," Sonjay approved.

"One wrinkle," Buttercup told him. "We have no foolproof weapon."

"He doesn't allow the people to have weapons," Crumpet explained. "But if I can catch him with his guard down, I believe I can stun him and then, well, then I have a chance. Maybe I can stab him with a knife or strangle him to death. If I can just stun him so he can't use his powers, then I stand a chance."

Doshmisi shuddered.

"Can he defend himself against poison darts?" Sonjay asked matter-of-factly.

"Not without armor. Certainly not straight from a bath," Crumpet said, his brow creasing with thought. "But only the Special Forces have darts. Sissrath makes the poison with his secret formula. We can't get a poison dart. Believe me, we've tried."

"You didn't try hard enough," Sonjay announced smugly. "We have one."

Crumpet's goldeny eyes grew round and large, "you what?"

"How?" Daisy asked.

"Impossible!" Buttercup exclaimed.

"A friend of my brother's hooked him up. Denzel's friend took one during the recent attack on the Passage Circle. Denzel has it. And a dart shooter too. And we, the Four, plan to use it against Sissrath," Sonjay added fiercely.

"If we can get you into Sissrath's chamber tomorrow night after he bathes, then you will kill him?" Buttercup hissed in a stage whisper.

"With pleasure," Sonjay answered. "He murdered our mother."

"Praise Debbie," the Mountain People spoke in unison.

"Can you meet us back here tomorrow in the late afternoon?" Buttercup asked.

Sonjay asked Jasper, "Can you find this house again?"

"Does a tree have leaves? I'm a guide. I'm trained to do this," Jasper replied with pride.

"You must have tigers near here. Leave them at the Whispering Pond on the mountain side of the city, just beyond the gate. We'll take care of them and have them ready for you should you need them quickly. One of us will meet you there to take care of them."

"Then we'll come here tomorrow, with my brother Denzel and my sister Maia," Sonjay promised.

"Let the work of the Four continue," Crumpet said solemnly.

The others in the room repeated, "Let the work of the Four continue."

Sonjay held up a fist in solidarity and also said, "Let the work of the Four continue."

Crumpet led Jasper, Sonjay, and Doshmisi up from the basement and opened the door to the alleyway. He looked carefully in both directions and then shooed them out.

Night had fallen during the basement meeting. Jasper took them back through the city, where people milled about and merchants closed up their booths for the day. They passed back through the tall gate and returned to their camping site, where Denzel and Maia anxiously awaited them.

"You had us worried," Maia said. "It got dark. What happened to you?"

"You'll never believe what happened to us in a million years!" Sonjay exclaimed jubilantly. "A plan happened to us," and he proceeded to tell them about Crumpet and Buttercup and the Mountain People in the basement.

"How do we know this isn't some kind of a trap?" Doshmisi worried.

Jasper reassured her, "I've heard stories about Crumpet and Buttercup. We learned about them in history class at school. We can trust them, and the others with them."

"If Jasper says to trust these people, then we can trust them," Denzel put in. "I promised Jasper I wouldn't doubt him again."

"How do you know he's really who he says he is? What if he's not Crumpet?" Doshmisi asked.

"Oh, he's Crumpet, alright," Sonjay told her. "I know. I have the Amulet of Heartfire, remember? I just know those folks are OK. Kind of rough, but OK. Don't worry Dosh. I don't know why you have a bad feeling, but you're wrong this time." Sonjay's words convinced Doshmisi to let it go.

The next day they decided stay out of the city until the appointed meeting time with the Mountain People. They didn't want to draw attention to themselves. They spent a restless day at the camp instead. Denzel must have checked the dart and his shooter a thousand times. They dreaded the thought of finally confronting Sissrath, of standing in the same room with him, even if his bath would strip him of his enchantments.

Finally the time came for them to take the tigers to the Whispering Pond and return to Crumpet and Buttercup's basement lair. When they arrived at the door in the alleyway the delicious smells of food greeted them. Lamps on the tables and along the walls lit the basement up like the marketplace in the noonday sun. The room was packed with people who sat on barrels, chairs, tables, sawhorses and wherever they could find a place to sit down, balancing plates of food in their laps.

Sonjay nearly fell to his knees in gratitude when he realized that the Mountain People were passing around plates loaded with some kind of breaded and fried meat. He didn't recognize it, but it sure smelled good. He picked up a piece and bit into it and groaned with pleasure. It was the first time the Four had seen any cooked meat during their entire time in Faracadar.

"Don't you want some?" Sonjay asked his brother.

"Mystery meat? No way," Denzel replied. "You don't know what kind of beast that stuff came from."

"I don't care. These people know how to throw down some food," Sonjay's face glazed over with satisfaction. Another plate went past and Sonjay took a handful of what looked like small meat balls.

Denzel stopped Daisy as she walked past him and asked her, "What is this stuff?" He pointed at Sonjay's plate.

"Those are slime bat fried in prong liver oil," she said, pointing at the fried meat, "and that," she pointed to the meat balls, "swamp pig eyeballs dipped in ground skeeter brains."

Sonjay stopped stuffing the meat into his mouth and stared at his plate in disbelief.

Denzel busted out laughing.

Sonjay looked daggers at his brother. Then he shrugged. "Tastes like fried chicken and meat balls," he said. And he put another piece of slime bat in his mouth.

Doshmisi and Maia exclaimed in unison, "Gross!"

"You've totally lost it!" Denzel laughed even harder.

Doshmisi, Maia, and Denzel stuck to the food they could recognize as bread, cheese, fruits, and vegetables. They had no appetite for the bizarre objects going into Sonjay's mouth, no matter what he claimed they tasted like.

When Daisy brought Sonjay a plate of skinny braided twisty things to try, Sonjay told her, "Don't tell me what these are. I don't want to know." And he helped himself to half a dozen. "You go ahead and eat okra and goat cheese if you want," he said to the others, "I'm having the meat, no matter what animal it came from."

After they ate dinner, Crumpet smoothed a worn and wrinkled map out on a table.

"Oh, I have one too," Sonjay informed. He produced the map Clover had given him and rolled it out on top of Crumpet's map.

The moment Crumpet laid eyes on Sonjay's map he demanded, "Where did you get this?" Without a moment's hesitation he grabbed a cup of coffee and threw the coffee on the map. Doshmisi tried to grab Crumpet's arm but she wasn't quick enough.

"What'd you do that for?" Sonjay snapped angrily.

"Cardamom made this map of the Big House. The map has a wet revealment on it," Crumpet explained excitedly. Before Sonjay could respond, a coffee-colored mist rose off the map and left the surface dry as a bone. When Sonjay looked at the map again he realized that the coffee had revealed many passageways not previously visible.

"You just throw liquid on a map with a wet revealment and more information appears. This one shows secret passageways. How did you get this?" Crumpet's gaze pierced Sonjay.

"From Clover the Griot on Whale Island. I don't think she knows that Cardamom made this map because she didn't tell me about the wet revealment," Sonjay replied.

Sonjay, Crumpet, Daisy, Jasper, and Denzel leaned over the map with excitement.

"Awesome," Crumpet exclaimed. "We had planned to go in here," he pointed to the spot, "but we would have to subdue the guards to do it. Instead, we can use this passageway over here." He pointed to a spot on Sonjay's map. "This is much better. This passageway starts outside the city gate, which makes it much safer. And it connects with this passage that I had hoped to use, which comes up right inside the fireplace in Sissrath's bedroom."

"Good thing it's summertime, Papa," Daisy chuckled, "and no fire in the fireplace."

"Right you are, baby," Crumpet stroked his daughter's hair

affectionately. "Well, time to get this show on the road." The light-hearted Daisy grew serious as she gave her father a hug, "come back to us safely, Papa," she whispered. Crumpet kissed the top of his daughter's head and then embraced Buttercup, stretching his arms all the way around her rotund middle. Then he called out to his comrades "may the work of the Four continue" and they echoed "may the work of the Four continue" in response. The travelers left their belongings, as well as Bayard and Cocoa, in Buttercup's safekeeping. Bayard perched on Daisy's shoulder and she stroked his throat gently.

Tense with apprehension, Crumpet and the travelers went up the stairs and out into the deserted and silent alley. They slipped quickly and quietly out of the city, walking briskly to the garden where they would find the door to the secret passageway indicated on Sonjay's map. In the garden they found the statue they wanted and at its base the large, flat, movable stone indicated on the map. No one would ever guess that the stone served as the door to a secret passageway. But when Crumpet pulled the stone aside, the mouth of a corridor yawned wide in front of them. Crumpet lit a lantern and entered, the others following close behind.

"We had better close this," Crumpet said. So they put the stone back in place behind them. Crumpet led them down the corridor. It sloped deep into the ground and droplets of moisture glistened on the damp walls. They walked for twenty minutes. Maia didn't like enclosed spaces and it made her anxious to plunge so far underground. She sighed with relief when the corridor opened into a larger cavern and she could feel more air and space around her. They took out the map and Crumpet immediately spit on it. Doshmisi cringed and Maia turned up her nose.

"What?" Crumpet asked them, his eyebrows raised. "It has a wet revealment on it. I have to make it wet. What do you want me to do? I don't have a lot of choices here." He turned back to the map.

"I think we want that passage there," he pointed at one of three openings. "What do you think?"

Jasper and Sonjay examined the map and agreed with Crumpet. They proceeded through the opening and in a short distance came to a chamber. As they approached the chamber, Crumpet blew out his lantern. He quickly held out an arm and pushed the others back. "Just as I thought," he whispered, "He has posted a guard in there. Wait here while I subdue the guard." Crumpet went forward on his own and returned swiftly. When they entered the chamber, they saw the guard lying on the ground in the dim light from a lantern hanging on the wall.

"Did you kill him?" Maia asked, wide-eyed.

"No, no, I don't know any enchantments that can kill. I used a sleeping enchantment. Pretty good, huh?" Crumpet said, puffing out his chest. He then held out his hand and from it flashed a greenish yellow current that looked like electricity. "That should hold him until the morning," Crumpet said with satisfaction.

In front of them rose a narrow flight of stairs. Before mounting the stairs, Crumpet turned to the others, "These stairs come up through the Big House and take us to the back of Sissrath's fireplace. Don't make a sound or someone might hear us in the walls. When we arrive at Sissrath's room, let me listen. I will open the door at the right time. Denzel, you must come in right behind me with the dart, ready to shoot. Sissrath is crafty, shrewd, and he has no scruples, don't give him time to act. Not even a split second. Don't fall for his tricks," Crumpet warned.

With their hearts pounding in their ears, the travelers climbed the stairs slowly and steadily behind Crumpet. This was the task they had come to do. This was their moment. Denzel wondered in the privacy of his deepest thoughts if he could really kill a person, even if the person was the evil and dangerous enchanter who had caused the death of his parents. He must make himself as cold as steel. He must do the work that needed to get done. He must be a man.

Crumpet stopped at the entrance to the fireplace. He peered through a crack in the stonework for a long moment. "He's in the bathroom," he whispered quietly to the others. "I'm going in. I'll stand behind the bathroom door and shut it behind him when he emerges so he can't escape. I'll use my stun enchantment to prevent him from using any of his enchantments and then Denzel can shoot."

"I hope he isn't naked when he comes out of the bathroom," Maia muttered.

"Now that would not be pretty," Sonjay whispered.

Jasper shushed them.

Crumpet slunk through a door that opened silently at the back of the fireplace. Denzel peered through a crack in the stonework. He could see Crumpet crouched behind a door on the other side of a big four-poster bed. Denzel had the dart loaded in the shooter and he held it steadily in his hands. He had practiced how to use it. He stood completely ready to avenge his mother and the people of the Passage Circle.

They must have waited like that for only a few minutes, but it seemed like hours. Finally, the door to the bathroom swung open and a tall, bony figure entered the room. Swiftly, Crumpet slammed the door shut behind Sissrath and held out a trembling hand to place his enchantment. Then something went wrong. Crumpet's hand glowed a phosphorescent yellow-green; and the phosphorescence spread up Crumpet's arm and across his whole body as his face took on a horrified look. An instant later a large rock sat on the floor where Crumpet had been.

Sissrath threw back his head and laughed furiously. "Fool, you can't even cast a simple enchantment on a defenseless enchanter straight from his bath. You should leave the real work to your brother."

Fortunately, the rock that had once been Crumpet blocked the closed door so Sissrath had no course for retreat when the Four burst into the room with Jasper close on their heels a moment later. The Four gasped at the sight of Sissrath. He had a long sharp nose, scraggly hair the color of old pee on dirty snow, and sallow skin that appeared sickly and dry like old parchment. The whites of his beady little eyes looked like smeared egg yolks. He wore a dull robe that was the dreary color of tobacco stains. Hoops embedded in his earlobes created holes in his ears as big around as quarters. The Four could see right through his ears to his greasy neck. He raised a hand slightly, and they saw his fingernails, long and curled under like claws. He stood more than seven feet tall. His lip twisted into a surly grin as his eyes passed over the intruders and came to rest on Denzel, who held the dart aimed at Sissrath's heart.

An instant later, Sissrath disappeared and in his place stood a young and vibrant Deborah Goodacre. She smiled at her children and held her arms open for them to run into them. "Give Mama some sugar," she said, laughing her warm and bubbly laugh. Maia took a step forward. Tears stung at the back of Doshmisi's eyes. Sonjay gasped like a dying fish. Denzel froze as he felt the blood stop flowing in his veins. Jasper shrieked urgently, "Denzel, shoot! Sissrath is a shape-changer! It's not Debbie. Shoot. Shoot!"

But Denzel could not shoot. He could not shoot this person who looked so completely and perfectly like his mother in her younger years and in the peak of health, who held her arms open and offered him his deepest heart's desire, to embrace his mother one more time. Sissrath seized the moment of Denzel's hesitation, and, in the form of Deborah Goodacre, he closed the short distance between himself and his would-be assassins in two swift strides, took the dart and shooter out of Denzel's hands, and turned it around so that the poison dart poised inches from Denzel's chest. The vision of Deborah Goodacre vanished.

It all happened so quickly. Just that fast, Sissrath had gained power over them. And so easily. He stepped back carefully, the dart pointed at Denzel, and pressed a button on the wall next to the bed. He grinned, revealing sharp little crooked teeth. Maia burst into tears. Denzel clenched his fists at his sides and did not look to the right or left. Sissrath gave Crumpet the rock a scornful kick.

The room filled with Sissrath's Special Forces, summoned by the button the enchanter had pressed. The smell of decomposing broccoli filled the room as Compost entered. "We have visitors of a high order," Sissrath told his men, without taking his eyes off the intruders. "Seize them." He waved his hand and golden sparks flew from his fingers in the direction of the Four, who turned instantly back to their regular color. "Did you think that a little color change powder would prevent me from recognizing you?" Sissrath asked. "I'm so disappointed that you so grossly underestimated me." If a snake could talk, it would sound like Sissrath.

Even though his Special Forces, fully armed, now filled the room and restrained the failed assassins, Sissrath still held the dart pointed at Denzel's chest, and Sonjay remembered the words of Clover: *beware, for those who carry weapons are likely to have weapons used against them.*

Chapter Fourteen

Into the Amber Mountains

Sissrath finally lowered the dart when he could see that the Special Forces had a firm grip on Jasper and the Four. He then approached Sonjay and put his hand out to touch the chain of the amulet that Sonjay wore around his neck. Sparks flew from the amulet and leapt at Sissrath's fingers. Sissrath quickly withdrew his hand and shook it in pain, his fingers stung by the sparks. "It is still true," he said with obvious annoyance. "The amulets cannot be taken while those who wear them live."

"But you can change that situation," Compost snarled menacingly. A puff of greenish gas hovered over his head.

"I certainly can," Sissrath agreed. "Compost, I congratulate you on providing such good advice. Burning the Passage Circle brought the Four right to my door. What a gaggle of predictable imbeciles. The last four were so much cleverer. I would have had a much more difficult time killing them." He curled his lip in a twisted smile.

"You can't kill us. We are the Four," Sonjay told Sissrath defiantly. He pulled one arm free of his captors and reached behind him in a flash, grabbing the nearest object at hand, which happened to be a bottle of perfume, and threw it at Sissrath. It flew wide of Sissrath and landed at Compost's feet where it shattered on the hard floor, dousing Compost's legs and feet with the strong scent of sweet honeysuckle.

Compost leapt in the air and screamed as if in terrible pain. "I've been hit," he screeched. He pinched his nose shut with his fingers as he hopped from one foot to the other, and then he fled from the room, acting like a skunk had sprayed him.

Sissrath threw back his head and laughed. When he laughed, Sissrath's earlobes, with the see-through holes, jiggled. "You of the Heartfire have some spunk. Lucky for me that you didn't hold the dart or I might be dead now, eh? But you didn't, and I'm not, and I *can* kill the Four. If someone has told you otherwise then they lied to you because you *can* be killed and guess what? You *will* be killed. Watch me do it. But not tonight. The people must have the opportunity to see that I have captured and removed the Four. For this reason, you will have a special public execution. I will send the word throughout the city and invite the people to witness the end of the Four at last. I hope they will find it entertaining to see you die. I look forward to having them see the amulets taken from your lifeless grasp and put into my hands. They will realize that Debbie's retreat to the Farland to mother you in safety came to nothing, because you have fallen into my hands in spite of it all. Then I can finally rid myself of that ninny Hyacinth and his disagreeable daughter, and take possession of the royal line. It belongs to me. The power rightfully belongs to me. In the name of the People of the Mountain Downs."

Sissrath commanded his Special Forces, "Take them to the courtyard and chain the Four to the posts then put their friend here into a cage. Oh, and put this rock into the cage too," he kicked at Crumpet. "I'll have to decide what to do with this traitor later. Now go, and leave me to reweave my enchantments. I must look my best tomorrow for the big day, perhaps the greatest day of my life."

The Special Forces fastened the prisoners' hands behind their backs and forced them to walk at a brisk pace as they whisked the travelers from the room and along a corridor lit with lanterns. Then they hurried them down a flight of stairs and along another corridor. They came out at the top of a huge, wide staircase, with elaborately carved banisters running down both sides. A plush gold-colored carpet covered the stairs. At the bottom of the staircase stood a pudgy, middle-aged man with hair graying at the temples. He wore a goldenrod bathrobe and fluffy bedroom slippers. In his arms he held a large, long-haired orange cat with enormous golden eyes. As the guards bustled down the stairs with their captives, the man asked them timidly, "What is this rumpus that has distributed my sleep?"

One of the guards told him briskly, "Sissrath's business. Go back to bed. He will inform you in the morning." But the man did not go back to bed. He watched, his eyes wide and frightened, as the guards rushed past him with the Four and Jasper and swept out through an enormous set of double doors that led into the night. After they had left, the man stood at the bottom of the stairs for a long time stroking his cat for comfort, staring after them, and trembling. Then he turned on his heel and resolutely hurried into the depths of the Big House.

After they chained the Four to a series of thick posts set firmly in the ground of the square, and after they locked Jasper and Crumpet into a cage beside the posts, the Special Forces retreated. Two guards remained to keep watch. They sat down in a little guard house and proceeded to play a game with tiles and stones, looking up frequently to confirm the security of their prisoners.

The Four wore chains on their hands and feet and a metal belt around the waist with a chain that went through a metal loop in the belt. Each of these chains was locked securely to a heavy wooden post. The four posts stood only a short distance apart; far enough apart so that they couldn't touch each other but close enough for them to talk in quiet voices amongst themselves. They had to speak up a little to talk to Jasper over in the cage. As soon as their captors left, Sonjay spoke to his brother, "Denzel, hey, don't blame yourself, man. None of us could have killed him when he looked exactly like Mama. What a despicable thing for him to do. Only a cowardly evil punk would even think of such a thing."

Denzel did not reply. He stared at his chained feet.

"You know Sonjay is right," Doshmisi added with concern. "It would have been hard enough to kill a person no matter what they looked like, but when the person looked and sounded and seemed exactly like Mama..."

"He tricked me. I should have been smarter and more cold-blooded," Denzel said evenly. "I should not have hesitated. I should have been man enough to kill him no matter what."

"Denzel," Doshmisi called to him, struggling to see his face in the dark, "listen, Sissrath is absolutely evil. That makes it hard for good people to fight him because good people hesitate at using the kind of evil necessary to defeat him. I'm glad you didn't shoot. How would I have ever forgotten the image of you shooting Mama?"

Then Maia spoke, "Any man can shoot and kill but it takes a real man to hold his fire out of love and compassion. Mama didn't want you to be just any man, Denzel. She wanted you to be a real man."

Maia had simply said it all. Doshmisi felt a rush of admiration for her little sister.

Sonjay announced, "OK, well, it happened and now we have to get over it and move on. We have to think how to get out of this mess. It's like a puzzle. We just have to solve it."

Jasper, who had stood clinging to the bars of the cage as he listened to this conversation, stepped back and sat down on Crumpet. "Sorry, old man," he muttered to the rock. Just then Bayard flew into the square and perched on Sonjay's shoulder. Sonjay lifted one chained hand and stroked the bird. Bayard butted Sonjay's neck with his head and for once kept his mouth shut. Sonjay petted Bayard absently.

Suddenly, they heard the sound of guards approaching. A group of the Special Forces entered the courtyard, led by the pudgy man who had stood at the foot of the stairs in the Big House. The man went to the guard house and spoke with the guards there, who left and headed up the street toward the Big House. The man waited until the guards from the guard house had left the courtyard and disappeared out of sight. Then he proceeded to the prisoners, followed by a dozen or more of the Special Forces. He came to stand in front of the Four. He looked them up and down and then his face broke into a child-like grin of absolute happiness. "Cousins!" he exclaimed and opened his arms wide.

A skinny girl with heavy black-rimmed glasses shushed him. "Daddy, keep your voice down. C'mon, we have to get them out of here." She turned to one of the Special Forces and ordered, "Toad, get the keys from the guard house."

"I have them," a large man, tall and broad, handed her a heavy key ring which he held in his muscular hands. His fingers bulged like sausages. She quickly approached Doshmisi and started looking for the correct key to fit the locks on the chains.

"Who are you?" Doshmisi asked the girl.

"Princess Honeydew, and this is my Daddy, High Chief Hyacinth," she found the correct key and released Doshmisi. "Don't mind him," she waved in the direction of her father, "he's a little goofy but he has a big heart. We're going to get you out of here, but we have to move fast."

While Princess Honeydew freed Doshmisi, her father rattled away in a whispered speech that made no sense. Doshmisi and the princess proceeded to find the keys and unlock the chains on Maia and Sonjay, while Hyacinth rambled on. The princess turned to her father and hissed, "Daddy, hush up." He fell silent and rocked back and forth on his feet, beaming with pleasure.

"Who are these soldiers?" Sonjay asked the princess. "Can we trust them?"

"Oh yes," the princess told him, "they're some of the Special Forces who have remained secretly loyal to my father. Toad is their leader. You will never know how we have waited for your return. We have lived as prisoners in our own home. Your presence tonight gave Daddy and his men the courage and the hope they needed to finally act."

Maia took the girl's hands in hers and looked into the princess's face. Close in age, they looked so much alike that as they stood across from each other their kinship was obvious. Then it dawned on Maia that Hyacinth and Honeydew had no rainbow colors in their skin, which was purely rich brown, just like the Four. "You are family," Maia said to Honeydew.

"Yes," Honeydew's previously business-like voice softened, and her eyes, behind her thick lenses, became moist. "We are cousins." The two girls embraced. Meanwhile Sonjay freed Denzel and began working on the lock of Jasper's cage with the large ring of keys. When the door finally swung open, Denzel entered and lifted the rock that was Crumpet, which measured approximately a foot across and a little less than a foot high, with a shape like a giant walnut only sort of flat on one side where it sat on the ground. He hugged the rock to him, cradling it in his arms.

"What's with the rock?" Honeydew asked Maia.

"It's a friend of ours," Maia told her, sadly. "He got turned into a rock."

"Anyone I know?" Honeydew asked.

"Do you know Crumpet? The enchanter?" Jasper asked.

Honeydew turned to her father, "Daddy, you'll never guess who that rock is! It's old Crumpet. Come see."

"Crumpet? A rock? Oh my, oh my. How unfortuous. What should we do with him?" Hyacinth fussed as he joined them.

"Does he mean unfortunate?" Maia asked, but no one answered her.

"We'll take him with us to have him changed back as soon as possible," Denzel stated firmly.

Jasper grasped Denzel around the upper arm and insisted, "It's not your fault. He would have tried and failed on his own tonight whether you came along with your dart or not and you know it."

"Whatever," Denzel still clutched the rock that was Crumpet.

"Then stop beating yourself up," Sonjay told his brother. "C'mon let's get out of here before Sissrath figures out what's going on and chains us up again."

"Yes, yes," Hyacinth agreed, "we have to get out of here. Come. My men will protect us. Where did you leave your tigers? You must have tigers, right?" They sped quickly out of the courtyard, following Toad and the other loyalist forces.

"We had planned to meet our friends at the Whispering Pond. Crumpet's wife, Buttercup, has the tigers and our belongings. We're late, but maybe they waited," Sonjay told Hyacinth.

Hyacinth instructed Toad "to the Whispering Pond." The party broke into a run. On their way out of the city gate, Hyacinth and Honeydew and their loyalist forces met up with a couple of men who awaited them with tigers for everyone.

At the Whispering Pond, Cocoa dashed out from between Buttercup's stout legs, quivering with happiness at the sight of Jasper. The travelers and their rescuers dismounted from the tigers.

"Buttercup!" Hyacinth exclaimed, "I should have figured you had a hand in this, old girl. I know I should have been more forcible and done something by now. But Sissrath implicates me. You understand, don't you?"

"He means 'intimidates'," Honeydew interjected.

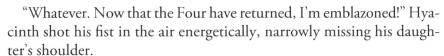
"Whatever. Now that the Four have returned, I'm emblazoned!" Hyacinth shot his fist in the air energetically, narrowly missing his daughter's shoulder.

"You're emboldened, Daddy, not emblazoned," Honeydew told him.

Suddenly Hyacinth's face fell, "Buttercup, I have bad news. Sissrath turned Crumpet into a rock. An attractive rock, nice shape and color, but a rock nonetheless." He pointed to the rock that Denzel carried.

Buttercup took Crumpet from Denzel and stroked the rock tenderly. "You always were terribly hard-headed," she told the rock gruffly, but her lower lip quivered and her eyes filled with tears. "Sissrath didn't turn him into a rock," she said. "You see, he has a hard time administering his stun enchantment. Crumpet did this to himself, the old dunderhead. He's not a very artful enchanter, you know. When he's under stress, he has trouble with his enchantments. I feared this might happen. Last time it took us six months to track down his brother and get him changed back."

"Don't worry, we'll find a way to change him back." Denzel put his hand on Buttercup's shoulder to comfort her.

"His brother could do it," Buttercup said hopefully.

"Then we'll take him with us," Honeydew assured her.

"With you? Where are *you* going?" Sonjay asked. Princess Honeydew annoyed him. She was too bossy.

"We're going with you to the Final Fortress in the Amber Mountains," Honeydew informed them.

"Whoa, whoa," Sonjay put up a hand as if to defend himself. "First-of-all, you're *not* coming with us, and second, we have no reason to go to the Amber Mountains."

"Oh yes you do," Honeydew tossed her one long braid over her shoulder and stepped up to Sonjay, who had started to get on her nerves, "because only one person can help us and that's the great enchanter Cardamom. Sissrath imprisoned him at the Final Fortress in the Amber Mountains, for your information, and it's about time that someone rescued him. With his help, we have a much better chance of defeating Sissrath."

Sonjay rolled his eyes. This girl thought she could tell him what to do next. He didn't feel as excited as Maia or Doshmisi about finding this long-lost cousin with the thick glasses and the attitude, but he kept his mouth shut for the time being.

"I should have rescued Cardamom years ago," Hyacinth said, looking crestfallen. His mood changed every other second. One moment he acted as excited as a cheerful little boy and the next he acted dejected and depressed. The Four watched him with fascination. "But Sissrath terribalizes me. I don't deserve to be the high chief. It should never have been me." He put his face in his hands.

"Hyacinth," Doshmisi pitied the poor fellow who had let himself become a slave to Sissrath. She liked him and she wanted him to be his excited and boyish self. "You rescued us. You snatched the Four right out of Sissrath's hands. That took courage."

"You're on your way to greatness," Maia assured him.

Hyacinth looked up hopefully, his face clearing and his smile returning.

Sonjay poked Bayard, who perched on his shoulder, and demanded, "Yeah, Hyacinth rescued us, you crazy bird, in fact he saved our lives, what have you got to say about him *now*?"

Bayard riffled his wings nonchalantly and pronounced, "Hyacinth is a *brave* fool."

"Don't pay him no mind," Sonjay told Hyacinth, "he's just a parrot." Bayard pecked Sonjay on the head. "Ouch! Chill out you vicious heap of feathers."

Tenderly holding the rock, Buttercup advised the others, "Hyacinth and Honeydew are right, you should go to the Final Fortress and try to release Cardamom. He is indeed a great enchanter. With him, the Four could overcome Sissrath. Now go quickly. Sissrath will pursue you as soon as he discovers your escape. I've brought your belongings for you and your tigers are well-rested."

Denzel stepped up to Buttercup and put his hands on Crumpet. "Let me take him with me. I'll do everything in my power to get him to Cardamom and have him changed back."

Buttercup reluctantly passed Crumpet back to Denzel. "Crumpet would give anything to go on this adventure, even if he has to travel as a rock." Buttercup knocked on the rock with her fist, "Hey baby, if you can hear me in there, I'm sending you to Cardamom with Denzel, and I love you." She kissed the rock.

"Buttercup," Jasper asked the woman, "would you do me a favor and keep Cocoa here with you until I return? I don't think the Final Fortress is a safe place for a dog with her tender disposition."

"I'd love to take care of her," Buttercup replied, as she kneeled down and stroked Cocoa's head fondly. Cocoa looked forlorn but she nuzzled into Buttercup's arms.

Denzel put some of his tools into Jasper's knapsack so that he could fit Crumpet into his own knapsack. Then the travelers mounted their tigers. The number of travelers had swelled, with High Chief Hyacinth and Princess Honeydew, Toad, more than a dozen warriors who had betrayed Sissrath, and, of course, Crumpet in the form of a rock. Buttercup waved them on and then disappeared into the shadows of the night. Toad and Jasper took the lead as the tigers broke into a run in the direction of the mysterious Amber Mountains.

The travelers rode through the night in a landscape of low rolling hills covered with heather-like plants and scrub. They reached the foothills of the Amber Mountains before sunrise. There they found few trees and nowhere to hide. Toad stopped once to show the others how to tie themselves to their tigers' necks so that they wouldn't fall if they dropped off to sleep. The devoted tigers pushed themselves hard, covering a great distance, putting as much time and space between their precious cargo and Sissrath as possible.

With the coming of dawn, a flock of skeeters circled overhead, marking the location of the travelers. Toad halted and looked behind them with a spyglass. The others stood around him in a circle, worried and expectant. He slowly lowered the spyglass from his eye and told them grimly, "Sissrath himself pursues us. He and his Special Forces follow not far behind, and if I can see him with my spyglass, then he can surely see me with his. Besides, these skeeters seem determined to lead him right to us. I don't see Compost. Sissrath must have left him in charge back at Big House City."

"How can we congeal ourselves?!" Hyacinth asked frantically.

"Conceal, Daddy," Honeydew corrected him calmly. "Congeal means to come together and thicken up. You mean conceal, like to hide."

"Thicken, hide, anything! If he catches us we're goners, history, vulture meat," Hyacinth grabbed himself by the neck and made dramatic choking noises. The others ignored him.

"We won't have much protection in the foothills because the land is too wide open and will give Sissrath good visibility. We could hide in the mountains, but it will take us a few hours to ride deep enough into them to find cover," Toad explained.

"Can we outride Sissrath?" Denzel asked.

"Yeah," Jasper liked that suggestion, "exactly. Maybe if we move fast enough we can reach the Amber Mountains far enough ahead of him and disappear into the trees."

"Let's give it a try. I can't think of any other plan," Toad agreed. He called out to the travelers, "Strap yourselves on securely, we're going to make a run for the Amber Mountains and look for a place to hide." Everyone leaned in low on their tigers, tightened the ropes that held them, and hugged the tigers' necks. Despite the fact that the tigers had been running at top speed all night, they leapt forward with a renewed burst of energy, their enormous padded feet propelling them across the ground. But as fast as they went, Sissrath and the Special Forces went faster. As the morning progressed, their pursuers gained on the travelers. By noon, no one needed a spyglass to see the army of Special Forces pressing after them across the scrubby moorlands. The swarm of bright white skeeters continued to swirl above them like a gigantic malignant halo as they began to ascend into the foot of the Amber Mountains.

The tigers panted hard, picking their way across rocks that became more dense at each step. Soon trees and boulders began to screen the travelers from Sissrath's view. Doshmisi could hear the voices of the trees inside her as they urgently insisted that she and her companions make haste and hide. *Where? Where?* She communicated back to them desperately, but they did not give her an answer.

As the travelers scrambled up the rocky slope, they could hear Sissrath's Special Forces closing in behind them. Pausing on a small, flat plateau, they had an excellent view of the land below that they had just crossed. They had gained more altitude than any of them realized. Looking down, they could see their pursuers moving between the trees, with Sissrath in the lead.

"Toad," Hyacinth called, "take us to the nearest opening of the Through-Tunnel."

"But your Highness..." Toad began to protest.

"We have no choiceness!" Hyacinth cut him off.

They had no time for discussion. Toad led the travelers on a thin path through dense evergreen trees. The branches reached out to snag their clothing and hair. The tigers scraped through, panting. They came to a clearing where a cave mouth yawned in the side of the mountain. Now they could hear Sissrath just behind them in the undergrowth. Hyacinth leapt off his tiger and hastened his daughter, Jasper, and the Four into the cave. Outside the mouth of the cave, Toad and the other warriors dismounted and took up positions from which to defend themselves. The released tigers bounded up the mountain, invigorated and light-footed without the burden of their riders. Bayard flew high up and disappeared into the trees.

Sissrath and his forces burst from the evergreen forest into the clearing with their poison darts at the ready. But Toad and his men had darts of their own. The air filled with darts zinging in all directions. Hyacinth herded the travelers deeper into the cave to relative safety, but he could not keep Denzel from returning to the mouth of the cave. Doshmisi called to him desperately to move back to safety. But Denzel would not obey her. From his vantage point, just inside the cave entrance, he could see Toad and the others hiding behind rocks and trees, jumping in and out to take aim and shoot at their attackers. Denzel wished he had a weapon. He would not fail this time.

Suddenly, Toad's body fell across the entrance to the cave. Denzel leapt forward, out of the mouth of the cave. Doshmisi saw him and screamed. Denzel put one of Toad's massive arms over his shoulders and attempted to drag him into the cave. Toad's protective armor had torn, exposing an island of naked skin at his hip, and three darts pierced the skin. As the poison began to do its deadly work, Toad collapsed, unable to stand. Denzel stood completely exposed for a brief moment as he hauled Toad inside the cave. Jasper and Doshmisi ran forward to help pull Toad into the depths of the cave. Honeydew brought a lantern.

"In here," Hyacinth directed. They followed Hyacinth and Honeydew down a tunnel that led for several yards and then opened into a small cavern.

"He's been hit," Denzel said, although they could see the row of darts protruding from Toad's hip.

"Sissrath's Special Forces are trained to look for weakness and to take advantage of it. They must have seen the rip in Toad's armor," Princess Honeydew said in a quavering voice.

"I know only too well how Sissrath takes advantage of a person's weakness," Denzel said through clenched teeth.

Doshmisi took out her herbal. They momentarily forgot the battle raging outside the mouth of the cave. From the cavern, they could no longer hear the sounds of the conflict. Doshmisi allowed the herbal to fall open on Toad's chest. When she read the words on the page, tears sprung to her eyes. Silver spark. And she had none. There quite possibly would never be any again. Sissrath's warriors had burned it out of existence.

Hyacinth kneeled down and took Toad's large hands in his own. The warrior looked up at his chief with eyes like a child's, frightened and distant.

"You have served your chief and your land like a true warrior," Hyacinth said. "I promise you, we *will* succeed; and when we do, your name will live on in history forever. Forever, Toad, forever."

A faint smile touched Toad's lips and then the light of life went out of his eyes.

Princess Honeydew choked "oh Toad" and she laid her head down on his wide chest and cried.

Sonjay put his hand on Hyacinth's shoulder. "I'm sorry," he said, "but we need to move on into the tunnel, into the mountain, before Sissrath defeats the rest of your men and catches up with us."

Hyacinth waved his hand distractedly. "They won't follow us in here."

"How do you know?" Maia asked.

"Same reason the tigers and your bird and my men wouldn't come in here. Geebachings. Sissrath's men would rather be turned into rocks than come in here."

"Geebachings?" Doshmisi asked, a new fear biting at her heels. "What are geebachings?"

But before anyone could answer, Princess Honeydew shrieked and pointed to Denzel's shoulder. Everyone followed her finger and, in the light cast from her lantern, they saw what had made her shriek. Sticking out of Denzel's shoulder was one, single red-and-yellow-feathered poison dart.

Chapter Fifteen

Geebachings

"No, no, no," Maia moaned. "Oh Denzel. No." Sonjay punched Denzel full in the chest and then put his skinny arms around his brother and squeezed him as hard as he could. "Fool, why'd you have to go and be a hero?"

Doshmisi reached over and plucked the dart out of Denzel's shoulder. She examined the end of it, which was coated in a black, sticky substance that resembled pine tar. "There must be an antidote," she said, looking at her brother in panic.

Denzel gently unwrapped his brother from his waist, pushing him away from him, and unbuttoned the front of his shirt. Then he knocked on his chest with his fist. It made a hollow clunking sound because his upper body was encased in a thin, tough, shiny shell that resembled the surface of a fresh acorn. The shell was flexible, like leather, but impenetrable. "Armor vest," Denzel told the others. "Mole gave it to me. Sorry, just didn't think to tell anyone I was wearing it."

Hyacinth embraced Denzel in absolute glee and slapped him on the back. "You had us terrificated for a moment! I myself was mortified. Did you see Honeydew's face?" He chuckled.

"It's not funny, Daddy," Honeydew had feared for Denzel's life and her father made her angry by making fun of her. "And mortified means embarrassed. You must mean something else. I wish you would get a grip on the use of language," she complained in exasperation.

"I meaned to say that I was scared to death," Hyacinth said, looking hurt.

"I was scared to death too," Sonjay wiped his eyes quickly with the back of his hand.

Maia patted Denzel's arm softly and asked, "You're really OK?"

"Yeah, I'm cool," Denzel reassured her sheepishly.

Having determined that Denzel would live, Doshmisi turned to Hyacinth, "So what's up with these geebachings?"

"Geebachings. Yes," Hyacinth looked thoughtful. "Very mirthful creatures."

"Does he mean murderous?" Denzel asked Jasper.

"Unfortunately, he really means mirthful," Honeydew responded grimly.

"No disrespect, Hyacinth, but would you mind if Honeydew explains about the geebachings? I can understand her a lot easier than I understand you," Denzel said, putting his hand on Hyacinth's shoulder.

Honeydew took a deep breath, "The geebachings are little creatures around so high…" She put her hand out at her waist, "…that live inside the Amber Mountains. They love to laugh. More than anything in the world. In fact, they live on laughter. It keeps them alive as much as food. And more than anything they love to capture other creatures and hold them prisoner and make them laugh. The harder their prisoners laugh, the more it tickles them. In their world, it's kind of a delicacy, like something special, to make others laugh with them."

"That doesn't sound so bad," Sonjay said hopefully.

"Except they never stop. They make their prisoners laugh to death," Honeydew continued. "They force their prisoners to laugh and laugh for hours and days on end until…." Hyacinth made a slashing motion against his throat with his hand. "They can't help themselves really. It's the geebachings' way in the world."

"And because of the geebachings no one will come in here? Not even Sissrath? You're sure?" Denzel asked.

"Especially not Sissrath," Honeydew emphasized. "He won't step foot in here. He hates geebachings. He couldn't think of a worse way to die."

"Couldn't he just use an enchantment on them?" Maia asked.

"No, enchantments roll right off a geebaching, like water off the back of a duck," Honeydew answered.

"If no one comes in here then how do the geebachings capture prisoners to laugh with them?" Doshmisi wanted to know.

"They kidnap people," Honeydew explained.

"Maybe we can hide and then sneak back out of here in a few days," Maia suggested.

"Not likely," Jasper told her dismally. "Sissrath will surely keep this entrance heavily guarded."

"And no one knows another way out, other than going through the mountain?" Sonjay questioned.

"No other way," Jasper confirmed. "This passage through the mountain could actually be done in less than a day, as opposed to going over the mountain, which could take us two to three days before we would get to the other side, depending. If we could just make it past the geebachings, we could come out the other side of the mountain long before Sissrath can get there. But there's no way around the geebachings."

"Well, wait," Hyacinth contradicted. "We might have one way to circumnavigate the geebachings."

"What?" the Four asked eagerly. Honeydew looked skeptical.

"High Chief Charles passed through the mountain safetally once when he had no choicement. He did it with quietude," Hyacinth pronounced.

"Of course," a look of comprehension spread over Honeydew's face. "Daddy's right. Charles really did it. It would be difficult to pass through in silence, but possible."

"In silence?" Sonjay asked.

"Yes. The geebachings have extra-sensitive hearing. They don't see very well, but they hear better than snarfles on a clear night. Chief Charles passed through the entire mountain once, and his tiger with him, by not making a sound. If we can travel through in absolute silence, we might make it." Honeydew explained. The Four wondered what snarfles were and why they could hear so well on a clear night, but no one asked about it.

"That won't work, we have my chatterbox brother with us," Denzel grinned broadly at Sonjay.

"Shut up, man," Sonjay said automatically, but he didn't really mind since he was still feeling glad that Denzel hadn't died from the poison dart.

"I think we have to try this," Doshmisi told the others. "I can't see any other option."

"And what if the geebachings capture us?" Maia asked, wide-eyed.

"Then I guess we'll die laughing," Jasper answered dryly.

"They won't capture us," Sonjay said with determination. "I know we can do this."

"Do you think the geebachings will come this close to the surface?" Jasper asked Honeydew.

"I'm not sure," she told him.

"Well, I vote that we take a chance and camp here, in this cavern, and get some sleep so that we're well-rested," Jasper suggested. "We don't want to go stumbling around inside the mountain. We'll need all our senses as alert as possible to do this." The others readily agreed. None of them had slept the night before and everyone felt thoroughly hungry and exhausted, even the lively high chief. So they sat down in a circle around Honeydew's lantern. Doshmisi produced mannafruit from her knapsack, which delighted Honeydew because she had never eaten it before. The high chief got so excited that he practically recited a poem to the mannafruit on the spot. "This rememberizes me of my youngsterhood," he proclaimed.

After they ate, the travelers laid down on the hard cavern floor. They were so tired that even their excitement and their precarious situation couldn't keep them awake.

Hours later, Doshmisi awoke before anyone else. Since coming to Faracadar, she didn't need as much sleep as she used to. She lay in the dark, listening to the even breathing of the others. Hyacinth muttered in his sleep but she couldn't make out what he said. She put a message out to the trees, to see if any would answer her inside the cave, but she received nothing. Wherever her thoughts wandered, her mind kept returning to the poison darts. What if she could discover an antidote, or better yet, a vaccine? She wondered if they knew about vaccines here. If only she could have spent time studying with the healers on the islands.

Jasper stirred restlessly and sat up slowly next to Doshmisi. "You awake?" she whispered to him.

"Almost," he whispered back. "What's up?"

Doshmisi smiled to herself in the dark. Jasper had acquired that "what's up" from Denzel.

"You know those poison darts?"

"How could I forget them?" Jasper replied.

"There must be an antidote or something. Tell me what you know about the poison, like what does Sissrath make it from?"

"Sap from the red oaks combined with sap from the Texas oil tree," Jasper answered.

"Texas? Why Texas? Do you know what Texas is?" Doshmisi asked incredulously. Why would anything in Faracadar be named after one of the United States?

"High Chief Charles called it that and the name stuck. When he saw the black sap that comes out of the tree, he said it looked like Texas oil and we've called it that ever since. I know Texas is a kind of tree in the Farland, if that's what you mean," Jasper told her.

She smiled with amusement, knowing full well that Texas was not a tree. "So the poison is made from tree sap?"

"Not exactly. The raw sap isn't poisonous. But Sissrath uses Shakabaz to change the chemistry of the sap. He makes it into a substance that enters the body through the blood and causes a person's heart to stop pumping." Jasper couldn't see Doshmisi in the dark. "Does that make sense?

"It makes perfect sense," Doshmisi said grimly.

"Sissrath developed the sap poison using Shakabaz. He produces the poison himself in a laboratory. No one else knows how to make the poison," Jasper concluded.

"So without Shakabaz, he couldn't make any more poison?" Doshmisi asked.

"Exactly," Jasper confirmed.

Doshmisi and Jasper had kept their voices down so as not to disturb the others. But now they could hear the others stirring to wakefulness.

"I wonder what time it is," Denzel said.

"We came in here during the afternoon so my guess is that it's around midnight," Jasper suggested.

Whatever the position of the sun outside the mountain, they were inside the mountain; and for them the time had arrived for their silent journey through to the other side. Honeydew lit the lantern. Tense and eager to get moving, they ate some mannafruit and gathered their things.

"How will we find our way through the mountain?" Maia asked.

Jasper pointed to the roof of the cavern, "We follow the glow. Honeydew, cover the lantern." Once Honeydew covered the lantern and their eyes adjusted, they could see a phosphorescent glow clinging to the ceiling. "The mountain contains lots of passageways but they taught me as a guide that the passageways that lead out have phosphorescent molds growing on them. In the dark, they make the directions obvious, you see?"

"I don't get it. Once we go deep inside, how do we know whether to turn right or left?" Sonjay wondered.

"Look closely at the glow," Jasper pointed. "See how it's made up of strips of phosphorescence, and the strips are shaped like arrow-tips? The pointy side, or front of the arrow tip, is the Mountain Settlement side, and the back of the arrow tip is the Big House City side. We basically just follow the arrows. Couldn't be simpler. But we can only see in the dark, so no lantern."

"By thunder, that's unutterably incredulous!" Hyacinth exclaimed.

Honeydew rolled her eyes and mumbled, "Incredible, Daddy, utterly incredible."

"They teach you that in guide school?" Denzel was impressed. "That's tight."

"OK, let's do it," Sonjay ordered.

Jasper organized them. "Form a line, holding hands. We'll have to walk for quite a few hours. If someone needs to stop for any reason, then squeeze the hand of the person in front of you. If you lose the hand of the person behind you, then squeeze the hand of the person in front of you. If you feel a squeeze of the hand then stop. If we hear or see any sign of geebachings then we stop and press back against the wall. Stay calm. Slow and easy will do it."

Denzel and Jasper put on their knapsacks and Maia hoisted her travel drum and her bag over her shoulder. Honeydew turned out the lantern and gave it to her father, who put it into his knapsack. Jasper stepped out in front and took Doshmisi's hand. She blushed but fortunately no one could see. She reached behind her for Maia, next in the chain. Then came Sonjay, Denzel, Honeydew, and the high chief brought up the rear. Stepping as quietly as they possibly could and paying attention so they wouldn't scrape against the walls, the travelers slowly started forward down the corridor leading out of the cavern and into the depths of the mountain.

It required tremendous concentration to make no sound. They stepped quietly, they breathed quietly. They avoided touching anything. The corridor led down and they felt increasing dampness surrounding them. Whenever they glanced up, they could see the phosphorescent arrows, guiding the way. Sometimes the corridor would open into larger rooms or caverns, pass through them, and continue out the other side.

After they had walked for a long, long time, and had just entered a cavern, Maia sent a squeeze through the chain and everyone froze. They followed Jasper's lead as he stepped back and clung to the wall. As they stood in silence, they realized why Maia had stopped their progress. They could hear, faintly, high-pitched giggles. The giggles became more distinct. To their horror, the travelers realized that the gigglers quickly approached. Jasper sent an urgent hand-squeeze down the chain as several geebachings passed through the cavern. They could not see them in the dark and the geebachings carried no light with them, but the travelers heard them only a few yards off.

The geebaching giggles were terribly infectious. One of them tee-hee-heed and another snorted through its nose. A third put its hand under its armpit and proceeded to make loud farty noises. The farty noises grew more and more raucous and the geebachings belly-laughed like tickled babies. At the end of the line, Hyacinth raised a hand to his face and covered his mouth, suppressing a laugh. His daughter pinched his arm hard, digging in with her fingernails. He rocked back on his feet in pain and held his silence. The geebachings abruptly grew quiet, listening in the dark. The travelers held their breath. The geebachings listened. Suddenly, one of the geebachings started burping to the tune of "Jingle Bells." If they hadn't been so terrified, the Four would have cracked up over that. Then the geebachings started to trip each other as they went out the passageway on the other side of the cavern. From the sound of it, they were holding out their feet in front of one another and falling on the ground. Their laughter grew fainter and fainter as they disappeared down the passageway.

No one dared speak. Jasper gave a gentle squeeze of Doshmisi's hand, Doshmisi sent the squeeze down the line, and the travelers stepped out, inching their way through the mountain once more. For the next few hours, they moved slowly through the underground passageways and caverns, stopping frequently whenever they heard geebachings nearby. Doshmisi remembered that Jasper had said it would only take a few hours to travel through the mountain, but it seemed like it took forever. Just as Doshmisi thought that their journey would never end, the corridor began to slope upward. With a rush of relief, the travelers realized they would soon reach the exit out of the mountain. They didn't know exactly how much further they had to go, but they began to hope that they might make it through without capture. Doshmisi's heart pounded in her ears and her spirits lifted.

Just at that moment when Doshmisi thought to herself that they might make it through the mountain, a large group of geebachings twittered into the passageway ahead. As they had done many times already, the travelers flattened themselves against the wall.

The geebachings skipped past, a few at a time, almost brushing against the travelers in the narrow passageway. They chuckled and giggled together. Most of them had passed when some of them burst into song, out of the blue. In high screechy voices they belted out an old Dionne Warwick song from the 1960s. How did they know that song? It was absurd. The Four recognized the song instantly and it nearly set them laughing hysterically to hear it sung in such a bizarre context.

"Do you know the way to San Jose?" the geebachings screeched. "Bum, bum, bum-bum, bum-bum, ba-bum bum, bummmm."

Sonjay bit his tongue. Denzel tried to think of the baseball scores from the last World Series. Maia stepped down sharply on her own toe and Doshmisi squeezed Jasper's hand so hard she cut off his circulation as they tried desperately not to laugh.

Most of the geebachings had progressed through the passageway now and had actually passed the travelers. Only the singers straggled at the back. Jasper, Honeydew, and Hyacinth could tell that something about that song had the Four on the verge of cracking. The travelers could practically reach out and touch the tension among them.

Then Jasper felt a little flurry of movement close to the ground. As it increased, he realized that a family of mice had crossed his feet, their claws scrabbling for a foothold. He reached around with his free arm and pressed Doshmisi even tighter against the wall, as if protecting her, and he grabbed Maia's upper arm in his hand to steady her as the mice scuttled down the line of the travelers, running across their feet and ankles, their tails brushing behind them. Denzel let go of Sonjay's hand and put his hand over the princess's mouth to keep her from making a noise. But at the moment when she recognized the creatures as mice, only one thought went through Honeydew's mind: she knew her father well and knew that he had a deep terror of mice and she knew that whenever he even saw a mouse, let alone touched a mouse, he couldn't help himself, he lost control and he...

Hyacinth screeched like a little girl and hopped up and down, waving his arms in the narrow passageway. Hyacinth's scream seemed to go on forever, echoing down the dark passageways of the mountain tunnels. Everyone cringed, realizing that the geebachings would find them in an instant. The sound reverberated against the walls. Doshmisi almost started crying. Oh, they had almost made it! They had come so close!

The geebachings immediately stopped in their tracks. The singers fell silent for a moment and then shouted in glee. The whole pack piled back into the passageway, falling over each other in their excitement as they ran their hands down the wall until they found the travelers. The moment the geebachings discovered the intruders, they jumped up and down and jabbered and some of them blew loud whistles. Jasper tried to run for it, but the geebachings clung to him and the others, dragging them down and sitting on them.

The geebachings fell out into gales of laughter as they pulled Hyacinth to the ground and bounced on his big belly playfully. Denzel, Sonjay, and Jasper struggled to free themselves of the geebachings so they could run away. But they struggled in vain. The geebachings were small and wiry and surprisingly strong and they had the advantage of numbers. So many of them crowded the corridor that they could easily restrain their prey. They soon tied the travelers' legs and hands together and stuffed them into little wire cages on wheels, brought by more geebachings, who swiftly joined the first group. The passageway overflowed with geebachings.

The creatures trollied their prey away in the little boxed cages, through many corridors and caverns, until they entered a large chamber, lit by a giant bonfire and absolutely packed to the gills with geebachings hopping around on rocks and boulders. The geebachings resembled monkeys more than anything else, but they had no tails. They had lots of orange-ish hair covering their entire bodies, but they could not be described as furry. They had large heads and long arms with long fingers, and tiny squinty eyes and large flapping ears. Each of them sported a unique, odd-shaped nose. They wore simple one-piece tunics and the travelers couldn't possibly tell the girls from the boys.

When the geebachings arrived in the chamber, they parked the cages containing the travelers against a wall in a row. None of the travelers had spoken for hours so it came as a shock when Hyacinth's voice apologized woefully, "I should never have come with you. This is all my faultness. You would have made it through the mountain without me. I am forensic when it comes to mice. They make me scream and I can't help myself. I just can't help it." He sobbed hopelessly into his hands.

Honeydew sighed and with her never-failing patience she corrected, "Phobic, Daddy, not forensic. Forensic means argumentative like in a debate in a courtroom. Phobic means you have an illogical and uncontrollable fear of something."

"I mean I hate mice," Hyacinth shivered.

The Four watched the geebachings intently in utter fascination. "Hush," said Denzel, "watch what they do, and maybe we'll figure out how to get out of this yet."

"Try not to look at their noses," Honeydew warned. "They can mold them into any shape and they will use this trick to make you laugh."

The geebachings opened the knapsacks that belonged to the travelers and went through them item by item. First they took out Denzel's tools and poked each other with them and one of them wired the solar panel to his forehead and marched around. They took out Crumpet and sat on him and tossed him back and forth. They giggled and guffawed and laughed with such wild abandon that the prisoners in the cages couldn't help but laugh with them. They were the silliest, funniest creatures with the most terribly contagious laughter.

Just as Honeydew warned, they stretched their noses into long bean poles and squished them flat into piggy snouts and bent them up to their eyebrows and bent them down under their chins.

They went through Doshmisi's knapsack and rummaged through her herbs. Two of them began juggling the mannafruit and soon they had six or seven going at once. They tossed them between their legs and caught them behind their backs and then they threw them and hit each other in the head with them. One of the geebachings made his nose into a ring like a little basketball hoop and the others slam dunked mannafruit through it. They found more of Denzel's tools in Jasper's knapsack and attempted to use them on each other, twisting each others' putty-like noses with wrenches and cleaning their teeth with the screwdrivers. Meanwhile, they put the articles of clothing they discovered in the knapsacks on all the wrong parts of their bodies. One of them wore Sonjay's boxers on his head, with his nose sticking out the fly and another wore Doshmisi's shirt on his legs, which made him fall over when he tried to walk. They looked hilarious and the prisoners couldn't stop laughing.

Princess Honeydew gasped, "Think of something terribly serious and terribly sad. Think about poor Toad. Try not to let them get to you." They tried to feel sad and solemn but they couldn't. The geebachings carried on with such ridiculous antics and their laughter had some sort of charm to it that forced the prisoners to sputter and screech with amusement.

When the geebachings came to Maia's bag, it caused a great deal of excitement. They played the drum, rather well actually. They took out the water organ and wore the larger cups on their heads. Eventually they put the water organ back together and put it away in its bag. Similarly they put the drum away too. In fact, they put the objects back quite carefully, except, Maia noticed, they kept her timber flute and handed it to one of the bigger geebachings who broke it in half deliberately over his knee. Maia winced. It appeared that they had left everything exactly as they found it in the end, except for the timber flute. They put the travelers' belongings into a little room off the great chamber.

Then they danced around in glee, bending and pulling their flexible noses into every shape and form imaginable, including pretzels, fish, cauliflowers, frying pans, and shovels. Their laughter more than anything else drove the prisoners half mad because no one could listen to it without laughing. They laughed until their sides ached and they gasped for air. They couldn't catch their breath. Maia had so much trouble breathing that she finally passed right out for lack of oxygen. After Maia fainted, the geebachings took the prisoners out of the cages and locked them into the little room with their belongings.

At first the travelers just lay still on the floor breathing deeply and resting their sides. Maia regained consciousness, but she could hardly move. Doshmisi cradled her sister's head in her lap while she asked Hyacinth and Honeydew to tell her everything they knew about geebachings.

"Well, they're sort of folklyrical creeptures," Hyacinth said, which made no sense and was no help. "We don't know much really about them, just heresy."

"Hearsay, Daddy," Honeydew took over. "We know what people say, like rumors, but so few people have come through the mountain alive that we don't know any cold facts about geebachings."

"Have you heard any rumor about how to defend against them or any weaknesses they have?" Sonjay asked. "Any at all?"

"Well," Honeydew grew thoughtful, "I heard from a traveling musician that geebachings can't tolerate music. He said they like drumming and singing, but that they can't stand music from musical instruments like horns or strings. And the more beautiful the music, the more strongly it disturbs them."

"Well then let's find out exactly how much it disturbs them," Maia said, sitting up resolutely. "Did you notice that the only one of our belongings that they kept was my flute? And they broke it." Maia lowered her voice so that the others had to lean in to hear her, "But I have another instrument that they didn't recognize. And I'm going to play it, before they try to make us spend another session laughing with them." Maia took out her water organ. None of the others had heard her play it, as she had only played it with Raffia in the Braiders Cottage. She poured water from her canteen into the cups and lined them up along the wall next to the door. Her amulet began to glow with blue light and Honeydew pointed at it.

"Yeah, they do that," Sonjay told Honeydew. "All of them except mine."

"Now we wait," Maia said. "The next time they open that door, you guys do whatever it takes to keep the door open while I play music."

They didn't have long to wait. In a short while, a couple of geebachings approached the prisoners with bowls of food. The moment they unlocked the door to the room, the travelers seized the geebachings, and before they had a chance to react, Maia closed her eyes, took a deep breath, and played the water organ.

An unspeakably beautiful sound emerged from the small cups. It sounded kind of like Calypso music from the Caribbean islands. The music had a deep, rich resonance and it filled the tiny room, bursting out into the large chamber beyond with the force of a church organ. The two geebachings in the cell flapped their ears shut and screeched. The travelers heard similar screeches echoing throughout the underground chambers and corridors. As she played, Maia said to the others in a low voice "the door." Denzel and Jasper blocked the doorway, so that no geebachings could enter or leave or lock the door shut. But they had no need to worry since the music completely incapacitated the geebachings. The two in the cell rolled their hairy bodies up into little balls and rocked back and forth.

All of a sudden the two little geebachings in the prison chamber seemed to blow up. First the travelers saw a puff of orange hair, and then in place of the geebachings sat two beautiful golden birds with orange crests and long, pointed beaks. Maia kept playing her celestial music, while her comrades cautiously emerged from their prison cell. In the great chamber, hundreds of geebachings rolled into balls, rocked back and forth, and then transformed into birds. The birds took no notice of their former prisoners, instead taking flight in the chamber in great swooping dives. Then they flew out into the corridors and one by one they all disappeared until the entire chamber had emptied. The bright golden orange birds warbled in the distance as they plunged upward toward the surface and their new life in the open air.

After the last geebaching bird had left, only Maia's sweet music continued to fill the air. The other travelers returned to the little room, where Maia sat cross-legged in front of the water organ, wrapped in intense concentration, her amulet throbbing with pulsating blue light in rhythm with the music. The princess touched Maia on the shoulder gently. Maia looked up, as if awakened from a trance, and the last exquisite notes of the water organ faded.

"Girl, that was outstanding," Denzel told her gently.

"Fabulous," Sonjay agreed.

"Obstreperous," Hyacinth blustered.

"Obstreperous means stubborn, Daddy," Honeydew told him.

"Well, I mean it was very, very lovely," Hyacinth grinned.

"You don't have to correct him all the time," Sonjay told Honeydew. She was such a know-it-all. She got on Sonjay's nerves sometimes. She gave him a hurt look.

Maia looked around shyly. "It worked, and that's what matters. Let's get out of here."

The travelers shouldered their bags and knapsacks and entered the great chamber. They looked at the corridor openings leading out.

"I think that we should make a pact to keep this a secret," Honeydew said thoughtfully.

"What do you mean?" Denzel asked.

"I mean that it may come in handy for us to know how to deal with geebachings and for Sissrath and a few other people I can think of *not* to know. We might need to escape inside the mountains again. Let's agree to keep what we've learned a royal secret, OK?" As the others agreed and swore themselves to secrecy, Honeydew turned to her father, "Daddy, you will remember not to tell, won't you."

"Absolutenly," he assured her.

Honeydew rolled her eyes, but she didn't attempt to correct her father.

"C'mon, let's find a passage with some phosphorescence and see if we can't rescue Cardamom sometime this year," Jasper said, as he led them up one of the corridors through which the new geebaching birds had departed. They followed Jasper's lead. Since Maia's music had transformed the pack of geebachings within earshot, the travelers had the relief of completing their passage through the mountain without having to keep silent.

Chapter Sixteen

The High Mountain People

When they reached an opening that led out of the mountain, Jasper left the others inside while he went to check for safety. He didn't think it possible for Sissrath to make it to the other side of the mountain before them, since he had to travel overland; but they agreed to proceed with caution in any case.

They emerged in a beautiful, serene forest right at the golden hour of sunset when each blade of grass and every leaf glowed iridescent as if they held a drop of the sun within their veins. Tall yellow and blue fir trees and other ancient trees of strange and unfamiliar shapes and colors with wide trunks and unusual leaves swept down the slope in front of them. They recognized some of the former geebachings with their new yellow and orange feathers and their long beaks. From where they stood atop a mountain slope, they had a panoramic view of other mountains surrounding them.

"We have arrived at the home of the High Mountain People," Hyacinth announced with satisfaction. "Directionally to your left-hand you will see the land of the Mountain People of the Downs and the Final Fortress is situational beyond there. Then that way," he pointed to the right, "you'll eventuality come to the ocean."

Jasper, ever a trained guide, had his bearings immediately, "So that means that directly behind us on the other side of the mountains is Akinowe Lake."

"Correct," the princess confirmed.

"Then we want to head that way, to the Final Fortress," Sonjay pointed toward the Downs.

"Not a good idea," Honeydew shook her head. "Not with Sissrath behind us. Those are his people."

Sonjay frowned. He didn't like Honeydew contradicting him. "We can't rescue Cardamom from the Final Fortress without going there," Sonjay said sarcastically.

"We've emergenated right near the Wolf Circle, where I met your mother," Hyacinth told his daughter. "The High Mountain People will help us. Let's go to them," Hyacinth clearly couldn't contain his delight at the thought of visiting the Wolf Circle.

Honeydew advised the other travelers, "Daddy has a good point. Let's go to the Wolf Circle. My mother grew up there and they know us. I think they can help us properly prepare to travel to the Final Fortress and consulting them will increase our chance of success in rescuing Cardamom. No disrespect to Jasper, but perhaps we can find a guide more familiar with the Amber Mountains."

"Does your mother stay at the Wolf Circle?" Doshmisi asked. She had been curious about Honeydew's mother and had restrained herself, but now her curiosity got the better of her.

Honeydew shook her head negative and offered no information. Hyacinth told them, "Honeydew's mother, Saffron, disappeared three years ago. She was a quietous, mysterious person. We don't know why she left us."

"She often went off on her own. She liked to be by herself. She didn't talk much," Honeydew volunteered. "She always knew things that no one else knew. Sort of clairvoyant, you know, like the intuits. One day she disappeared." The princess clenched her jaw shut to keep her lip from trembling.

Maia put her hand on Honeydew's shoulder, "Our father disappeared also when we were very young." Honeydew stared down at her feet in silence.

"Which way to the Wolf Circle?" Jasper asked. "We should try to make it there before dark."

"Yes, yes, right down there," Hyacinth pointed down the slope and the others could make out evidence of a vague path through the trees. "The ancient spirits made us emergenate here absolutely."

In no time at all, the weary travelers arrived at the Wolf Circle. As they approached the circle, a dozen or more large white wolves appeared out of the shadows and trotted swiftly toward them. The Four turned on their heels in an instant, poised to flee, until Hyacinth delightedly called out to the beasts and fell to his knees. The wolves surrounded him and licked his face happily while he petted them and cooed over them. Honeydew embraced one of the wolves around its thick neck and buried her face in its fur. Hyacinth talked to the animals in a guttural sort of growling language and the wolves became even more excited and howled and yipped, which brought people out from the circle. Just as they had predicted, the people from the circle recognized Hyacinth and Honeydew and greeted them warmly. Not only people greeted them, but also an assortment of animals, mostly wolves, dogs, birds, and a small furry ball of an animal the Four had never seen before.

The people from the Wolf Circle escorted the travelers into the circle's community room, where they gratefully sat down at a big round table. Two of the wolves came right into the room with Hyacinth, refusing to leave his side for an instant. Hyacinth introduced a tall man with skin a shade lighter than cider and straight, amber-colored hair as his brother-in-law, Goldenrod. A small, colorful parakeet perched on Goldenrod's shoulder and squawked "welcome Hyacinth" over and over again. Goldenrod sat down at the table next to the princess and took her hand affectionately and asked her about her studies and her pets. She apparently had a pair of canaries that sang beautifully and Goldenrod wanted to hear all about the birds. Honeydew patted the parakeet and chatted with her uncle about the canaries and her dog and her two tigers and numerous other pets she had left behind at the Big House. Hearing Honeydew talk about the many animals she and her father kept as pets at the Big House amazed the Four. They began to understand what Clover had meant when she said that the high chief would prefer to live quietly with his animals than to rule the land.

Meanwhile, Mountain People bustled to and from the table, offering food to the royals and their companions. Many of them had devoted dogs following closely at their heels. When they brought around a platter with a roasted greenish animal resembling a large lizard, dribbling juice and sliced in thin slabs, Sonjay started drooling. He, the high chief, and the princess took several pieces each. Denzel disgustedly muttered something about eating dragon meat, while Sonjay ignored him and put another green slice into his mouth.

The mountain people provided more than enough to eat, with or without the green meat, and the travelers ate well.

"So when do you come to us for your apprenticeship?" Goldenrod asked Honeydew.

"Next year, when I turn thirteen," she told him proudly.

Goldenrod explained to the others, "Honeydew will come to our circle to study to become an enchantress when she comes of age. She has the mark of an enchantress and we hope she will become an accomplished and great one. Show them the mark," Goldenrod urged her.

Honeydew blushed with embarrassment, but she obeyed, rolling up her sleeve to reveal a reddish-brown crescent birthmark on the inside of her wrist. "It's the mark of the gift of enchantment," she said. "My mother had it too."

When the Four saw the mark, they sucked in their breath in astonishment. Doshmisi, Maia, and Denzel immediately looked at Sonjay, who silently rolled up his sleeve and turned his hand over to reveal an identical mark on his own wrist. Honeydew ran a finger over it gently and then looked at Sonjay in delight. "Cousin," she said, "it looks as though you too bear the mark of an enchanter."

Honeydew's know-it-all attitude annoyed Sonjay, but the fact that they shared the mark of the enchanter bound him to her in kinship and from that moment on he had more tolerance for her bossiness. Their shared mark made him feel as though he wanted to protect her and at the same time as if he had a powerful ally in his cousin.

"Sonjay has never shown any sign of having the powers of an enchanter," Denzel commented with a glint in his eye, "unless you count mysteriously making Mama's chocolate chip cookies disappear before anyone else can get at them."

Sonjay ignored Denzel as he repeated to Goldenrod, "I've never shown any signs of being an enchanter."

"That's because you're too young," Goldenrod explained. "Your gift won't come into strength until you go through puberty."

"What's that mean?" Sonjay asked.

"He means when you become a teenager," Doshmisi told him.

Sonjay mulled this over in his mind.

When they couldn't eat another bite, they each had a steamy mug of hot cocoa. The warm drink after the big meal made them so sleepy that they could hardly keep their eyes open. All of them except for Hyacinth. The high chief was having the time of his life reacquainting himself with old friends and members of his wife's family, all the while petting and fawning over the great white wolves that flanked his chair.

Goldenrod got Hyacinth's attention and volunteered, "I'll take your young people to some rooms so they can go to sleep. They look beat." Just as he said this, a strikingly beautiful woman approached the table. She had jet black hair that fell straight to her waist, golden eyes, long slender hands, and perfect almond-colored skin lightly tinged with a yellow-gold glow like all the Mountain People. She moved with unusual grace and Doshmisi and Maia thought her the most beautiful woman they had ever seen. She completely charmed Hyacinth the moment he laid eyes on her. "Let me introduce you before I go," Goldenrod said, watching his brother-in-law intently as the woman glided up to the table.

Goldenrod held out both his hands to the woman, who took them in hers and flashed a smile that revealed perfect teeth. "Who are your friends?" she asked Goldenrod, with her eyes fixed on Hyacinth. Sonjay had the feeling that even though the woman looked at Hyacinth, she was examining every inch of the other travelers who sat at the table.

"This is High Chief Hyacinth. He has just come from the Big House," Goldenrod told her. Then he turned to Hyacinth, "This is Amaranth, recently come to the circle to study animal enchantments."

"Ah, animal enchantments," Hyacinth said, obviously pleased to meet this unusual woman, "I have a peacock at home who used to be my butler. I've been meaning to change him back but can't get the knack of it. I never had much skill at enchantment. It's a shame really. He was a good butler."

Goldenrod helped the travelers gather their things to take to their rooms. As he led them out, they could see Hyacinth settling in with Amaranth for a long, cozy chat. Princess Honeydew could not disguise her disapproval of her father for flirting with the woman, but she held her tongue.

The weary travelers fell into bed, still wearing their traveling clothes, and slept soundly through the night. In the morning, Doshmisi woke up refreshed. She, Maia, and Honeydew had spent the night in a room with cheerful black-eyed-Susan wallpaper. The boys had shared a room across the hall. The first one up, Doshmisi went outside for a little walk before breakfast. The circle glittered damp and fresh in the early morning sunshine. Doshmisi watched the hypnotic movements of a group of women gathered on a patch of grass as they engaged in some type of martial arts routine.

Goldenrod found her there and steered her to the community room for breakfast with the others. By the time Doshmisi arrived, Sonjay had already piled a plate high with sausages made from who knew what. The sausages looked normal enough from the outside, but Doshmisi could not imagine what weird animal's guts filled the inside.

"You have some eggs and juice with that, too," Doshmisi told Sonjay sternly.

"I will," he grumbled. Then he brightened and asked Goldenrod, "You folks wouldn't happen to have any of those round little bat eyes in smashed slime pig sauce, would you? I had something like that at Big House City and it tasted great."

"Sonjay!" Denzel tried to snap his brother back to his senses. "Give it a rest. You don't need anymore slime pig sauce!"

Sonjay turned his concentration back to his breakfast plate in defeat. Goldenrod laughed. "I think you would enjoy our broiled goose-chicken eyeballs if you have a craving for something round and crunchy," he told Sonjay.

Just then, Hyacinth arrived with Amaranth on his arm, the two great wolves from the night before at his side, and a gleam in his eye. "You will never guess," Hyacinth eagerly addressed the others. "Amaranth here knows the Final Fortress well. She was stationeered there when she serviced in the army. Last night she offered to provide us with accompaniment to the Final Fortress and she suggestively proposaled a plan to free Cardamom."

"I'll bet she suggestively proposaled," Honeydew grumbled under her breath. Denzel, the only one who overheard her, had to suppress his laughter by pretending to choke on a piece of egg. Honeydew didn't even bother to correct her father's massacre of words.

"Explicate, please," Hyacinth requested, turning to Amaranth.

Amaranth spoke to the others in a syrupy hypnotic voice, "A guard house stands outside the main entrance to the Final Fortress. At night, it is the weakest point of the fortress. Only one guard works the guard house and he holds a key ring with the main keys. An enchantment protects him, and one of Sissrath's commanders changes the enchantment every night. But I know the anti-charm that breaks the code of the enchantment, because I used to be that guard. Hyacinth has entrusted me with the knowledge of your intentions. I can help you reach Cardamom and free him."

"And why would you do that?" Honeydew asked Amaranth rudely, with suspicion.

A flash of anger flickered for the tiniest second in Amaranth's golden eyes before she suppressed it. Only Sonjay caught it and it made him suddenly wary. Amaranth answered, "Because I wish to defeat Sissrath as much as you do. He murdered my family."

"So it's a settlement," Hyacinth said. "Amaranth will departure with us for the Final Fortress."

"You mean it's settled, Daddy," Honeydew corrected him, "a settlement is a collection of circles in the land."

Before anyone could question Amaranth further or object to Hyacinth's plan, a commotion occurred in the doorway. With a flap of feathers and a burst of color, a small flock of parrots whisked into the room. One of them flew directly to Sonjay where it perched on his shoulder. "Bayard Rustin!" Sonjay exclaimed. Everyone was so happy to see him that they forgot about Amaranth.

"How did you find us?" Sonjay asked as he petted Bayard fondly.

"Hyacinth is a brave fool," Bayard squawked.

"I'll take that as a compilement," Hyacinth said good-naturedly.

"Compliment, Daddy, compliment," the princess corrected.

Bayard flew to Hyacinth's shoulder, as if to confirm that it was a compliment, and Hyacinth stroked the brilliant bird's head. The other birds alighted on various perches near the travelers and Hyacinth pointed out, "It looks like Bayard brought some friends with him."

"Sorry to cut this reunion short," Jasper said, "but we need to hit the road."

Sonjay rose from the table with Bayard once again sitting on his shoulder. He surveyed the food. "I don't suppose I can get a doggy bag for later?"

"Don't push your luck, man. They'd probably put a real doggy in it," Denzel teased his brother. Sonjay dropped the subject.

When Doshmisi, Maia, and the princess returned to the privacy of their room to prepare for their journey, Honeydew told the other two, "I don't like Amaranth. I don't trust her. I wish that Daddy had not befriended her or given her so much information about us. She gives me the creeps."

"Maybe it's just that she's so frightfully beautiful," Maia said.

"Frightful is the right word," Honeydew remarked with a snort. "She must dye her hair, because no High Mountain People would have hair that dark. The combination of her High Mountain features and that jet black hair looks kind of scary, particularly if you know what High Mountain People usually look like, the way I do. It makes her seem like she's wearing a fright wig or something."

"But you have to admit that it's striking," Maia pointed out. "In a Morticia Adams sort of way," Maia added.

"Who's Morticia Adams?" Honeydew asked.

"Never mind," Maia didn't know how to explain.

"Well, if she can help us rescue Cardamom then I don't care what she looks like," Doshmisi told the others.

The travelers left the friendly circle with reluctance as they set out on their journey over the mountains into enemy territory in the Downs.

They had no tigers to ride, but tigers would not have been much help anyway on the rocky, irregular mountain trails. Fortunately, Jasper and Amaranth found some worn paths that led them through in the easiest possible places. They walked for a full day, spent the night in a grove of short stubby red trees with enormous crinkly leaves that smelled like vanilla, and then walked again. Late in the evening of the second day, they came over a ridge and could see the towers of the Final Fortress in the distance. The fortress looked ancient and the grayish land surrounding it looked prehistoric as it revealed itself in glimpses through drifting banks of mist.

The fortress was a large, ominous stone structure, with gigantic birds of prey swooping between its turrets. Pale yellow flags flew from the topmost point. Just the appearance of the fortress gave Maia the shivers and made Denzel's blood run cold. It put them in mind of old Frankenstein movies. Amaranth stood forward on a bluff with her hair streaming behind her in the wind. "It looks impenetrable," she said, "but it's as easy as pie to get in when you know the secrets it holds. We wait until dark and then we move forward."

They set up a camp halfway down the slope and near the fortress but far enough away to conceal themselves from view. Bayard had traveled with them as had the two white wolves, who would not leave Hyacinth's side. Doshmisi had the feeling that other wolves lurked invisibly in the shadows around them, following the lead of Hyacinth's friendly escort, but she never actually saw any.

When darkness fell, Amaranth suggested that they wait until midnight to make their move, since the fewest number of guards patrolled at that hour. Hyacinth told them to try to sleep. He said he would keep watch. But everyone felt so anxious that they couldn't possibly fall asleep. Denzel paced like a caged lion. Sonjay fidgeted with pieces of wood, tossing them into the campfire Jasper had built. Maia played with Honeydew's hair. Jasper shared stories from his home with Doshmisi, talking quietly where they sat apart from the others. Amaranth's laughter floated on the cold breeze as she flirted with Hyacinth.

Finally, in the dead of night, Amaranth gave the word and they approached the fortress on silent feet. As she had predicted, they saw a guard house at the entrance. She motioned to the others to fall back and she walked up to the guard house, the hood of her cloak pulled up over her head. After exchanging a word with the guard, she raised a slender hand and the guard slumped to the floor of the guard house. She then waved the others to join her, which they did.

They entered a cobblestone courtyard containing a fountain in the center and stone statues of fierce warrior kings and steely enchantresses in long robes around the edges. The eerie silence of the courtyard in the overbearing presence of the statues of the ancestors sent chills down the spines of the travelers. Amaranth had taken a large metal ring of keys from the guard and she thumbed through the keys as she glided toward a flight of stairs that led up to a large wooden door with the face of a fierce lion carved on the front. As Amaranth made for the stairs, Maia happened to look up above at the ominous towers and walls of the fortress. She saw a man standing on the balcony of a room high up in a tower that overlooked the Amber Mountains. A clean yellow light spilled from the doorway behind him and his long beard and hair blew in the breeze. He raised a hand and Maia touched Honeydew's arm, pointing up above them at the man. Honeydew gasped and whispered to her father one word: "Cardamom."

Hyacinth hissed in hushed tones at Amaranth, who turned midway up the stairs and followed his gaze up to the tower where Cardamom stood bathed in the light from his chamber. Hyacinth pointed and Honeydew said, "We see Cardamom; look up there."

Amaranth seemed strangely irritated to discover Cardamom in the tower, but she came back down the stairs and assured them, "We'll have him out in a jiffy." She rifled through the keys until she found the one she wanted, which opened a door at the bottom of the tower. Cardamom had gone back inside and closed the door so they could no longer see the light of his room. His rescuers climbed a long winding staircase that passed many doors and landings until it ended at the very top where Amaranth fitted a small iron key to the lock in a thick wooden door. The door creaked back slowly on stiff hinges.

A tall, regal enchanter stood in the center of the room. He wore long yellow robes and looked like the embodiment of wisdom itself.

His sparkly yellow eyes twinkled like a tiger's in a face creased with age yet still glowing and vigorous. His presence filled the room, filled the tower, filled the night.

Sonjay entered and knelt before Cardamom while the others crowded into the room behind him. He looked up into the enchanter's face, as if in prayer. Cardamom reached his large hands out to Sonjay, who took them in his own small ones and allowed himself to be pulled back to his feet. "Never kneel to me, youngest born of the Four. You are destined to rule with greatness and *I* will serve *you*, not the other way around."

"Not until you have taught me what I need to know," Sonjay replied in awe.

"Enough," Amaranth broke the reverent mood between the two. "We must go before someone discovers us. Quickly."

"Do you need to pack anything to take with you?" Doshmisi asked Cardamom.

The enchanter shook his head, "Everything of value to me is forbidden here." Honeydew shyly took Cardamom's hand in her own. "Too much time has passed since we have seen each other," Cardamom said to her in a kind voice. "You have grown into a beautiful young woman."

"Come, come with us quickly," Honeydew stammered, "before we lose you again."

The rescue party retreated rapidly down the stairs. Amaranth stood back to lock the room and followed at the rear. When they reached the bottom of the stairs and spilled into the courtyard, they discovered that they had lost Amaranth. They hugged the shadow of the tower, anxiously waiting for her. Sonjay started to go back up the stairs to find her. But then she appeared, breathless and flushed, looking anxiously behind her. Cardamom's forehead furrowed in thought, and he looked as if he was figuring out a problem that he couldn't quite grasp because of a crucial missing piece. But just then, guards appeared at the entrance to the courtyard. They began to sweep around the square.

The travelers panicked. "Quick," Amaranth told them, "this way." She led them across the courtyard silently, clinging to one statue and then another, until they arrived back at the bottom of the stairs leading to the door with the lion on it.

"How do we get out with those guards posted?" Jasper wondered aloud.

Amaranth smiled a winning smile, "Follow me." She skipped lightly and noiselessly up the stairs and without even fitting a key to the great door with the lion carved on it, she led the travelers through it as quickly as possible. They found themselves in a vast, high-ceilinged, tiled entranceway. Amaranth locked the door behind them. Then she herded them swiftly across the entranceway and into a large room, brightly lit, with a loud black and white checkered shiny floor and animal skin rugs. Amaranth gave the travelers her most alluring smile as the Special Forces surrounded them. An enormous, heavy desk stood in front of a wide picture window and behind the desk, in front of the window, stood Sissrath.

He looked much younger and healthier than when they last had seen him at the Big House with his enchantments unwoven. Now he wore the false appearances he wove to make himself look all-powerful. He still had long hair and long fingernails and those rings in his earlobes. But the unmarked, clear skin of his face glowed with youth and his shiny hair fell across his shoulders, thick and well-oiled. He stood broad and tall, emulating strength. He did not seem as thin as they remembered him and his skin did not appear sallow but rather vibrant. His evil presence was unmistakable, but his outside appearance was quite different from that of their last encounter.

"Thank you, Amaranth," Sissrath said. "You will receive generous payment for a job well done."

"Oh, I know," Amaranth purred as she slithered across the room. "They made it so easy, I almost feel guilty taking credit. Oh, and sorry about the enchanter," she apologized. "He was standing out in plain view so I had to let them rescue him before I could bring them down to you. I asked some of the guards to encircle us in the courtyard so I could herd them in here. Do you want me to take Cardamom back to his cell?"

Sissrath waved a hand in dismissal. "That's quite alright. I don't think I want Cardamom here anymore. I had toyed with the idea of taking him back to the Big House with me anyway. Now we can all go to the execution of the Four together."

He smiled his sly smile, revealing perfect white teeth. "Welcome to my home away from home," he said to his captives. "So nice of you to drop by."

The travelers blinked in the bright light. Once again they had fallen for a trick. Amaranth had led them by the nose straight into Sissrath's net.

Sonjay stamped his foot on the floor in fury and lunged at Amaranth, but a dozen hands of the Special Forces restrained him.

"Go ahead, son of Debbie. See if you can find some perfume to sling at her," Sissrath taunted Sonjay. "She won't mind nearly as much as Compost did."

Chapter Seventeen

The Final Fortress

The Special Forces surrounded the travelers. Two of them restrained Sonjay, while the others stood poised to respond if the Four so much as raised a finger. Hyacinth moaned and hit himself in the forehead with his hand, as if attempting to knock the stupidity out of his head.

Meanwhile, the gaze of each of the Four was drawn to an object standing behind Sissrath's desk and just to the right of the tall glass picture window. The object that commanded their attention and transfixed them was a polished, shiny, carved wooden branch. It bulged at the top as thick around as the upper arm of a grown man with strong biceps and it tapered down to a thickness of no more than the wrist of a young girl at the bottom. The branch was held upright in a metal stand. Bristling feathers that stood out more than six inches in each direction from the wood decorated the top of the branch. An expert hand had woven these red, yellow, blue, and green feathers into a wiry material attached to the branch by wooden struts. Feathers covered at least a foot at the top of the branch, sticking out from it in all directions. Below the feathers, small shells hung down on strings in a cascade. The wood of the branch itself had faces of people and animals carved into it. The faces peeked out from strands of the wood that entwined around the main branch like vines, or smaller branches, or sinews of a mighty muscle. The Four had no question in their minds about the identity of this object. They knew they gazed upon the Staff of Shakabaz.

Shakabaz reminded Sonjay of the *kahilis*, or giant standards of the great kings and queens of Hawaii. He had studied about them at school.

The kings and queens used them as royal scepters, and the size and magnificence of the *kahilis* increased the perceived size and magnificence of those who held them. The Bishop Museum in Honolulu housed a whole room full of them. Sonjay had a book filled with pictures of the Hawaiian *kahilis*.

Denzel, who could easily judge sizes and distances at a glance, figured Shakabaz stood more than nine feet tall. It looked extremely heavy.

Doshmisi could hear a faint murmur coming to her from the wood itself and the faces carved into it seemed to move. "Do you hear it?" she whispered to Maia.

"I hear it," Maia answered. "It's calling."

"Me too," echoed Denzel.

"I hear the call too," Sonjay said incredulously.

Doshmisi sensed the spirit of the Staff of Shakabaz, as well as the spirit of the legendary tree from which it came. She sensed it so strongly that she took a step in the direction of the staff. But the Special Forces blocked her path.

"Impressive, isn't it?" Sissrath hissed, gesturing toward Shakabaz with his hand.

"Beautiful beyond all beauty," Maia whispered.

Just then Hyacinth let out a high-pitched screech that pierced the air and penetrated the night. The others jumped and winced at the pain in their ears. Sissrath stepped forward and struck Hyacinth across the face and he fell silent as he hung his head.

"Oh shut up," Sissrath told Hyacinth. "Your mangy dogs can't hear you in this place. You're beyond help. Tell me something, did you really believe that a beauty such as Amaranth would find you attractive?" Sissrath threw back his head and laughed.

Just at that moment, the glass picture window smashed to bits as several balls of white fur hurtled through it. Hyacinth's favorite wolves, leading the rest of the pack, came flying into the room. His screech had called them to his aid. Sissrath reached for Shakabaz while his Special Forces attempted to secure the prisoners as the wolves poured into the room. They leapt at the throats of Hyacinth's enemies and bared their long teeth in fury. They brought down four of the guards. Two of the wolves snarled and growled at Sissrath, who removed Shakabaz from the stand and tilted it in their direction.

Cardamom held his hands out in front of him and muttered under his breath. Sissrath instantly turned on him, interrupting him mid-incantation, by pointing Shakabaz at him. Denzel, with his quick reflexes, ripped the mirror off the wall behind him and held it in front of Cardamom as a shield just as a blast of electric light flew from Shakabaz. The electric light bounced off the mirror and hit Amaranth full in the chest. She slumped to the floor, where one of the wolves pounced on her and sunk his teeth into her neck. All of this happened in a heartbeat. As soon as the wolf bit into Amaranth, one of the guards stabbed it in the side with a knife. Guards stabbed wolves as Maia and Honeydew screamed in horror. The white fur of the wolves grew sticky with blood and the floor became slippery and littered with the bodies of the Special Forces and the wolves. None of the wolves dared attack Sissrath while he held Shakabaz. As the Special Forces killed the outnumbered pack that had attacked them, a few of the wolves fled through the broken window. The skirmish ended swiftly. Hyacinth knelt beside a wolf body and stroked the soft fur of the wolf's side in despair, tears running down his cheeks.

Sissrath kneeled on the floor and held the hem of his gown to Amaranth's neck to stanch the flow of blood.

"I want them in the dungeon," Sissrath ordered hoarsely. "Now! Take Amaranth to her room. Bring that one with Amaranth," he pointed at Doshmisi. "She is the healer."

The guards rapidly hauled everyone but Doshmisi back out to the courtyard.

They rushed Doshmisi up a flight of stairs and into a large room filled with heavy, old furniture. Intricate tapestries depicting enchanters in long robes hung on the walls. Sissrath carried Amaranth up the stairs while pressing her bleeding neck against his arm. He placed her on the bed with a gentleness that Doshmisi would not have guessed him capable of showing. He pressed a towel against the wound. "Bring hot water and more towels," he roared. The Special Forces jumped to obey.

"You," Sissrath ordered Doshmisi, "Healer; come here."

Doshmisi approached the bed.

"This should be easy for you, with your powers," he snarled at Doshmisi.

Slowly, Doshmisi unstrapped her herbal and laid it on Amaranth's chest. The pages riffled and flapped and then fell open. Sissrath leaned over to look at the open page. "Useless," he cried. "Absolutely useless piece of junk! It's blank."

Doshmisi looked at the page in confusion; it didn't look blank to her. It had a recipe on it. "I can read it," she said. Then it occurred to her that Sissrath could not see any words in the book. At the same time, Sissrath also understood that the knowledge of the book would not open to him. "Cursed book! Tell me what it says," he demanded.

Doshmisi scanned the short recipe. Her eye fell on the last item on the list. It did not surprise her that it was silver spark. She swallowed hard, terrified of the response she expected when she gave the enchanter this news.

"Well?"

"It has a recipe," Doshmisi told him.

"Then let's hop to it," he demanded impatiently.

"But we have a problem," Doshmisi met his eyes with hers and for a single instant he was just another anxious relative, like the many she had spoken to in the clinic at the Passage Circle, and she didn't know how to tell him that Amaranth would not live.

"What problem?" he thundered.

"The herbal offers a recipe that calls for silver spark. And there is no silver spark in the land."

"No silver spark?" he looked truly puzzled.

"You don't know what happened to the silver spark?" she asked. "Your Special Forces burned the silver spark fields at the Passage Circle. It is a delicate plant and only works when it is fresh. But now there is none left. It can frequently save a person whose life hangs in the balance by a slim thread."

Sissrath looked at Doshmisi with loathing, as if she had burned the silver spark fields, while the meaning of her words sunk in.

"Is there anything you can do for her?" he asked gruffly. "I would spare your life if you could save her."

It shocked Doshmisi to realize that even Sissrath had someone whom he cared about. She looked back into the herbal. As often happened with the mysterious book, a sentence she had not seen before seemed to have appeared at the bottom of the page in tiny print. Doshmisi peered closely at the words and her heart leapt. "Yes," she said.

"Yes, what?" Sissrath asked, his voice lifting.

"Yes, there is another treatment. It suggests that we use the life-giving properties of the Staff of Shakabaz."

Sissrath put his head back and howled. It was not the joyous whoop that Doshmisi expected, but instead a howl of torment. He fell on Amaranth then and held her in his arms. Doshmisi did not know what to do.

Finally, Sissrath looked up and spat out the words, "I am bound by an agreement with your dear mother; a deep binding enchantment of the oldest and strongest kind prevents me from using Shakabaz in direct matters of life and death. Even if I knew how to use it to give life, and I don't, your mother's bond denies me that power."

Although Amaranth had betrayed them, put them into the hands of their enemy, Doshmisi somehow could not wish for Amaranth's death. The bleeding had slowed, but Amaranth's once goldeny brown skin had turned pale gray. Her lips seemed tinged with ash and had lost all color. Her nail beds were blue. She remained unconscious and Doshmisi didn't think she would live through the hour. "Perhaps I can use Shakabaz to..." Doshmisi began to suggest.

Sissrath struck Doshmisi hard across the cheek with the back of his hand. "Do I look stupid?" he cried. "You think you can steal Shakabaz from me in a moment of weakness? Well I have no weakness, you fool! I have no weakness!"

Doshmisi reeled under his blow. No one had ever hit her in the face. The violence of it stunned her and knocked all words from her mouth as she cradled her cheek in her trembling hand.

"Make the recipe without the silver spark. Perhaps it will work enough to save her," Sissrath commanded. Doshmisi said nothing as four guards seized her and guided her to the fortress kitchen. They returned her bag, with her herbs in it, to her.

In the kitchen a plump, quiet mountain woman showed her where they kept the medicinal herbs. At first Doshmisi didn't pay any attention to the woman, but after she asked her to boil some water, she couldn't help noticing something familiar about the silent helper. She resembled Honeydew. She had the same arched eyebrows and the same high cheekbones, and most of all, the same eyes. Doshmisi thought about this while she gathered the herbs needed for the brew, crushed them, measured them, and prepared the medicine. She placed the ingredients in a large glass and then poured the boiling water over them. All this time, the kitchen helper sat wordlessly at the table and cracked walnuts, placing the nut meats into a jar. As she waited for the medicine to brew, Doshmisi asked the kitchen helper, "Do you know Princess Honeydew who lives at Big House City?"

The woman looked puzzled as she repeated key words to herself, "Honeydew. Big House City. Princess?" She appeared to be trying to remember something. "I'm afraid I don't know."

When she had prepared the medicine, Doshmisi informed the guards and they took her back to Amaranth. Sissrath sat in a chair next to the bed. He had applied a pressure poultice to the wound, from which blood continued to ooze. Doshmisi used a dropper to slowly feed the medicine to Amaranth drop by drop, like feeding an orphaned baby bird, until Amaranth had swallowed all of it.

Sissrath locked Doshmisi to the heavy metal bed with a chain and left her under guard. "I'm going to my rooms. Send for me if anything changes," he ordered. After he left, Doshmisi wearily laid across the foot of Amaranth's bed where she dozed off, her cheek still throbbing from Sissrath's blow.

While Doshmisi tended to Amaranth, the Special Forces took the other captives down damp stone stairs into the deep belly of the fortress where they threw them into a cold, stone cell. The dungeon cell had no beds or even blankets in it. They sat in a row, leaning their backs against the wall despondently.

Hyacinth apologized yet again, "You would have been much better off without me. I've been disasterment for you. Pure disasterment. I'm totally incompliment."

The princess emitted a sigh and said, "Daddy, I think you mean to say that you're incompetent, which means you aren't good at your job. But that's not true."

"Yes it is. I'm a terrible chief. I trusted Amaranth simply because of her outer beauty and because she flattered me. I put all of us in danger." A big tear trickled out of Hyacinth's eye and drizzled down his cheek.

"We all trusted her," Jasper consoled him. "Not just you."

"And I never should have called the wolves. My beautiful wolves are dead and now I made Sissrath really mad," Hyacinth continued.

"Ask me if I care how mad Sissrath is," Denzel said.

"I never do anything right. Never," Hyacinth wrung his hands.

"At least we have Cardamom with us. Hey, Chief, you made the best choices you could make at the time," Sonjay assured him. "You're brave, and besides that, you're a good person. The opposite of Sissrath."

Hyacinth stared at Sonjay and repeated, "I'm a good person," as if he didn't believe it, as if it had never occurred to him before.

"Yeah," Sonjay assured him, "you're a good person, I mean you treat everyone respectfully, even though you're the high chief and all, and you try to do the right thing. Always."

"It's more important to be a good person than to be a good high chief," Maia said.

"But you're both," Denzel added. "You're a good person and a good high chief. You just need a break."

"He's right, Daddy," Honeydew said, stroking her father's arm.

Hyacinth burst into tears, "No one ever called me a good high chief before."

Cardamom's lips curved in a faint smile, "Well, the Four have pronounced you a good high chief. Now we have to figure out how to extricate ourselves from this mess and place you back on your throne, without Sissrath interfering anymore."

"Oh yes, if only I could be the high chief without Sissrath. If you helpered me instead, Cardamom, I could figurize it out and I think I could do a better job," Hyacinth said hopefully.

"Sissrath has used Shakabaz to put a blocking enchantment on me so that I cannot use my higher powers," Cardamom said. "But we can defeat him without enchantment. I know we can. Think, think." The enchanter pressed two fingers hard into the center of his forehead as if this would push a smart idea into his head.

The captives sat side-by-side, leaning on each others' shoulders, thinking hard for a way to trick Sissrath or to escape from the situation. But no one had an idea and the night wore on and nothing happened and eventually, one by one, they each drifted off into an uncomfortable sleep propped against one another.

Some time later, while the others dozed, Sonjay swam up from sleep to hear a voice chanting faintly in the distance. A deep, rumbling voice, jagged and resolute. He carefully disentangled himself from Maia on his left and Hyacinth who snored faintly on his right, and crept to the door of the cell. He put his ear against the door. He could hear the voice a little more distinctly. At first he thought perhaps it was the Staff of Shakabaz calling to him. Then he thought the voice sounded vaguely familiar, but he couldn't place it. What did it say? He strained to hear it. Goosebumps rose on the back of his neck because it sounded like the voice kept saying "Doshmisi, Denzel, Maia, Sonjay," over and over again, slowly, deliberately, and with purpose. Who in Sissrath's dungeon would know his name or the names of the others? A prisoner? Why would a prisoner say their names like that? He listened as hard as he could to the faded, tattered voice, until he realized what it was.

Footsteps clanged in the corridor and the voice stopped abruptly. Sissrath himself, backed by his men, flung open the door to the cell, awakening the others. His guards tossed their belongings to the prisoners and Sissrath said roughly, "We depart for Big House City within the hour. The execution of the Four will be the greatest single event of our time and I look forward to mounting the spectacle. I would welcome the presence of the high chief and his daughter as well as the great enchanter Cardamom at this momentous occasion. Consider that a personal invitation."

"How is Amaranth?" Cardamom asked gently.

Sissrath turned on his heel and flew out the door. As he went, he called over his shoulder, "Amaranth is dead."

Cardamom looked sadly at his feet, "She was a gifted enchantress, just led astray, as sometimes happens." Hyacinth nodded gravely in agreement.

The captives looked through their belongings but surprisingly did not find anything missing. Sissrath or his Special Forces had clearly rifled through everything, but apparently nothing in them looked particularly threatening or useful to Sissrath. It pleased Maia to have her water organ and drum back. Denzel had kept the crystal that Violet had given to him hidden in his clothing and in this way had prevented its discovery. He might need it soon to call for help, but he didn't know yet whom he would call or what he would ask them to do. His first concern at the moment was old Crumpet, in his rock-like form, who still weighted down the bottom of Denzel's bag.

Denzel carefully removed Crumpet from the bag and put him down in the middle of the cell. They all stood around the rock and stared at it.

"I forgot about him," Jasper said.

Cardamom looked at the rock thoughtfully, "I'm afraid to ask."

"Well," Denzel hesitated, "that's actually your brother Crumpet."

This news made Cardamom laugh until tears ran down his face. Between guffaws, he wheezed out, "I knew that. Somehow, I knew that. Oh not again."

"I'm afraid so," Maia finally told him. "And you must change him back."

"Do I have to?" Cardamom asked. "He'll only get himself into trouble again in the shake of a tail. He's safer as a rock. Oh, I suppose I should. It's an easy one for me." Cardamom closed his eyes and, pointing his hands at the rock, he uttered "reformion buffoonus." In a puff of yellow smoke, the rock turned back into Crumpet, full-sized.

Crumpet patted himself all over and with a cry of excitement he gave his brother a tremendous hug. "Where am I? What's happened? Are you freed? Did we kill Sissrath? Oh no, doesn't look like it. We're in prison, right?" he babbled.

"We're at the Final Fortress and Sissrath is about to take us back to Big House City under guard to kill us," Sonjay told him matter-of-factly. "But not you, he's not going to kill you, just the Four. Well, maybe he plans to kill you, but he probably has some other form of creative torture in mind for you. We did manage to rescue Cardamom, as you can see. He's coming with us. You've been a rock for a awhile. Denzel carried you through the Amber Mountains with us to find Cardamom so you could get turned back into a person."

"Denzel carried me here?" Crumpet asked in amazement, choosing to ignore the news that he might face death or torture by Sissrath. He trapped Denzel in a giant bear hug while Denzel grimaced because Crumpet smelled somewhat like old apples and dirty socks after spending so much time in the bottom of Denzel's knapsack.

"I felt responsible since I didn't shoot Sissrath like I was supposed to," Denzel said, wincing and prying Crumpet off.

Just then, some of the Special Forces arrived to escort them from the cell. And of course it gave the soldiers a shock to discover Crumpet with the prisoners. People sometimes escaped out of prison cells, but they had never seen anyone escape into one.

They took the captives back upstairs, to the courtyard of the fountain and the many statues. There they chained them together at the feet, waist, and hands, like prisoners on a chain gang. When Sissrath saw Crumpet he remarked, "Ah yes, I knew that rock looked familiar. Frankly, you looked better as a rock."

Crumpet started to reply, but Cardamom clapped his hand over his brother's mouth.

Guards brought Doshmisi from somewhere within Sissrath's citadel. She had not slept much and she had circles under her eyes. A bluish welt had appeared on her cheek. Despite her weariness, she stood proudly at the top of the stairs when she emerged from the building. Her short hair covered by her embroidered kufi hat made her neck look long and her dolphin earrings dangled gently from her ears. She had the wise eyes and compassionate face of one of the Four. Jasper remembered what she had looked like when she had first arrived in the land, tentative and timid, and he looked at her where she stood now and admired the change in her. He flinched when he saw the welt on her cheek.

"Sissrath," Doshmisi demanded. The enchanter looked up from gathering his followers and belongings, including the Staff of Shakabaz, which was quite unwieldy to take on a road trip. He turned, startled from his activity, when Doshmisi called his name. "Sissrath," Doshmisi repeated boldly, "a kitchen maid helped me last night. I would like to take her with us to Big House City."

A devilish smile slowly curved on Sissrath's lips. "You would, would you? How sweet. Well, I think that's actually a superb idea. I wish I had thought of it myself." He sent the Special Forces to fetch the kitchen maid and then he chained Doshmisi to the end of the line of prisoners. "Some healer you are," he snorted as he walked away.

Doshmisi squeezed Honeydew's hand and said to her, "I have a feeling about the woman who helped me in the kitchen. Tell me if you know her." The shy woman appeared at the top of the steps, blinking in the bright morning sun. At the sight of her, Hyacinth sunk to his knees and a sob came from his throat.

"Daddy, what is it?" Honeydew asked in alarm.

"Look," he croaked. Honeydew squinted against the sun and peered up the steps at the woman, who gazed serenely down on them showing no sign of recognition.

"Is it? Is that?" Honeydew choked.

"Saffron," Hyacinth called. "Saffron, it's me. Hyacinth."

The woman, Saffron, descended the stairs and stood before Hyacinth and asked him kindly, "Do you know me? Do I know you?"

"A memory enchantment," Cardamom informed the others quietly. "Sissrath has put her under a memory enchantment. She can't remember you."

Hyacinth looked bewildered.

"What did you eat for dinner last night?" Cardamom asked Saffron.

She looked at him vacantly, twisted up her face in thought, and told him, "I just can't recall." Then she smiled, "But whatever I ate, I found it tasty and I liked it."

Sissrath threw back his head and roared with wicked glee. "She was always too smart, so I recalibrated her a bit. Now she suits my tastes. She's always a blank slate rubbed clean. I think you'll enjoy her. She's more your speed now, Hyacinth."

"How could you do such a thing to the high chieftess of Faracadar?" Crumpet burst forth in fury. Cardamom reached out to restrain his brother, but he couldn't grab him fast enough. Crumpet held up his hand and threw an enchantment at Sissrath, except, just as in Sissrath's room in the Big House, the spell turned backwards on Crumpet, traveling up his arms and arriving at his head with a popping sound. Where Crumpet had stood, a small gold-colored chicken scratched the ground with bright red claws.

"You must do something about that brother of yours," Sissrath called to Cardamom, who had covered his face with his hand in disgust. "Shall I change him back?" Sissrath grinned.

"Don't bother," Cardamom replied. "He'll just do it again. Would you bring me a chicken cage?" The devastating affect that Saffron had on her family and Crumpet's antics had now put Sissrath in a rather good humor so he obliged Cardamom by providing a chicken cage. Meanwhile, Sissrath placed Saffron on a tiger and patronizingly told her she must go on a journey, while Hyacinth and Honeydew watched with helpless frustration.

"I guessed that she was related to you," Doshmisi told the princess quietly, "she looks so much like you. I didn't mean to cause any pain."

"Don't worry. She's better off coming with us," Cardamom whispered to Doshmisi and Honeydew, "because I can reverse a memory enchantment easily if I have my higher powers restored, and we're going to find a way to escape. We have to." His determination encouraged the others. "Think, we have to keep our wits about us and think."

Sissrath turned the tigers out to the path that led across the mountain pass to the upper shore of Akinowe Lake. They could not proceed with any speed since the prisoners as well as many of Sissrath's men traveled on foot. But now that he had captured his prey, Sissrath did not seem in a hurry. Perhaps he still grieved for Amaranth and his distraction with this kept him from forcing them to make haste. Although he did not seem like the kind of person who would grieve long for anyone. More likely he simply savored watching the captives as they suffered the grueling march through the mountains.

Hyacinth whispered to Cardamom, "I thought my wife abandled me because I wasn't smart enough for her, and instead Sissrath had kidnicked her."

"Kidnapped. High Chief, she loves you very much. She never would have abandoned you of her own free will," Cardamom replied. "When I regain my higher powers, I'll set her right."

They traveled on a beautiful day, clear and fresh, with the heavy fragrance of flowers in the air. Despite the fact that Sissrath had chained them to each other, the travelers felt their spirits lift with the beauty of the forest. It gave them hope to have Cardamom with them. Maybe he would think of a way to thwart Sissrath or at least escape from him. The Four were encouraged to hear the call of Shakabaz whispering to them from time to time.

Princess Honeydew could not help smiling to herself as she stole glances at her mother riding high on a tiger, with Crumpet the chicken in a little wooden cage strapped behind her. Honeydew had almost forgotten how her mother looked and sounded. It delighted her to see her mother again, even if Saffron couldn't recognize her own daughter.

Sissrath led his caravan through the mountains for three days. Preoccupied, he paid little attention to his prisoners. He set up a tent each night and retired to it alone. He left the prisoners heavily guarded and never unchained them from each other. Saffron cooked dinner for them in the evenings. Bone weary by nightfall from walking all day, they slept soundly. On the morning of the fourth day they wound their way around the rim of Akinowe Lake with a warm summer rain soaking them. That night they made camp in the fragrant Marini Hills. The Four and Jasper thought back to the last time they had traveled through these hills. So much had happened since then.

The trees spoke in their language to Doshmisi, telling her to keep hope alive. She took comfort in their communication. They sang her to sleep when darkness fell. She awoke later in the blackness of deep night to find a tiny hand covering her mouth. A tiny voice whispered, "We can help, don't make a sound, no sound no sound." Doshmisi did not move. She knew immediately who had wakened her. Bumblebee danced in front of her with a wide grin on his face and pointed next to him, where Sonjay stood, unchained and free.

Then Doshmisi saw Maia in the arms of a man with long dreadlocks. He rubbed her back noiselessly in happiness. Doshmisi recognized him as one of Maia's drummer friends from the Passage Circle. The sprites released Doshmisi from her shackles, and led her away from Sissrath's encampment. "Quickly, quickly," the sprites repeated in their tiny, hushed voices. Doshmisi ran behind them, not looking back. The sprites stopped in front of a huge oak tree. Bumblebee touched the trunk with his hands and whispered "in the name of Shakabaz." The tree's branches sighed in the breeze and then suddenly it opened at the base, between two large roots, with an enormous creaking sound. The sprites scurried into the entrance revealed by the parted roots and the Four followed them. The tree snapped shut behind them.

They scurried down a dimly lit corridor that tilted into the ground sharply. Down they went until the corridor opened into a great underground town square, with passageways leading from it in all directions and small cozy homes embedded in the earth around it. Sprites filled the square and cheered when the visitors arrived.

Not until she entered the square and paused for breath did Doshmisi look around her and realize that not all her traveling companions had escaped. She saw Denzel, Maia, and Sonjay. And there was Jasper. But it appeared that the sprites had not freed any of Sissrath's other prisoners. Doshmisi's heart sank. What would Sissrath do to the others when he found the Four missing?

"Isn't it wonderful?" Maia shouted to her sister above the rejoicing. "The drummers are in hiding here and they brought the sprites to free us."

"What about the others?" Doshmisi exploded. She rounded on Bumblebee, who was gleefully accepting congratulations coming noisily on all sides from his followers. "Why did you leave the others behind?" Silence dropped like a curtain around Doshmisi as sprites stopped rejoicing and stared humbly at their feet. Bumblebee looked hurt.

"Why didn't you rescue everyone?" Doshmisi demanded.

Maia's drummer friend stepped forward, "You must understand, sprites never allow people in their home. But they took in the drummers of the Passage Circle after the attack. Taking us in was a very generous and courageous thing for them to do and they only did it because of the precarious and dangerous times we live in. This night, they agreed to rescue you. The Four. They even brought your guide, because they trust him. But to ask them to trust enchanters and royals, well, that is too much to ask. It could not be done."

"Dosh, be grateful," Denzel pleaded with his sister. "The sprites have risked their lives for us. Now that we are free we can form an army. We can fight Sissrath. We can help the others."

Sonjay took Doshmisi's hands in his and looked up into her face with his earnest brown eyes, "Poor Dosh, always thinking about everyone else; just take a minute to be happy that you are free, free to do something. We can win this. But first we must show our gratitude to these sprites, who bewitched Sissrath's Special Forces to save our lives."

Sonjay was right. Doshmisi took off her woven cap and made a slight curtsy to Bumblebee and told him, "I'm sorry I yelled at you; thank you for your brave rescue." Bumblebee absolutely beamed. The little sprites beamed. Then one of the drummers began to tap on his drum and the others joined him in an instant, and Maia produced her own drum and sat down on the spot, and before Doshmisi could blink, the sprites started dancing and bumping and bouncing to the infectious beat of the drummers.

Meanwhile, aboveground, Sissrath awoke in the Marini Hills to find his prize snatched from his grasp. In his rage, he tore up the forest. He knew that the remaining captives had nothing to do with the escape. It was clearly the work of sprites. Sprites had robbed Sissrath and in his fury he bashed and shattered his way back and forth through the forests of the Marini Hills. Finally, unable to unlock the secret of the entrances into Spriteland, Sissrath returned to Big House City empty-handed and fuming, leaving a trail of damage in the forest behind him. He could do nothing but wait for the Four to make a move so that he could capture them again. The next time he would not stand on ceremony. He wanted the Four dead and he would take care of it as soon as he had the chance.

Chapter Eighteen

Satyagraha

Under different circumstances, the Four and Jasper would have had the time of their lives staying with the sprites in their magical land under the forest, but they could not enjoy the pleasures of Spriteland because they were worried about Cardamom, Hyacinth, the princess, Saffron, Crumpet, and the many people of the land suffering under Sissrath. What if they couldn't figure out a way to defeat Sissrath? They felt like they had missed something important, something that could help them. But they couldn't see it. It was frustrating and frightening.

Sonjay repeated Cardamom's word "think, think, think," to himself all day long. They knew that Cardamom believed that if they thought hard enough, they would know what to do. But nothing they thought up seemed powerful enough or big enough or strong enough to overpower the absolute evil of Sissrath. While they struggled to figure out what to do, they received tender care from Bumblebee's people.

Maia and her drummer friends beat their rhythms with a desperate frenzy day and night. Sprite musicians joined them with flutes and stringed instruments and their own delicate voices. While Maia drummed, Denzel and Jasper investigated every device and gadget used in Spriteland, from grain mills to water pumps, in search of an idea for some kind of weapon that might work against Sissrath. While Sonjay accompanied Bumblebee wherever he went, his mind kept returning to the problem of defeating Sissrath, the problem he couldn't solve.

Restless and anxious, Doshmisi could not concentrate on any activity. She sat alone for long hours by the side of a peaceful cove of water fed by an underground mountain spring. The roots of trees hung down from the forest above into the roof of the cavern that arched over the cove. In this place, if she sat perfectly still beside the water with her eyes closed and cleared her mind of thoughts, she could receive the communication of the trees.

For three days she sat in stillness in the cove, sending one question only to the trees, "How do we free the land from the grip of Sissrath?" She discovered that, not surprisingly, trees take a long time to consider a question and to provide an answer. Three days is shorter than the blink of an eye to a tree, who lives for thousands of years. Doshmisi forced herself to remain patient. She forced herself to sit quietly and wait for the trees to communicate. But their suggestion, when it finally came, disappointed her because it did not seem helpful in the least. The trees told her to go ask the whales. She had not expected this. Why couldn't the trees provide a solution? They were wise beyond measure. But, if they said to ask the whales, then she would obey their instructions.

On the evening of their third day in Spriteland, Doshmisi announced to the others that the trees had instructed her to speak with the whales so she intended to disguise herself and travel to Emerald Island.

"A tree told you to ask a whale how to defeat Sissrath?" Denzel asked her incredulously. "And now you're going off to find a whale?"

"I know that you believe in the scientific laws of the universe, Denzel," Doshmisi countered hotly, "and that you think that you can invent a weapon or devise a military attack that will destroy Sissrath. But that way hasn't worked so far. Clever weapons and hard battles are not the only way. I think the trees know another way to fight, a way of the spirit. I want to hear what the whales say. I can't just stay here and hide and rack my brains for an idea. Maybe while I'm gone you'll come up with something and maybe not. Maybe I can bring something back that will help." Doshmisi stood firm in her resolve to seek the whales.

"Then we're going with you," Denzel insisted.

"Oh no," Bumblebee interjected in alarm, "very bad idea. Bad, bad. Very bad. Mister Jasper talk them out of it. They'll all be captured again. All. Captured." The little sprite leader tugged on his long beard in worry.

"You know he's right. The Four together stand out like an elephant in a petunia patch. I'll go with her and the rest of you stay here and see what you can come up with," Jasper agreed with Bumblebee.

But Doshmisi put her hand on Jasper's arm. "No," she told him, "I have to do this alone. It's OK. I know the way. If I leave at dawn tomorrow I can make Emerald Island before dark. I'll use the color change powder and dress like a boy. If Sissrath does find me, then at least I will know that the rest of you are here together and that you'll try to rescue me."

Jasper smiled at his determined friend. "You'll need a tiger," he said softly.

"You think she should go?" Denzel rounded on Jasper.

"I think she's one of the Four and she knows what she needs to do," Jasper answered. Doshmisi could have kissed Jasper for taking her side.

Denzel looked from one to the other of them. "OK," he said reluctantly, "you the man, Jasper. I told you I would listen to your advice and I will. But I don't like this one bit. Here," Denzel unbuttoned his shirt and removed his armor vest, "wear this at least." He held the vest out to Doshmisi.

"Please," he pleaded, "it will make me feel better."

Doshmisi took the vest.

Maia sent the drummers to find her sister a tiger.

She took with her some food and water. She left her herbal behind in Maia's care. She wondered long and hard whether or not to take the amulet and in the end decided she had better wear it, even though it was a dead giveaway of her identity. She borrowed some of Jasper's clothing and wore Denzel's armor vest.

As the gray-blue mists of dawn embraced the Marini Hills in the early morning, Bumblebee and Jasper escorted Doshmisi to one of the entrances to Spriteland to point her in the direction of the Passage Circle and the sea. The instant they emerged from Spriteland, a flutter of wings engulfed them as a brightly colored bird perched on Doshmisi's shoulder and rubbed his head joyously against her cheek. It was Bayard Rustin, of course! Doshmisi laughed with happiness at the sight of him.

"You just don't quit," she told the bird as she stroked his head. "You can't come with me today, but if you go with Jasper, he'll take you to Sonjay and the others." The bird seemed reluctant to be passed off to Jasper, but he went obediently.

Doshmisi solemnly embraced Jasper and bent down to embrace little Bumblebee. With a quick wave they returned to the arms of the tree roots and disappeared. Doshmisi pulled her large gray cloak around her, hiding her face in the deep hood, and set off toward the open sea. Her tiger, Brianna, carried her swiftly and silently out of the hills and down the slope to the Passage Circle, then along the edge of the circle and out to the shoreline. She reached the sea even before the fog had lifted from the ground for the day. As Doshmisi approached the bridge to Gull Island, she discovered a guard posted at the entrance. This was a new development. No guards had stood at the entrance to the bridge the last time they had traveled to the islands. A makeshift little shack housed three uniformed officers. It was so early in the morning that the bridge was deserted.

Doshmisi drew to a halt at the little guardhouse. Fortunately, the officers were not Sissrath's Special Forces, but just some of the regular army, young people from outlying circles sent to serve at Big House City most likely. Doshmisi told them she was going to visit her mother on Emerald Island. They didn't even think to question her. They waved her through sleepily as they sipped hot cocoa in the brisk morning air. They had no reason to mistrust her. She rode across the bridge to Gull Island and without stopping continued on to Seal Island, where the bridge guards were equally as friendly and disinterested. On the edge of Seal Island, Brianna had a break from carrying her passenger while they waited for the ferry. Doshmisi could see it coming across the water. A flock of skeeters flew overhead and circled in the sky above the incoming ferry. Doshmisi pulled her hood further over her face. The skeeters made her nervous, but they continued on their way without stopping and she felt confident that they had no clue who she was.

When the ferry arrived, it docked and unloaded. By now it was the middle of the afternoon and Doshmisi couldn't wait to get far enough out to find the whales. The closer she got to the whales, the more she felt hopeful that they would give her the key to Sissrath's destruction. Perhaps they knew a secret weakness of the great enchanter that would cause his defeat.

She boarded the ferry. As it sliced through the water it flung up a salty spray that felt good on Doshmisi's face. She eagerly scanned the distance for whales. None appeared, but she soon heard the silly singing of the dolphins and sighed with relief that she could still understand the Seaspeak of the water creatures. She would have loved to see Fern and to spend the night in the comfort of the Willow-wisp Inn, but she dared not allow herself to go where anyone could recognize her. So she rode out to the far shore of Seal Island, facing Dolphin Island, released Brianna, and sat far up on the beach, gazing out at the water. She had perhaps one more hour of sunlight. Was she far enough out toward the ocean to hear the whales? Maybe she needed to go on to Dolphin Island in the morning?

Doshmisi wrapped her arms around her knees and huddled into her cloak. She had found a secluded, rather rocky spot, away from the nicer beaches where people might come for an evening stroll. She sat alone and apart, waiting for any sign of whales. Her thoughts wandered to Mama. She remembered Mama in her green apron with the sunflowers all over it, cooking dinner in the evening while Doshmisi and Denzel did their homework on the kitchen table. Maia would be practicing the piano and Sonjay would be outside playing basketball down the street. Mama would poke her head out of the open window and call to him when dinner was ready. The sound of the piano, the sound of her brother and his friends playing in the street, the smell of spaghetti sauce, the peacefulness. The familiarity. That's what love feels like, Doshmisi thought as she hugged her knees to her chest. Her worries back then had been so small compared to her worries now. Saving Faracadar from the clutches of Sissrath. She closed her eyes tight and sent her thoughts out over the water. She called to the whales with her thoughts.

How long had she sent her thoughts across the water before she saw that first spout out in the distance? As the greenish ball of the setting sun fell to meet the sparkling waters of the ocean, she could definitely see sprays of water spurting up as whales spouted from their blowholes.

She couldn't tell how many. It seemed like a lot of them. The water lapped loudly at the shoreline with rougher waves caused by the presence of the large creatures.

The light in the sky faded and the horizon blended into the ocean, with the clear blue of night spreading like spilled ink above and the glittering stars intensifying in color. Although she could understand the Seaspeak of the dolphins, she couldn't speak it. She also could not converse with the whales in Seaspeak so she didn't know how to tell them why she had come.

We know why you have come.

You cannot find the key.

Two voices spoke together, one like a song, a cheerful female voice, that sounded like a brook tumbling over rocks, the other deep and booming like the waves themselves, heavy and full of meaning. The voices twined together in Seaspeak, dancing a duet as they communicated.

You will never conquer while you seek to conquer.

No change will come while you seek to destroy.

Creation brings change.

The new circle begins the new way.

Dang, Doshmisi thought to herself, they're speaking in poetry. She had never been good at figuring out the meaning of poetry. It had too many meanings. She should have known they would speak like this and that even though she understood the words, she wouldn't be able to figure out what they meant. But just as she thought this, the double-braided whale voices encouraged her.

Trust yourself.

Trust your ability to understand.

She closed her eyes against the ocean, the beach, the evening, all thoughts, and tried to let the words of the whales be the only thing in the world that she knew for just this instant.

Negative energy feeds the spirit of evil.

Negative thoughts and deeds; destructive and hurtful actions feed the spirit of evil. And the power of evil grows like a strangling tumor as it feeds.

Positive energy feeds the spirit of good.

Positive thoughts and positive deeds; creation and loving actions feed the spirit of good. And the power of good grows like abundant love as it feeds.

Violence and destruction will never defeat evil. Violence only makes more violence. Violence cannot defeat evil because it IS evil. You cannot fight evil in combat, you can only move it to another place. You must uproot evil. You must transform it. Use goodness as your tool and love as your shield, destroy no life, destroy no shred of creation. Destroy nothing. Only heal and create anew.

Transform evil.

With purely positive energy.

The whale voices fell silent. Doshmisi opened her eyes and looked for the spouts of water out at sea. The beach had grown completely dark now. She ran to the water's edge. But she could see nothing in the water. "Come back," she called in desperation. She ran frantically up and down the beach, shouting and waving her arms. "I don't understand. Please. Come back." But the whales had gone.

Doshmisi stood still and gazed across the water for a long time before she trudged wearily back to her spot among the rocks and burrowed into a sandy niche with Brianna for the night. She slept curled up with her tiger, and awoke stiff and despairing at first gray light. She knew that the whales had nothing more to say. She could chase them out to the far tip of Whale Island, to the edge of Faracadar, and they would tell her no more than they had already told. But what did it mean? Defeat Sissrath with goodness and love? Goodness and love wouldn't cut it. Sissrath would shoot them down. How did you use purely positive energy against overwhelming evil?

She turned the words of the whales over and over in her mind as she rode the ferry and traveled the long distance back across islands and bridges to the beaches that licked the edges of the Passage Circle, and she wondered at the words of the whales as she ascended into the Marini Hills, where she entered the forest. The trees around her celebrated her return and she could sense their delight as they rejoiced that she had received the words of the whales. They seemed oblivious to her mood and her inability to decipher the meaning of what the whales had spoken.

She returned to the spot where she had emerged from Spriteland and waited there until complete darkness fell. Then she heard voices below the tree and the roots separated and sprung open to reveal Jasper, Denzel, and Bumblebee, who stared at her in shock since they had not expected her to return so quickly.

"You went out to Emerald Island and back?" Denzel asked.

"I told you she'd do it," Jasper pummeled Denzel's arm playfully. "You owe me a skateboard." He turned to Doshmisi, "What did you find out? What did they say?"

Bone-weary and disheartened, Doshmisi answered, "I'll tell you with the others. The whales spoke to me alright, but I haven't a clue what they said."

"You didn't understand the Seaspeak?" Jasper asked.

"No, I understood the Seaspeak well enough," Doshmisi answered.

"You don't remember what they said?" Bumblebee's eyes grew wide.

"No, I remember. I just don't get it." Doshmisi patted the little sprite on the shoulder. "I could use a good meal. Do you have any soup made down there?"

"Oh yes, yes, good soup." Bumblebee hopped from one foot to the other. "Very good soup. Come. Soup."

When Doshmisi arrived in the central chamber of Spriteland, a crowd of hushed voices followed her. The crowd parted to let Maia and Sonjay through to her. Everyone turned to her with hope in their eyes. Not too long ago, their looks of respect and awe would have flattered and pleased her and made her feel important, but now she felt a terrible weight of responsibility and dreaded letting them down by telling them that she had learned nothing.

Bumblebee ordered soup and bread brought for Doshmisi. Maia returned the herbal to her sister and Doshmisi strapped it back around her waist. It felt good to wear it again. Its very presence gave her courage. While she ate, the others leapt into a conversation that had obviously been going on for the past two days. They were trying to figure out how to fight against the army at Big House City when the people had nothing more than kitchen knives and pitchforks and tools not meant for battle. Denzel maintained that they should build weapons. He wanted to contact Mole and try to make a prototype for a cannon or something that would shoot an explosive device, which was previously unheard of in Faracadar.

"I think that with a few strong cannons, and one group of fighters with something like bows and arrows, we could disorient Sissrath's army. We have sheer numbers on our side. Maybe I can put together a gun. If we bring in an army, from all over the land, with whatever household tools can serve as weapons, and we combine that with cannons and bow-and-arrow regiments then even without guns we would have strength in numbers, right?" Denzel thought out loud.

Jasper looked skeptical, "But it's going to take time to make cannons and bows and arrows. What if Sissrath discovers us? What if you can't invent a cannon that fast?"

"Maybe we could bring other battery makers here and make a weapons factory," Denzel considered this possibility.

Bumblebee shook his head anxiously, "No, no more people in Spriteland," he told them. "No weapons in Spriteland."

Sonjay remained deep in thought, with his eyebrows puckered and his forehead tense. He repeated to himself Denzel's words "strength in numbers."

Doshmisi put down her soup spoon. She knew Denzel wouldn't want to hear it, but the one thing she had understood for sure from the whales was the fact that shooting up Sissrath and his army was not the answer. "Hey," she said to get the attention of the others. "We don't want to be responsible for introducing guns and cannons into Faracadar. That's not why we came. Besides, making more weapons won't work anyway."

"Why not?" All this talk and no action was getting on Denzel's last nerve. He was the only one suggesting any kind of plan at all and everyone else just seemed to want to knock his ideas down as soon as he had them.

"The whales said that violence won't work. Shooting arrows and guns and cannons and whatever is violence," Doshmisi explained. And then she told them everything she could remember of the words of the whales, right down to the end: transform evil with purely positive energy.

After Doshmisi finished talking, the others pondered the words of the whales.

Maia echoed Doshmisi's thoughts when she asked, dumbfounded, "Defeat Sissrath with goodness and love?"

"How is that supposed to work?" Denzel fumed. "He don't play that."

"Exactly," Doshmisi agreed grimly. "What do you think I've been asking myself all day? Sissrath will strangle goodness. He'll crush love. He'll poison positive energy. What do the whales want us to do, walk up to Sissrath with goodness in our hearts? He'll shoot a poison dart or zap us with Shakabaz or whatever else he has up his filthy sleeves and it will be all over."

Sonjay's face cleared and he leapt in the air with a whoop of excitement. "That's it," he shouted. "That's it. That's what the whales told you!"

"To walk up to Sissrath with goodness and love in our hearts?" Doshmisi figured that the pressure of the situation had finally gotten to Sonjay and he had cracked.

"Yes! Yes," Sonjay exclaimed. "That's exactly what we have to do. Don't you get what the whales told you? It's just plain what goes around comes around. That simple."

"What goes around comes around?" Jasper asked in confusion.

"It's a saying we have at home," Sonjay told him.

"It means that you have to treat other people the way you want them to treat you and that the way you act and the things that you do have a way of coming back to you," Maia explained.

"That's exactly it," Sonjay continued. "If you do bad then you get bad back. If you do good then you get good back. As long as we keep using weapons at each other then weapons will keep getting used. We have to break the pattern. That's what the whales told Doshmisi. And that's what I've been trying to figure out. And now I know the answer. We have a stronger weapon than any weapon Sissrath can invent and it's not even a weapon at all."

"What?" asked Denzel, "You've got me on the edge of my seat, man."

Sonjay said one word: "satyagraha."

"Satyagraha?" Denzel repeated.

"Satyagraha?" Doshmisi wondered what it meant.

But Maia remembered the beautiful picture of Dr. Martin Luther King, Jr. at home and she quickly began to piece together in her mind what Sonjay was getting at. She jumped up and gave him a big hug. "Boy, you've got game. That's it. Satyagraha. It's the way. You tell it."

"Go on, what is this stuff, how does it work, and where can we get some?" Jasper prodded Sonjay.

"You have it inside you," Maia told Jasper.

"OK," Sonjay tried to contain his excitement in order to explain. "In the Farland, there was once a great man, in fact, a great chief. Martin Luther King. He taught the people how to resist evil with the power of the courageous, loving spirit, standing up against what is wrong. It is the way of nonviolence and fearless determination. He learned this way from a great leader named Mahatma Gandhi. Gandhi used what he called satyagraha, or truth force. It means that you know the truth in your heart and no one can turn you away from it. You know it so strongly, that you will stand by it courageously to your death, without lifting a finger to harm your enemy."

"So you just go marching up to Sissrath with truth and love in your heart?" Denzel exploded. "He'll kill you."

Maia hopped from one foot to the other, fit to burst with excitement, "No, no, Denzel, think about Dr. King. Think how he did it. He got a lot of people. A huge number of people, to march with truth and love in their hearts. All we need is people. Loving, nonviolent people. And Faracadar is full of them. Farmers and healers and drummers and braiders and children and parents and, well, everyone."

Denzel stared at her in amazement as what she and Sonjay proposed fully dawned on him. He had studied the civil rights movement and the work of Dr. King. One time, Dr. King had inspired the Black people in Montgomery, Alabama to stop riding the buses until they were allowed to sit anywhere they wanted on them. Before that, the Black people had to sit at the back of the bus. But after the bus boycott, when they said they wouldn't ride the bus unless they received due respect, they won the right to sit anywhere. Dr. King did that without firing a single shot. He went to jail for it. But in the end, he won. Maybe Sonjay's idea could work. They could use nonviolent protest just like Dr. King had done. But they would need a lot of people. Denzel whistled through his teeth, "Maia's right. We need a lot of people. In fact, we need everyone."

Jasper stared at Denzel in complete puzzlement. "I don't get it," he said.

"I do," Doshmisi said, her hopes soaring at last. "I understand what the whales told me. If you have to bomb someone or shoot someone or harm someone to turn them from evil then you have lost the battle already because you have become evil yourself. The only way to really win is through nonviolence. A combination of love and courage. Satyagraha has to work. Because if it doesn't, then there's no other way and really we're all lost."

Bumblebee grinned from ear to ear and burst out with "Bad things are still bad even if they make good things happen."

"Exactly," Doshmisi agreed. "Who said that before?"

Bumblebee pointed shyly at Sonjay.

"Me. I said that," Sonjay giggled with delight. "Remember when the sprites took our things to show to the people at the Passage Circle? And when we got them back I told Bumblebee not to steal, even for a good reason. That's what I said. He remembered."

"I remembered," Bumblebee beamed.

"We won't use any weapons at all," Doshmisi told Jasper. "We'll use ourselves and our own courage and the courage of the people. We'll use the satyagraha, the truth force in each of us. But Denzel sure said it when he said we need everyone. And they'll have to be very, very brave. We'll all have to be very, very brave. Because some of us will lose our lives. Perhaps many of us. But Sissrath can't kill everyone."

"You know that we, the Four, will have to stand at the front, to give the people courage," Sonjay told his sisters and brother. The others nodded to show that they understood exactly what he meant and exactly what kind of danger they would face.

"I will stand with you," said Jasper.

"And I," chimed in Bumblebee.

"Now we need to find a way to communicate to the people throughout the land. Someone will have to travel to the Crystal Dome to send a message," Sonjay pointed out.

Denzel cleared his throat. "No, not really. I have a way to communicate with Violet at the Dome right from the forest above us. I just need a little sunlight." The others looked on in amazement as Denzel produced from his pocket the tiny crystal that Violet had given to him and held it out on the palm of his hand for them to see.

"Denzel, you're full of surprises," Sonjay said with admiration.

"Thanks to Violet," Denzel gave credit where credit was due.

From his perch on Sonjay's shoulder, Bayard called out in his clear voice "satyagraha, satyagraha, satyagraha."

Chapter Nineteen

The Battle of Truth

Their bold plan made the travelers too excited to sleep. They stayed up late into the night, discussing exactly what they should say in their message to the people. They had to find a way to explain satyagraha and nonviolent protest simply and convincingly in a short crystal communication transmission. They worked on this for hours.

They decided that they would assemble the people on the beach at the Passage Circle. From there it would take them two days to travel to Big House City. Denzel had his own plans to sneak into the Passage Circle at night to work with Mole to build an amplifier so that they could speak to a large crowd through a microphone. Doshmisi and Jasper discussed crowd control, marching formations, how to keep people from trampling each other, and how to keep a large group of people as safe as possible. They speculated on how many people would actually come.

They had so many things to consider, so many things to plan. What if Sissrath chose to march out from Big House City and attack them on their way to meet him? They must prepare for this possibility. Doshmisi wondered how they would get all the people to agree not to fight but to rely on truth force. How could they get everyone to practice nonviolence? She thought that Dr. King did it by example, mainly. She made up one speech after another in her head. What could she possibly say to the people to give them some sense of what Dr. King and Mahatma Gandhi had accomplished with nonviolence?

At first light, they went up to the surface for Denzel to catch the sun with his crystal so that he could send the message to Violet. They had developed a strong, clear message and had written it down. Denzel read it for the transmission in a mighty James Earl Jones sort of voice. He called for the people to assemble on the beach in five days and to prepare to take back their land with the power of truth. He told them not to bring any weapons.

They planned to start the march to Big House City in five days. They feared what Sissrath would do when he realized that people were on the move all over the land. Surely he would see the crystal communication they had sent to everyone. But they could not anticipate his response so they would just have to wait and deal with new problems as they arose in their path. For the time being, they had no other plan, no other idea, no other hope.

Maia and the drummers drummed up a storm to release the tension in Spriteland. The sprites, by nature timid creatures, intended to march with the people and the thought of this petrified them. Doshmisi borrowed a drum and joined the drumming to take her mind off the call they had sent out to the people. At nightfall, Denzel sprinkled himself with color change powder and he and Jasper slunk into the darkness to find Mole so they could begin their work building an amplifier. They did this for the next few nights, sleeping during the day, and sneaking out to the Passage Circle as soon as daylight fled. After three nights, they arrived at the entrance to Spriteland bursting with the news: people had started streaming into the Passage Circle from everywhere. The roads had swelled to bursting. Throughout the land people had answered the call to come to the beach to march on Big House City with the Four.

"What about Sissrath? Have you heard anything about his reaction?" Doshmisi asked anxiously.

"They say he has shut down communication to and from Big House City and my guess is that he has lied to his army about who we are and why we are coming," Denzel said. "He has to know about this whole thing. I'm sure he has seen our crystal transmission by now. I bet it seems like a big joke to him. I mean think about it. The people planning to confront him with the power of truth? I bet he can hardly wait for us to arrive so that he can shoot us with his darts. We have no weapons, no trained soldiers, no power at all."

"No doubt he's ecstatic," Doshmisi noted grimly. "He expects to get his big chance to finally kill the Four in front of all the people. If he does kill us, you know it would pretty much clinch his power over the land. He and his stinky buddy Compost are probably dancing around in glee."

"That's an image I don't want to have stuck in my mind," Maia shuddered.

"I'll try to communicate with Violet from the Passage Circle tonight," Denzel promised.

"I hope she's safe," Doshmisi worried.

"I hope the Crystal Communication Dome is safe," Maia added.

"Sissrath wouldn't destroy the Communication Dome," Jasper said, "because then he would lose the ability to communicate with his Special Forces wherever they go. And Violet knows more about the Dome than anyone so I don't think he would harm her."

"People from the islands have started camping out on the beach, and today a lot of the People Beyond the Lake joined them," Denzel related. The following day, Denzel returned with the news that Diamond had joined them to work on the amplification system. Jasper' parents had arrived, and Crystal looked well.

Bumblebee awakened the Four before dawn on the fifth day. They wanted to arrive on the beach by sunrise. The Four prepared for their departure in silence, each caught up in their own thoughts. They put on their best clothes, which they had received as gifts from people they had met in Faracadar. Doshmisi wore her herbal and a small shoulder bag with a few herbs and some mannafruit in it. Maia carried her travel drum over her shoulder and her bag with her water organ. Denzel put his bulging knapsack on his back. It had everything under the sun in it. Sonjay carried nothing but a canteen. Bayard perched on his shoulder, as usual. Doshmisi attempted to return the armor vest to Denzel but he wouldn't take it.

"If one of us falls, we all fall. I don't see any point in wearing the vest now. It can't cover everyone," Denzel told his sister. They left it leaning against the wall in Spriteland.

They emerged from Spriteland in the expectant milky blue darkness that precedes the dawn. With Jasper and Bumblebee at their sides and a host of sprites fluttering nervously behind, they descended the hillside to the Passage Circle and the beaches. As they arrived within sight of the beaches, the rising sun crested the horizon out over the ocean, shooting golden rays across the water. They stopped and stared in awe at the people, people, and more people. People filled the beaches as far as they could see. Up and down the coast. Hundreds of thousands of people. The sheer numbers filled the travelers and their sprite companions with pride and wonder.

As the people began to realize that the Four approached from the hill, a tremendous thunder of cheering arose from the sandy water's edge and swept through the people in waves, back and forth, a mighty roar. Denzel pointed out the platform with the amplification system that he had built with Jasper, Mole, and Diamond. "It's portable," Denzel informed them. "We'll take it with us to Big House City."

The Four made their way toward the platform. By now the sun poured over them proclaiming the glory of the new morning and warming the beach under an electric blue sky. Tufts of wispy clouds floated out toward Gull Island in the distance. Island People continued to stream over the sea bridge and pour into the area.

At the platform, Iris from Whale Island waited for them. She embraced each of the Four and whispered to them softly, "Clover did not come. She doesn't leave the island. But she sent me to tell you that she is proud of you for finding another way, one that does not use violence, and she sends her love."

"Jack. What happened to Jack?" Doshmisi asked Iris.

"He came with me. Over there," she pointed down into the front of the crowd where Jack waved enthusiastically at them with both his little hands. They waved back.

Sonjay turned away from Iris and asked Denzel tensely, "How do I use that speaker thing? I need to talk to the people."

Denzel handed Sonjay a microphone and then he bustled around with Mole as they turned the system on. Then he nodded at Sonjay who spoke into the microphone, "Can you hear me?" His voice boomed and echoed out over the ocean, startling him with its magnificent volume.

The people cheered and hollered, "Yes, yes, we hear you, speak to us."

Sonjay looked out at the sea of faces, all different colors, from everywhere in the land. Doshmisi, Maia, and Denzel stood with him, deeply moved by the resplendent sight. They all thought the same thing: these are my people. This land, that had seemed so strange to them only a short time ago, felt like their land and their home.

Sonjay spoke into the microphone that he held in his small but sure hand, "Welcome to all of you. Welcome. Where are my friends Crystal and Granite? Are you out there?" From a part of the crowd several yards away he could see motion and a group of People Beyond the Lake waving their arms. "Crystal and Granite from Debbie's Circle and the People Beyond the Lake out here today, thank you for coming," Sonjay boomed. A tremendous cheer went up for the People Beyond the Lake. "Crystal and Granite, come march with me." Jasper's parents pushed through the crowd, that parted to let them walk up to the platform.

Then Sonjay asked, "Jelly, the innkeeper from the Crystal Dome Circle, Jelly and Mrs. Jelly, and Violet the great communicator, are you out there?" From a different part of the crowd there came cheering and tiny Violet was raised up by some people. Sonjay could see her looking terribly embarrassed where she teetered on her neighbors' shoulders. "Solferinos, thank you for coming today," Sonjay called to them. The crowd gave them a cheer. "Violet, Jelly, Mrs. Jelly, come join me to march today." And they too proceeded through the parting crowd to meet Sonjay.

"I wish that Governor Jay could stand here with us to see this great morning," Sonjay said. "But before we rest, we will free him from his prison cell at Big House City and he will return to his people. Cinnamon and Ginger, wherever you are out there, know that we will free your husbands from Sissrath's prison." After the deafening shouts and cheers died down, Sonjay continued, "Thank you to the people of the Passage Circle and all the Coast People for coming out here today." The crowd cheered for the Coast People.

"Iris from the library on Whale Island stands here by my side and I'm sure that our friend Fern who keeps the Willow-wisp Inn is out there somewhere. Thank you to the Island People, for coming to march with me today. We must also honor the sprites who have left their safe home in the hills behind us to march with us to Big House City. And the people from the distant Wolf Circle in the Amber Mountains, where are you? Is Goldenrod here, and Buttercup, the wife of the brave enchanter Crumpet? Thank you to the Wolf Circle and the Mountain People who came today." As he named each of the peoples, the crowd went wild and Sonjay had to wait for the uproar to subside. When Buttercup pushed her ample body through the crowd to join the Four, she brought Cocoa with her, causing a brief commotion as the dog was reunited with Jasper.

"We are the Four," Sonjay declared. The shouting and hooting began again, but Sonjay shushed the crowd with a wave of his hand. "We are the Four," he repeated, "and we have friends here from every people of this land. We stand together today to march to Big House City to reclaim Shakabaz and remove Sissrath from power. We will take back our land. Not with the same violence that Sissrath has used to rule Faracadar, but with the power of truth in our hearts and with love. Violence only makes more violence. We don't want a land built on violence. If we must kill to defeat him then we are as bad as he is! Everyone here must swear an oath that there will be no violence from this gathering of the people. None. If the person next to you is killed, you will continue to move forward peacefully. You will not act in anger or from fear. You will move forward with love in your heart and the knowledge that we have the truth on our side."

The crowd became so quiet that each person could hear his or her own heart beating. Doshmisi could not even swallow, as she watched the people accept the meaning of Sonjay's words and she wondered if all of them, if the people, if she, Doshmisi, would have the courage and the strength to do this thing.

Sonjay continued, "Put your hands in the air. Everyone." The Four raised their hands. Jasper and Bumblebee raised their hands. Iris and Mole raised their hands. A sea of hands went up in the crowd, rippling to the far edges, as everyone raised their hands. "Swear on everything that you hold dear, on the heads of your children and on the heads of your elders, swear that you will not act in anger. Say it. Say: I will not use violence. I will move forward in peace with love in my heart and truth on my side."

The people repeated Sonjay's words.

The Four could hear his words echoing in the crowd as the people swore the oath. The words reverberated from the ocean before them to the sand dunes behind them. Then everyone fell silent. The weight of the task before them came to rest heavily on their shoulders. Sonjay raised his fist in the air and shouted, "Onward to Big House City with truth on our side!" He turned to the others, sweat poured from his face and soaked the front of his shirt. "Let's do it," he said.

Denzel, Mole, and Jasper scrambled to pack up the sound system and put it on the back of a tiger. It took them no time at all. They had done an excellent job and the system really was portable. Doshmisi gently grasped Sonjay's skinny upper arm. He turned his face toward her questioningly and she said to him, "My baby brother Sonjay: you've become a great leader. Mama would have been very proud of you." Sonjay blinked hard several times and swallowed a big lump in his throat. Bayard, who had perched on Sonjay's shoulder while he addressed the people, butted Sonjay in the ear with the top of his head. The Four headed out in the direction of Big House City, with the multitudes following behind.

Maia and the drummers carried travel drums and they beat a rhythm that spread throughout the crowd as other musicians joined them. Many of the people raised their voices in song. Music surrounded the people as they marched, like a protective shield. It comforted them and gave them courage.

Many families had brought their dogs with them and the Mountain People had their wolves and parrots, as well as other birds. Some of the colorful exotic birds flew together in a flock above the crowd; but Bayard preferred to stay on his accustomed perch on Sonjay's shoulder.

Food and drink passed among the crowd. Those who grew weary or were very young or very old were lifted up onto tigers or on the shoulders of the strong. The people did not falter but continued their journey until nightfall, when they halted and made camp, sleeping wherever they could, wrapped in blankets or sweaters, leaning against friends or tigers or into the cradle of the land itself. While the people slept, Dosh-misi went into the forest with Maia and many of their friends, including Iris, Fern, Jelly, Crystal, Goldenrod, and others. Together they collect-ed mannafruit, enough for the entire multitude, before they finally laid down to sleep for the night. When morning dawned, mannafruit circu-lated in the crowd and the people ate it greedily and joyously. Most of them had never seen or tasted it before and they marveled over it, tell-ing their children to remember it well for the rest of their lives.

After breakfast, the march continued. The people sang while they walked. Maia had them all singing "ain't gonna let nobody turn me 'round." In the late afternoon, as they approached the final hill separat-ing them from the plain that swept down to Big House City, swarms of bright orange, red, and turquoise butterflies arrived in the air above them. "Percival," Maia exclaimed in delight. In their own fashion, the butterflies marched with the people.

The Four, who remained at the front of the march, crested the final hill first. As they looked at the scene spread out below them, their hearts sank. They stood at the top of a long, high ridge. The land sloped down away from their feet toward Big House City. On the plain that stretched across the distance to the city, Sissrath's army stood waiting for them. The bravest and strongest sons and daughters of the land, in full bat-tle dress, with swords, on tigerback, poised at the ready to attack on one word from Sissrath. Behind the army, they could see Sissrath him-self. He stood, clearly visible from the ridge top, in front of the main entrance gate to the city, which rose up behind the army. In his right hand he held the Staff of Shakabaz. Next to him stood Compost and also Cardamom in chains with Crumpet still in the form of a chick-en scratching and pecking beside him. They could also see the royal family, Hyacinth, Princess Honeydew, and Saffron, under guard, just behind Sissrath. A long, long regiment of the Special Forces, also on tigers and in full battle armor with swords in their belts and carrying, clearly visible, the deadly poison dart shooters, extended in both direc-tions from their leader, poised to obey his every command. The sight of the Special Forces terrified and overwhelmed the Four, their com-panions, and the people.

As the weaponless army of the people and sprites flowed up and over the hill with their dogs, tigers, wolves, birds, and butterfly escort, and the fully equipped army beneath them came into view, everyone stopped and gaped in dumbstruck silence.

"They won't do it," Maia said quietly. "The people won't walk straight into that. Sissrath will kill us all."

"Quick, give me the microphone," Doshmisi ordered, and Denzel and Mole scrambled to unpack the system and set it up.

"I have an idea," Doshmisi explained, "remember when Denzel couldn't shoot Sissrath because he looked just like Mama? Well, those soldiers down on the plain there are preparing to attack their own parents, but they don't know it. By the time they figure it out themselves, it might be too late. I'm going to help them figure it out."

Doshmisi summoned Crystal and Granite to her side and handed them the microphone, "Call out to Mica, your son. He must be in that army somewhere. Call out and tell him to put his weapons down and join us. Both of you. Call out to him." Crystal and Granite followed Doshmisi's instructions and pleaded with Mica to come out from the army to join his parents and the rest of their people from Debbie's Circle. Doshmisi scanned the army on the plain with her eyes until she saw what she looked for. One soldier. Far back and to the right. He had taken off his helmet and put down his sword and was breaking ranks, driving his tiger forward toward Crystal and Granite on the ridge.

Doshmisi turned to the people around her and asked, "Who has a child in the royal army? Anyone." A couple stepped forward. Doshmisi took the microphone and handed it to them. They called to their daughter. And then another set of parents called to their son.

As Mica continued to make his way through the army ranks and up the hill toward his parents, Sissrath commanded, "Stop him. Stop the traitor!"

The other soldiers on the plain paused in surprise and confusion. They didn't move, even at Sissrath's command.

Doshmisi passed the microphone to another set of parents, but before they could speak, Sissrath raised the Staff of Shakabaz, tilted it forward, and sent a lightning bolt of energy crackling above the crowd.

Enchanted energy permeated the army and jolted through the people on the ridge top.

For a dreadful second, Doshmisi feared that Sissrath had struck everyone dead. But then she remembered that he could not use Shakabaz to kill them. She opened her mouth to say something, but no words came out. No words came from anyone's mouth. A deadly silence drifted in the crowd. Sissrath had not struck them dead, he had struck them speechless.

Mica, who had reached the strip of land between the army and the people on the ridge top, leapt off his tiger and stood uncertainly, searching the crowd for his parents who had spoken to him through the microphone only moments before.

The army had their swords raised, but they too seemed on the edge of uncertainty, as a few of them broke ranks and headed toward the crowd to find their parents. Everything hung in the balance. Doshmisi held her breath. What could they do now? They couldn't speak. They couldn't encourage the army to join them or tell them that their parents and families stood on the ridge top. What could they do to sway the army?

Suddenly a little brown and tan heap of fur flew out from between the legs of the people on the ridge top and bounded down the slope. Cocoa jumped up on Mica, shivering and barking with all her little might in pure happiness at seeing her beloved Mica again. Mica knelt down to embrace the dog who licked his face wildly, barking with joy. Then Mica walked up the slope as his parents came down to meet him. Sissrath had silenced the people, but not the animals. Cocoa's gleeful yelps reverberated in the still air.

The sight of the family's dog reunited with Mica reminded the army that their families, parents, grandparents, dogs, stood before them in the crowd and they knew they could not attack. The army lowered their weapons, removed their helmets, dismounted, and began walking up the hill to find their families. Cocoa's dash at Mica had tipped the balance. The royal army joined the people's march.

But Doshmisi thought in panic that now they couldn't speak. How could they organize the crowd?

While everyone watched the reunion of Cocoa and Mica, Maia took down her bag, opened her water organ, and filled the little cups with water from her canteen. Her amulet began to glow as she sat down on the ground and put her fingertips on the instrument. The sound of the water organ's exquisite music rolled and swelled over the crowd.

Sissrath frantically shouted orders to his rapidly disintegrating army from his position on the hill behind them. But his words had no effect. He had no microphone and his raspy voice could not compete with the beauty of Maia's music. Finally, in utter frustration, Sissrath raised Shakabaz and banged the heavy standard on the ground, which cracked beneath it as a clap of thunder sounded over the city.

Then Sonjay stepped forward with Bayard on his shoulder. Denzel stood up next to his brother with Jasper at his side. Doshmisi stood beside Jasper. Jack, Ginger, Cinnamon, Diamond, Mole, Crystal, Granite, Fern, Jelly, Mrs. Jelly, Violet, Iris, Goldenrod, Buttercup, and other friends of the Four formed a line alongside Sonjay, Denzel, Jasper, and Doshmisi. They knew without any words passing between them that the moment of truth had come. The line moved out in front, the army parted, the Four and the people behind them headed out to confront Sissrath.

The music of the water organ melted Sissrath's curse of silence. When Maia realized that her voice had returned, she picked up the microphone, took a deep breath, and then she sang out the best song she could think of to give the people the courage they needed. It was Mama's favorite song and it had the famous words written by James Weldon Johnson. Maia sang:

Lift ev'ry voice and sing,
Till earth and heaven ring,
Ring with the harmonies of Liberty;
Let our rejoicing rise
High as the list'ning skies,
Let it resound loud as the rolling sea.
Sing a song full of the faith that the dark past has taught us;
Sing a song full of the hope that the present has brought us;

Facing the rising sun of our new day begun,
Let us march on till victory is won.

Maia sang one verse of "Lift Ev'ry Voice and Sing," and then she fell silent as she concentrated her whole being on the scene unfolding in front of the city gate.

While she had been singing, her sister and brothers, with the line of people alongside them and the enormous crowd of people, sprites, animals, and winged creatures following, had walked with determination and focus, down the hill. Sonjay walked slightly in the lead, and as he and his followers proceeded down the slope, the army parted before them like the waters of the Red Sea. They walked evenly and deliberately toward the raised dart shooters of the Special Forces and toward Sissrath, who tilted Shakabaz toward them menacingly. But Sonjay held out his arms in front of him, bent at the elbow, with the palms of his hands facing outward, his fingers curving in the direction of Shakabaz.

Thunder boomed around them again.

Sissrath shrieked in agony and withdrew his hand from Shakabaz, which had burned him as it began to glow with red-orange light. Then Shakabaz rose up into the air of its own accord and shot bolts of lightning that arched up above the heads of the people. Sonjay continued to move forward, with the army opening before him, his brother and sister by his side, their many friends stretched out in a firm line walking with them, and the people, sprites, and butterflies following them in rows behind.

Shakabaz hung in the air. Sissrath attempted to retrieve it, but each time he raised his hand to touch it, his hand sizzled and he jerked it back. Sissrath could not grasp control of Shakabaz. Sonjay and his followers closed in on him. The enraged enchanter tried to touch the floating staff again, but again it flashed and burned his hands. If he could not control Shakabaz, he could still control the Special Forces. He ordered, "shoot, shoot, SHOOT," a vein in his temple throbbing in fury. The Special Forces let fly a fleet of poison darts that took the first line of people full in the chest, piercing every one of them.

With a row of darts sticking out of his chest, Sonjay continued to walk forward. He did not so much as hesitate or break his stride for a second. When Maia, who remained behind on the ridge top, realized that Sissrath had shot her family she began to weep. Doshmisi looked down at the darts in her chest in disbelief, grasping them between her fingers and pulling them from her skin, as she began to struggle to breathe. Jasper clutched his chest but continued forward. The front line of marchers that had been hit contained many of the friends the Four had made during their time in Faracadar and all these people fell to their knees as they desperately clutched at the darts that pierced their chests.

Sissrath threw back his head and laughed loudly. Compost applauded as if at the theater.

As Denzel looked around him at the darts in Sonjay's chest, and looked at Mole, Diamond, Granite, Crystal, Jelly, and so many other friends pierced with the deadly weapons, a blind rage filled him and he raised his fists, poised to batter Sissrath to death with his bare hands if it was the last thing he did. He would go out fighting, he thought to himself. But, without turning his head, Sonjay said to his brother quietly, "satyagraha; no violence."

Denzel dropped his hands to his sides and then dropped to one knee as the poison began to take effect. Denzel's amulet began to glow with a blinding red light. At the same time, Doshmisi's amulet pierced the air with vibrant green; while up on the ridge top, Maia's amulet glowed iridescent blue.

The second row of people, with terrible bravery, stepped out in front of the fallen first row. Doshmisi felt so proud of the people and wondered if they would continue to come, wave upon wave, until Sissrath killed everyone and ruled over an empty land.

At that moment Honeydew and High Chief Hyacinth broke away from their distracted armed guard and crossed the line to join the marchers. Honeydew ran to Doshmisi and wrapped her cousin in her arms. The second row of people continued to advance on Sissrath where the first row had left off, as the Special Forces fitted fresh darts to their shooters. Tears ran down Doshmisi's cheeks and the princess sobbed. High Chief Hyacinth joined the second row of people that advanced on Sissrath. He tore open his shirt and hollered at the Special Forces, "Go ahead, sink one here," as he pounded his bare chest.

The marchers in the first row had fallen, except for Sonjay, who continued to march forward, the line of darts in his chest making him look absolutely ferocious, until he stood only a few feet from Sissrath. He faced his enemy with blazing eyes as, for the first time since he had arrived in Faracadar, Sonjay's amulet glowed, and it didn't just glow a little bit but it burst forth with eye-shattering brilliance, throwing bright golden rays of light in all directions.

Then Sonjay called, with a shout from his soul, to the Staff of Shakabaz as he reached up and plucked it out of the air where it floated above his head. It came to his hand easily. Without breaking eye contact with Sissrath, he told the enchanter, "I believe this belongs to me." Doshmisi thought to herself that she would never see another moment when Sonjay would be more filled with satyagraha, for the force of truth blazed from his face and filled his presence and his being, just as the golden light blazed from the Amulet of Heartfire.

The people gasped. The light from Sonjay's amulet beamed above his head and joined with the light from the other three amulets to make a resplendent diamond-bright shape, which slowly turned on its axis high above the heads of the people.

Sonjay held the enormous, heavy wooden Staff of Shakabaz as if it were as light as a feather. The Special Forces knew the tremendous weight and bulk and unwieldiness of Shakabaz because they had helped move it many times, so they realized it was a miracle that a little boy could hold it upright. His ability to do so terrified them. They became even more terrified when the row of poison darts suddenly flew out of Sonjay's chest and fell to the ground, useless, leaving no mark on Sonjay's body and not even the tiniest mark on his shirt.

Doshmisi remembered the night that the herbal had told her she could save Amaranth's life with the power of Shakabaz and she called to her brother with her last breath, "Use Shakabaz to heal the others." Darkness began to engulf her.

Sonjay heard his sister's words and he tilted Shakabaz to his right. The darts that had pierced his friends who stood to his right fell from their chests. He tilted Shakabaz to his left, and the darts that had pierced his friends who stood to his left fell from their chests. The darts flew from all the victims and left them clean and whole.

He looked Sissrath in the eye and taunted him, "You are bound by the deep enchantment of my mother so that you can not use the Staff of Shakabaz in matters of life and death, but I can use it in these matters, and I choose to use it for life."

Sissrath's Special Forces broke ranks and wildly fled the reach of Shakabaz. Compost attempted to mount a tiger, but Sissrath shoved him aside and jumped on it himself, then he took off down the hill in a puff of dust. Compost pushed one of the soldiers of the Special Forces off his tiger, mounted, and beat a hasty retreat close on Sissrath's heels. Bewildered and frightened, the Special Forces followed Sissrath and Compost. In a matter of moments, Sissrath, Compost, and the Special Forces had disappeared over the hill as fast as their tigers could carry them, in the direction of the Amber Mountains.

Hyacinth shouted to no one in particular "arrestimate them."

But Doshmisi, who had revived instantly as a result of the healing power of Shakabaz, put a calming arm around Hyacinth and told him, "Never mind him. He has lost his power. Let him go." Then she fell into Princess Honeydew's arms and the cousins laughed and cried at the same time, so happy to see each other safe and sound.

Cardamom held his manacled hands up in front of his face and stared at them in wonder, "I can feel my full powers returning. Sissrath's work unravels." And it appeared that Sissrath's work truly did unravel, because Saffron seemed to have come to her senses as if awakening from a deep sleep and, embracing her husband, she asked, "What happened? What was wrong with me? Where is my baby girl? Are we alright?"

Cardamom reassured her, "We are better than alright, now. Sissrath cast a memory enchantment on you. He has held you in his power at the Final Fortress. Here is your baby," and he pointed at Honeydew. Saffron burst into tears, "Why she's almost a woman; and I've missed everything!" Hyacinth put his arms around the high chieftess and, for perhaps the first time in his life, couldn't think of a word to say.

Sonjay turned to face the people, his people, and he held the Staff of Shakabaz high above his head in victory as cheers rose up all around him. Maia came down from the ridge top to join the rest of the Four.

Cardamom suggested to the royal family, "We should declare today, the thirty-fourth day of Loma, as a holiday throughout the land in every year to come, to celebrate this great event."

As he said these words, the smile faded from Doshmisi's lips. "Did you say today is the thirty-fourth day of Loma?" she asked the enchanter.

"Yes, yes, today is the thirty-fourth. A day that will go down in history forever," he proclaimed.

Doshmisi turned to Denzel, but before she could say a word, her brother spoke, "I know. I heard him. The thirty-fourth day of Loma." Sonjay lowered the Staff of Shakabaz to the ground and turned to Cardamom, "Where is Angel's Gate?"

Cardamom pointed in the direction of the ocean, where they could see a wooden structure set off from the city. The structure stood like a giant doorway to nowhere. "Is today the day of your return?" Cardamom asked.

Maia shook her head, "No, not today. Tomorrow. The thirty-fifth day of Loma."

Cardamom brightened. "Tomorrow is tomorrow and today is today. We still have all night to celebrate before you make your journey home."

"This is our home," Sonjay replied. But even as he said it, he knew it wasn't entirely true. He thought of Aunt Alice and Manzanita Ranch and what it felt like to play basketball all afternoon without having to make any big decisions or take responsibility for a land and its people. Sonjay suddenly felt overwhelmingly tired and he wished to go back to Manzanita Ranch and have a really fun summer and make new friends and eat pizza and look forward to starting fifth grade in the fall.

Cardamom put his hand on Sonjay's shoulder, "Tomorrow is tomorrow and today is today. Let's go celebrate, youngest son of Debbie." Sonjay nodded wearily and put his skinny little brown arms around Cardamom's waist and squeezed.

Chapter Twenty

The Return Of the Four

Sissrath's departure changed everything.

Cardamom transformed Crumpet from his fowl state back into his old self so that he could join the festivities. Overjoyed to find Sissrath gone and his friends and family safe and sound, Crumpet bent his plump wife backwards so far that the tippy ends of her long, straight hair brushed the ground and then he gave her a romantic kiss to end all kisses. After the kiss, Crumpet crowed like a rooster (perhaps he had been a chicken for a little too long). Buttercup couldn't straighten her bent back after that kiss.

"I'm too old for this sort of thing," she scolded Crumpet. Daisy had to help her mother unbend.

Once he restored Crumpet, Cardamom went with Hyacinth down into the Big House Jail and freed the prisoners, including Governor Jay. When they saw their beloved governor again, the Coast People did what they always did to celebrate, they made music. Once the music started, and Maia and her drummer friends got their groove on, the wheels came off and the freedom party kicked into full swing. Saffron took Fern, Jelly, and Mrs. Jelly into the kitchens with her and they supervised a feast like none other while the music and dancing in the courtyards and marketplace square and streets of Big House City swelled and overflowed. Food poured out of the Big House and the people shared whatever they had brought with them from their circles. Big House City filled with rejoicing and the celebration continued on into the night.

Denzel made a new skateboard for Jack and the little intuit gave a dramatic demonstration. A handful of intuits took turns at skateboarding on some makeshift equipment that Denzel, Mole, and Diamond put together for them. Many intuits had died in the preceding weeks and the people would especially need the gifts of this small group of intuits for a time until more intuits were born and came of age.

Maia spent her last night in Faracadar drumming. Denzel spent the night with the rapt attention of Mole, Diamond, Mica, and a group of intent battery makers, as he attempted to describe to them some of the inventions of the Farland, like cars, computers, and telephones. Princess Honeydew gave Sonjay a grand tour of the Big House and the city itself, introduced him to everyone she could think of who held a responsible position in Big House City, and afterward they wound up dancing and singing with the revelers.

Doshmisi melted into the shadows and watched these things unfold around her. She found a table in a quiet corner of the banquet room in the Big House. From there she listened to the drumming and observed the happiness of the people glorying in the feeling of freedom left in the wake of Sissrath's disappearance. After awhile Jasper found her. She knew he would. He slid into the seat next to her and they talked for awhile, remembering their adventures and marveling at how everything had turned out.

When they finally fell silent, Jasper put his arm around Doshmisi and she laid her head on his shoulder and they leaned on each other and watched the people together, until Doshmisi, despite her efforts to keep her eyes open, nodded off to sleep. Jasper awakened her and walked her to her room. At the door, he wrapped his arms around her waist and kissed her, right on the lips. He tasted like sweet peaches. After the kiss, he turned abruptly without a word and ran away. She had never kissed a boy for real before. She was glad to have her first kiss from Jasper.

The next morning, Doshmisi awoke in the Green Room of the Big House. She stretched comfortably between soft, clean sheets in the heavy four-poster bed and allowed herself the luxury of feeling like a chieftess. The sunlight poured in through the tall windows that overlooked the courtyard where only a short time ago she had stood chained to a post in the dead of night. On this morning, festive sounds and cheerful voices rose from the courtyard. She heard tigers roaring and a dog barked. Remembering that dreadful night when Sissrath had captured them and then thinking about the way things had turned out, she thought to herself how easily everything can change in a heartbeat.

She left the comfy bed reluctantly and went to the bathroom where she showered and put on her clothes. She wore her dolphin earrings and her woven green kufi hat. When she descended the stairs to the main dining room she discovered the others already eating breakfast.

"Some of us wish to walk out to Angel's Gate with you," Cardamom told Doshmisi when she joined them.

Sonjay had a plate piled high with purple sausages and little round crusty things. His cheeks bulged.

"I'm afraid to ask," Doshmisi cringed.

"Pond snake and goose-chicken eyeballs," Sonjay sputtered through an overstuffed mouth. "These people can throw down some food."

The travelers and their friends sat around the table like one big family, eating and talking and joking around. Doshmisi glanced at Jasper shyly. He was subdued and didn't say much. She would miss him.

After breakfast the Four prepared for their departure.

Doshmisi went through her belongings and chose what to take back home with her. Not much. The herbal of course. Her water canteen. Some herbs and medicines wrapped in cloth, a couple of shirts, a sweater, a little jewelry. She placed her few remaining pieces of mannafruit on the night stand next to the bed. Then she thought better of it and put them back into her bag as a gift for her aunt and uncles.

Maia put her water organ and a new timber flute given to her by the sprites into her embroidered bag. She would sling her drum over her shoulder. She took nothing else other than the clothes on her back.

Denzel's knapsack bulged at the seams with all manner of unidentifiable objects and he also had a duffle bag full of an assortment of tools and materials and gadgets and pieces of things.

Sonjay had taken nothing with him to Faracadar and he prepared to return the same way. He disappeared after breakfast and came back into the room soon after carrying the enormous Staff of Shakabaz, still able to lift the tremendous *kahili*-like standard as if it had no weight to it at all. He carried it solemnly to Cardamom and held it out to the enchanter.

"Take care of this for me while I'm gone in the Farland, OK? You may need it here. I can't think of anyone better to look after it," he told Cardamom. "Learn how it works and then you can teach me when I return."

Cardamom bowed his head. "As you wish Prince Sonjay. Long have I wished to study the healing powers of the Staff of Shakabaz. I hope I will have much to share with you about its properties when next we meet. I will protect this with my life." Sonjay handed Shakabaz to Cardamom who leaned into the weight of it.

"I think you will have to make a stand for it, the way Sissrath did, but one that honors its beauty more than its power," Sonjay instructed Cardamom.

Cardamom nodded in agreement. Then he asked Sonjay, "May I request a favor?"

"Of course," Sonjay said without hesitation. "Anything."

"Please tell your Aunt Alice..." Cardamom paused and they realized that the great enchanter was blushing an orange color. "Tell her that, well," he cleared his throat.

Honeydew affectionately put a hand on the tall enchanter's arm and interrupted him, "Tell her that Cardamom is still in love with her and he will wait for her until his last sunset."

Cardamom coughed and smiled bashfully, "Yes, yes, to the last sunset, tell her that."

Doshmisi and Maia stared at Cardamom in amazement as it dawned on them that he and their Aunt Alice must be in love with each other. They had never imagined a man in Aunt Alice's life. She never had anyone around. Now they understood why. Her man lived in Faracadar.

"Why doesn't she come to you now?" Maia asked.

Cardamom looked at his feet. Saffron answered, "Because she must stay in the Farland to take care of you."

"Because of us?" Doshmisi exclaimed.

"Your aunt stayed in the Farland so that someone would be there to care for you when your mother's years ended. Alice knew the bargain Debbie made with Sissrath and she knew that the day would come when you would need a new home. But don't you worry. The time is not far away when she will be able to retire here. With Cardamom. Right, old man?" Saffron patted Cardamom's shoulder and he smiled weakly.

"Absolutely right," Cardamom said. "You go back to her and tell her I'm still waiting." He slipped a thin silvery-green metal bracelet with tiny emerald stones embedded in it from his pocket and gave it to Doshmisi. "Give this to her, from me."

The bracelet was beautiful and delicate and Doshmisi knew just how much Aunt Alice would treasure it. She put it carefully into her bag.

Then Sonjay called Bayard to him and he told the bird, "You would probably be much happier staying here until I come back. Princess Honeydew would take good care of you. What do you think?"

The bird peered at Sonjay first from one beady eye and then from the other and then he pronounced, "Sonjay is a fool." He didn't budge from Sonjay's shoulder.

"Oh now I'm a fool?" Sonjay grabbed the bird's beak. Bayard flapped his wings. When Sonjay let go of Bayard's beak, the bird squawked, "There's no place like home," and he pecked Sonjay on the head.

"Bayard's right," Denzel said, "it's time for us to get on up outta here."

The Four, escorted by their friends, walked slowly out to Angel's Gate when the sun stood high in the sky.

"We will eggerly await your returnment," Hyacinth told them when they reached the enormous, unusual wooden structure. Saffron patted his arm tenderly.

Jasper and his parents gave each of the Four a hug. When Jasper hugged Doshmisi, he whispered in her ear, "I will wait for you too." And then he definitely blushed bright scarlet, no mistake.

Maia cried and cried as she embraced her drummer friends again and again, until it became comical, and they laughed and cried at the same time.

The Four walked into the wooden doorway of Angel's Gate. They looked out at their friends. Suddenly Mole ran up to them and pushed a metal box with wires and buttons protruding from it into Denzel's hands. The two of them saluted each other as Mole stepped clear of the doorway.

Sonjay held up his arm, wrist outward, revealing the crescent sign of the enchanter and Princess Honeydew held her arm up as well, revealing her mark that matched his.

For one moment in time they stood looking at each other and then a puff of colorful smoke billowed out of Angel's Gate and the Four vanished from view in Faracadar.

At the very moment that they disappeared from Angel's Gate, Doshmisi, Denzel, Maia, and Sonjay appeared in the little cabin in the woods at Manzanita Ranch. The first pale wisps of dawn swept the sky outside the cabin windows.

"Have a good trip, did you?" Amethyst asked.

"Very good, thank you," Sonjay told her.

"And does Sissrath still strangle that fool of a high chief in Big House City?" Amethyst asked.

"Hyacinth is no fool," Bayard squawked. Everyone laughed with surprise.

"Bayard sure changed his tune!" Amethyst snorted.

"Well, a lot of things have changed," Doshmisi told her, "Sissrath and Compost have run away to hide and Cardamom keeps the Staff of Shakabaz for my brother at the Big House until Sonjay's return."

"What a relief," Amethyst commented. "Then you succeeded and I best be getting home."

"Crystal and Granite have joined Jasper at Big House City right now," Maia told Amethyst. "They left Ruby at home. Please tell her we said hello."

"Thank you my dear. I'll give your message to Ruby and I'm sure the others will tell me everything soon enough."

"Jasper traveled all the way with us," Doshmisi told his grandmother. "He is an awesome guide. And a brave one."

Amethyst glowed with pride. "Well, well, well," she muttered.

"What day is it here?" Sonjay asked. "Is it still summer?"

"Oh my, yes," Amethyst exclaimed, "you have only been gone for one night. Your aunt and uncles await your return right outside. We have had a lovely visit. They just stepped out to look at the sunrise."

Amethyst flung the cabin door open and they could see the figures of their aunt and uncles just beyond the doorstep.

"Aunt Alice, we're in the house," Sonjay called to them.

Aunt Alice, Uncle Martin, and Uncle Bobby hastened into the cabin. As they appeared inside the doorway, they stopped short, staring. Aunt Alice caught her breath sharply while she looked at her nieces and nephews. Doshmisi's hair was cropped short with her cap covering her head. She wore a beautifully woven green and blue tunic over lightweight forest green pants. Her herbal was strapped around her waist and over her shoulder she carried a cloth bag full of herbs. Her dolphin earrings hung at her neck and a small green stud glimmered in her nose. Denzel's hands were worn and nicked with small cuts, and his fingernails were dirty. He had a backpack bursting at the seams on his back and a giant duffle bag full of unidentifiable lumps at his feet. In his hands, he still held the strange box that Mole had given him. He wore a red and black plaid work shirt over his undershirt and his once-prized sneakers were spattered with grease. He had not combed his hair very well and it looked a little lopsided, his eyes shone brightly. He looked the very picture of a genius inventor. Maia's multitude of long braids fell to her waist. She had lost some weight and didn't look heavy anymore. Her travel drum hung over one shoulder and she carried her small embroidered bag with her water organ and timber flute in it. She wore a sweater as blue as the sea over her overalls. Finally, their eyes came to rest on Sonjay, with no possessions at all, his hair in twisted dreadlocks, Bayard on his shoulder, and the Amulet of Heartfire openly visible where it rested against the front of his vibrant yellow T-shirt.

"You have become the Four," Aunt Alice whispered. "Oh let me have a look at you. You have truly become the Four."

"You have certainly become the Four," Uncle Bobby echoed.

"I wish Debbie could see this," Uncle Martin added.

Doshmisi remembered her night on Akinowe Lake and she said with certainty, "Mama can see us alright, we just can't see her." Then she handed Aunt Alice the bracelet from Cardamom. "He says he awaits your return, until his last sunset." Aunt Alice put the bracelet on her wrist as she blinked hard and her eyes glistened. Doshmisi reached in her bag and produced the mannafruit she had taken with her and gave it to her aunt. "This is for you too. And Uncle Bobby and Uncle Martin. From me."

"Oh my," Aunt Alice exclaimed, as she passed mannafruit to her brothers. "There are so many flavors from Faracadar that I could wish for. This will require some thought."

"We have a few questions for you," Sonjay said accusingly, putting one hand on his hip.

"I guess so," Aunt Alice answered.

"And for Uncle Martin and Uncle Bobby," Sonjay added. "I need some answers. Next year when I go back, I'm rescuing my father."

They all stared at him in amazement.

"You heard me," Sonjay told them. "Our father is alive and being held prisoner in the Final Fortress. I heard him saying our names over and over again during the night that Sissrath locked us in that cell. I'm sure it was our father." He turned to his aunt and uncles, "But I need to know some more about a lot of things before I go back to the Final Fortress to free him. And I need a map."

Aunt Alice exchanged glances with Uncle Bobby and Uncle Martin. Then Uncle Martin told Sonjay gently, "Don't depend on it, son. It may or may not have been him."

"Oh, I know it was him," Sonjay replied firmly. "And when I know something is the truth, I really know it."

"You better believe him," Denzel told them with a wide grin. "You don't know the half of it. He's got game." Denzel gave Sonjay a high five.

"So give us the four-one-one. What happened over there?" Uncle Bobby asked eagerly.

Before any of the Goodacres could say a word, Amethyst interjected, "I really must leave before it gets any lighter out. See you next Midsummer's Eve my dears." Amethyst gave everyone a warm hug, then she stood in front of the fireplace on a pillow surrounded by the wooden sticks, sprinkled a bit of powder on her head, and promptly disappeared, as did everything in the cottage, which reverted back to the drab and unused appearance it normally had for the rest of the year.

After Amethyst disappeared, the family walked lazily up the raspberry-studded path that led to the driveway and back to the house. Aunt Alice put one arm around Maia's waist and the other around Doshmisi's waist. Uncle Martin carried Denzel's duffel bag, secretly feeling around at the lumps inside when he thought no one would notice. Sonjay realized why his cousins had not come to Manzanita Ranch this year. They would never have understood why the Goodacres looked so different this morning from the way they had looked last night.

As the sun rose in the East, the family sat in the country kitchen and the new Four told the remaining three of the old Four the story of their adventures, weaving a new history.

A summer at Manzanita Ranch looked totally different to the Goodacres after their adventure in Faracadar. Aunt Alice's library seemed like a candy shop full of delicious treats. Doshmisi ran her fingers over the shelves and shelves of books on the topic of healing and tried to decide where to start studying so that she could use the herbal to its full power. As for the TV, well she didn't give it a second thought. She had more important things to do than watch those tired old stories where people had silly problems that could not compare to Sissrath destroying villages and trying to control an entire land with Special Forces and poison darts and enchantments.

Denzel claimed Uncle Martin's books for himself. In Faracadar he had longed to have *A Beginner's Guide to the Way Things Work* with him and now he could spend hours poring over the diagrams and pictures. It didn't matter to him anymore that his computer games wouldn't play on the computer. And when he noticed Aunt Alice's old Toyota sitting in the yard, a glint came into his eye as he remembered that he had permission to take it apart.

When Maia returned to Aunt Alice's house, she gazed lovingly at the stacks of sheet music. She couldn't imagine a better summer than one spent playing the piano, teaching herself the timber flute, and listening to music. When it came to drumming, well Aunt Alice told her that a group of people from the Ranch drummed under the stars every Friday night at a neighbor's house and Maia planned to attend every one of those drumming sessions.

As for Sonjay, he picked up the fattest book in Aunt Alice's library, entitled *A Complete History of Faracadar*, and propped the giant volume up against his skinny knees every night in bed. But during the day, he left the book behind and he went to day camp. He swam and jumped off the diving board at the deep end a million times and played basketball and skateboarded and made friends with as many guys as he could. For Sonjay was the youngest son of Debbie and the keeper of the Amulet of Heartfire and he knew in his own heart that he had a limited amount of time to play because it was his destiny to one day become a great leader and a powerful enchanter in a place on the other side of Angel's Gate. He would need memories of fun-in-the-sun summer days to remind him of what peace and freedom felt like, since the day would come when he must stop playing and work very hard to protect that feeling and preserve peace and freedom for people of many colors in a faraway land called Faracadar.

The Call to Shakabaz

Dear Reader:
If you liked my book, please tell your friends about it. If you know someone who might enjoy reading it, please recommend it to them or better yet give them a copy.
I am depending on you to help me get the word out to people about *The Call to Shakabaz*.
Thanks!

Order *The Call to Shakabaz* by requesting it at your favorite bookstore or through Amazon. Additional ordering information is provided on our website: www.wozabooks.com.

Acknowledgments

In the spring of 2003, Hopland Elementary School Teacher Chris Gibson took a chance and accepted my offer to read *The Call to Shakabaz* aloud to his fifth/sixth grade class. My son Sudi was in Chris's class that year. Reading the story aloud to this multi-ethnic and multilingual group of children in an early draft was a tremendous eye-opener and I recommend it to any writer of children's fiction. The ideas, energy, enthusiasm, creativity, and support of these children have woven themselves inextricably into this book. I would be negligent if I did not thank each and every one of Mr. Gibson's students of the class of 2002/2003:

Tessa Behnke	*Joshua Biaggi*
Anthony Billy	*Jacob Carter*
Mercedes Cruz	*Ameyalli Dominguez*
Frankie Dutra	*Joshua Eller*
Karla Esquivel	*Juliana Garcia*
Yeraldin Gonzalez	*Btaaka Hernandez*
Christopher Hiatt	*Juvenal Jaimes*
Gabriela Kong	*Freddie Loupy*
Johnny Maik	*Evelyn Puentes*
Jerry Robinson	*Salvador Romero*
Eustacio Ruiz	*Gavin Sherling Marvin*
Lisa Vasquez	*J. Sudi Reed Wachspress*

I especially owe a debt of gratitude to Chris, who is one of the most extraordinary teachers I have ever had the privilege to watch in action. His observations and suggestions have been invaluable. I also thank my adult draft readers on this book: my husband Ron Reed, my parents Eugene and Natalie Wachspress, Lesley Barkley, and my brother Dan. Dan read the book out loud to my precocious nephew Jacob when Jacob was six years old and their suggestions have added to the final product (Jacob dreamed up the goose-chicken eyeballs). Thank you to my college pal Julia Alvarez who has always believed in me and treated me as her peer even as she herself became an internationally recognized author while I continued to plod along mired in the day-to-day trivialities and stresses of family life out here on the ranch. I also want to thank J. K. Rowling for restoring the lustrous magic of reading as a favorite childhood pastime during an era when it was in danger of fading.

Thank you and a huge shout out to Cynthia Frank, who has served as my guide in this extraordinary enterprise of publication, and to the Cypress House team of enchanters who dedicated many hours to the effort to allow my words to make the leap from the page into the world.

As I have raised my own children, and struggled to give them an enchanted childhood in the midst of a world gone mad, I have come to have a greater appreciation for the delight and wonder of the childhood my parents gave me and my brothers. I thank them for that gift.

I am grateful daily for the opportunity to spend my life in the company of the wisest and most talented person I have ever known, my husband Ron Reed. Without his love, humor, and insight, *The Call to Shakabaz* would never have taken hold in my imagination.

Study Questions for The Call to Shakabaz

1. Doshmisi communicates with trees. If trees could talk, what do you think they would say?

2. Even though the butterflies are very small, they protect the travelers from harm. Can you think of an example of many small things using the strength of numbers to accomplish something that they could not each accomplish alone?

3. Things are not always as they appear. Do you think Denzel had a right to get angry at Jasper in the Marini Hills? Do you think the Four had a right to blame Jasper for the robbery?

4. Clover warns Sonjay, "Beware, for those who carry weapons are likely to have weapons used against them." What does she mean by this? Do you think a person who owns a gun is more likely or less likely to be shot than a person who doesn't own one? (Look up the statistics.)

5. The Bible says "an eye for an eye and a tooth for a tooth." Gandhi said that if everyone followed this belief then the whole world would be blind and toothless. What did he mean by that? What purpose, if any, is served by revenge?

6. Music is important to the Coast People. How can music be healing? How can music help people make positive changes? Why do you think music is so powerful?

7. Hyacinth regrets trusting Amaranth, who was a double agent. He apologizes to the others. What is the value of an apology? Why is forgiveness important?

8. Denzel leaves the armor vest behind in Spriteland. He says, "If one of us falls, we all fall. I don't see any point in wearing the vest now." What does he mean by this?

9. The whales tell Doshmisi that violence will make more violence and that she must find a way to fight without engaging in violence or making negative energy. She must create positive energy. In what ways can people work for change without using violence? What alternatives are there to war? If, as the whales say, violence will make more violence and bad energy will make more bad energy, then how do you fight a powerful leader who intends to use violence against you? To learn more about the practice of nonviolence, visit the website for the Metta Center at **www.mettacenter.org**.

(Visit the Woza Books website at **www.wozabooks.com** for a free comprehensive *Teachers' Study Guide*.)

About the Author

One of my favorite things in the whole world is traveling through the pages of fantasy adventures while reading aloud to young people. I have read aloud to my two stepsons (Mort and Brian) and to my three children (Yael, Akili, and Sudi) for nearly thirty years. Because my stepsons and two of my three children are all grown up, I will have to find other children to read to soon (so look out). Before I had any children, I went to college and got a masters degree in English. I have been a scenic artist, carpenter, welder, magazine editor, Head Start administrator, grant writer, peace and justice activist, tomato farmer, quilter, and pie baker. I like to play with my cats, watch my youngest son skateboard or play baseball, and watch football on TV (go Raiders). I have been married

for a very long time to Ron Reed, better known as DJ Reed (as in disc jockey). He and his terrific family on the Southside of Chicago have given me a passion for R&B and Soul music. I live in an ancient forest on a dirt road leading to a magical cherry orchard in Mendocino County, California. Ancient trees stand guard at my gate.

Photo: Yael Reed Wachspress

green press

INITIATIVE

Woza Books is committed to preserving ancient forests and natural resources. We elected to print *The Call to Shakabaz* on 100% post consumer recycled paper, processed chlorine-free.

As a result, for this printing, we have saved:

35 TREES (40' TALL, 6-8" IN DIAMETER)

12,600 GALLONS OF WATER

24 million BTUs of total energy

1,618 POUNDS OF SOLID WASTE

3,036 POUNDS OF GREENHOUSE GASES

Woza Books made this choice because we are a member of Green Press Initiative, a nonprofit program dedicated to supporting authors, publishers, and suppliers in their efforts to reduce their use of fiber obtained from endangered forests.

For more information, visit
www.greenpressinitiative.org

Calculations from **www.papercalculator.org**